QUEEN

KAREN LYNCH

For Alex

ACKNOWLEDGMENTS

Thank you to my family and friends for your love and support. Amber Shepherd for everything you do, my beta readers (Amber, Irina, April and Sarah), my editor, Kelly, my cover designer, Melissa, and all the readers who make this possible.

1

———————

I STARED AT my father, waiting for him to say something after the bombshell he'd dropped on me. The torment in his eyes was too much to bear, and it was almost a relief when he turned his head away.

My mind whirled as I tried to think of a response to his declaration that the Seelie crown prince was my brother. My brother, who had died twenty years ago, when he was two months old. The only plausible explanation was that the stress of my near-death had caused Dad to have a mental setback.

Guilt pressed down on me. The doctors had warned me this could happen if he didn't take it slowly. I needed to call them. The possibility of Dad having to go back to the treatment facility gutted me, but we couldn't risk his health. Fifty percent of recovering goren addicts went back to using within the first year, and my father would not be one of them.

I laid my hand over his. "Dad, you look pale. Maybe you should lie down for a few minutes."

"I don't need to lie down. I've slept enough in the last four months."

"But –"

He swung his gaze back to me. "I'm okay, Jesse. It's a shock and a lot to take in, but it's not a delusion."

I stared into his clear eyes. His tone was rational, and he didn't look like someone on the verge of a mental breakdown. But his claim that a faerie prince was his dead son was the kind of thing that got people admitted to a psych ward. All I could think of to do was hear him out and see where it went.

"Can you tell me about it?"

Dad drew in a shaky breath. "I don't know where to start."

I reached over to take his hand. "Why do you think Prince Rhys is Caleb? Did someone tell you that?"

"No. Your mom recognized the prince when she saw Tennin's photos of him. She said the hair is different, but the prince has my eyes, and he looks like I did when I was twenty." Dad let out a weak laugh. "I know how that sounds because I thought the same thing at first."

"Why didn't Tennin tell me this?"

Dad shook his head. "He didn't know. Your mother didn't tell me until we were back in the car. I thought she was imagining the resemblance until she pulled out an old photo of me she keeps under the visor."

I realized I was holding my breath. "And?"

"If my hair was blond, I could have been Prince Rhys's twin when I was his age."

I had to see this for myself. Standing, I went to the cabinet where Mom kept all the photo albums. They were labeled by year, and I pulled out the one for my parents' late teens. My heart thudded as I carried the album back to the couch and sat beside Dad. I stared down at the cover, afraid of what I would see when I opened it.

"Do you want me to do it?" Dad asked when I made no move to look inside.

"No." I lifted the cover. The first few pages were of Mom with her high school girlfriends, followed by an 8x10 photo of her in her cap and gown. I turned the page slowly to reveal Dad's graduation picture, and it was as if someone had punched all the air from my lungs.

"Oh, my God," I whispered. Whipping out my phone, I brought up one of the thousands of online pictures of the Seelie crown prince. I laid the phone beside Dad's photo, and my world tilted on its axis. It wasn't only the eyes that were the same. Prince Rhys and the eighteen-year-old version of my father had identical smiles and the same tiny cleft in their chins. The prince had more refined features, like a marble statue with all its imperfections polished away, but Dad was right. They could have been twins.

I looked at Dad, who was watching me expectantly. Twenty-three years had passed since that photo was taken, and his face was leaner now with crow's feet near his eyes and lines around his mouth. When I looked past those things, all I could see was the young man smiling up at me from the album.

"How did I not see it? The first time I talked to Prince Rhys, I felt like I'd met him before, but I thought that was because his face was everywhere." I shook my head. "What about Bruce, Maurice, and your other friends who knew you back then? None of them saw a resemblance between you and the most famous faerie in the world?"

Dad shrugged. "I doubt they would remember exactly what I looked like back then without seeing a photo. That happens when you age together. As for everyone else, people don't always see what is in front of them, especially when they aren't looking for it. Who would think to make a connection between me and the Seelie prince? You didn't."

I looked down at the two photos. I knew from personal experience how easy it was not to see something that was right in front of your eyes. I still wondered how I hadn't realized who Lukas was until Rogin Havas had let it slip.

I pursed my lips as I searched for the right words to phrase what had to be said. "Prince Rhys looks like you, but that doesn't mean he's Caleb. I mean...Caleb died. You and Mom saw him, and there was an autopsy and a funeral."

I flinched internally and saw an answering expression on Dad's face. He and Mom never liked to talk about that time, but there was no way around it now.

He shifted position and glanced away before meeting my eyes again. "The medical examiner said Caleb died from pulmonary atresia, which is almost always diagnosed soon after the baby is born. Caleb was two months old, and he didn't have any of the symptoms. He looked like a normal, healthy baby. Your mom..." He swallowed. "She didn't believe the dead baby she found in the crib was ours. She said a mother knows her own child, and that someone had switched her baby for a dead one."

Dad's voice cracked on the last word. Tears pricked my eyes, and I blinked them away.

"The baby looked like Caleb, and the M.E. said there was nothing suspicious about his death. I explained that to your mom, but she was too distraught to believe it. Nothing would convince her Caleb was dead."

"What did you do?" I asked around the rock lodged in my throat. I had always seen the sadness in Mom's eyes when Caleb's name came up, but my parents had never gone into detail about his death, other than the cause.

He cleared his throat. "I thought she would come to accept it after a few days, but she refused to even make the funeral arrangements. And then she started going up to strangers with babies to check that their baby wasn't Caleb." Dad paused, his face etched in pain. "It was bad for the first year. After a while, she started to be more like her old self, but I don't think she was happy again until we found out she was pregnant with you."

"You guys never told me any of this," I said hoarsely.

"Your mom didn't want you to know. It was a very dark time in our lives, and she was ashamed of how she behaved." His face twisted in agony. "No one believed her when she said the baby wasn't Caleb – not even me. And all this time, she was right."

Needing to do something, I laid the album on the coffee table and got up to walk around the room. It hurt too much to think about what my parents had suffered back then, so I focused on their disappearance.

"What happened the night you disappeared, Dad?"

He straightened his shoulders as if he was shaking off the pain. "Your mom wanted to see the prince in person. We called one of our contacts at the Ralston and found out he was doing a photo shoot in the small ballroom on the sixth floor. The odds of getting near him were slim, but we had to try." Dad stared past me as he remembered the events of that night. "The moment we stepped off the elevator, I knew your mom was right. Prince Rhys is Caleb."

A new wave of shock rolled through me. "You saw him?"

"Not the prince. The ballroom door was open and a group was leaving. There were two male faeries in front, and as soon as they saw us, they came to intercept us. They knew who we were before we could even show them our IDs. One of them said he knew they should have killed us twenty years ago when they took the boy.

I pressed a hand to my mouth as he continued. "They restrained us and told the prince's guard to take him to his suite while they dealt with the prob-lem. The next thing I knew, we were in the ballroom and they were calling Rogin Havas to dispose of us. They didn't want the death of two well-known bounty hunters to draw any attention to Prince Rhys and risk reporters making a connection between him and us. They had no idea Rogin's sister would intercept the call and save us."

"You remember seeing her?" I'd told him that Raisa had been the one who gave them the goren to keep them alive. Until now, he had no memory of her part in it.

"Yes. I woke up in her house. She said she would do whatever she could to keep us alive. After that, all my memories are foggy. I can't tell the real ones from the goren dreams."

I continued pacing. I couldn't think about the possibility that my brother was alive or about everything my parents had been through. It was too much for my brain to process all at once. Instead, I focused on the person at the root of it all, the one who had caused my family so much pain.

"What I don't get is *why*? Why would Queen Anwyn steal a human baby, convert him, and raise him as her son? Her *heir*? One thing I know about Fae politics is that they only want the bluest blood in the royal line. I can't believe any Seelie faerie with an ounce of royal blood would be okay with someone who isn't even Fae-born being their king someday."

"They would if they don't know he isn't Fae-born."

"That's it!" I whipped my head toward my father. "That's why her guard tried to have you and Mom killed, and why they don't want you to remember. I thought they were worried you knew about them stealing the ke'tain, but all along it was about Prince Rhys…Caleb…"

My voice trailed off, and a knife twisted in my gut at the fresh pain in Dad's eyes. I couldn't imagine what he was going through. His son had been ripped from him and raised as a faerie with no knowledge of his real parents. Even if Prince Rhys somehow learned the truth and wanted to know his family, we could never get back the life that had been stolen from us.

I went back to pacing. "It still doesn't explain why she would take a human baby and pass him off as her own. What could she gain from that?"

"I don't know." Dad stared down at his hands. "But she went through a lot of trouble to do it and to cover it up."

He was right. Her guards had done a lot more than steal Caleb. They'd switched him with a changeling made to look like my brother, which required a lot of magic. They also would have had to glamour the medical examiner to make sure the autopsy report confirmed the dead baby was Caleb and that he'd died of a heart defect.

After all of that, the guards couldn't bring a human baby to Faerie. Their magic wasn't strong enough to do a conversion, which meant Queen Anwyn had secretly come to our realm to perform it herself.

But why Caleb? Of the millions of male babies in the world, why had they chosen my brother? Had they been looking for something specific, or were we the first family they found with a baby boy? We'd probably never know the answer to that, and I feared it would haunt my parents for the rest of their lives.

Helpless anger flared inside me. The Seelie queen had done nothing but bring pain to the people I loved, and she was virtually untouchable. Not that we had evidence of her crime. The prince's resemblance to Dad could be passed off as coincidence, and we had no proof of his real identity. Once a human became Fae, none of our human DNA remained. It was one of the things I'd been struggling with this past week.

There was the body Mom and Dad had buried, but it would take a lot more than a crazy story about changelings to get the authorities to exhume it.

And something like that would not go unnoticed. My family would be dead before the ink was dry on the order.

A soft whistle drew my attention to Finch, who stood at the end of the hallway. His eyes were wide and worried as he signed, *Is Dad okay?*

I followed his gaze to where Dad sat with his head in his hands, and then I signed back, *Yes. He's just figuring out something.*

Okay. He turned and disappeared again.

Dad moved his head from side to side. "It's my fault. I should have kept him safe."

"How can you say that?" I went to sit beside him. "No human is a match for the Seelie royal guard. You know that better than anyone."

"You don't understand. I had the apartment warded, but only against the kinds of faeries we hunted. I never thought to protect us from Court faeries. If I had, they wouldn't have gotten in and taken Caleb."

"You can't blame yourself for that. No one would have thought to ward against the royal guard." I laid my head against his shoulder, lost as to how to comfort the strongest man I'd ever known. My father was a protector, and he'd carry this guilt on his shoulders forever. It was one more reason for me to despise the Seelie queen.

Neither of us spoke for a long moment, and it was Dad who broke the silence. "We need to make a plan."

"A plan for what?" I straightened. Surely, he wasn't going to suggest we tell Prince Rhys who he really was. As much as I wanted my parents to be happy, I was terrified of what the queen would do to them.

"To protect our family. If Queen Anwyn learns the prince has been here and met me, she's not going to take it well. And if her guards find out I have my memories back, they –"

"No." Fear sent me to my feet. "We can't tell anyone about this. The Seelie guard will come after you and Mom, and I can't lose you again. I can't."

"Jesse." Dad stood and put his hands on my trembling shoulders. "I'm not talking about going public with this. But if the prince keeps showing interest in us, the queen will take notice, and her guard will come snooping around. We need to prepare for that."

"How?"

He pressed his lips together, and his grip on my shoulders tightened a fraction. "The first thing we have to do is tell Lukas."

"No." I shook my head so hard it almost gave me whiplash.

Dad stopped me when I would have pulled away from him. "Listen to me. I know you're still angry at him, but he cares about you. He'll protect you."

I had no idea what I felt for Lukas anymore. At first, I'd been furious at him because he'd made me Fae without giving me a choice, even though there had been no way I could have made that decision. Then I'd hated myself for being unfair to the person who had saved my life. I'd spent the last week alternating between hoping he would come assure me everything would be okay and not wanting to see him. Not that he had tried to see me – or talk to me. The others had been taking turns calling to check on me, but I hadn't heard a word from him since the day he brought me home.

There was one thing I did know. If we told him about Caleb and what Queen Anwyn had done, he wouldn't let me stay here. He'd most likely send me to Unseelie to keep me safe, and it could be months or years before I saw my family again. After everything I'd gone through to get them back, I wasn't letting anyone separate us.

I shared my fears with Dad and waited for several long minutes while he paced the room deep in thought. His face was still pale, but he looked more like himself as he worked out things in his head.

He stopped walking midstride and turned to me. "We'll tell people the doctor said our memories are gone for good. That usually only happens with long-term goren addiction, but we were given high doses and put into comas, so it will be believable. If the guard is watching, they'll get wind of it."

"What about Mom? What if she gets her memory back and tells someone?"

Dad nodded. "I'll talk to her. She'll be okay."

I didn't ask what he would say to her. If he said he would take care of it, he would. My parents' marriage was built on a deep foundation of trust and mutual understanding. They were best friends and partners and knew each other better than anyone else ever could. Whatever Dad told her, she would trust him and follow his example without question.

"That takes care of Mom. How do we protect you if the queen's guard comes around?"

A gleam entered his eyes. "The guard took me by surprise last time, but now I know what I'm up against. I'll make some preparations and call in favors from a few friends. Don't worry about me."

The pressure on my chest eased. "Are you going to tell Maurice the truth?"

"Yes. I'll ask him to come by this evening."

Maurice normally didn't stay in town this long, and I'd assumed he'd be off on another big job now that the ke'tain had been found. He felt guilty that he hadn't been there for us when Mom and Dad were missing, and he wanted to make up for that by sticking around for another month or so. I'd never been so happy to know he was next door.

"Now what do we do about you?" Dad asked, startling me from my thoughts.

"What about me?"

"It's you Prince Rhys came to see. Even if the queen believes my memories are gone for good, she's not going to allow you two to continue seeing each other." Dad paused. "Especially if she thinks his interest in you is more than platonic."

My stomach rolled at the mere suggestion that Prince Rhys might have any romantic interest in me. He was raised a Faerie, but he was still my brother. The fact that I'd never been attracted to him didn't ease the ick factor one bit.

It made much more sense now why Queen Anwyn had sent her guards to warn me away from him. It had nothing to do with me being a lowly bounty hunter and everything to do with me being his sister.

"I doubt we'll be seeing that much of him anymore. You heard what he said when he was here. He's Seelie and I'm Unseelie, so it wouldn't be right for him to visit me." I let out a breath. "And I don't think the queen will come after me now that I'm Unseelie. She knows I'm friends with Lukas, and after the whole ke'tain thing, he would suspect her if anything happened to me."

"That's true." Dad smiled, but there was no mistaking the flicker of sadness in his eyes. His focus was on keeping our family safe, but at the root of all of this was the child who had been stolen from him. What turmoil he must be feeling. To protect the rest of his family, he had to pretend he didn't know his son was alive and well.

He cleared his throat. "I'm going to the office to make a few calls."

"I'll make us some coffee," I said a little too cheerfully. "That is if you haven't used up my stash."

"I wouldn't dare." He chuckled, and the sound warmed me.

As soon as he left the room, the weight of everything I'd learned pressed down on me again. I moved on autopilot as I put the coffee on and took down two large mugs. The last week I'd wallowed in my misery, thinking about what I'd lost. That was nothing compared to what my parents had suffered and the loss to our family.

Caleb is alive. I wondered how many times I'd have to repeat those three words before they sank in. I thought back on all the years of visiting his grave with my parents, of looking at that tiny, white headstone and imagining what my life would have been like if my brother had lived. Not in a hundred years could I have envisioned a scenario where he was stolen by faeries and raised as the crown prince of Seelie. Or that if I breathed a word of it to anyone, the monster he called a mother would have my entire family killed.

The coffee finished brewing, and I inhaled the rich aroma as I poured it into our mugs. At least some things didn't change. I made my father's just how he liked it and then my own. I had been so depressed for the last week I couldn't even think about food, and the smell of the coffee made me realize how much I'd missed it.

I raised the cup to my mouth and closed my eyes to savor the first sip.

And then I sprayed coffee across the kitchen.

I set the mug on the counter and ran to the sink, ducking my head under the faucet to rinse the awful taste from my mouth. It was bitter and ashy and made me think this must be what burnt dirt tasted like. No matter how much water I gargled, I couldn't get rid of it.

Raising my head, I wiped my mouth with my sleeve and stared at the coffee left in the pot. Someone was pranking me. They'd switched out my coffee for this horrid stuff and...

Realization hit me like a blast of cold air, and I let out a cry that would have put a banshee to shame. Dad came running into the kitchen, wild-eyed like he expected to find the entire Seelie guard attacking me.

"What's wrong?" he asked a little breathlessly.

"I hate coffee," I wailed.

He stared at me in confusion until understanding dawned on his face. "I'm sorry, honey. It was bound to happen."

I bent my head so he couldn't see the tears burning my eyes.

"Jesse," Dad said at the same time the doorbell rang. I grabbed some paper towels and cleaned up my mess while he went to see who else was paying us a visit. The way this day was going, it was probably Queen Anwyn.

I didn't look to see who it was, but I could hear the murmur of male voices. Seconds later, footsteps approached, and I looked up at Faolin's scowling face. I would have preferred the Seelie queen.

"Are you crying?" he asked brusquely.

I tossed the wet paper towels in the trash. "I'm just *that* happy to see you."

He scoffed, but I caught a glimmer of amusement in his eyes, which only annoyed me more. His sharp gaze moved past me to the coffee machine and the two mugs on the counter. He quickly put two and two together, and in typical Faolin fashion, he said, "You're crying because you can no longer drink that stuff?"

I glared at him. "It's not about the coffee." I didn't need to add the words "you insensitive jerk" because my tone more than implied them.

"Then what is it?"

"It's nothing." He was the last person I wanted to confide in. I hadn't even told Dad about it. That ever since I'd woken up and learned I was Fae, I had taken comfort in the fact that I still looked and felt human. I had no magic or Fae strength, and iron didn't affect me thanks to my goddess stone. As long as none of that changed, I could pretend I was the same old Jesse.

I crossed my arms. "Why are you here, Faolin?"

"I brought you some food." He set a bulging cloth bag on the counter.

I eyed the bag warily. "We have plenty of food."

"Human food." He loosened the drawstring and took out various Fae fruits, a few of which I recognized, along with a bottle of green juice and two small, round loaves of dark bread. The juice looked like the same stuff Faris had drunk during his convalescence.

Faolin finished his task and looked at me. "Your father said you have barely eaten since you came home."

"Did he?" I shot Dad an accusing look. He hadn't been at the door long enough to discuss my eating habits, which meant he'd talked to Faolin before his unexpected visit.

Dad leaned his shoulder against the wall, not looking the least bit contrite. "You have certain nutritional needs you didn't have before, and I wasn't sure exactly what to buy."

"Faeries can eat human food," I reminded them.

"Yes, but we also require Fae nourishment." Faolin picked up something that resembled an elongated pink pear. "Fruits and juice will be the easiest for you to digest until your body adjusts to the change. You can have Fae bread but only in small portions at first."

"What? No crukk steak?" I quipped. Crukks were the main source of meat in Faerie. They looked like a shrunken version of a wooly mammoth and they were raised domestically like our cattle.

He gave me a mocking smile. "You can eat crukk if you don't mind it coming back up an hour later."

I made a face. "I'll stick to beef."

"As long as you make sure to include enough Fae foods in your daily diet." He waved a hand over the food. "You can get any of this at the local Fae market, or you can call us, and we will bring you what you need."

"Thanks," I said without much enthusiasm.

"Do you need anything else?" he asked.

Yes. I want to know why Lukas didn't bring the food, and why he is the only one who hasn't called me, I thought, but all I said was, "No."

"Then I'll be going."

Dad stepped back to let Faolin pass. "Thank you for coming by. We appreciate everything you and the others have done for us, and when my daughter gets her manners back, she will tell you the same."

I scowled at my father. What was he talking about? I'd thanked them. Hadn't I?

"You're welcome," Faolin said. His back was to me, but there was no missing the note of laughter in his voice. At the door, he turned to face me. "Don't think your new status means you no longer have to train. We will resume that after you build up your strength."

"Oh, joy. I can't wait."

"Neither can I." He flashed me a devious smile as he left. "See you soon, Jesse."

Dad followed me back to the kitchen. "It was nice of him to bring you food."

"He's a real boy scout." I opened the bottle of juice and sniffed. It *was* the same stuff Faris used to drink. I capped it and put it in the fridge then grabbed a basket from the cabinet for the fruit.

"You're not going to eat any of it now?" Dad asked when I was done.

"Not hungry." I picked up my mug and gave it a longing look before I poured the coffee down the drain. After rinsing the mug, I placed it in the draining rack to dry. "Well, I guess I'll save a lot of money on coffee."

He came over to put an arm across my shoulders and gave them a small squeeze. "There's the Jesse I know."

I heaved a sigh. "I'm sorry I've been so hard to live with this week."

"You had a good excuse, so I'll let you off easy this –"

The floor vibrated beneath our feet, and a rumbling sound filled the air as if a plane was flying low over our building. I clung to Dad as the windows rattled, and car alarms started to go off down on the street.

It was over as fast as it had started, leaving the two of us staring at each other in stunned silence.

I was the first to find my voice. "Did we just have an earthquake?"

2

———

Before he could answer, flashes of colored lights outside drew my gaze to the window. I ran over to look up at the sky and saw the familiar light display. We weren't having an earthquake. It was a Fae storm. Only, this time, it was over land instead of the Hudson.

I twitched as static electricity moved across my skin. That was new and not at all pleasant. Shaking it off, I said, "Dad, come look at this."

"Jesse!" Dad's voice held a note of alarm that had me spinning to face him. Or I tried to. It's a little hard to turn when you are suddenly weightless and floating a foot off the floor.

"What the hell?" I grabbed for the window ledge, but it was out of reach as I drifted upward like a helium balloon. My head bumped gently against the ceiling, and I put my hands up to brace against it. I fought to keep the panic out of my voice. "Dad?"

He had barely taken three steps toward me when the door opened, and Faolin burst in as if he expected to find us under attack. He came up short, and his serious expression relaxed into one of amusement at the sight of my predicament.

I glared at him. "Don't just stand there. Get me down from here."

He made a sound suspiciously like a laugh as he came over to place his hands on my waist. Pale blue magic poured from his fingers, and the uncomfortable tingling sensation disappeared. Seconds later, gravity took over, and I floated back to the floor.

"Thanks," I said, too happy to be back on solid ground to care about the smirk he wore. "What was that?"

He stepped back and gave me a once-over. "Your body reacted to the storm. Humans can't feel a storm's energy. Faeries feel it, but it doesn't affect us. You, on the other hand, are newly converted, and you have barely developed your magic. That makes you susceptible to it."

"Great," I muttered. "I hope I'm not outside the next time there's a storm, or I'll be the first faerie in orbit."

Faolin actually chuckled. "I think we can give you something to carry with you when you go out that will suppress your magic until you can control it."

"Like a dampening ward?" Dad asked.

Faolin nodded. "We can't ward Jesse, but she should be able to carry something on her person. It will allow her to feel other magic while not reacting to it."

Dad folded his arms across his chest. "I thought the storms were supposed to get weaker now that the ke'tain is back in Faerie."

"It's taking longer than we expected," Faolin said. His phone rang, and he walked away to answer it.

"I can't wait to see how the Agency tries to spin this one with the public." I glanced out the window and saw that the lights were gone from the sky. The Hudson storm had been passed off as a freak tornado that had happened at the exact same time as the aurora borealis. I still couldn't believe people had accepted that explanation.

"I don't think they can." Dad turned to the hallway. "I'm going to check on Finch and Aisla. I'll be back in a minute."

Now that I was alone with Faolin, snatches of his phone conversation reached me. "She's okay. I was outside when it hit."

I didn't need to hear the other person's voice to guess who it was. Anger and hurt licked at me. If Lukas was concerned about me, why didn't he call me instead of Faolin? Was the thought of talking to me that abhorrent to him now?

Faolin ended the call and looked at me. "One of us will bring the ward to you later today. It will most likely be a bracelet or something to wear around your neck. Try not to go outside until then."

"I won't. Thanks."

"Thank you for your help," Dad said, rejoining us.

We said our goodbyes again, and Faolin left for the second time today. Dad and I went downstairs to check on Mrs. Russo and the other residents who were shaken by the storm. As scary as it had been, it was nothing compared to the violent one I'd experienced on the ferry two months ago. I was more rattled by the whole floating thing than the storm itself.

I *was* unnerved when we checked the news reports an hour later and learned Los Angeles, London, Hong Kong, and Tokyo had all experienced similar storms around the same time. It was no coincidence that these five cities were the most popular in the world for faerie portals. Our storm had set off a citywide panic that had prompted both the mayor and the governor to go on the air to reassure people they were safe.

Two hours after the storm, the White House and the Agency did a joint press conference. Without going into too much detail, they informed the country about an artifact that had been brought here from Faerie, causing some instability in the barrier between the two realms. After telling viewers the object was safely back in Faerie, they assured people the barrier was healing, but there could be more storms until the damage was repaired.

"The worst is over," said the national head of the Agency during the barrage of questions fired at them by reporters.

I looked over at my father. "Do you believe that?"

"No."

I rubbed my suddenly cold arms. "Me either."

"Are you ready for this?" Dad asked as he reached for the door handle.

I smiled at him. "Are you?"

"Guess we'll find out." Grinning, he opened the door, and we stepped into the lobby of the Plaza. It felt like it had been a lot longer than three weeks since the last time I'd been here. I couldn't imagine what it was like for him coming back after a four-month absence.

There were at least a dozen hunters in the lobby, and all heads turned in our direction. It surprised me to realize I knew everyone there. So much had changed since the first time I'd set foot in this building all those months ago.

A cheer went up, and some of the hunters clapped as they called out to Dad. In the next instant, we were surrounded by his old friends clamoring to welcome him back.

Warmth filled me as I watched him talking and laughing and looking more like his old self than he had since he'd come home. I'd been a little worried it was too soon for him to come here with me today, but this was exactly what he needed.

I spotted Maurice, Bruce, and Trey standing on one side of the room, and I walked over to join them. Maurice dropped by our apartment every day, but

I hadn't seen Bruce or Trey since before the day I'd nearly died from a bullet to the chest. As far as they and the other bounty hunters were concerned, I had been shot in the arm and had taken time off to heal. Outside of my family, the only humans who knew the real story were Maurice, Violet, and the Agency.

"Jesse, good to have you back," Bruce said as Maurice gave me a one-armed hug.

"It's good to be back," I replied lightly. I had been practically floating since I got a call from the Agency this morning letting me know my license had been reinstated. I'd immediately called Levi, who told me to drop by this afternoon.

Trey pushed away from the wall he was leaning against. "How's the arm?"

"Like it was never shot."

He gave a slow shake of his head. "I can't believe you were shot by Davian Woods, of all people."

My jaw went slack. "How do you know about Davian?" I was under the impression the Agency hadn't released any details of that day.

Trey smirked. "You should know by now that word travels around here. We heard you found the ke'tain, and Woods tried to take it from you."

The rumor was close enough to the truth, so I nodded. "Good thing he's a lousy shot."

Trey's eyes widened. "It's true? You were the one who found the ke'tain?" He whistled. "A hundred thousand dollars. What are you going to do with all that money?"

A hand came to rest on my shoulder, and Dad said, "She's going to college."

He moved to stand beside me, and we shared a smile. In the week since his life-changing revelation that Caleb was alive, Dad and I had spent a lot of time talking about the future and making plans. He'd insisted I use the ke'tain bounty for school, which meant I had enough to start college in the fall. Come September, I would be a fulltime student at Harvard University.

I wasn't sure how I felt about leaving my family after all that had happened. Every time I brought it up, Dad said college was months away and everything would be back to normal by then. I wanted to believe that more than anything.

Trey made a face. "College? I thought you were going to hunt from now on."

"Harvard," Dad corrected him proudly. "She'll keep hunting until the fall."

Maurice beamed at me. "Harvard? That's wonderful!"

"You don't mind her hunting alone?" Trey asked.

"I wouldn't say that." Dad smiled at me. "But Jesse's proven more than capable of taking care of herself. And things seem to have calmed down here now that the ke'tain is back in Faerie."

"If by *normal* you mean except for the storms." Bruce's voice was laced with resentment. "How could they have kept that from us?"

His anger was justified. Maurice had told Dad and me the bounty hunters were furious they had been left in the dark. They understood why the Agency wanted to keep it from the general public, but this vital information should have been shared with the hunters. The Agency's actions had created a layer of tension between them and the hunters, who now viewed them with distrust.

Guilt gnawed at me. I'd learned the truth about the storms from Lukas, but I hadn't told anyone. Thinking back, I wasn't sure why I'd kept it to myself. And now the Agency and I were keeping another secret from my fellow bounty hunters. How would they react when the news of my conversion came out?

The elevator dinged, and I looked over to see the Mercer twins walk out. When Adrian saw us, he poked his brother, and the two of them headed our way.

"Are those Joe and Leah Mercer's boys?" Maurice asked. "I think the last time I saw them, they were in middle school."

Dad nodded. "They've been hunting for two years."

"Lord, I feel old." Maurice rubbed the back of his neck. Dad and Bruce laughed.

Aaron and Adrian exchanged hellos with us, and then Adrian grinned. "We just landed our first Four from Silas."

"That's awesome!" I fist-bumped him.

"We did a few Fours with Mom and Dad, but this is our first since we went on our own," Aaron said.

"What kind of Four did you get?" Dad asked them.

They puffed out their chests and spoke in unison. "Banshee."

"No way!" Envy pricked me. Banshees didn't show up much, maybe one or two a year. I'd read up on them, but I knew I'd never be assigned one because they were not a one-person job. It took at least two people to capture a banshee.

Adrian looked at Maurice with something akin to hero worship. "Any advice?"

"If it's your first banshee, partner up with another team," Maurice said.

Bruce nodded. "Don't let your guard down for a second. They're slippery even when they're in shackles."

"And don't look her straight in the eyes when she's wailing," Dad added. "She'll be able to control you, and you do not want a banshee in your head."

A shiver went through me at his words, and Aaron and Adrian shuddered as they exchanged a look. They did their weird twin communication thing before they turned to me with identical earnest expressions.

"Jesse, you want to help us catch a banshee tonight?" Aaron asked.

"Are you kidding?" A grin split my face until I remembered what Maurice had told them. "But I don't have a partner."

Trey quietly cleared his throat. Aaron and Adrian ignored him, but I made the mistake of meeting his hopeful eyes. Ah, hell. I didn't want to work another job with him, but I'd feel like a total jerk for leaving him out.

"If Bruce doesn't need Trey, I guess he could be my partner for this one," I said without much enthusiasm.

"Sure," Trey blurted.

Bruce shot me a grateful smile. "He's all yours."

The twins looked less happy about it, so I added, "Trey and Bruce did bring in a banshee last year."

I didn't mention they had worked with Phil Griffin on that one, and that Trey had been more of a bystander. He *had* witnessed a banshee capture in person, which was more than the rest of us could say.

The twins did their silent look again and nodded at the same time. Was I the only one who found it a little creepy when they did that?

"Okay," they said together.

"Great." My excitement built up again. "Where and when?"

Aaron took out his phone. "I'll send you the details."

I texted him my number since I already had theirs. Trey and I agreed to meet up at my place and drive together since it made no sense to go separately when we lived a few streets apart. He and Bruce headed out, leaving me with Dad and Maurice.

Amusement sparkled in Dad's eyes. "Didn't you tell me working with Trey would drive you insane?"

"I said I'd go insane after a week of working with him. I think I can survive a few hours."

Maurice chuckled. "The question is, will Trey survive?"

I let out a puff of air. "I make no promises."

Three hours later, Aaron, Adrian, Trey, and I stood across the street from a twenty-five-story high-rise in the Upper East Side as Aaron explained the situation to us.

"Here's what we know. A woman committed suicide here in January. She jumped from her apartment on the top floor. Last week, contractors started renovations up there, and a few days ago a banshee appeared. She's been sticking to the top level, and so far, she hasn't hurt anyone, but she has been keeping everyone off the floor."

"Was the woman's name Claire...something?" I asked because the story sounded familiar.

Aaron glanced down at his phone. "Claire Parker. How did you know that?"

"I remember seeing it on the news." I'd watched a lot of TV when I visited my parents during their first two weeks in the hospital. The story about Claire Parker had been all over the local news the first week of January. She had been an up-and-coming model, who had recently signed a contract with one of the big cosmetic companies.

"Good memory," Adrian said.

I craned my neck to look up at the top floors of the building. "Maybe the police were wrong about it being a suicide."

Trey nudged me. "What makes you say that?"

"A banshee only haunts a place this long after a death if it's a violent death like a murder." I lowered my gaze to meet his. "And that means –"

"This banshee is going to be angry," he finished for me.

I nodded grimly. "She is not going without a fight."

Banshees appeared for two reasons. The most common one was when someone, usually a female, was dying. No one knew why they were attracted to some deaths and not others, but they would wail mournfully every night until the person was dead.

The second reason was to lament the violent death of a female. Faeries said the banshee was drawn to the angry, restless spirit of the deceased, and her keening forced the spirit to sever its final ties to the mortal world. The banshee could feel all of the spirit's grief and rage, which made her angry as well. And an angry banshee was a dangerous one.

"Great," Trey muttered.

I looked at Aaron and Adrian. "Let's do this."

We crossed the street and entered the building. As we rode the elevator up, we talked strategy. There weren't many options when dealing with a banshee, so it didn't take long to plan our attack. It was the execution of the plan that would be the hard part.

On the twenty-fifth floor, the doors slid open to a dark cavernous space. Most of the interior walls were gone, leaving support beams, hanging electrical wires, and sheets of thick plastic that fluttered like wraiths in the cold breeze whistling eerily through the empty floor.

I opened the small backpack I'd brought with me and pulled out my headlamp as the others went for theirs. The second I flicked mine on, a high-pitched wail came from somewhere on the floor, making the four of us jump. I'd seen videos of banshees before, but none of them had prepared me for this. The sound was so mournful and angry it raised gooseflesh on every inch of my body. Shouldn't I be immune to this now that I was Fae?

I waved my hand to get their attention and pointed in the direction of the sound. They all nodded, and we started toward it with me in the lead. I wasn't sure how I had somehow become the unspoken leader of our mission, but I didn't mention it. I was more comfortable leading than following.

We maneuvered around piles of debris and building supplies, following the growing volume of the banshee's cry. The closer we got, the colder the air became until our breaths were clouding the air around us.

The wail ended abruptly. I froze mid step, and Trey collided with me. He grabbed my shoulders to stop my fall, and I mouthed a silent thank you.

Covering my headlamp so it didn't blind them, I pointed two fingers at my eyes and at the space around us. They nodded, and we started moving again but at a slower pace.

A sheet of plastic to our left suddenly billowed like a sail in the wind before it was split down the center. I spun toward it as two gnarled hands with pointed fingernails shoved the pieces of plastic aside, and the stuff of nightmares came through it.

It resembled the corpse of an old woman with dead, milky eyes and gray skin hanging off her sunken cheeks. I averted my gaze from hers, but it was her mouth that made a scream rise in my throat. It gaped open impossibly wide until it took up half her face, and the shriek that poured out of it was so horrible I was sure it had pierced my soul.

The creature flew straight at me, her ghastly maw stretching as if to swallow me whole. I tripped backward over a piece of lumber and got tangled in some dangling electrical wires. I struggled to free myself, but I was a fly trapped in a spider's web.

"Get her," I shouted above her screeching.

The banshee veered away from me toward Aaron and Adrian. One of them howled in fear, and then came the sound of running feet. The banshee gave chase, her angry wails mixing with their screams.

Something grabbed me from behind, and I let out a small scream, whirling to strike out at it. My fist hit flesh, and it staggered back a step.

"Ow! Damn it, it's me." Trey rubbed his cheek. "You nearly took my head off. Where did you learn to punch that hard?"

"Sorry." Apparently, my Fae strength was starting to kick in. I freed myself from the wiring. "Let's go."

We ran after Aaron, Adrian, and the banshee. It wasn't hard to track them with all the noise they were making, and we found the twins cowering in a corner with the banshee shrieking her rage at them.

I tugged on Trey's sleeve and held up my shackles. He nodded, and we rushed in at the same time. I grabbed onto one of the banshee's arms, and he went for the other one. The intent was to shackle and hold her long enough for the twins to gag her. Shackles could slow down a banshee, but the only way to subdue one was to silence her. This was why it took multiple people to bring one in.

I almost had the shackle on her wrist when she screamed so loud it was like needles pricking my eardrums. I lost my grip and fell to my hands and knees, and she disappeared into the darkness.

It took a minute for my ears to stop ringing enough to hear Adrian calling his brother's name. I lifted my head and saw Aaron lying on the floor while Adrian bent over him. A few feet to my right, Trey sat on the floor, shaking his head and looking a little dazed.

I crawled over to Aaron, who had a bloody gash on his forehead. "What happened?" I asked too loudly.

"I think he ran into a two-by-four." Adrian shook his brother gently. "Come on, bro. You're scaring the shit out of me."

I checked Aaron's pulse and breathing and opened his eyes to look at his pupils. They reacted to the light, which was a good sign. I was debating what to do next when he blinked and let out a low moan. My breath left me in a relieved whoosh, and I sat back on my heels.

A few seconds later, he put a hand up to feel the goose egg on his head. "Did anyone get the license plate of that truck?"

From the far end of the floor, the banshee keened. Aaron sat up and nearly fell over, clutching his head.

"Take it slowly," Adrian told him.

Aaron looked at his brother with haunted eyes. "Did you see her? It was Emmy but not."

Adrian nodded sadly. "I saw her."

I didn't say anything. Emmy was their sister, who had been two years behind me in school. She'd died from leukemia a year and a half ago.

"Do you guys want to keep going or come back tomorrow?" Trey asked from behind me.

"Keep going," Aaron, Adrian, and I said together.

Aaron stood, pressed his mouth into a hard line, and tossed away his busted headlamp. "That bitch is going down."

We headed back toward the other end of the building where we'd heard the banshee the first time. Halfway there, she started up her keening again, and a shudder went through me. I reminded myself it was all in my head, and she couldn't hurt me if I didn't let her. A glance at the other three told me they were dealing with their own fears. I didn't know what Trey had seen, but our visions couldn't have been anywhere near as bad as seeing a dead sister.

As with before, the banshee went silent when we drew near. This time, though, we were expecting her attack. We stood together with our hands over our ears as she flew screaming at us out of the darkness. She circled us a few times and took off when she saw she wasn't going to scare us away.

We resumed walking. She kept returning to the same spot, and I suspected it might be where Claire Parker's apartment had been. If so, that was the best place to corner her. She was drawn to it, and she would make her stand there.

I could hear the howl of the wind the closer we got to our destination, and the sheets of hanging plastic danced like ghostly figures. For a moment, I imagined one of them was the ghost of Claire Parker, and I quickly shook off the thought. The banshee was terrifying enough without me scaring myself more.

Trey touched my arm and pointed at something up ahead. I squinted through the gloom and spotted a figure standing in front of a window, or the place where a window used to be. Her gray cloak and long gray hair fluttered wildly, and she had her head bent forward, her hands clasped as if in prayer.

"Same plan as before?" I asked as we approached her.

Aaron didn't take his eyes off the banshee. "Yes."

I swallowed dryly and moved ahead of them. The plan we'd come up with was for me to distract the banshee. While I took the brunt of her anger, the three of them would subdue her. It had sounded like a great plan before I'd experienced her wrath firsthand.

She started a low keening when I was ten feet from her, but she didn't lift her head to look at me. My heartbeats pounded in my ears as I slowly closed the distance between us. She didn't move.

I glanced over my shoulder at the others, and Adrian shrugged. They couldn't sneak up on her if she stayed where she was, but she didn't seem inclined to leave the spot.

Then it hit me. If this had been Claire's apartment, the banshee was probably standing exactly where the woman had fallen from. I shivered at the realization.

None of the books I'd read had mentioned what to do when a banshee just stood there like this. Dad had said she would go after whomever got close to her, which was me in this case.

"Hey," I said to her, feeling stupid talking to a banshee. Could she even understand me? Too bad becoming faerie didn't give me command of their language. That probably would have come in handy.

She didn't move, so I spoke again. "Hey?"

Still no response. I took a breath and tried a different tactic. "Claire?"

Her head shot up, and she fixed her dead eyes on me. I backed up as her face twisted in rage, and her keening grew louder. In the blink of an eye, she was so close I could feel the cold emanating from her. She began to circle me, and I moved with her until I was now the one with my back to the windows. Her mouth gaped, and I clapped my hands over my ears before the shriek came.

I couldn't hear the others moving, but suddenly, the banshee whirled away from me. The twins grabbed her arms, and I caught the glint of metal in Trey's hands. I didn't breathe as they wrestled her to the floor.

The banshee exploded from the tangle of bodies with an earsplitting screech. I flinched at the thud of two bodies hitting the wall as she rounded on me. She flew at me so fast there was no time to evade her attack. I pitched backward, but there was nothing to grab onto. Terror slammed into me as I fell through the opening and into the night.

3

"Jesse!"

Trey's frantic shout sounded a long way off as I flailed wildly, reaching for anything to stop my fall to my death. The fingers of my right hand touched the lip of the opening, and I grabbed it, holding on with everything in me. I swung helplessly in the wind as I reached up with my other hand.

It took four tries for my hand to latch onto the raised edge. Above me, the banshee screeched and Trey shouted. I couldn't hear Aaron and Adrian, which meant Trey was on his own against her.

I tried to climb up, but there were no footholds, and the more I moved, the more the metal edge bit into my fingers. I didn't dare look down. This was nothing like hanging from the ferry. I would have survived hitting the river. There would be no surviving a twenty-five-story fall, even for a faerie.

An agonized scream came from above. *Trey.*

Strength surged through me. I pulled my body upward with such force that I cleared the bottom of the window and flew through it. I hit the floor in a roll and came to my feet in front of the banshee and Trey. He was on his knees facing me, and she was behind him with her gnarled, hands on either side of his head.

Her head snapped up, and her dead eyes locked with mine. I felt a frisson of fear until I realized her stare had no effect on me because I was no longer human. I rushed at her, and she released Trey as she backed away from me.

"Jesse! Jesus, I thought you were dead," Trey said between gasps. "How...?"

The banshee whirled to flee, and I leaped, tackling her. We went down in a tangle of limbs, and she shrieked so loudly in my ear it sent needles of pain through the side of my head. I managed to clamp a hand over her mouth, but even my new strength wasn't going to hold her for long.

"Trey, shackles," I grunted. I heard movement behind me, and it seemed to take forever before Trey appeared holding a pair of shackles.

The banshee screamed against my hand and bucked viciously to throw me off her. I lost my grip, and one of her arms flailed, hitting my cheek with such force that I saw stars.

Trey dived into the fight, and between the two of us, we finally managed to pin her down. Looking around, I found the shackles three feet away, and I was the closest to them. I moved my hand so Trey could put his over her mouth, and then I went for the shackles.

My head jerked back violently when the banshee's bony fingers snagged my hair. Tears pricked my eyes as I pulled out of her clutches and felt my hair coming free from my ponytail. Ignoring the pain in my scalp, I reached for the shackles and snatched them up.

Waves of cold nausea slammed into me, and I swayed on my legs, which were suddenly unable to bear my weight. I fell to my hands and knees, gasping for air and fighting not to pass out.

"Jesse!"

Trey's shout penetrated the roaring in my ears. I lifted my head to see him staring at me as he struggled with the banshee. I tried to push up off the floor, but I was like steel stuck to a powerful magnet.

It wasn't until I caught a glimpse of strands of red hair in the banshee's fist that I realized what was wrong with me. When she'd grabbed my hair, she had pulled the goddess stone from it as I had done with the kelpie.

A horrifying thought hit me. The goddess stone was the only thing protecting me from the iron in this world. What if the stone passed to her now? Without it, I didn't know how long I could last.

Fear propelled me forward, and I crawled the few feet to Trey and the banshee. It took supreme effort to reach up and catch her hand, but as soon as I made contact with her fist, energy flowed into me like rainwater into parched soil. I forced her fingers open, and there on her palm was the stone in the exact same shade of red as my hair. I touched it, and it disappeared. The strength flooding my body told me the stone was back in my hair where it belonged.

"The shackles," Trey shouted.

I snatched up the shackles from the floor and made short work of securing the banshee's wrists. Her thrashing stopped, and she lay weakly in Trey's hold while I pulled off my backpack and found the muzzle I'd stuffed in there earlier. Trey took his hand off her mouth, and I fitted the muzzle in place, ignoring the hateful glare she shot me. She might have been scary when I first saw her, but she was no danger to anyone now.

Sitting on the floor, I stretched my jaw to relieve my ears that still ached from her wailing. My fingers touched the cold head of a hammer, and I jerked my hand away as if the metal had burned me. A shudder went through me, and I tried not to think of what it must feel like for the banshee to wear those shackles.

I stood. "Watch her. I'm going to check on the others."

Trey grabbed my arm before I could leave, and I met his eyes, which were round with shock. "You... You're a faerie," he whispered. "But how?"

"Don't be ridiculous, Trey." I pulled away from him.

He scowled at me. "I know I'm not as smart as you, but I'm not an idiot either. I saw what just happened to you, and the banshee didn't affect you at all when you looked at her."

I shook my head, intending to deny it, but his expression told me it wouldn't work. Any explanation I came up with would sound lame after what he'd witnessed.

"You can't tell anyone about this," I said.

His eyes grew even wider. "You're really a faerie? When? How?" He paled as he connected the dots. "You were shot. Oh, Jesse..."

One of the twins groaned somewhere off to our left.

"Yes," I hissed at Trey. "Can we not talk about this here?"

His look was incredulous. "It's not like you can keep it a secret."

"I will for as long as I can. And you are not going to tell a soul, not even your dad."

"But..."

I leaned in to whisper, "If you breathe a word of this, I will tell the whole Plaza about the time you were so afraid of the clown at the neighborhood Halloween party that you peed your pants."

He stared at me aghast. "I was a little kid, and he was dressed like *Pennywise*."

"You were fourteen." I gave him an evil smirk. "I have the pictures to prove it."

I left him sputtering and went to check on Adrian and Aaron. That clown incident was Trey's most embarrassing secret, and I had happened to be in the right place at the right time to witness it. I wasn't lying about the pictures, but I would never humiliate him that way. He didn't know that, though.

Adrian was out cold, but Aaron was coming to when I found them. It took half an hour to get them both on their feet. I suggested they go to the hospital, but they wouldn't hear of it. Neither of them was happy when they saw the bound banshee and Trey's smug look. We'd all get credit for the capture, but this was going to leave a bad taste in their mouths for a long time.

We gathered our stuff and got into the elevator with the banshee between Aaron and Adrian. It was their job, so it was only right for them to bring her out of the building. Trey grumbled under his breath until I shot him a warning look.

Out on the street, we got plenty of stares from passersby who gave us a wide berth. Bounty hunters were common, but it wasn't every day you saw a real live banshee.

"Our van is around the corner," Aaron said. "Do you guys want to follow us to the Plaza?"

"Not unless you need us to go," I said, speaking for Trey and me.

Adrian shook his head. "We can handle her from here. We'll leave your shackles and muzzle and your share of the bounty with Silas."

"Sounds good."

We said our goodbyes, and they limped away with the banshee between them. Aaron looked like he'd gone a few rounds with a prizefighter. Adrian hadn't fared much better than his brother. Trey was sporting a black eye, but that was from me, not the banshee. He'd gotten off the easiest among us. I didn't have any facial bruises, but my ribs felt like they'd been kicked by a kelpie. I'd soon find out if faeries healed as fast as I'd heard they did.

"Hey, isn't that one of the faeries who was at your apartment on Christmas Eve?" Trey asked.

My stomach did a little tumble as I followed his gaze to the other side of the street where a lone figure stood outside a restaurant. I let out my breath when I saw it was Faolin, not Lukas.

Faolin's head turned slowly as if he was doing a sweep of his surroundings. His eyes met mine, and he frowned. I couldn't tell if it was from displeasure or surprise.

I gave him a cheeky grin and a little wave that was sure to annoy him. I was rewarded with a scowl as a large black car pulled up in front of him. He made no move to get in, and I realized too late that he was waiting for someone.

The door behind him opened, and a couple walked out. The man was handsome, in his thirties, and he looked a little familiar. A celebrity maybe? His companion was blonde, beautiful, and Fae.

Another person appeared behind them, and my gut clenched when I saw Lukas. The female faerie turned to say something to him, and he laughed.

The day after Faolin's visit, I had summoned the nerve to call Lukas and thank him for what he'd done for me. I'd gotten his voice mail instead of him, and I'd left him a short, rambling message to which he'd never replied. I had been telling myself that the reason I hadn't seen or heard from him in the last two weeks was that he was busy dealing with the barrier problems. Apparently, I was mistaken.

Faolin leaned over to say something to Lukas. Seconds later, Lukas's head swung in my direction, and his gaze locked with mine. His smile was gone, but that didn't stop the quickening of my heart or the physical pull toward him. It felt like months, not weeks, since I'd last seen him, and I was relieved for the traffic that prevented me from giving in to the urge to go to him.

The female faerie said something to him. When he didn't respond, she followed his gaze to me. She clearly wasn't happy that someone else was stealing his attention from her, and I could feel the hostility she directed at me. If not for the street between us, her glare might have reduced me to cinders.

"Jesse?"

I tore my eyes from Lukas to look at Trey, whom I realized had said my name a few times. He glanced between Lukas and me, and I could almost see the light come on over his head.

"Was he the one who...?"

"I'll tell you about it on the way home." Pasting on a smile, I hooked my arm through his. I don't know what compelled me to do it. Maybe I wanted to show Lukas that I was doing fine without him, too.

I cast one last glance across the street. Faolin now sported a knowing smirk, but Lukas's mouth had formed a thin line. I might have allowed myself to believe he was jealous if he hadn't avoided me for two weeks. My anger flared. He had been ignoring me, and now he looked annoyed that I wasn't sitting at home waiting for him to finally have time for me. He couldn't have it both ways.

I turned my back on him and tugged on Trey's arm. "Let's go."

"Do I want to know what that was about?" he asked as we started back to where the Jeep was parked.

"Nope."

We walked in silence for a few minutes before he spoke. "Why don't you want anyone to know about... what happened to you?"

"Because the media will go nuts, and I can't put Mom and Dad through that." Dad had been doing well this week, but I'd seen the strain around his eyes a few times when he thought I wasn't looking. It had to be killing him to know his son was alive but to not be able to reach out to him. I'd never been a vengeful person, but every time I saw what this was doing to my father, I wanted to hunt Queen Anwyn down and make her pay for what she'd done to my family.

Trey stopped walking and turned to face me. "I swear I won't tell anyone – even without the blackmail. I like your parents, and I wouldn't do anything to hurt them."

"Thanks." I smiled. "I wouldn't have told anyone about Pennywise."

He laughed. "I know. Otherwise, you would have done it back in school."

We started walking again, and we'd barely gone ten steps when he asked, "Can I have those pictures?"

"No." I grinned, feeling lighter.

He sighed heavily. "Can't blame a guy for trying."

Finch whistled, pulling my attention from the spreadsheet I was working on. I looked up as he sat on a stack of books on the corner of the desk.

I thought we were going to see Mom today, he signed.

"We're going when Dad gets back." I glanced at the time on the computer monitor. "He's only been gone an hour."

Finch's big eyes sparkled. *Do you think he's getting your present?*

"Probably." I laughed. Finch was more excited about my birthday than I was.

A series of soft whistles came from the top of the shelves where we kept our gear. Aisla had started coming into the office with Finch, but she was still too timid to sit on the desk.

"What's she saying?" I asked Finch.

She said maybe Dad will bring Gus home. Finch gave me such a hopeful look that my chest squeezed in response.

I cleared my throat. "Gus went home to Faerie to live with all the other drakkans, remember?"

Finch's eyes grew sad. *We miss him. Do you think he misses us?*

"Of course. How could he not miss you?" I couldn't tell my brother that Gus had most likely forgotten all about us and his time here. Faris had said that would happen once he was among the wild drakkans.

The doorbell rang, and I jumped up. I had no idea who could be calling, but I was glad for the interruption.

I peered through the peephole, but all I saw was a wrapped box sporting a large, blue bow. *Dad.* I rolled my eyes at his antics as I opened the door.

"Happy birthday!" shouted a voice that was definitely not my father's.

I gaped at my visitor. "Violet! What are you doing here?"

"Some welcome home that is." She threw one of her arms around me and hugged me while awkwardly holding the present. I pulled her into the apartment, took the box, and tossed it on the table. Then I hugged her until she grunted that I was crushing her.

I let her go. "Sorry."

She pretended to shake out her arms. "I see the faerie strength is finally kicking in."

"It comes and goes." I couldn't stop smiling. "You're home!"

"You didn't think I was going to miss your birthday." She took off her coat and hung it over the back of a chair. "Where is everyone?"

"Finch and Aisla are in the office, and Dad had to run out. He should be back soon."

She walked into the living room and sank down on the couch. "Perfect. That gives us time to catch up before the birthday festivities begin."

"Tell me everything about the movie. What was it like being on an actual movie set?" She and I had texted every day, but she hadn't gone into a lot of detail.

"It was exciting at first, but it gets old fast. This movie has a ton of CGI, so there's a lot of green screen shooting. I was able to get away for a few days because they won't be shooting the rest of my scenes until later." Her face lit up. "Oh! I'm doing two extra scenes I wasn't supposed to have. The director thought there weren't enough females in them, so they're switching out a male actor for me."

"That's amazing!"

She lifted a shoulder. "I would rather have gotten them because of my awesome acting skills, but this will give me twice as much screen time."

"And it will give everyone more time to see how awesome you are," I added.

"Exactly."

I threw up my arms. "My best friend is a movie star!"

The two of us squealed and jumped up and down like we were thirteen and I'd gotten a valentine from Josh Warren, the cutest boy in our class.

We fell back onto the couch, laughing, and I reached over to take her hand. "I missed you."

Her smile waned. "I wish I could have been here with you. The timing for this movie could not have been worse."

"I wasn't exactly a fun person to be around for the first two weeks. It's good to be hunting again because it keeps me busy."

"You must have been desperate to hunt if you went on a job with Trey." She snickered. "I wish I'd seen his face when you blackmailed him with the clown story."

I laughed with her. "He's been pretty cool about it, actually, and he kept my secret."

Violet tucked her legs under her and fixed me with a searching look. "Soooo?"

"So, what?"

"You've been texting about hunting, Harvard, and the fact you can no longer drink coffee – which is tragic, by the way." She gave a sorrowful shake of her head. "But one thing you haven't said a word about is a certain Unseelie prince."

I ignored the tiny pinpricks of pain in my chest. "Because there's nothing to tell you. I haven't spoken to him since he brought me home. I'm starting to wonder if he regrets making me Fae."

"You don't believe that, and neither do I. I saw him at the hospital, and I think he would have attempted the conversion even if your dad hadn't said yes."

"Then why haven't I heard from him?" I asked glumly.

She pursed her lips. "Have you tried calling him?"

"Once." I puffed out a breath. "I left him a message, but he never called back."

Her brow furrowed. "That doesn't make sense."

"I've given up trying to make sense of it," I lied. I wouldn't admit that his absence consumed my thoughts every night when I lay in bed. I could have asked Faris or Conlan about it, but my pride wouldn't let me. If Lukas wanted to ghost me, I wasn't going to chase after him.

"You know what? We should go out one night before I have to go back to Utah." Violet's eyes gleamed with mischief. "We can meet up with Lorelle at Va'sha or go somewhere else."

"I don't know." I bit my lip. Except for work, I hadn't gone out much lately. I didn't know if I was ready to be around a lot of people.

My phone rang, and I was grateful for the reprieve until I saw Ben Stewart's name on the screen. My stomach tightened. The only time the Agency's head of the Special Crimes division called me was when he had bad news.

"I don't suppose this is a social call," I said.

He chuckled. "No, although I do believe a happy birthday is in order."

Of course, the Agency knew everything there was to know about me – except for a few closely guarded secrets. "Thank you."

There was a brief silence on the line, and then he said, "I'm calling to give you a heads-up. There's been a leak from someone at the hospital."

"A leak?" My pulse leapt.

"We got a call today from a reporter asking about a Fae conversion that supposedly happened there. They didn't have any names, and they wouldn't give us the name of their source. We're looking into it, but I don't think there's anything to worry about. All they have is a rumor, but even a hint of a conversion is too much for them to pass up." He paused to take a breath. "The network is going to run the story. I didn't want you to be blindsided by it."

"Thanks for letting me know," I said as a cold knot formed in my gut. The truth was going to come out eventually, but I'd hoped I would have more time before the media got wind of it. It didn't matter that it was only a rumor. That was enough for the paparazzi and the reporters to start digging until one of them found something.

"Why do you look like someone kicked your puppy?" Violet asked when I ended the call.

I picked up the remote and turned on the television. I flipped through the channels until I found a local news station with a picture of the hospital in one corner of the screen. The words DEVELOPING STORY were displayed across the bottom.

My fingers gripped the remote as I listened to the two anchors discussing the information provided by an unnamed hospital insider. The details were so vague that if it had been about anything other than a conversion, it wouldn't have gotten air time. It had only been a few months since Jackson Chase's death, and another conversion so soon would send the media into a feeding frenzy. Already they were speculating about the identity of the new faerie and why the conversion was being kept hush-hush.

"Jesse," Violet said sharply.

I tore my eyes from the television. "What?"

She tugged at the remote in my hand. "Unless you want to buy your parents a new one of these, hand it over."

I opened my hand to reveal two cracks in the remote's plastic casing. "Crap."

She took it from me and studied the damage before she turned off the television. "Remind me not to hold your hand the next time you're upset or angry."

"This new strength takes a while to get used to." I flexed my fingers. "I accidentally crushed a carton of eggs the other day. What a mess."

She snickered. "Bet it comes in handy when you're hunting, though. Wait until you have Fae strength *and* magic."

I made a face. "Faris said it's different for every new faerie. Some wake up one day, and they have their magic. Others get it in spurts, and it can be unpredictable at first. I appear to be in the latter group."

Violet's laugh warmed me. She set the remote on the coffee table and faced me. "You're good at everything you put your mind to. Before you know it, you'll be throwing around glamours like a pro."

"I would never glamour someone!"

"Wrong choice of words." She smiled sheepishly. "But you know what I mean."

I sighed heavily. "Sorry. I'm a little sensitive about it."

She let out a mock gasp. "Really? I never would have guessed." She fingered the ends of her hair, which was back to its natural shiny black. "You know, pretty much every actor and model in the world would love to have your problems if it meant never aging."

I gave her a pointed look. "*Every* actor?"

"Well... except for Paul Rudd. The guy *never* ages."

I tapped a finger against my chin. "True."

"I think he is a faeman," she said.

"A what?"

She grinned. "Part faerie and part human. I know they say it's impossible for a faerie and a human to make a baby, but you have to wonder about him."

I snorted, and a laugh slipped out. She joined in, and I suddenly felt lighter.

"Was that someone from the Agency on the phone?" she asked.

"Ben Stewart." I filled her in on what he'd told me.

"All they have is a rumor. They don't know it was you."

"Not yet, but they will." I slumped against the cushion. "I need a distraction. Tell me more about the hot actors you worked with."

Violet rolled her eyes. "You hang out with the Unseelie prince and his royal guard, and you want to hear about a bunch of actors?"

"I don't hang out with them," I replied grumpily.

She opened her mouth to retort just as the doorbell rang. I hopped off the couch and went to answer it with her trailing behind me. Peering through the peephole, I wasn't all that surprised to see Conlan and Faris. It had been a few days since any of them had dropped by to check on me.

I opened the door, and the two faeries greeted me with smiles and arms full of wrapped presents.

"Happy birthday," they said together.

I frowned as I stepped back to let them in. "I thought faeries didn't celebrate birthdays."

"We don't." Faris set four presents on the table. "But we know it's an important human tradition, and we wanted to help you celebrate yours."

My heart constricted. "Thanks."

Violet caught my eye and gave me a look that said, *"You don't hang out with them, huh?"*

Faris pointed to two boxes wrapped in shiny blue paper. "Those are from Faolin and me. The other two are from Iian and Kerr."

"And these are from Lukas and me," Conlan said, drawing my attention to the large wrapped rectangular box he carried. He handed a smaller wrapped gift to me. "This one is from me."

"Thank you," I said thickly, deliberately not looking at the large box he propped against the table. "You guys didn't have to get me anything."

"We wanted to. Not every day our *li'fachan* has a birthday." He wrapped an arm around my shoulders like he'd done the night we met. Unlike that time, I didn't shrug him off.

"You're not starting the party without us, are you?" Dad said from the doorway, startling me. "Sorry I'm late. It took longer than I thought to pick up your birthday gift."

"Dad, you didn't have to get me anything," I protested.

He only smiled and moved to one side.

A red-haired woman stepped into view and smiled at me. "Happy birthday, Jesse."

4

———————

"Mom!" I ran to her and wrapped her in a tight hug. "They let you out for the day?"

She patted my back. "Not exactly. It's more of a permanent thing."

I pulled away to look at her. "Are you serious? You're home for good?"

A series of shrill whistles made my ears ache as a tiny blue figure sped toward us. Finch reached us and scampered up Mom's body to cling to her neck. She placed a hand over his small back and smiled, looking the happiest I'd seen her since she woke up in the hospital.

"Welcome home, Mrs. J," Violet called from behind me. "Looking good!"

Mom laughed softly. "It's great to see you, Violet." Her gaze shifted to Faris and Conlan. "I saw you at the hospital, but I'm sorry, I don't remember your names."

I made the introductions, and she clasped Faris's hand and then Conlan's. "I don't know if I thanked you that night for saving Jesse's life. We will be forever grateful for what you did."

"We're happy we could be there for her," Faris said humbly.

Conlan ruffled my hair. "Life would be too boring without our Jesse."

I stepped out of his reach and scowled at him, which only made him chuckle. Some things hadn't changed.

Mom laughed as she unbuttoned her coat. Dad helped her remove it because Finch was still hugging her neck. Seeing the three of them together here for the first time in months made my heart swell until I thought it would burst from my chest. Our family had been through so much since that awful

34

November night, and finally, we were all home. I couldn't ask for a better birthday present.

Faris looked at me. "We'll be going now and leave you to enjoy your celebration."

"Please stay," Mom said. "You can't go until after we have cake."

I looked between her and Dad. "There's cake?"

"Of course." Dad went across the hall and unlocked Maurice's door. He disappeared inside and returned a minute later with a large, pink bakery box. Sneaky.

"Where's Maurice?" I asked when he shut our apartment door.

Dad set the cake on the kitchen counter. "He's on a job, and he'll stop by later."

While my parents went into the kitchen to get plates and forks, I hurriedly whispered to Conlan and Faris about the call from Ben Stewart and what I'd seen on TV. Neither of them was surprised by the news.

"We've been monitoring the hospital and the media. You have nothing to worry about," Conlan said in a low voice.

I looked at my parents. "I'm not worried about me."

Mom turned toward us, and I noticed the changes in her face since the last time she had stood in our kitchen. She looked tired, and her complexion was pale from so much time indoors. The doctors had deemed her well enough to come home, but she still had months of recovery ahead of her.

After we'd all enjoyed the triple layer chocolate cake, Violet declared it was time for me to open my gifts. I started with hers, which contained a crimson Harvard hoodie.

I held it against me. "It's perfect."

"I know." She lifted one shoulder. "It's scary how well I know you."

"Mine next," Conlan said eagerly. "I've never given a birthday present, so I hope you like it."

"I'm sure I will." I opened the small gift he handed me, and Violet gasped at the leaf-shaped pendant on a delicate chain. The pendant and chain were made of eyranth, a Fae metal that resembled platinum but with a faint bluish glow. Eyranth was rare and valuable in our realm because faeries didn't part with it often.

"This is too much, Conlan," I protested weakly.

"No, it's not." Violet reached out and wriggled her fingers at the pendant. "Can I touch it?"

I handed her the box and gave Conlan a quick hug. "Thank you."

"If you're going to reward me with hugs, I'll be giving you more gifts," he teased.

I opened Faris's gift next and sucked in a breath when I saw the red and gold drakkan figurine. The detail in the tiny piece was so good I wouldn't have been surprised if it had opened its snout and sent out a puff of smoke and sparks.

"It looks exactly like him," I said quietly. "Thank you."

Finch whistled, and I looked at him standing on the table with his eyes wide in recognition. He stretched out his arms, and I placed the figurine in them. Cradling it reverently, he jumped off the table and ran to the treehouse where Aisla was hiding from our visitors.

"He and Aisla miss Gus a lot," I said to Faris, who was watching Finch scamper up the ladder to the treehouse.

Faris gave me a knowing smile. "I can tell he is missed."

"Open the rest!" Violet picked up one of the other gifts and shoved it into my hands.

Grinning, I tore off the wrapping paper to reveal a rolled-up pouch of soft leather. I opened it to find six sharp double-ended spikes made from a charcoal gray metal.

"Ummm. Thanks?"

Conlan laughed. "These are from Iian. They're throwing spikes for when you progress to weapons training."

"Oh." I looked at them with new interest. "I figured you'd start me with something less...pointy."

"Open Kerr's gift," Faris said.

I did and found a cylinder sheath about a foot long. Uncapping the sheath, I tipped it, and a polished wooden object slid out. It had metal tips and looked like a piece of a staff I'd seen in their training room.

Faris took it and pressed one of the metal parts, and the piece extended until it was a full-length staff. He handed it back, and I marveled over how light it was.

"This is a combat staff," he said when I balanced the staff on one finger. "The wood is very strong, and it is a lethal weapon in the hands of a trained fighter."

Dad came to stand beside me, and I passed the staff to him. He gripped it in both hands and stared at it appreciatively. "I always wanted to learn to fight with a staff."

"Why didn't you?" I asked.

"Never got around to it. I focused on other training that was more practical for the job."

Leaving him to admire the weapon, I turned back to the table where a flat box lay. One of the last people I would expect to receive a birthday gift from was Faolin, and I was intensely curious about what was inside.

I removed the plain blue paper to see a dark wooden box with a hinged cover. Lifting the lid, I gasped at the pair of knives nestled on a bed of silky material. They were about ten inches long with wooden handles and wickedly sharp blades made of the same dark metal as Iian's throwing spikes.

"Wow," I breathed. I looked up at Faris and Conlan, who appeared as surprised as I was.

"Those are glaefere blades," Faris said after a moment of silence.

"The finest weapons a warrior owns after their sword," Conlan explained. "It is said that the first glaefere blades were crafted by the Asrai."

I stared at him. "Are you sure Faolin meant to give these to *me*?"

Conlan's eyes sparkled with laughter. "Anyone who can land a strike against the Unseelie prince *and* his head of security is deserving of such a gift."

"You hit the Unseelie prince?" Mom asked sharply. "And one of the royal guards?"

I winced because it sounded bad when she said it. "It's kind of a long story. I'll explain it all later."

She fixed me with her no-nonsense look. "I see we have a lot of catching up to do."

"You still have to open the big gift from Lukas," Violet blurted.

I eyed the box with a mix of curiosity and resentment. For weeks, Lukas had acted like I didn't exist, yet he'd taken the time to get me a birthday gift. I wasn't sure how to feel about that.

I snagged the wrapping paper on the top end and tore it down the length of the gift that was over three feet long. Underneath was a plain cardboard box, and I lifted a flap to see the outline of a black guitar case inside.

Violet peered over my shoulder. "He got you a new guitar. I bet it's a nice one."

"Are you going to open it?" Dad asked, and I realized I'd been staring at the case a little too long.

I took the guitar case from the box and set it down on the table. Unhooking the latches, I lifted the cover and stared at the instrument inside. It took me a long moment to realize what I was looking at.

Tears blurred my vision as I reached out to touch the guitar my grandfather had taught me to play on, the guitar that had been one of my prized possessions until two men had broken in here and destroyed it. I hadn't been able to bring myself to throw it out, so I'd shoved it under my bed where I didn't have to see it.

"How?" I whispered.

"Lukas asked me for it, and I gave it to him," Dad said. "I wasn't sure it could be repaired, but he said he could do it."

"Try it out," Violet said, and Finch whistled in agreement.

I took the guitar from the case and sat. After a minute of tuning the strings, I played a few lines of Finch's favorite song. It played and sounded exactly like it had before it was broken.

I pretended to adjust the strings some more so I didn't have to look up at everyone watching me. I didn't understand how Lukas cared enough to give me something that meant so much to me, when at the same time he didn't want to see me or even pick up a phone to call me. It made no sense, and I was more confused than ever.

"Do you like it?" Conlan asked.

"It's perfect," I said honestly, and I played until the ache in my chest went away.

I shivered and pulled my cap down to shield my ears from the icy wind that sliced through the cemetery. This winter felt like it had been going on forever, and it wasn't ready to release its grip on us yet.

Beside me, Mom seemed impervious to the cold as she crouched to replace the old flowers at the base of the white marble headstone with fresh ones. She arranged the flowers as she spoke softly to the son she still believed was buried here.

I met Dad's eyes over her head and saw how hard this was for him. He and Mom had spent the last twenty years grieving for their lost son, and now he had to watch her continued suffering. He had asked their doctors how much to reveal to her about the things she didn't remember, and the doctors said small things were okay. To avoid a relapse, we needed to let her regain her memories at her own pace.

Dad and I had decided that one of us would be with Mom at all times because we couldn't risk her remembering something traumatic when she was alone. So far, it had been relatively easy to do because this was the first time she'd left the apartment since coming home three days ago.

My mother was not stupid. She knew we were keeping something from her, but Dad had asked her to trust him, and she did so without question. I think, for her, having us all together was enough for now.

I dropped my gaze to the name engraved into the small headstone. My whole life, this had been the only place I'd felt somewhat connected to my brother. Being here now, knowing it wasn't Caleb's body in the grave, I didn't know what to feel other than a simmering anger at the person who had torn my family apart.

Mom stood and ran a gloved hand lovingly over the little angel atop the headstone. She straightened her shoulders and smiled at me, but I caught the sadness in her eyes before she could hide it like she always did.

"Your nose is so red it's almost glowing," she teased.

"Just the look I was going for."

Laughing, she looped an arm through mine. "Let's stop for Thai on the way home. I've been dying for something spicy, and that will heat us up."

I forgot all about the cold. She had been eating like a bird since she'd come home, and this was the first time she'd shown interest in food. Thai was her favorite, not mine, but I'd have it seven days a week if that was what it took to get her to eat.

"I could go for some Pad Thai." I looked over at Dad. "You can have that mango rice you love."

He smiled at us. "What's a meal without dessert?"

I started to ask what our trainer, Maren, would think of his love of desserts when an unpleasant tingle spread across my skin. My whole body tensed because I knew this sensation. My first instinct was to make sure I was wearing my dampening amulet. Then I lifted my head to look at the colored lights in the sky a few miles away.

There hadn't been any Fae storms in New York since the big one a few weeks ago. This one had the light display and some electricity, but it was mild compared to the last storm. Thanks to my handy amulet, my feet stayed planted on the ground.

"It's okay," Dad called to a young couple standing by a grave a few rows over. "Looks like it's already moving off."

I shifted restlessly. He was right that the storm was dissipating, but why did I still feel the magic?

Mom tugged gently on my arm and whispered. "You alright?"

"I don't know." I rubbed my arms through my coat sleeves. "Something doesn't feel right."

The words had barely left my mouth when the tingling intensified into pins and needles. Mom sucked in a breath, and I followed her gaze to the lights that had appeared in the sky above us. Was this a second storm or the same one?

The light dimmed as if a cloud had blocked out the sun, and my scalp prickled with a new sensation. Dread.

"We need to go." I grabbed Dad's arm and started toward the car, pulling him and Mom with me. I would have run, but Mom wasn't strong enough for that yet.

"Jesse, what is it?" Dad asked.

A loud crackling filled the air, which felt charged with static electricity and made my hair stand on end. The cemetery was suddenly bathed in a purple glow that caused memories of another storm to flash through my mind. Fear threatened to choke me, and all I could think of was getting my parents away from here.

Behind us, someone shouted. A second later, there was a snap followed by a small explosion. We turned to see pieces of black marble spraying out from where a headstone had stood a few dozen yards away.

"My God," Mom uttered.

Magic surged around me again. Before I could move, a bolt of purple lightning obliterated a statue, sending stone shrapnel in every direction. I watched in horror as a jagged column of electricity scorched the grass and sped away from the destroyed statue.

Toward us.

I spun and grabbed Mom. Throwing her over my shoulder, I ran.

We'd barely gone ten feet when another explosion rocked the air. I pushed Dad to the ground and dropped Mom beside him. Throwing myself on top of them, I tried to shield them with my body as pieces of stone and debris pelted me.

It took a minute for me to register the silence. Rolling off my parents, I lay on the grass and blinked up at the puffy white clouds in the blue sky. My breath came out in ragged pants that had more to do with the adrenaline coursing through me than exertion.

"Jesse!" Dad scrambled over to kneel beside me. "Are you hurt?"

"No." I gave him a reassuring smile and sat up.

His eyes went to the side of my head, and he frowned. "You're bleeding. Let me look at it."

I reached up to gingerly touch my head and realized I'd lost my cap. The area was tender, but there was only a small cut. "It's nothing. You know head wounds bleed a lot." I lowered my voice. "And I heal fast."

"I don't care. I still want to check it." He pushed my hand away and examined the cut. "You'll live."

I shot him a sideways look. "Told you."

"Caleb," Mom said in a choked voice that had the two of us jerking our heads in her direction. She was on her knees, her face a mask of anguish as she stared at what remained of his grave.

I jumped up and ran to the edge of the crater where the tiny grave had been. Shock rippled through me when I saw the fragments of white marble littering the hole. Only a piece of angel wing identified it as the headstone that had stood there minutes ago.

My stomach knotted as I scanned the hole, praying I would not see pieces of the coffin or its contents in the debris. The last thing my mother needed in her fragile state was to see the skeletal remains of the baby she'd buried.

I let out a breath when I couldn't find any coffin remnants. The crater looked to be about five feet deep. Maybe the lightning hadn't reached the coffin at all. It was hard to tell with the loose dirt at the bottom.

Something glittered at the far edge of the hole, partially buried beneath a small chunk of marble. I leaned forward for a closer look and frowned when the object refracted the sunlight like a prism. A crystal of some kind?

"Help! Someone, please help!" called a woman's voice.

I swung my gaze in the direction of the young couple Dad had spoken to. The man lay on the ground, and the woman knelt beside him. Less than ten feet away from them was the remains of a shattered headstone.

Looking behind me, I saw Dad with his arms around Mom. Neither of them appeared injured, and she needed him more than she did me.

I skirted the hole and ran to the couple. The man's eyes were closed, and a shard of stone protruded from his chest. The woman had her bloody fingers wrapped around the piece of shrapnel, about to pull it out.

I placed my hand over hers to stop her. "No. We can't move it." I racked my brain for everything I knew about first aid and looked around for something to staunch the bleeding. Of course, there was nothing because we were in the middle of a cemetery.

Unzipping my coat, I yanked it off. Thankfully, I'd dressed in layers. I pulled my hoodie over my head and used it for padding around the stone shard. I instructed the woman, who told me her name was Julie, to hold the padding in place while I reached for my phone in my coat pocket.

A fortysomething woman hurried toward us. She dropped to her knees beside me, and the first words out of her mouth sent relief washing over me. "I'm a doctor. The paramedics are on the way."

I stood to give her room to work. Shivering, I pulled on my coat and zipped it up to my chin as I got my first good look at the carnage around me. A statue and three graves, including Caleb's, had been destroyed. A zigzagging trail of gouges and scorched grass showed the lightning's path of destruction.

The dozen or so other people in the cemetery had recovered from their own shock and were making their way toward us. We were lucky there hadn't been more casualties.

The doctor had control of the situation, so I went back to my parents, who now stood at the edge of the hole where Caleb's grave had been. Mom's face was ashen, and Dad's arm was around her shoulders, supporting her.

"He's... he's gone." Her body looked ready to crumple in on itself. I'd seen and endured a lot in the last few months, but nothing gutted me more than seeing my formidable mother so vulnerable.

"We don't know that," Dad said softly, his helpless gaze meeting mine. "I don't think the lightning went that deep."

I swallowed around the lump in my throat. "He's right. All I see is bits of headstone."

She straightened a little. "How could lightning do this? I've never seen anything like it."

"I have." As bad as this had been, the storm wasn't half as strong as the one I'd been in on the ferry. I kept that to myself. I seemed to have the extraordinarily bad luck to always be around when a storm occurred. If not for the fact that they were happening in other cities around the world, I'd be a little paranoid.

The sound of sirens reached us and quickly grew louder. Within minutes, the cemetery was overrun by emergency vehicles and police cars. Mom, Dad, and I talked to a police officer as the injured man was tended to by paramedics and loaded onto a stretcher. I found my cap and covered the blood in my hair so the paramedic who came to check on us wouldn't see that my head wound was healing already.

We were still talking to the police when half a dozen agents arrived to take command of the situation. Two of them started in our direction, and I scowled when I recognized Agent Daniel Curry. There had to be a hundred agents in this city, yet somehow, I always ended up with this one.

"Agent Curry, good to see you," said my father, who had no clue about my dealings with the man. As far as my parents knew, Curry had merely been the agent who'd rescued us from Rogin Havas's basement. I saw no reason to tarnish their good opinion of the agent because I didn't like him.

"I'm glad to see you both recovered." Curry smiled and shook their hands, and then he introduced Agent Will Ryan. I'd met Ryan before and liked him despite his partner.

Agent Curry sent the police officer away to question someone else, and then he turned to me. "You seem to have adapted well to your new circumstances."

I resisted the urge to roll my eyes. "It's not as if I have a choice."

"I've heard it takes months for new faeries to adapt to the iron in a city." He eyed me shrewdly. "You don't appear to be bothered by it at all."

I shrugged. The Agency knew nothing of my goddess stone, and I intended to keep it that way. "We Jameses are very resilient. Look at my parents. They finished their treatment months faster than the doctors said they would."

Dad smiled at me. "Jesse excels at everything she does."

"So it would seem." Agent Curry looked around. "You were all here when the storm hit?"

Mom nodded. "We were visiting our son's grave, and..." Her voice trailed off as tears filled her eyes.

"Your son?" For the first time since I'd met him, Agent Curry's businesslike mask slipped, revealing his surprise. My guess was his investigation into my parents hadn't gone that far into their background. When he'd followed me to the cemetery in December, I'd assumed he knew I was visiting my brother's grave.

"Caleb," Mom said, recovering her composure. She pointed to the hole a few feet away. "That was his grave."

Both agents turned to look at what was left of the grave, and Agent Ryan walked over to peer into the hole. "The lightning ended here. Where did it strike first?"

I pointed out the first headstone that had exploded. "The statue was next. After that, we ran and hit the ground."

"Then we'll start over there," Agent Curry said. "I'm glad you're all okay."

Dad nodded. "We're very lucky."

The agents said their goodbyes and walked off. I watched them go for a moment before I faced my parents. "I'm ready to go home. How about you?"

Mom shook her head. "We have to take care of Caleb's grave. We can't leave it like this."

"The cemetery has people who will do that," Dad said. "We should get out of their way so they can get to work."

"You're right." She gave the hole one more look and smiled wanly at me. "I don't feel like going for Thai anymore. How about I make my meatloaf and mashed potatoes for dinner?"

"Even better." My stomach let out a loud growl, and Dad laughed. I felt lighter when some of the old spark replaced the sadness in Mom's eyes.

We headed for our car, which was parked on the now crowded road that cut through the cemetery. There were no less than two ambulances, three fire engines, and half a dozen police cars with their lights flashing. I spotted three shiny black SUVs that must belong to the agents and two news vans.

The police were blocking the media and a small crowd of spectators from entering the scene, so the reporters and their cameramen were forced to record from the road. One of the reporters saw us and started our way, prompting us to pick up our pace. Even Mom was laughing when we reached the car and jumped in.

Dad started the car and maneuvered around the other vehicles, but he had to stop for the people who were in no hurry to move out of the way. We had to wait until a police officer came over to herd them off the road.

A lone figure standing in the shadows beside a tall headstone on the other side of the road caught my eye. At first, I dismissed him as another one of the curious onlookers until I realized his attention was not on the area where the storm had hit. His head was turned slightly, and he was watching us instead.

The sun came out from behind a cloud, bathing the mysterious man in light. My stomach lurched.

It was one of Queen Anwyn's personal guards.

5

———————

I WOULD KNOW that face anywhere. He was one of the two faeries who had warned me to stay away from Prince Rhys.

I stared into his cold eyes, unable to look away until the car started to move again and the faerie disappeared from view. I let out a breath and sank back against the seat, but my heart still beat a rapid tattoo against my ribs.

There was no way his presence here was a coincidence. Was he tailing us to report back to the queen, or did he have a darker reason for being in the cemetery today?

We were halfway home before I calmed my racing mind enough to remember the odd crystal I'd glimpsed in Caleb's grave. I'd completely forgotten about it after I'd gone to help the injured man. I hadn't thought much of it when I saw it, but now I had a chilling suspicion it had been put there deliberately. Some Fae crystals could store and generate enough energy to light a room or power an entire building. Could they also be used in other ways? Such as attracting an electrical storm full of Fae magic to a specific location?

I tucked my suddenly cold hands between my thighs. We hadn't told anyone we were going to Caleb's grave today, so there was no way the Seelie guard could have known we'd be there. But what if my parents and I hadn't been the target? What if the queen had seized upon an opportunity to destroy the only physical evidence that could prove my brother was not dead? Us being there when the storm struck would have been a bonus.

I should tell Dad, but the thought of adding to his burdens made me feel

45

sick. He was still recovering from his goren addiction and trying to cope with the truth about Caleb. On top of that, he was helping Mom, who needed him more than ever now.

We stopped for groceries on the way home, and I shivered when we pulled into the exact same spot I'd parked in the day the queen's guard had warned me to stay away from Prince Rhys. As we left the store, I couldn't help but scan the parking lot, afraid to find one of them waiting for us.

I was so wound up by the time we parked on our street that I jumped when Dad's phone rang. He picked it up from the console and hesitated a second before he answered it. I knew something was up when his eyes flicked to me in the rearview mirror before he averted his gaze.

"How did you hear about it so fast? No, the paramedics checked us out. We're all okay. We just got home." His voice lowered a notch. "She had a small cut on her head, but it's probably healed by now. A healer? I don't think that's necessary."

My suspicion about the call morphed into anger as Dad spoke, and the anger quickly boiled into fury. Lukas couldn't talk to me, but he had no problem calling my father to check up on me. Oh, hell no.

I unhooked my seat belt, nearly ripping it out of the seat, and leaned forward to snatch the phone from Dad. "If you want to know how I'm doing or anything else about me, you ask me."

The only response was silence from the other end of the line, and that got to me more than anything he could have said.

"That's what I thought." I hung up and thrust the phone at my father, who watched me with a mix of concern and admiration. Grabbing the two bags of groceries on the seat beside me, I opened the car door. "I don't know about you guys, but I'm starving."

Mom's soft laugh cut through some of the tension in the car. "We'll be up in a few minutes."

I barely felt the cold as I stalked toward our building. I knew my parents had stayed behind to talk about me, and I didn't care. I was so over this. Over *him*.

Letting myself into the apartment, I set the bags on the table and pulled out my phone to text Violet. **Let's go out tomorrow night. Somewhere fun.**

Her response was immediate. **Who are you, and what are you doing with Jesse's phone?**

Ha, ha. You in?

Her answer was an eyeroll emoji followed by **Do you even have to ask?**

"You're not having fun." Violet's mouth turned down in a pout.

"I am."

Lorelle, Violet's Fae girlfriend, smiled from across the tall bar table we stood around. "If you don't like Navi, there are other clubs we can go to."

"Navi is great. I was just thinking about something."

Violet leaned in. "Your mom?"

"Is it that obvious?" I let out a sigh. Today, Dad had gotten word that the storm at the cemetery had completely destroyed Caleb's coffin. We hadn't told Mom, but we couldn't keep it from her forever. The news had put a damper on my plan to go out, and I would have canceled if Dad had let me.

"Your mother is one of the toughest people I know," Violet said. "She'll be back to kicking ass in no time."

I straightened my shoulders. "You're right."

"I'm always right." She waved over a waitress and ordered another round of nonalcoholic drinks for our table. Normally, she'd be drinking some fruity cocktail, but she'd passed on that because Lorelle and I didn't drink alcohol.

After the waitress returned with our drinks, Violet excused herself to go to the restroom, leaving me alone with Lorelle. Lorelle knew about my conversion, and she'd taken me under her wing tonight when I had confessed I hadn't been out to a club since becoming a faerie. I wished she wasn't Seelie because it would have been nice to have at least one female friend in Unseelie when I finally went to court.

I studied Lorelle's face as she watched Violet walk away, and there was no mistaking the tenderness in her expression. She cared for my best friend as much as Violet did for her. I was happy for Violet, but I was also worried. I couldn't help but think about Jackson Chase and Princess Nerissa's tragic story. They'd fallen in love, and it had destroyed them.

"She's crazy about you," I said quietly.

"She is unlike anyone I've met." Lorelle swung her gaze to me, and her eyes held a sadness I hadn't seen there before. "I know what you are thinking. You are afraid she will be hurt when we have to part."

"Violet seems worldly to people who don't know her well, but she has a big heart, and she feels things deeply." I turned more to face Lorelle. "I like you, and I can see you care about her. All I'm asking is for you to try not to hurt her."

She smiled wistfully. "Violet and I have already talked, and we both know this has to end. I am going home to Seelie when she returns to her movie. This is our last week together, and we plan to make the most of the time we have left."

My throat tightened. "She didn't tell me."

"I am not surprised. She loves you and does not want you to worry." As if sensing Violet's presence, Lorelle looked in the direction she'd gone. "She is a beautiful person."

I followed her gaze to Violet, who beamed at us as she made her way back to our table. Tonight, she wore a jade green Fae dress – a gift from Lorelle – that fit her like a second skin and drew admiring looks from everyone she passed. She looked every bit the celebrity she was on the verge of becoming.

Lorelle stepped toward Violet when she reached us and took her hand. Without a word, she led Violet to the dance floor, and they began a slow, sensual dance, completely lost in each other. They looked so perfect together. It was cruel of fate to let them find each other only to tear them apart.

I averted my eyes because it felt like an intrusion to watch them like this. My gaze swept the club and landed on a dark-haired man on the other side of the dance floor who was watching me. He smiled when our eyes met, and I looked away because I didn't want to encourage him. I was here to spend time with Violet and to try to forget the one male I thought about way too much.

My phone vibrated from my tiny purse. Unlike Va'sha, Navi didn't prohibit phones or cameras, except on the VIP level. It was one of the reasons I'd chosen this club. Less privacy meant less chance of running into high profile celebrities and certain Fae royals. Cowardly, maybe, but I didn't think my heart was ready to see Lukas with someone.

Pulling out my phone, I was surprised to see Tennin's name on the screen. I hadn't seen or heard from him since the day he took photos of Lukas and me. That felt like a lifetime ago. I'd called him weeks ago to tell him I was sorry about what happened to his friend Angela, but his voice mail said he was in Faerie. Why on earth was he calling me at this hour?

"Tennin, hi. It's so great to hear from you."

"Jesse, listen to me very carefully," he said in a voice that was all business. "Go to the VIP section of the club. The stairs are behind you to your left."

"What are you talking about? Are you here?" I craned my neck to search the crowded club for him.

"Yes. Don't ask questions. I'll explain when I meet you up there."

Something in his tone told me to do as he said. "What about Violet?"

"I'll bring her to you," he said. "Go. *Now.*"

"Okay." I grabbed my purse and stepped back from the table just as I spotted the man who'd caught my eye approaching. He looked harmless enough, but Tennin's call had unnerved me. I gave the man a curt smile to discourage him and turned toward the stairs to the VIP section.

"Jesse James?" someone called in a friendly, disarming voice.

Hearing my name made me stop abruptly and frown over my shoulder at the man. Did I know him from somewhere?

His smile broadened. He was a good-looking guy, mid-twenties, nice eyes. There was nothing exceptional about him, but I would have remembered if I'd met him before.

"Mark Jansen." He held out a hand, which I took out of politeness, a second before he blindsided me with his next words. "So, Jesse, how do you feel since your conversion?"

I stared at him. "W-what?"

He flashed a press ID. "I'm with *The Fae Chronicle*, and my readers want to know all about you. Who did your conversion? Are they here with you?"

"I don't know what you're talking about. Excuse me. I need to –"

A camera flashed in front of my eyes. It was followed by a second and then a third.

"Jesse, have you been to Faerie yet?" someone yelled.

"How did you survive the conversion?"

"Why did they change the rules for you?"

"Is it true your Fae lover changed you so you could be together?"

"Who is he, Jesse? Is he here with you tonight?"

The questions came at me rapid-fire from all sides, punctuated by the blinding camera flashes. I shielded my eyes with my arm, but it was impossible to see through the throng of paparazzi surrounding me. Panic choked me, and I tried to back away, but escape was blocked from all sides.

A few paps shouted angry words at someone who shoved past them. I jerked when an arm was thrown across my shoulders.

"Stay close. I'll get you out of here," Tennin said in my ear.

I clung to him like a lifeline as he tried to push through the mob. His fellow paps weren't having it, swearing at him and calling him a traitor. Tennin was unfazed by their insults and didn't falter, even when one of them snatched his camera and threw it to the floor. This was insane. Why wasn't the club's security doing something to help us?

Two paps directly in our path suddenly disappeared as if they'd been picked up by a strong wind. The rest backed off with expressions that ranged from fear to excitement. I saw the reason for their reactions when three of Prince Rhys's stone-faced personal guards appeared before us. I didn't know whether to be relieved or unhappy to see them.

"Come with us," growled Bayard, the blond, fearsome head of Prince Rhys's security.

The other two guards took up positions behind us, and they ushered us through the crowds of paparazzi and onlookers to the VIP section. The muscled security guy at the bottom of the stairs took one look at us and moved aside to let us pass. I stayed glued to Tennin as we ascended the stairs, acutely aware of the hundreds of eyes following us.

At the top, people scurried out of our way, making it easy to see Prince Rhys and his two other guards waiting for us at a corner booth. As soon as we reached him, the five guards formed a scowling wall between us and the rest of the club.

"Jesse, are you okay?" the prince asked. "Did they harm you?"

"I-I'm fine." My legs felt like rubber. How did celebrities deal with that every day?

I took some deep breaths to regain my composure. Tennin kept his arm around me, and I was grateful for his solid presence.

"She's a little overwhelmed," he said. "Thank you for your assistance."

Prince Rhys looked at my savior as if noticing him for the first time. "Tennin, right? Aren't you a paparazzo as well?"

Tennin laughed. "When it suits me. Jesse is a friend of mine, and her welfare is more important than a few photos."

The prince nodded approvingly. "Jesse chooses her friends well."

My phone rang, and I blew out a breath when I saw it was Violet.

"Jesse? Jesse, can you hear me?" she yelled when I answered. I had no trouble hearing her over the background noise.

"Calm down, Vi," I said with more composure than I felt. "I'm okay."

"Oh, thank God! Where are you? I couldn't get to you, and then you were gone."

I grimaced at the panic in her voice. "My friend Tennin and Prince Rhys's guard got me away. I'm upstairs in the VIP section. Can you and Lorelle meet us up here?"

She huffed loudly. "Yes. As soon as I give these asshole paps a piece of my mind. They don't know who they're messing with." There was a slight scuffle followed by Violet's muffled, "That's right. I'm talking to you."

I rubbed my temple. "Vi, please don't start a fight with the paparazzi." But she'd hung up.

Tennin and Prince Rhys laughed, and my glower did nothing to stop them. I turned to push through the guards, but Tennin put up an arm to block me.

"You are not going down there," he said firmly. "I'll get your friend for you."

"You've never even met her. She won't listen to you."

He grinned. "I can be very persuasive, and I'm the best one to deal with that mob down there."

He had a point. I stepped back, and he tapped one of the guards on the back to let him pass. As soon as he was gone, I realized I was alone with Prince Rhys – my *brother* – for the first time since I'd learned his real identity. I had no idea how to talk to him now, and I was afraid of saying something I shouldn't.

"Please, sit." He waved at the plush leather couch behind me. "Would you like something to drink?"

"I'd rather stand, but water would be nice." The initial shock of the incident was wearing off, and embarrassment was setting in. I couldn't believe I'd gotten so frazzled because of a few paparazzi. Those guys would run screaming if they came face-to-face with some of the things I'd seen. It was a good thing Faolin hadn't been here to witness this. He'd never let me forget it.

Prince Rhys poured a glass of water from a carafe on a small table and handed it to me. "I'm sorry you had to go through that."

"I guess it had to come out eventually." I'd wondered what it would be like when the press got wind of it, but this was worse than what I had imagined.

"When I first came to this realm, the cameras and shouts were disconcerting," he admitted. "I still don't like them, but my guards shield me from the worst of it."

"As a prince, you must be used to being in the public eye at court."

He smiled. "Yes, but we have no cameras in Faerie. And no one there would dare to shout at the crown prince that way."

"You have a point." I relaxed a little and sipped my water.

"I have a confession to make," he said. "I've been hoping we would run into each other, although I wish it had been under different circumstances."

My fingers tightened around the glass. "Oh?"

"I enjoyed meeting your father very much, and I've been reading the books he recommended to me. I'd love to talk to him again and hear more of his bounty hunting stories." Prince Rhys sighed. "I cannot explain it, but you are the only people in this realm with whom I feel a real connection."

I tried to think of a response, but I had nothing. Was it possible for someone to be drawn to the family they didn't know existed? What would he say if he knew the truth?

"Now I've made you uncomfortable." His smile fell, and his expression turned sheepish. "I won't impose on you and your family. It would not be appropriate for me to seek out a new Unseelie faerie."

Bayard gave a low snort, reminding us Prince Rhys had done exactly that a week after I'd come home. Something told me the head of security was the real reason the prince hadn't come to call on us again.

My ears picked up a small commotion from the other side of the VIP section. I could feel tension build in the wall of guards blocking us from view, and my first thought was that some of the paparazzi had managed to sneak upstairs. I braced myself for a confrontation, but not for the arrival of the last person I expected to see.

When the guards parted to let Lukas through, I took an involuntary step backward. I hadn't been this close to him since the day he'd brought me home, and his presence was almost overpowering. The hard set of his jaw didn't help. I couldn't tell if he was angry at me, Prince Rhys, the paps, or all of the above.

"Rhys." Lukas gave a head tilt in acknowledgement. "Thank you for coming to the rescue of my ward."

His *ward*? What was I – ten years old? I glared at him, but he either didn't notice or he didn't care.

"I am glad I could help," Prince Rhys said without any of the arrogance he'd had the last time I'd seen the two of them together. "The paparazzi were quite aggressive with her."

Lukas's gaze finally met mine. "Did they hurt you?"

"No." I bristled under his demanding tone. "How did you know about it?"

"Tennin called me."

I pressed my lips together. My favorite photog and I were going to have words later.

"Come. Let's get you out of here." Lukas took my arm in a firm grip, and I nearly jumped at the spark of electricity that shot through me. I opened my mouth to tell him I wasn't going anywhere with him, but his whole countenance said this wasn't up for negotiation. The last thing I needed was to create another spectacle, so I held my tongue. For now.

I smiled tightly at Prince Rhys. "Thank you for your help."

He started to extend a hand toward me and dropped it. "Anytime, Jesse. However, you might want to avoid the paparazzi for a while."

"She will," Lukas said before I could reply. I clenched my jaw so I didn't embarrass myself by telling him he wasn't the boss of me.

Prince Rhys's guards moved aside to let us pass, and I wasn't surprised to see Conlan and Faolin waiting for us. I expected us to walk to the stairs, but Lukas steered me toward a door on this level.

I walked with my head up, pretending not to be aware that every person in this section was staring at us, but it was impossible not to hear the whispers. They all wanted to know about the new faerie who clearly had more than a passing acquaintance with the Seelie prince. One comment about the sexual nature of our relationship was so ugly that only my pride kept me from breaking into a run.

Lukas made a sound deep in his chest, and the whispers died as people averted their eyes. He opened the door and ushered me into a small private lounge with white leather couches. I expected Conlan and Faolin to join us, but they took up positions outside the door. As the door shut behind us, I felt a moment of panic at being alone with Lukas. For over a month I'd thought of all the things I'd say to him if I saw him again, but I couldn't remember a single one of them.

Instead of sitting on one of the couches, he held up his hands and murmured a few Fae words. Within seconds, the air shimmered as a portal began to form.

"What are you doing?"

"We can't exactly leave by the front exit." He lowered his hands, and I saw what looked like a stone wall beyond.

I took a step back. "What about Violet? I can't leave without her."

"Violet is with Tennin and Lorelle. They will protect her from the paparazzi."

"Who will protect the paps from Violet?" I could imagine my best friend unloading on the mob of photographers.

Lukas chuckled and pressed a hand to my back. The next thing I knew, we were in an open stone courtyard filled with flowering vines and a view of glittering stars in a dark sky. I didn't have time to wonder at the fact that there were stars in Faerie before another portal opened and we were in the living room of his Williamsburg building.

I whirled on him as the portal closed. "I thought you were taking me home."

"I will. First, we need to talk." He walked toward the kitchen, tossing his jacket onto one of the bar stools. "Would you like something to drink?"

I threw up my arms. "Oh, *now* you want to talk?"

He poured a glass of ghillie juice from a carafe on the counter and brought it to me. When I didn't take it, he sighed softly.

"I know you're hurt and angry with me, and I'm sorry."

"I'm not hurt." I snatched the glass from his hand and went to sit in a chair. I forgot I was wearing a dress and had to hurriedly adjust it when the blue material slid precariously up my thighs.

He took the chair across from me. "You are, and you have every right to feel that way. You've been through a traumatic experience, and I should have been there for you."

My chest squeezed, and I looked away from the sincerity in his eyes. Only pride kept me from asking why he hadn't been there and why he'd finally shown up tonight. If he told me he'd come to the club for me out of obligation, I wasn't sure my heart could take it.

"Do you know how many successful Fae conversions there have been?" he asked.

"Nineteen." I frowned at him. What did that have to do with anything?

"Twenty," he corrected me with a smile. "Out of billions of humans, only twenty have become Fae, and it's been a learning experience for us as well as the new faeries. We've made some mistakes, but most have settled happily into their new lives."

I met his eyes directly as a tiny knot formed in my gut. "Most?"

"The first two faeries had trouble adjusting, and they formed a deep attachment with the one who performed the conversion."

I relaxed a little. "They were children, so it makes sense that they would bond with the faerie."

"Yes, but these were not normal, healthy bonds. The children became attached to the point of obsession. They followed the adults who converted them everywhere and became distraught and inconsolable when separated from them. It was like a drug addiction that caused severe withdrawal symptoms."

I sucked in a breath. "Are you saying that's going to happen to me?"

"No. I would never allow that." He leaned forward with his elbows resting on his knees. "I'm telling you this so you'll understand why you haven't seen or heard from me until now. After I brought you home, my father's advisors warned me of the consequences of not staying away from you during the first month of your adjustment. Even the sound of my voice could have affected you, which is why I never called you."

I remembered the night I saw him across the street in Manhattan and the strange physical pull I'd felt toward him. A shiver went through me. That had been a brief encounter from a distance. How powerful would the attraction have been if I'd had normal contact with him? The thought of having no control over my mind or body, of having an unnatural bond with anyone, terrified me.

"What about Conlan and Faris and the others? They've been to see me multiple times, and it didn't affect me."

Lukas shook his head. "They took part in your conversion, but we used my blood."

"Your blood...is in me?" I stared at him. The conversion process was so secret that no human knew what it entailed. I had no recollection of it because I had been close to death when it happened.

"My blood is the strongest," he said matter-of-factly.

This was too much. I got up to pace the room. "You couldn't tell me any of this before? You let me think…"

He stood and came over to me. I didn't know whether to punch him or throw myself at him. He made the decision by wrapping his arms around me and holding me against his warm chest. To my mortification, tears burned my eyes. I blinked, refusing to let them fall.

"I'm sorry, *mi'calaech*," he murmured against my hair. "It had to be this way. If we'd told you the truth, it might have triggered you into seeking me out. I couldn't take that chance."

"It's safe now? I'm not going to turn into some mindless, obsessed stalker?"

His chest rumbled with laughter. "You might, but it won't be a side effect of the conversion."

"In your dreams." I pushed at him, and I didn't miss his playful grin when he released me. It had been so long since I'd seen him smile, and my stomach quivered in response. I was suddenly very aware that we were alone but also that I had no idea where things stood between us now. Did he see me as a friend or something more?

I wasn't sure I wanted to know the answer to that question yet, so I moved back into safer territory. "What happened to the new faeries who became attached? Did they recover?"

"Yes. It was difficult for them at first, but they are both happy in their new lives now. It is believed that their age played a factor in their recovery. The younger you are when converted, the easier it is to adapt to being Fae."

I let out a breath. The last month didn't seem so bad when I thought of what could have happened. An involuntary shiver went through me, and I rubbed my arms for warmth.

"Are you cold?" Lukas's gaze dipped to take in my short dress, and I shivered again but for a whole other reason.

"A little. I left my coat at the club."

He went to retrieve his jacket from the bar stool and draped it over my shoulders. "I'll have someone get your coat for you."

"Thanks." The jacket smelled of him, and I resisted the urge to inhale deeply. That wouldn't look stalkerish at all.

He smiled ruefully. "I'm sorry your night out was ruined. If it's any consolation, you'll look beautiful in all the paparazzi photos."

I groaned. "Thanks for reminding me. For a minute there, I'd totally forgotten that disaster. How did they find out?"

"I don't know." His expression hardened. "The Agency assured me they had it under control, but I should have known this would happen and protected you from it. A story like this is too big to keep under wraps for long."

"It's not your fault. You can't control every situation, and I knew it would come out eventually." I let out a sigh of resignation. This was my life now, and I had no choice but to deal with it. "How long do you think it will take them to get bored and move on to another story?"

He shook his head, and his expression told me I wasn't going to like the answer to that question.

"I won't lie. It's going to be bad for a while. A conversion is big news on its own. Add to that your age and it happening so soon after the Jackson Chase story..."

My stomach churned, and I held up a hand. "You don't need to say any more."

He crossed his arms. "It won't be safe for you until this calms down. You should stay here where the reporters can't get to you."

"I'm not leaving my parents to deal with this alone. If the reporters can't get to me, they'll go after my family."

Lukas frowned. "Your father is more than capable of taking care of them. And if the media knows you aren't there, it will draw them away."

"Dad is barely recovered from a goren addiction," I reminded him. "Now he's taking care of my mom, who just got out of the hospital. They are nowhere near ready to deal with this."

I couldn't tell him the rest – that my father was also coping with his recovered memories and the truth about Caleb. Or that we were afraid of what would happen when Mom got her memories back, too. The timing for this could not have been worse.

As if to punctuate my words, my phone rang, and I saw it was Dad calling. I should have called him as soon as I got here. Those paps would already have uploaded their photos and videos, and the story was probably everywhere by now.

"Jesse! Oh, thank God," Dad said when I answered. "Bruce called and said he saw you on TV. Where are you? Are you okay?"

My gut twisted at the strain in his voice. "I'm okay, Dad. I'm at Lukas's, and I'll be home in a few minutes."

"Maybe you should stay there," he said in a calmer tone. "Our street is already filling up with news vans."

I glanced at Lukas, who raised his eyebrows as if to say, "I told you so." I scowled at him and said, "Lukas will create a portal to our floor."

"That's good. We'll see you in a few minutes then."

I hung up and picked up my purse. "Will you take me home?"

For a few seconds, I thought he would say no, but he raised his hands to form the portal. As the image of the same courtyard appeared, I couldn't help but wonder when I would be able to do this. I hadn't yet embraced the idea of being Fae, but the thought of being able to travel anywhere in seconds was very appealing.

Lukas took my hand, and we stepped through the portal. I managed to see a little more of the courtyard that appeared to be made entirely of stone. Not stone blocks but carved from stone, including the thick pillars and railing. This was nothing like the gray foggy place I'd been in when I went through Conlan's portal, and I wondered if each faerie had a special location they went to when they traveled this way.

The next thing I saw was my apartment door. It amazed me how precisely he targeted this location, and I wanted to ask how it worked. Did he have to be familiar with a place in order to create a portal to it? Or was it another faerie ability that allowed them to sense where they wanted to go?

The door swung open before I could reach for it, and Mom rushed out to pull me into what would have been a crushing hug if she were back to her full health. It was a stark reminder that she had months of recovery left, and it wouldn't take much to upset her. I swore silently at whomever had leaked my story and caused her so much distress.

"Thank you for getting her out of there." Dad held out a hand to Lukas.

Lukas accepted his hand. "I'm sorry it came to this."

Mom released me and faced Lukas. "You have nothing to apologize for."

We entered the apartment, and I was relieved to see the TV was off. We had been shielding Mom from all entertainment news, which she'd never been that interested in anyway. Seeing me being ambushed by the paparazzi would have stressed her, and Lord only knew what would have happened if she'd seen me with Prince Rhys.

I tossed my purse on the table and kicked off my heels. Letting out an audible sigh of relief, I turned to find Lukas watching me.

The corners of his mouth turned up. "You are handling this well."

"Did you expect me to be overcome by all the excitement?" I lifted a shoulder. "I've never been the swooning type."

"That you're not." He laughed, and warmth rippled through me. I hadn't realized until this moment how much I'd missed that sound.

"Lukas, would you like something to drink?" Mom asked, reminding me that he and I weren't the only people in the room.

His gaze shifted to her. "Thank you, but I can't stay."

I busied myself with removing his jacket to hide my disappointment. "Thanks for bringing me home and for explaining things to me."

Lukas smiled as he took the jacket from me. "I need to talk to the Agency and take care of some things. I'll be back tomorrow."

"Okay," I replied, embarrassed by how happy I was to hear him say that.

He opened the door and turned back to me. "Don't go out tomorrow. If any of you need something, call, and one of us will get it for you."

"We plan to stick close to home for a few days," Dad said for all of us.

"I'll do everything I can to help." Lukas looked at me. "Get some rest, Jesse. I'll see you soon."

6

MY BREATH CAME out in steamy puffs that I could barely see in the gloomy cave. The air was cold, but for some reason I wasn't shivering even though all I was wearing was my T-shirt and sleep pants. Strange.

I tried to peer through the darkness and wished I had a flashlight. Out of nowhere, a glowing crystal appeared, floating in the air before me. I reached for it, and as soon as my fingers closed around it, it grew bright enough to illuminate the cave.

I turned in a full circle. The cave was small with an uneven floor and two branches veering off in opposite directions. I had no idea which way led out, but something tugged toward the one on my left. Deciding to follow my gut, I headed down that tunnel.

After a few minutes of walking, the floor sloped downward, and I knew this was not the way out. But I couldn't make myself turn around. Something down here was calling to me, and I couldn't go back until I found it.

I slowed at a section of the tunnel that was so low I had to duck to pass through. On the other side, I straightened and came up short when the crystal's light revealed a dead end. I checked to be sure, but all I found was a solid wall of rock.

"That's just great." I laid my free hand against the wall. "I discovered rock."

It took me a few seconds to realize the rock, which should be cold, was warm under my hand. Leaning closer, I pressed my cheek against the wall and felt a hum of energy beneath the surface. It was muted by the rock, but I could sense immense power that comforted and terrified me at the same time.

A distant sound had me turning back the way I'd come. I took two steps, and *suddenly I was in a different cave, or maybe at the mouth of this cave system. The air was frigid, and wind tossed my hair wildly as I walked to the wide ledge where the view stole my breath away.*

I was in the mountains, high above the snow line, and all I could see was blue sky and mountain tops rising above the clouds. Something circled in the distance near one craggy peak, and I squinted at what looked like giant birds.

I was contemplating how the hell I got here and how to get down when the sky turned a sickly green. The air became charged with electricity, and I backed away from the ledge as foreboding washed over me.

A crack resonated through the mountains, and I jumped when a bolt of lightning struck the mountain above me. The cave shook, and I struggled to keep my footing while chunks of rock fell from the ceiling. I braced myself against a wall as the mountain started to topple around me.

I bolted upright in bed and stared wildly at my bedroom walls. My heart thudded against my ribs like I'd run five miles, but I had no idea what I'd dreamed to cause it. I fell back onto the mattress with a groan and closed my eyes, even though I already knew I wasn't getting back to sleep.

I became aware of voices coming from the living room and easily identified my father and Maurice. They were talking about Maurice's plans to visit his family in Louisiana next week, and it was a minute before I realized I heard them clearly through my closed bedroom door. My Fae hearing must be kicking in.

Tossing off the covers, I got up, dressed, and pulled my hair into a ponytail. One of the things that never failed to amaze me was how soft and manageable my hair had become. It used to take a stiff brush and a prayer to wrangle my hair after waking up, but apparently, faeries did not get bedhead.

I wrinkled my nose at the smell of burnt dirt that hit me as I walked down the hallway. Entering the living room, I cast a longing glance at the two mugs on the coffee table. I hated even the smell of coffee now, but I still remembered how it used to taste to me. I sighed and went to the kitchen to pour a glass of ghillie juice.

I took a seat on the couch. "Where's Mom?"

"Still asleep," Dad said.

"You're up early," I said to Maurice. He was a night owl and preferred to sleep late unless he was on a job that required different hours.

He picked up his mug and took a drink. "It's the only way to beat the reporters to the Plaza. Like bloody gnats they are."

"Why are there reporters at the Plaza?" It had been three days since the story about my conversion broke, and I'd spent that time holed up in the apartment with my family. We had been avoiding the TV and the internet, so I had no idea what was going on out there.

"Trying to dig up dirt on you." Maurice's lips thinned. "Once they found out you were a bounty hunter, they started hanging around, harassing everyone. Didn't take long to get some of the guys riled up. Yesterday, Ambrose punched out a guy who shoved a camera in his face."

"Oh, no. Did he get in trouble?" Guilt sliced through me. I knew from personal experience how much bounty hunters disliked outsiders. I could imagine how angry they were to have a bunch of nosy reporters prying into their business.

"Only a fine. The Agency announced that the Plaza is off-limits to reporters and the general public until further notice. That doesn't stop them from hanging around outside, though."

A car horn blared. I went to the window and looked down at the dozen or so news vans parked along our street and the throng of reporters blocking a taxi trying to pull up. The back door of the taxi opened, and an elderly woman with flaming red hair got out.

Mrs. Russo turned toward the building and was immediately confronted by the reporters. Someone stuck a microphone in her face, and I put a hand to my mouth when she lost her balance and nearly fell. What was wrong with them, going after an old woman like that?

Steadying herself with more speed than one would expect from a woman her age, Mrs. Russo swung her large handbag at the reporters. A laugh burst from me when several mics went flying and her bag connected with at least two reporters' faces. She yelled something I couldn't hear, straightened her shoulders, and marched past them toward the building.

No one followed her. Lukas had put a ward on the building to allow only residents and their invited guests to enter. He and his men could enter too, of course.

"What's so funny?" Dad asked.

"Mrs. Russo clocked some reporters with that big bag she's always carrying." I snickered. "That'll teach them to mess with her."

Dad and Maurice laughed. Mrs. Russo used to work on Broadway when she was young, and she was not shy about speaking her mind. She also liked to carry a stun gun. Those reporters were lucky she hadn't used that on them.

"I'd better get going. I'll have to face them sooner or later." Maurice drained his coffee and stood. "Maybe I should ask Mrs. Russo to walk me to my van."

I grinned. "She'd probably take pleasure in doing it."

The kitchen phone rang as the door closed behind him. Dad and I shared a look before he went to answer it. Two days ago, we had changed all our numbers to unlisted ones because of the nonstop calls from reporters and crackpots. You never knew how many sickos there were until you found yourself the center of media attention. Somehow, the reporters kept getting the new land line number. We'd agreed that only Dad would answer the phone until this blew over.

I listened to him decline an offer for an exclusive interview and waited for him to return to the living room. His face gave nothing away, but I caught the flash of worry in his eyes when he looked at me.

"How much did this one offer?" I asked in an attempt at levity.

"Nine-fifty," he said as he sat.

I huffed dramatically. "Did you tell them I refuse to go lower than a cool million."

Dad shook his head at me and picked up the remote. "I think we should see what they are saying before your mom wakes up."

It wasn't hard to find a channel talking about me or showing footage from that night at Navi. I winced at my deer-in-the-headlights expression as I'd stared at the sea of cameras and lights. Then Tennin was there, ushering me away, and the stone-faced royal guards were blocking anyone from coming after us.

If that wasn't bad enough, we found a panel on one entertainment show speculating about what the Seelie queen thought of her son's torrid affair with a bounty hunter. Apparently, Prince Rhys had converted me because he couldn't bear to give me up.

"What I'd like to know is how she survived the conversion at all," said one of the female hosts. "She was almost nineteen when it happened."

The others nodded and murmured solemnly, and a male host said, "That leads you to wonder if faeries have been misleading people all along about the age limit for conversions."

"Why did the Agency keep it a secret?" the first one asked. "What is so special about Jesse James?"

Another male host tittered. "I guess being the Seelie crown prince's lover comes with more than a few perks."

"Turn it off," I said, my stomach roiling.

Dad clicked the button on the remote just as we heard their bedroom door open. When Mom entered the living room, Dad was sipping his coffee and I was playing with my phone.

Before any of us could speak, we were startled by a knock at the door. Dad stood, but I motioned for him to sit as I went to answer it. It had to be someone we knew because no one else could get into the building.

My heart did a little flutter when I opened the door to Lukas. I'd seen him only once since the night he'd brought me home, but he called daily to check in. Things were a lot better between us since he'd explained his absence, and I couldn't imagine having to go through this craziness without him.

I wished I knew if his attentiveness was out of friendship or something more. Before my conversion, he'd admitted he cared about me but that there could be no future for us because I was human at the time. I had understood and accepted that. I was Fae now, and my mortality was no longer a barrier, but Lukas had given me no sign he wanted more than friendship even though we were free to be together.

He smiled and held up the bag he was carrying. "I brought more food and juice."

"Thanks." I stepped back to let him enter. "Finch and Aisla have been drinking all my ghillie juice."

A whistle came from the treehouse, and I spied Finch's grinning face in his window. He was getting used to Lukas and the others dropping by every other day.

"I saw you were going through it faster, so I brought an extra bottle." Lukas set the bag on the kitchen counter. "I also got more berries and yikkas."

"That's so thoughtful," Mom said. She smiled, but it didn't hide the strain around her mouth and eyes.

Lukas shot me a questioning look, and I moved into the kitchen where my parents couldn't hear us. In whispers, I told him about what Dad and I had watched before his arrival.

"I'm so afraid this will cause a setback for her," I confided as I put the food away. "She's supposed to take it easy and avoid stress. What if she has a relapse and has to go back to the facility because of me?"

He put his hands on my shoulders and spoke in a low, firm voice. "None of this is your fault. I should have handled this better from the beginning."

"You two are awfully quiet in there," Dad called, a note of amusement in his voice.

Lukas's fingers squeezed my shoulders. "I won't let anything happen to your family. Do you trust me?"

"Yes," I answered without hesitation, earning a smile from him.

"Good." He released me, and we went to the living room. "I've been thinking that it's unfair for you to have to stay cooped up here until the media craze dies down. I have several properties that would allow you more freedom and privacy, and they are available to you for as long as you need them. I can arrange private transportation as well so the media won't know where you are going."

Mom's eyes widened. "That's very generous of you."

"Are they in the city?" Dad asked.

"Not New York." Lukas sat in the armchair, looking completely at home. "There is a villa in the Italian countryside, an estate in the Scottish Highlands, and a small island in Brazil. They are all private, and the staff can be trusted not to reveal your whereabouts to anyone."

I stared at him. I knew he must be rich as the crown prince of Unseelie, but he never showed off his wealth. This was the first time he'd ever mentioned owning properties other than his Williamsburg building. He was also a private person, for a Court faerie, and here he was offering up one of his personal properties to my family.

Mom and Dad shared a stunned look, and Dad said, "All of those sound perfect. I think we'll need to talk it over first."

"The offer is open whenever you're ready," Lukas said.

"An island?" was all I could think to ask.

He smiled. "Sometimes, I like to be alone."

Mom rubbed her hands on her thighs, something she did now whenever she was feeling overwhelmed or disquieted. "How long do you think it will take for this to die down?"

Lukas's eyes met mine briefly before he answered her. "If we do nothing, it could take months unless a bigger story comes along."

My stomach fell. She couldn't deal with this kind of stress for that long even if we did go to one of his private properties. Dad knew it, too.

I sent Lukas a pleading look. "There has to be something we can do."

"We could do an interview," he suggested.

Some of the pressure on my chest eased. "We?"

"It won't be enough for them to hear from you. They'll want to talk to the faerie who did the conversion. Once we tell them our story, there won't be any exclusives for them to chase after. They won't back off completely, but they'll ease up. And it will kill all their stories about you and the Seelie prince."

Dad nodded. "I think he's right, Jesse, but it's up to you. We will go along with whatever you decide."

"They'll want to know how she survived the conversion," Mom said anxiously. "If people find out about her goddess stone, that will put her in more danger."

Lukas shook his head. "We are not telling anyone about the goddess stone. The only people who know about it are those Jesse has told, and we are keeping it that way."

I stared at him. "You didn't tell the king?"

"The goddess stone is your secret to tell," Lukas said, his tone softening. "You trusted me with it, and I will never break that trust."

My heart sped up as I felt something pass between us. "We would do the interview together?"

"If that's what you want." One side of his mouth lifted. "They'll give you whatever you ask for to secure this interview."

I inhaled and slowly let out the breath. I did not want to go on camera and share details of my private life with the world. But there was *nothing* I wouldn't do for my mother, and this was a small price to pay for her peace of mind.

"How do we do this?" I said at last.

"You decide who you want to do the interview with, and I'll make the arrangements. They'll want to do a sit-down interview and a photo shoot. We can work out the details."

"No live interview," I blurted. This was going to be bad enough without doing it in front of millions of people. "I want Tennin to do the photo shoot."

Lukas's eyes lit with amusement. "Anything else?"

I pursed my lips, starting to warm to the idea. If this was my only option, I was going to make the most of it. "Maybe. I'll let you know."

"Jesse, Jesse, over here!"

"Are you going back to work as a bounty hunter?"

"Don't you think it's wrong for a faerie to hunt other faeries?"

I tossed a friendly smile at the small group of paparazzi, let them snag a few photos, and jogged up the steps to the Plaza. I was used to them dogging me, and thanks to some advice from Tennin, I could handle them like a pro now.

It had been two weeks since Lukas and my exclusive two-hour interview aired. We'd spun a story of how we'd met and worked together during the search for the ke'tain, which the whole world had heard of by now. We kept the host on the edge of her seat with a thrilling tale of how I'd been kidnapped and shot by one of Davian Woods's men while trying to bring the ke'tain to Lukas.

Since I had been unconscious during the conversion, the host directed her questions at Lukas. She'd dabbed her tears away when he told her how I'd nearly died. Out of gratitude for my heroism, a group of Fae royals had attempted a conversion, and by Aedhna's blessing, it had worked.

Now that the whole country saw me as a hero and we'd killed the rumors of a love affair with the Seelie crown prince, the media was kinder to me. The story wouldn't go away anytime soon, but the situation was bearable now. A national hero was a lot less exciting than a Fae crown prince's secret lover. Some paparazzi still followed me and tried to provoke me into giving them fodder for a new story, but they weren't nearly as aggressive.

I entered the Plaza lobby, relieved they couldn't follow me inside. The first people I saw were brother and sister team, Kim and Ambrose, and I smiled at them. Ambrose had been in a perpetual bad mood since the day I'd met him, but Kim and I got along well. I expected the scowl he shot my way, but hers took me aback.

A few feet from them stood a group of four hunters that included Aaron and Adrian. The Mercer twins smiled, and Aaron gave a friendly wave, but the two other hunters, whom I knew by name only, glared at me. I looked to the other side of the lobby and was met by more cold stares.

I'd heard from Maurice how unhappy the other bounty hunters were about the media attention, but that hadn't prepared me for this chilly reception. Though I didn't blame them for being upset, I had hoped they would be a little more forgiving. It wasn't as if I'd gotten shot on purpose and asked for the conversion or the publicity that came with it.

I crossed the lobby to the elevators. Before I reached them, a hunter named Sean Murphy stepped in front of me to block my way. Sean was in his late twenties, wiry with long, sandy blond hair in a ponytail. He was one of the hunters who had challenged my story when I'd brought in a goblin as my first capture, but I hadn't spoken to him since that day.

He crossed his arms. "What are you doing here?"

I bristled at his tone. "Same as you, I would imagine."

"You're not the same as me," he bit out. "You're one of them now, and you don't belong here."

"Yeah," one of his friends called. "The only faeries in this building should be the ones in iron."

Their open hostility was like a slap to the face, but I refused to let them see how much it bothered me. I looked at the second man. "There's no law against a faerie being a bounty hunter."

Sean's lip curled. "There should be. How do we know you won't take their side against us?"

"Whose side?"

"Faeries," Ambrose spat from the other side of the room. "They look out for their own, and we look out for ours."

Anger sparked inside me. "Is that so? I must have missed all of you looking out for my parents when they went missing in December. You know, the two *human* bounty hunters who almost died at the hands of faeries."

"That's different," Sean protested. "The Agency opened an investigation and –"

"And you did nothing." I shot them all a scathing look. "You know who helped me look for my parents? Faeries. So, don't talk to me about how you take care of your own."

The lobby went quiet, and everyone averted their eyes. I thought we were done with the conversation until Sean spoke. "That doesn't change the fact that you lied to us. You didn't tell us about the conversion, and then we got mobbed by reporters while you hid out at home."

"I'm sorry about the reporters, but you can't blame me for their actions." I looked around the room and met the eyes that were watching me. "If any of you were in my shoes, would you want the world to know?"

"I sure wouldn't," said a new voice.

I turned to face Trey, who had entered the lobby without my notice. He gave me a small smile of solidarity and came to stand beside me.

"Jesse jumped into the East River to save me from a kelpie. I wouldn't be here if not for her. I'd take her as a partner any day."

"She was still human then," Sean argued like a dog with a bone.

Trey waved a hand at Aaron and Adrian. "She was a faerie when she saved all of our asses on a banshee job." He turned back to Sean. "You know what? I found out about her conversion weeks ago, and it didn't change a thing. I'd still choose her as a partner."

I nudged his arm with mine. "Aw, shucks."

"It's one thing to bring in lower Fae," Ambrose said. "What happens if you ever have to deal with a Court faerie?"

I let out an aggravated huff. "Do cops and agents refuse to arrest human criminals because they're human? And when was the last time there was a bounty on a Court faerie?"

The other hunters looked among themselves, but not one could answer me.

I walked over to the elevator and pushed the button. "Listen; I didn't ask for this, but I'm not going to apologize for being alive or for doing my job. If you don't like that, that's your issue, not mine."

The elevator doors opened, and I stepped inside. I turned and faced the room impassively. Some still wore their angry expressions while others regarded me thoughtfully. I'd said all I was going to on the subject, and it was up to them to accept me or not. This wasn't the first time they'd challenged my right to be here. Their opinions hadn't stopped me then, and they wouldn't stop me now.

Thirty minutes later, I left the building with three new jobs from Levi, who said he didn't care what I was as long as I kept earning him money. The paparazzi were waiting for me at the bottom of the steps, and I gave them a friendly wave as I ignored their usual shouts and headed for the Jeep.

I got in and started it, keeping my eyes averted from the camera lens nearly pressed to my window. They'd get bored with me eventually. Until then, I would make sure they got nothing newsworthy from me.

My phone rang, and I answered without looking at the number. The Agency had gotten me one of the special unlisted numbers reserved for Fae royals, and only a handful of people outside of my family knew it.

"Hello," I said as I pulled away, careful not to hit one of the paps who was slow to move out of the way.

"Jesse James, you are not an easy person to reach," said a man's voice.

An ugly jolt of recognition hit me, and I nearly slammed on the brakes. He was the last person I'd ever expected to speak to again. My knuckles turned white, and I eased my grip on the wheel before I spoke.

"Davian," I replied with a cool voice that belied the shock rippling through me. I scanned my surroundings, expecting to find him there. "How did you get my number?"

His laugh was the same charming one I'd heard the night we met at his party. "You must know by now that I have ways of getting the things I want."

"Not all of them," I retorted. The satisfaction it gave me was only a fraction of what I deserved after what he'd done to me.

"Not yet," he said in a less amused tone. "But you don't get where I am without being a patient man."

"Where is that?" I couldn't resist the gibe. "I hope you are well-stocked in your secret hideaway and planning on an extended stay."

"I am quite comfortable, thank you, and this is only a temporary inconvenience until everything blows over."

I shook my head. Did he honestly believe that? Aside from the fact that he'd conspired to obtain a stolen Fae artifact for his own gain, he'd also kidnapped and shot an Unseelie royal guard, who happened to be one of Lukas's best friends. None of them would forget that, much less forgive Davian. And they would long outlive him.

Instead of pointing out the obvious to him, I said, "Is there a reason why you called, besides wanting to catch up?"

"I want to know how you did it?"

I didn't have to ask what *it* was. "I didn't do anything. I'm sure you've seen our interview, and you heard what Lukas said."

"I heard the story you two gave the world, but we both know it was a fabrication. If all it took to convert an adult was a group of faeries, I would have done that already." His voice took on a note of excitement. "It was the ke'tain, wasn't it? They used it to amplify their magic so they could perform the conversion."

"You know faeries can't touch the ke'tain," I reminded him.

"Then you held it and used its power while they did the conversion," he persisted. "Tell me how it works."

Angry heat spread through me. "I have no clue what happened during the conversion because I was nearly dead from a bullet, no thanks to you."

"I'm sorry about that. I never meant to harm you. Things got out of hand." He sounded contrite, but I knew the real Davian Woods. He was only sorry he hadn't gotten what he wanted.

I gritted my teeth. "You hired mercenaries who murdered an innocent woman. Then you called the Seelie guard to come for Conlan and me. They would have done more than harm us."

"I made some mistakes," he replied casually. "I plan to make reparations to her family."

I had no response. What did you say to someone who had no remorse and believed money was the answer to everything? Davian was so blinded by his wealth and his obsession that he'd lost touch with reality. Did he honestly believe a check could ease Angela Moore's parents' devastation over their daughter's murder?

"Name your price, Jesse."

I blinked, suddenly aware he had been speaking. "What?"

"How much will it take for you to share your secret with me?" he asked. "Five million, ten million? Your parents will never want for anything. Say the word."

"I told you I don't know what happened in the conversion. I can't give you what you want."

What I didn't tell him was that my family had no need of his money, thanks to the three-million dollar deal I'd negotiated with the network for my exclusive interview. Mom and Dad could take all the time they needed to recover before going back to work, and that was worth every second of the uncomfortable interview.

"Is that your final word?" Davian's voice was tight as he tried to restrain his anger.

"Yes."

"Then I guess there's nothing else for us to say to each other. Goodbye, Jesse." He hung up before I could respond.

I gripped the steering wheel hard, and it was only then that I realized my hands were trembling. Too shaken to drive, I looked around for a place to pull over. I needed to call Lukas. We'd thought Davian was no longer a threat after he'd fled the country and gone into hiding, but we'd underestimated his obsession with becoming Fae.

A block later, I pulled onto a quiet street lined with brick apartment buildings and found an empty parking spot. I was no longer trembling, but my whole body was as jittery as it had been the time Violet and I drank three espressos in a row. Oh, what I wouldn't do for a coffee now. That was one more thing Davian Woods had taken from me.

I picked up my phone and called Lukas, letting out a frustrated breath when I got his voice mail. I didn't want to tell him about Davian in a message, so I asked him to call me as soon as possible. He was occupied with Faerie business lately, but he always responded quickly to my calls.

I laid my head against the headrest. Since the night he and I had cleared the air, we seemed to have fallen back into our old friendship – the pre-kiss one. Lukas was attentive and supportive to my family and me, and he'd completely won over my mother, despite her earlier reservations about him. At times, I thought I saw a flicker of something more in his eyes when he looked at me, but it was gone before I could read it. I was starting to think I'd imagined there had ever been more between us.

A vehicle slowed to a stop beside me, and I glanced out the driver's window at a blue van with tinted windows. My stomach gave a sickening lurch, and I held my breath as flashbacks filled my mind of another van and the day Conlan and I were abducted.

Relax, I told myself even as my hand moved to make sure the door was locked. I was going to feel pretty foolish in a few seconds when someone got out of the van and went into the apartment building. It wasn't as if they had me boxed in. The space behind me was empty, so I could back out that way if I wanted to.

Half a minute later, I frowned when no one exited the van. What were they waiting for?

Movement drew my eyes to the rearview mirror where I saw a second identical van approaching. My heart began to race when the van slowed as if to pull in behind me, and my mind screamed a single word.

Run!

7

I HAD MY seat belt off and was over the console into the passenger seat before I had made the conscious decision to move. Throwing the door open, I jumped from the Jeep and took off down the sidewalk without looking back. Male shouts and the sound of running feet behind me told me all I needed to know.

I reached the end of the block and tore around the corner of the last building. Another street stretched before me with more of the same brick buildings and not a person in sight. Where were the paparazzi who dogged me day and night? I spent my days trying to avoid them, and now when I could have used them, there wasn't a single one around.

I sped around another corner and came up short at the sight of two men running toward me. They were too far away to make out their features, but their build and clothing screamed "hired guns," and they were headed straight for me.

I looked around frantically, but there was no avenue of escape. If I crossed the street, the men coming at me from both directions would cut me off. I was trapped.

My desperate gaze fell on a metal fire escape across the street, and I looked up at the building beside me. There was a similar fire escape directly above me, but the bottom landing was a good twelve feet off the ground. The sliding ladder that hung down was still at least four feet out of reach unless you were a pro basketball star.

Or a faerie.

Feet pounded the pavement behind me too close for comfort. I shoved my phone into my pocket and bent my knees. *Don't fail me now*, I begged my body. My Fae strength and speed kicked in at random times, and this was the first time I prayed for it.

I leaped straight up into the air and nearly sobbed when my fingers closed around cold metal. Instead of sliding down as I'd expected it to, the ladder stayed in place with me dangling from it. I looked toward the running men. The glint of metal in the hands of one had me grappling for the ladder rung with my other hand.

I didn't know if it was adrenaline or a burst of Fae strength, but I pulled myself up to grab the second rung. I reached for the third one. Almost there.

I jerked at a sharp sting in my left thigh, but I didn't stop to look down. I grasped the next ladder rung and dragged my upper body onto the metal grate of the fire escape.

"Are you sure she's a faerie?" One of the men asked as I swung my legs up onto the landing.

My left leg dragged a little, and I found out why when I noticed the dart protruding from my thigh. I yanked it out and saw a bead of gray liquid at the tip. Iron, probably mixed with a sedative like the one used on Conlan. If not for my goddess stone, I'd be out cold.

"Lift me up," a man barked.

I looked down and found four men below me. Two of them bent and grabbed a third by the legs, preparing to help him reach the ladder. Davian's backup plan, no doubt. He didn't like to take no for an answer.

Leaning out, I threw the dart at the men. It struck one of the lifters at the corner of his eye, making him yell in pain and let go of his friend. The two of them landed on the sidewalk, and the other two rushed to help them up.

"Hurts, doesn't it?" I yelled down at them, and I was met with angry glares.

I stood and tested my leg. It was a tiny bit numb where the dart had struck me, but I could climb with it, and that was all that mattered. Ignoring the men's shouts, I ran up the stairs. The building was six stories high, and I didn't stop until I reached the top. Metal clanged below, and my stomach plummeted to the ground when one of the men pulled himself onto the bottom landing.

I tilted my head back to look at the roof. The fire escape didn't go that far, and there was nothing for me to grab onto if I managed to jump and reach it. The roof of the next building was lower, but I couldn't jump to it from here. That left me with only one option.

"I should have stayed in bed," I mumbled as I climbed over the rail and stepped onto the eight-inch ledge that lined up with the adjoining building. I immediately flattened my back against the bricks and kept one hand on the rail, refusing to look down.

Sucking in a breath, I let go of the rail and shuffled carefully along the ledge. Shouts came from the men on the ground, but I ignored them and the man racing up the fire escape. I was barely three feet from the landing when he reached it and lunged for me. His fingers brushed my coat, but I took another step before he could latch on.

I turned my head to meet his furious eyes. He didn't speak, but the determination on his hard face told me he wouldn't give up that easily. I wondered why he didn't reach for the gun that was visible in a side holster beneath his coat until I remembered that Davian wanted me alive.

Noise below alerted me to the fact that a second man was being lifted onto the ladder. Time to get the hell out of here.

I inched toward the end of the ledge until I was able to reach out and grab the edge of the roof next door. I turned quickly and grasped it in both hands, throwing myself onto the roof. I didn't take a moment to catch my breath before I was on my feet and running.

I jumped to the connecting building and had to climb onto a utility box to reach the slightly higher roof after that one. I pulled myself over the top and glanced back the way I'd come in time to see the man who'd grabbed for me pull himself onto the first roof.

I took off. Most of the remaining buildings on the block were the same height, which made running easier. It also meant my pursuers would have less trouble chasing me.

Some roofs had metal access doors, but every door I tried was locked. I tried kicking a few, but they wouldn't budge. Thinking I could jump down to the fire escape, I went to the edge of one building, only to see two of the men on the street following my progress.

My phone rang. It was most likely Lukas returning my call, but there was no time to answer it. There wasn't much he could do for me. Even if I knew what street I was on, he couldn't portal to me in time. I was on my own for this one.

I was two buildings away from the end of the block when I skidded to a stop at the sight of two men climbing onto the last roof. I spun the other way and saw the first two men four buildings away and gaining on me.

I ran to the back of my roof and faced the rear of another row of buildings. Below was a green area with some trees and benches and not much else. I stared at the opposite buildings and judged the distance to be at least thirty feet – impossible to jump even with a running start.

Think, Jesse.

I looked around. The building I'd just crossed jutted out in a stunted T-shape, closing the gap by half. A Court faerie could make that jump so I should be able to...maybe.

Blood pounded in my ears as I hopped over the ledge to the next roof, very aware of the men closing in on both sides. There was no time to second-guess or give myself more than a dozen feet to take off from. I sprinted toward the rear of the building, passing so close to two of the men that I heard their grunting breaths and felt the shift in the air when they grabbed for me. Their curses fell behind me as I reached the edge of the roof and leaped.

The world seemed to slow, and in that time, I pictured myself falling, crashing into the ground below. Would my pursuers leave my broken body there for someone to find or take me away to be another object in Davian Wood's Fae collection? My family would never know what had happened to me. I'd never see them or Violet or Lukas again.

My feet made contact with the ledge, and I windmilled for several terrifying seconds before I pitched forward onto my hands and knees. It wasn't one of my more graceful moves, but I wasn't trying to impress anyone. I couldn't believe I'd done it.

Standing on slightly rubbery legs, I turned toward the other building where the four men stared at me in surprise and frustration. We all knew the only reason I'd made that jump was because I was Fae, and none of them was stupid enough to attempt it.

One of them spoke into a radio. I swore softly. It wouldn't take long for their accomplices on the street to run around the block to this side. Hell, for all I knew, there could be a dozen more of them down there.

A little giddy from my escape, I couldn't resist giving them a cheeky wave before I ran to the other side of my building. Ten feet below me was the top landing of the fire escape, and I wasted no time lowering myself down to it.

I started down the stairs at a run. I reached the third floor of the building and was about to keep going when music drifted from a window that was cracked open a few inches. I didn't hesitate and knocked on the window.

Seconds later, a teenage girl, who looked no older than fifteen, appeared on the other side of the window. She stared at me with trepidation that quickly changed to shock.

"OMGEEE!" she squealed, opening the window all the way. "You're Jesse James!"

I nodded. "Can I come in?"

"Are you kidding?" She stepped aside, dancing on the spot as I climbed into her apartment. "What are you doing here? My friends will never believe this! Can I get a picture with you?"

I straightened and closed the window before I faced her. "I need to make a quick call to a friend for a ride, and then we can take a picture."

Her squeal pierced my newly sensitive eardrums. I winced and pulled out my phone, glad I hadn't lost it with all the running and jumping. I had a missed call and a voice mail from Lukas. I hit dial without listening to his message.

He picked up on the first ring. "Why didn't you answer my call? Are you okay?"

"I'll explain later," I said, aware of the girl listening to my every word. "Can you come pick me up?"

"Did you break down?"

"Not exactly. More like the Jeep is boxed in by a friend's vans, and I had to leave it." I couldn't think of any other way of saying I needed help without coming right out and speaking the words.

"A friend's vans? What friend?"

"Our friend Davian. You know what a joker he is."

Lukas said something in Fae that I was glad I didn't understand. His next words came out as a growl. "Where?"

"One sec." I asked the girl for her address and relayed it to him.

"Stay in the apartment. We're on the way."

I hung up and smiled at the girl, who had her own phone out and pointed at me. I tugged the phone from her hands.

"No posts until after I go." I gave her a conspiratorial look. "Can't have the paparazzi finding me."

Her eyes went impossibly round. "Are you hiding from them? Are they outside?" She went to the window I'd entered through and started to open it.

I stopped her before she could lean out and give my location away. "How about those pictures? What's your name?"

"It's Avery." She squealed again. I used to tease Violet for doing that, but she had nothing on this girl. We took some photos with her phone, and she asked me a bunch of questions I evaded by asking about her instead.

Less than five minutes after my call to Lukas, I got a text from him. **We're here.** It was followed by a sharp rap on the door. I checked the peephole and opened the door to admit Lukas, Faolin, and Faris. Normally, it was Faolin who wore the stony expression, but today, Lukas looked downright scary.

I'd told Avery Lukas was coming, and she knew who he was from our interview. But the sight of all three of them was too much for her. She let out a small squeak and swayed on her feet. She would have fallen if I hadn't been close enough to catch her.

"Is she ill?" Faris asked.

I smirked at him. "You guys just have that effect on us girls."

Faolin gave a surly shake of his head and stepped back into the hall. "I will wait out here."

I snapped my fingers in front of Avery's face, and she blinked before she turned bright pink and stammered, "I...uh...hi."

I introduced her to Lukas and Faris, and Lukas gave her a smile that nearly sent her into a full swoon. He thanked her for helping me out and graciously submitted to several photos with her and me, which were taken by a grinning Faris.

"Thank you, Jesse, for making my whole year!" she said when we opened the door to leave. "My friends will go insane when I post these pics."

I gave her a quick hug. "Thanks for helping me out."

The door had barely closed behind us when Lukas said, "What happened?"

I quickly told them about the call from Davian Woods and running from the men. As soon as I finished, Lukas exchanged a look with Faris and Faolin, and the brothers headed for the stairwell.

"Where are they going?" I asked.

"To look for the men and get your Jeep." Lukas raised his hands to create a portal. The set of his mouth told me he was keeping his anger in check, so I decided not to speak again until we got home. Only we didn't go to my apartment.

"Why did you bring me here?" I asked as he tossed his phone on the kitchen island at his place. "And how were we able to bring our phones through the portal? I didn't think you could bring stuff like that to Faerie."

"I shielded them with my magic." He raked a hand through his hair. "Tell me exactly what Davian said to you."

The conversation was still fresh in my mind, so I was able to recall it word for word. When I was done, he made me give him a play-by-play of what had happen from the moment the men showed up to when he had arrived at Avery's apartment. Back in Avery's building, I hadn't mentioned the dart the men had shot me with, and I could practically see the thundercloud forming above Lukas when I brought it up now.

"They shot you?" he ground out.

I raised my hands to placate him. "It didn't work, and I got away."

Lukas gripped the edge of the island. "You could have died. Your strength is still too unpredictable, and you could have missed that jump."

I went over and laid a hand on his arm, which was so tense it felt like granite. "I didn't, and thinking about what-ifs doesn't help."

He placed one of his warm hands over mine, and the heat spread through me. I was almost overwhelmed by the need to be held by him. I missed the closeness and intimacy we'd shared during the times we'd kissed. I wished he would kiss me and tell me he wanted me as much as I did him.

"This changes everything." He let out a harsh breath. "I thought Davian Woods was no longer a threat, but I underestimated him. That won't happen again."

"We all thought that. I'll be more careful from now on."

"That's not enough." He straightened to fix me with a determined stare. "You're staying here."

I took a step back. "No, I'm not."

"Yes, you are." He crossed his arms. "I allowed you to stay at your apartment after the story broke because of your mother's health, but Davian is too dangerous for you to continue living there."

"You *allowed* me?" I sputtered. "News flash, Lukas. You don't have any say in where I live or what I do."

"Actually, he does," Faolin said, causing me to jump. I turned to see him stepping out of a portal.

I sputtered. "Since when?"

"Since you became Fae. You're Unseelie, and Lukas is your crown prince. He can command you to do whatever he wishes."

I waited for him to smirk or say something to tell me he was pulling my leg. He didn't.

"You're joking, right?"

Faolin shook his head.

"What?" I whirled on Lukas. "No one told me this! I'm not going to spend the rest of my life being ordered around like I have no mind of my own. And if you think I'm going to bow down to you because you're going to be king someday, you have another thing coming."

"Females don't bow. They curtsy," Faolin said, and there was no mistaking the humor in his voice. Jerk.

Lukas came around the island and sat on one of the bar stools facing me. Most of the anger had left his eyes, but his tone was still firm. "No one is going to order you around, but there will be times when I'll make decisions you won't agree with. I refuse to take risks with your safety."

"But the ward –"

"The ward only protects you while you are inside your building," he reminded me. "Do you plan to stay at home for however long it takes us or the authorities to locate Davian? And what of your parents? Do you think Davian won't try to use them to get to you?"

Fear lanced through me. Since Davian's call, I hadn't had time to consider that he might go after Mom and Dad, but it was exactly what he would do.

I fumbled for my phone. "I need to call and warn them. Those men could be headed there now."

"Faolin?" Lukas said evenly. How was he so calm when my family could be in danger?

"Iian and Kerr are already there," Faolin replied, walking into the kitchen. "I called them after you left. No sign of trouble, but we travel faster than the humans."

I relaxed my tense muscles, but not by much. "They didn't tell my parents what happened to me, did they?"

Faolin opened the refrigerator. "No. Kerr told them it was a routine check-in to see if they needed anything."

I looked at Lukas. "I need to be the one to tell them."

He nodded. "I'll take you home to pack some clothes and whatever else you want to bring with you. You can fill them in while we're there."

"But –"

"You staying here is not up for debate." Standing, he walked into the living room and created the portal. He looked back at me. "Are you coming?"

I went to stand beside him. "We are not done discussing this."

"I expected nothing less," he replied wryly. Then he took my arm, and we stepped through the portal.

I halfheartedly strummed a few chords on my guitar and stood it on the floor propped against the bed. Flopping onto my back, I stared at the ceiling without seeing it. I thought about reading a book or watching a movie on my laptop, but I couldn't summon enough energy to do either.

The door creaked softly. A few seconds later, Kaia jumped gracefully onto the bed and lay beside me with her large head on my stomach. I scratched behind her ear, and her loud purr filled the room. She'd taken to hanging out in here and had even slept on my bed last night. I wasn't the best company, but she didn't seem to mind.

I stared at the high ceiling and wondered what my family was doing now. Mom and Dad were probably lounging on the deck of Lukas's island home while Finch and Aisla ate fruit until they passed out. I smiled at the image even as my chest tightened. They'd been gone less than a day, and I missed them so much it hurt.

When I'd told my parents about Davian, they had agreed with Lukas that the best place for me was at his building. Lukas suggested this was the perfect time for them to take him up on his offer to use one of his properties. Mom had always wanted to see Italy, but they chose the Brazilian island instead. It was tropical, private, and the perfect place for my parents to rest. Also, it wasn't listed among Lukas's holdings, so there was no way anyone could find them there.

Lukas had made all the arrangements, and they'd left yesterday after a tearful goodbye. I wanted to go with them, but Lukas said I needed to resume training now that my Fae magic was growing stronger. I'd been here for four days, and all I'd done so far was the same conditioning workout from before my conversion. I could leave the building but only with him or one of the others, which meant hunting was out of the question. I felt useless, and I was bored out of my mind.

"Knock, knock."

I raised my head to look at Conlan standing in the doorway of the library...or should I say my bedroom? They had completely transformed the room for me. Except for the new bed and wardrobe, it held most of my things from home. It was a comfortable space, and I loved the fireplace and queen bed. I just needed to get used to thinking of it as my room.

"Hey." I sat up, earning an unhappy growl from Kaia.

"Faris and I are thinking about trying an Italian place for lunch. What do you think?"

I stroked the lamal's fur, and she stretched contentedly. "Whatever you bring back will be good. I'm not fussy."

Conlan walked over to stand at the foot of the bed. "We thought you might want to come with us. There is a restaurant in Venice we've been wanting to try."

That got my attention. "Venice...as in the city in Italy? You're going to create a portal to Italy just to visit a restaurant? I thought you didn't use magic for portals unless you have to."

"We make some exceptions."

I shot him a knowing look that said he wasn't fooling me. They knew today was hard on me, and they were planning this outing to cheer me up.

A smile pulled at my lips. "I'd like that."

"Good." He turned to the door. "It's still cool there at night, so you might want a light coat."

I scrambled off the bed and changed into fresh jeans and a nice top. Grabbing a coat, I went to the living room where Conlan waited with Faris. Lukas had gone to the Agency with Iian and Kerr earlier and hadn't yet returned.

"I had another thought while we were waiting for you," Conlan said.

I raised my eyebrows. "Must have been a quick thought. I didn't take that long."

He laughed. "Since we're using a portal, it would be a good time to show you how it's done."

"Really?" I asked eagerly. I'd seen Lukas create them a number of times, but he did it too fast to follow his actions.

"She's not ready for that," Faolin said from the kitchen, putting a damper on my newfound happiness.

"I'm not going to have her create it." Conlan winked at me. "But I think she can handle learning the basics."

I was quick to agree. "Yes, I can."

He pointed at the door. "The wards on the building require more complicated magic. Let's do this outside."

"Okay." I followed him out to the private parking lot. It was an overcast day, but there was no cold nip in the air. Spring had finally arrived.

Conlan turned to face me. "What do you know about the barrier between this realm and ours?"

"I know it's made up of a balance of energy from both worlds. Our atmospheres are so different because of the amount of magic in Faerie that they form a layer where they meet." I shrugged. "I'm sure there is a more scientific explanation."

"Yours will do." He waved a hand through the air, leaving a scattered trail of glittering particles in its wake. "The barrier is not a solid thing, so some of the energy from Faerie leaches through to this side. The trace amounts are so small they can't affect this world, but a faerie with enough magic can isolate and manipulate them. Watch."

He raised both hands, palms facing me, and moved them apart. I stared at the soft blue magic pouring from his hands and attaching to the particles in the air. He moved slowly enough for me to see how he used the traces of magic in the barrier as building blocks and filled in the blank spaces with his own.

"Wow," I whispered. "That's amazing."

"There is more to it than harnessing the magic in the barrier," said Faolin, who had followed us outside with Faris. "It requires both strength and concentration to not only open the portal but to open it where you want to go."

I watched Conlan release the magic and lower his hands. "That makes sense. You wouldn't want to make a mistake and end up in the Seelie court."

"That wouldn't happen because citizens of one court cannot create a portal to the other without permission," Faolin said. "But you could end up in the middle of nowhere if you don't know where you're going."

Faris snorted. "It's no wonder you are the life of all the parties at court, Brother. Stop ruining our fun."

Faolin didn't smile, but I caught a flicker of amusement in his eyes. He waved a hand at us. "Carry on."

Conlan looked at me. "You give it a try."

I shook my head, laughing. "I can't do that. I don't know how to use my magic."

"Here, let me help you." He took my hand and raised it. My fingers twitched as a light stream of magic came from his.

"Do you feel anything?" he asked.

"It tingles."

"Good. That means you can feel my magic. I'm going to slowly pull away, and I want you to keep reaching out for the magic." He did as he'd said, and the flow of his magic trickled away.

I could still sense something, but it was too indistinct to touch. After a minute, I dropped my arm. "I felt it, but I couldn't connect the way you did."

Conlan chuckled. "I'd be shocked if you could on your first try. As Faolin said, it takes a lot of strength, more than a new faerie has. Do you remember how weak I was after Davian's men had me in iron shackles? I didn't have the strength to create a portal, and I have been doing it for years."

I thought back to that day. He'd barely been able to produce magic until I'd put the goddess stone in his hand. It had restored his strength, and he'd had no problem creating the portal. I was a faerie now, but the stone wasn't affecting me the same way. Why was that?

"Can we try that again?" I asked.

He lifted my hand and used his magic. This time, when he released me, I took the stone from my hair and held it in my other hand. The effect was instant. It was like a massive adrenaline rush along with a feeling of euphoria that made me lightheaded.

After the initial shock of it passed, I concentrated on the particles of magic Conlan had exposed to me. This time, they came into focus with crystal clarity. "Whoa!" I breathed when lavender magic poured from my hands. "Are you guys seeing this?"

Someone spoke, but I was too mesmerized by the sight of my own magic to focus on the words. I thought about touching the particles in the barrier, and my magic moved to do my bidding.

My body thrummed with a low current of electricity when I connected with the barrier, and instinct took over. I remembered what Conlan had done, and I emulated it. Only I didn't stop. I imagined a portal like the ones I'd seen him and Lukas create. A hole formed before me.

"Jesse, no," Conlan shouted. I felt his hand brush my arm.

Then I was sucked into a gray void.

8

I STUMBLED AND righted myself. Spinning, I looked for the portal, but it was gone. There was nothing but a thick gray fog.

Panic threatened to choke me, but I pushed it down. I'd been here before with Conlan, which meant it had to be a part of Faerie. And he'd created a portal out of here, so I could, too.

I still had the stone in my hand, so I did exactly what I'd done to create my first portal. It was much easier to connect to the magic from this side of the barrier, and an outline of a portal began to appear. I imagined the parking lot behind Lukas's building. I could do this.

"Jesse."

I spun around at the woman's voice, but all I saw was fog. Thinking I had imagined it, I returned my focus to the portal. It grew as big as a door, and I could make out the faint shape of a building on the other side.

The fog swirled, and I thought I saw a shape coming toward me. My heart thudded, and I lost my concentration. The portal began to close.

No. I pushed my magic into the portal. As soon as it reopened, I jumped through it.

I nearly fell when my feet hit uneven ground instead of flat pavement. Dread coiled in my stomach, and I straightened to look at my surroundings.

I was standing on a beach, facing the ocean where huge swells rose and rolled toward the shore under the first light of day. Turning, I found trees and greenery and noticed a few tall palm trees. A dozen feet away, a large turtle left a trail in the sand as he made his way to the water.

The roar of the waves drew my gaze back to the ocean. I squinted, and this time, I could pick out the dark shapes of people on boards. Surfers.

Relief filled me. If there were people here, I hadn't landed on some deserted island. My shock had worn off enough for me to take stock of my surroundings. It was windy but warm, and the sky told me it was not long after sunrise. That meant I had travelled west to an earlier time zone. California maybe?

I did a quick calculation. California was three hours behind New York, which would make it mid-morning there. It was definitely earlier than that here. That left...Hawaii. I was in Hawaii. The question was which one of the islands was I on?

I reached for my phone. No need to panic. I'd call Faolin, and he'd trace my phone. Then one of them would come and get me.

Only my phone wasn't in my back pocket where I'd put it before I left my room. I patted all my jeans pockets frantically as if the phone would magically appear in one of them. It took a whole minute for me to realize what had happened. I'd entered the portal without warding the phone like Lukas did, and Faerie had destroyed it.

"Okay, now you can panic." I looked both ways on the beach, but I was alone. Those surfers had to come in somewhere, so I jogged along the beach until I came upon a duffle bag and some men's sandals. I sat in the sand beside the bag and waited.

Forty-five minutes later, two of the surfers walked out of the water with their boards under their arms and headed to where I sat. When they drew near, the men slowed and shot me suspicious looks. Both looked to be in their early twenties with dark hair and the tanned glow of people who spent a lot of time in the sun.

"Can we help you?" one of them asked warily.

I stood and brushed sand off my jeans, which looked out of place here. "I hope so. Do either of you have a phone I can use?"

"You broke down?" the other asked.

"More like stranded." I wrinkled my nose. "It's a long story."

"Ah." The first one smirked and bent to unzip the bag. "I have a few of those to tell." He unlocked a silver phone and handed it to me.

"Thanks." I punched in Conlan's number and let out a breath when it started to ring. I hoped he didn't reject the call because of the unknown number.

"Hello?" he said in a voice laden with tension. I cringed at the thought of what he'd been going through in the last hour.

"It's me."

"Jesse? Oh, thank the goddess!" There was a rustling sound and a muffled, "It's her."

The next voice to come out of the phone was Lukas's. I couldn't tell if he was furious or worried when he said, "Where are you?"

"Uh...one second." I pressed the phone to my chest and looked at the two men who were watching me. "Where are we exactly?"

The two of them shared a look, and the one who had loaned me his phone snickered. "You really did have a fun night. We're at Pua'ena Point on the North Shore."

I repeated that to Lukas, and he, in turn, said it to someone else. I waited for an awkward thirty seconds before he said, "I'm on my way."

I handed the phone back to its owner. "You're a lifesaver. Thanks."

"Whoa!" he said, his eyes going wide at something behind me.

I spun and saw Lukas stepping from a portal a few dozen yards away. He looked angry enough to uproot the trees as he strode toward us, but I didn't think I'd ever been so happy to see him. I ran across the sand, meeting him halfway, and threw my arms around him.

I was prepared to be yelled at and scolded, and I wouldn't complain because I deserved it. What I didn't expect was for him to wrap me in his arms and hold me tightly against him like I might vanish at any moment.

He murmured something in Fae I couldn't understand, but no translation was needed to hear the worry in his voice. Guilt racked me for being reckless and making him and the others worry.

"We had no idea where you'd gone, and there was no way to trace you."

"I'm sorry. I'm so sorry," I said against his chest. "I was stupid, and I never should have tried that."

Lukas released a ragged sigh. "Sometimes, *mi'calaech*, I don't know if Aedhna sent you as a kindness or a test of my sanity."

I smiled. "Maybe I'm both."

He dropped his arms and took my face in his hands. I tilted my head back to meet his blue eyes, and my belly did a flip at the flare of heat in his gaze. His head lowered, and I held my breath in anticipation of the first brush of his lips against mine.

Someone hooted nearby, and the moment was gone. I wanted to cry when I turned to see the two grinning surfers watching us. More people had left the water and were walking over to join the men. This quiet beach was suddenly getting a little too crowded.

Lukas took my hand and led me down the beach, away from the men. We entered the privacy of the trees, and a thrill went through me at being alone with him.

My hopes of a kiss were crushed when he turned away and created a portal. I tried to hide my disappointment when he took my hand and we entered the stone courtyard. For the first time, I had no interest in seeing more of the place before he opened the second portal to his living room.

To my mortification, the whole gang was there waiting for us, and I had to explain what happened after I apologized for my little stunt.

"If it's possible to shorten a life, you did it with me," Conlan teased good-naturedly.

Heat crept up my neck. "I swear I'll never do that again."

"Lukas," Faolin said in a more serious tone. "The king sent a summons for you. You're needed at court."

"I've been expecting that. Send word that we'll be there within the hour."

I relaxed, grateful for a reprieve from the scolding for my reckless behavior. At the same time, I hated the thought of him leaving. "How long will you be gone?"

"Several weeks, at least." He paused. "We are all going."

"Oh." I tried not to show my dismay at the thought of being here alone for weeks. Kaia entered the room and came up to rub against my hip, and I reached down to stroke her head. "I guess it'll just be us girls."

Lukas's brows drew together, and then his eyes widened slightly as if he'd made some realization. "When I say all, that includes you. You're coming to Faerie with us."

"You don't have to be nervous," Faris said when I rejoined them in the living room, less than an hour after Lukas's little bombshell. "We will be with you."

I swallowed dryly. "I'm not nervous."

I was terrified, but I was too proud to tell any of them that. This wasn't like travelling to another country, which I'd also never done. We were going to a whole different world where I knew only a handful of people and very little about their customs and way of life. Plus, the little I'd heard about court didn't make me eager to go there.

Faris's expression said he knew I was lying, but he let it go. He gave me a reassuring smile and took my small bag from me. There wasn't much I could bring with me aside from some photos and a few books. Anything with metal in it was left here, including my guitar.

They'd even given me a Fae shirt, pants, and shoes to wear with the assurance I'd get a new wardrobe there. The clothes were made of a fine material that felt cool against my skin, but I already missed my jeans.

Lukas walked over to me, and I relaxed a bit. I didn't want to be dependent on him for anything, but his nearness eased my anxiety.

"You ready?" He took my hand, sending a delicious shiver through me.

I smiled up at him. "Lead the way."

Faolin stepped up and quickly created a portal. Iian, Kerr, and Conlan went through first, followed by Lukas and me. Faris and Faolin came last with Kaia. We emerged in the now familiar courtyard, and I felt a few seconds of panic when the portal to my world closed behind us.

Lukas's warm hand squeezed mine, and he lowered his head to whisper softly, "Breathe, *li'fachan*."

His use of their nickname for me reminded me I was a hunter – a good one – and I'd faced much scarier things than this. I straightened my shoulders and smiled to let him know I was okay.

I turned to get my first good look at the courtyard I'd only seen flashes of. It appeared to be built into a rock wall with two open sides protected by a stone railing. On one of the inner walls was a pair of closed doors, and on the other was an arched doorway that led to a hallway.

I tilted my head back to look up at the blue sky and gasped softly at the rock wall above us. It was black like obsidian, and it reflected the sunlight as it went on for hundreds of feet.

I opened my mouth to ask about it, but I was cut off when a faerie in a pale blue tunic with silver trim approached us and bowed to Lukas. His long dark hair hung to his waist, and his green eyes flicked to my hand in Lukas's before he addressed Lukas in Fae. The only word I could make out was Vaerik, Lukas's real name. Lukas replied to him in Fae. The faerie bowed again and left.

Lukas met my questioning look. "My father asked for me to go see him immediately upon my arrival. I told him I will be there after I have seen you settled into your rooms."

"It sounds important. You should go." I hated for him to leave, but I understood why he had to. He wasn't just Lukas here. He was the king's son and the crown prince of Unseelie.

Conlan spoke up. "We'll take care of her."

Lukas looked undecided for a moment, and then he nodded. "I'll see you for the evening meal, if not before." He smiled, and his thumb stroked the back of my hand. Heat pooled in my belly at the tiny gesture.

"Okay," I managed to say.

He walked to the arched doorway with Kaia padding after him. I watched them go before I turned back to the others.

"Vaerik has many duties and responsibilities when he is at court," Faris said, reminding me that even his closest friends used his real name here. That would take some getting used to.

"I know." I put on a cheerful face. "Guess that means you're stuck giving me the grand tour."

He bowed. "It would be my honor."

We were interrupted by the arrival of another faerie dressed in a similar outfit to the first one. He spoke to Conlan and the others in Fae, and by their tones, it sounded like they were having a disagreement. Lukas had told me the language would come to me as my magic had, but it was frustrating not to be able to understand what people were saying around me.

Faolin spoke sharply, and the new faerie backed down with a small bow. He said something and hurried away without a glance in my direction. What a welcoming bunch.

"Is there a problem?" I asked them.

Faris smiled. "There was some confusion about your quarters, but it's been sorted out."

"Speaking of." Conlan took my hand and laid it on his arm. "Let us show you to your quarters. We'll save the big tour for later."

The six of us left the courtyard through the same door Lukas had used and walked down the hallway. The floor and walls were as smooth as marble, but they appeared to have been carved from natural rock. From the ceiling hung glass orbs containing the same crystals I'd seen in Davian's penthouse. I knew now that they were called *laevik* crystals. They gave off a softer light than the electric bulbs I was used to, but they lit the place well.

Halfway down the hallway, we reached a large open space with a wall of windows that made it look like an indoor terrace. It had high ceilings hung with delicate light fixtures, tapestries on the walls, and flowered plants and trees scattered around the room. Couches, chairs, and small tables were arranged to allow for private or group conversations, and the space had an elegant yet homey feel.

Conlan steered me toward a small alcove on our left that was guarded by two male faeries, who exchanged nods with my escort. The faeries were dressed in black and wore swords and daggers on their hips. Other than their brief acknowledgement of us, they stood at attention with serious, alert expressions that sent a little shiver through me.

We stepped into the alcove that could fit maybe four people, and I faltered when the floor moved beneath my feet. Looking down, I was shocked to find the floor was a large stone disk that appeared to float.

"You can think of it as our version of an elevator," he said. "It has no buttons or doors, and you merely have to think of what level you want to go to."

"You don't have stairs?" I asked.

"We do, and we normally use them unless we need to go up or down many levels."

The floor started to descend, and I looked at the others who stood outside the alcove. "You're not coming?"

"We'll meet you there," Faris said as he disappeared from view.

We didn't go far. The lift passed one level and stopped at the one below it. We got off and walked down another wide hallway past closed doors that Conlan said were personal quarters, slowing when we came to what looked like a large indoor courtyard. There were couches and small tables and at least ten faeries alone or in small groups talking. A male servant poured a beverage into several glasses at a side table, and I recognized the white-blond hair and pointed ears of an elf.

I looked at the assembled faeries. The males wore pants and tunics or shirts. The females wore pants and tops similar to what I was wearing or flowing dresses. They were all so elegant and refined, exactly how I'd imagined faeries at court, and I felt a bit like *Eliza Doolittle* in her new finery.

All conversation in the courtyard stopped as everyone watched me with open curiosity. I supposed I couldn't blame them. New faeries were rare, and I wasn't a child like the others. The first faeries to arrive in my world had been subjected to more intense scrutiny than this.

While most of the faces wore expressions of interest, one stared at me with undisguised dislike that bordered on hostility. I thought I recognized the blonde female from somewhere, and it took me a moment to remember where I'd seen her before. She had been with Lukas and Faolin the night I'd seen them across the street in Manhattan. She hadn't been happy to see me then either. Whatever the reason for her animosity toward me, it was her problem, not mine. I met her gaze and held it until she looked away.

"There are many communal areas like this," Conlan said as we continued past the courtyard. "As well as larger rooms on several levels for bigger gatherings."

We walked down another hallway and passed a male faerie who tilted his head at Conlan. It wasn't until after he'd gone by that I recognized him as the one who'd argued with Conlan and the others about my room.

Conlan stopped at a door. "Here we are."

I looked at the door that had no distinct markings or numbers to distinguish it from any other door we'd passed. "How do you know? They all look the same."

"To you they appear identical, but not to the trained eye." He pointed to the door lintel where elegant script was etched into the stone. I'd mistaken it for design, but upon closer inspection, I realized it was Fae writing.

"What does it say?" I asked him.

"It's your name in Fae. Place your hand against the door."

I did as he ordered, expecting to feel magic, but there was nothing. The door simply clicked and swung inward an inch. "Nice."

"The doors are warded for the occupants. The royal guard can enter any room at court, but we only do that when it's absolutely necessary." He pushed the door open. "Welcome to your new home, Jesse."

I entered the room and stopped so abruptly that he nearly collided with me. There had to be some mistake because there was no way *this* was mine.

The large room was bright and airy with plush couches and thick rugs covering the stone floor. The walls were decorated with colorful tapestries depicting nature scenes, and there was a doorway on one end leading to what I assumed was the bedroom. At the other end of the room was a small dining area with a table and chairs that could seat six. There was no kitchen, which meant all food was prepared elsewhere.

Directly across from me was a set of open doors showing a wide expanse of blue sky. I crossed the room and walked out onto the private balcony, eager for my first real look at Faerie.

Spread out before me was a wide, green, horseshoe-shaped valley dotted with fields and hills. On the right, the valley was bordered by a thick forest, and on the left was a row of shiny black cliffs that gave me an odd sense of déjà vu. A sparkling river wound through the valley to meet the distant cerulean ocean that stretched as far as the horizon.

"Wow," I murmured at a loss for words. I leaned out over the stone railing to look down, and the height made me dizzy. Below was a wall of sheer black rock with balconies like mine built into it. There had to be at least thirty levels, maybe more, and that didn't count those above me. How big was this place?

Far below in the valley, there was movement in some of the fields. Through some trees I could make out buildings and roads. A town?

I straightened and caught sight of a dark shape against the sky, miles away. It dipped and soared with the grace of an eagle, but it had to be huge to be visible from here. I squinted, trying to see it better, and caught a glint of sunlight against it. My hand flew to my mouth. It couldn't be.

"It's a drakkan," Faris said from behind me.

I turned to find him, Iian, Kerr, and Conlan watching me in amusement. Faolin was nowhere to be seen.

"But it's so big!" I spun back to the rail to watch the winged shape fly to a distant cliff where others perched. "Gus was no bigger than a cat."

Faris came to stand beside me. "That is the normal size for drakkans. Gus was born in the human world, and the lack of Fae energy stunted his growth. He will grow to his full size here if he hasn't already."

I tried to imagine little Gus as big as one of these dragon-sized creatures and couldn't. A conversation with Lukas came back to me from the night he'd seen Gus at the apartment. He'd been surprised Gus stayed there because they were fierce creatures that protected the borders of Unseelie. I'd laughed, but that was before I'd seen them here.

"Is all of this Unseelie?" I asked.

"Only a small part of it." Faris pointed to our right. "You can only see a little of the forest from here, but it is bigger than the valley. Beyond this mountain, there are plains and more mountain ranges all within our borders."

I looked down at the wall of rock. "The people of Unseelie live inside a mountain?"

Conlan sat on the wide rail, making my stomach lurch. "The court is in the mountain. People also live in towns and villages and family estates."

This whole mountain was just the court? "How big is this place?"

"There are forty levels if you include the two below ground. Those are used by the servants and house the kitchens and cellars." Conlan's eyes gleamed. "And the cells for anyone foolish enough to commit a punishable offense."

Despite his grin, a shiver went through me. I didn't ask what kind of offense got you sent to a cell.

"The royal family lives on the top level," Faris said. "We – the royal guard – live on the floor below them. After that, occupancy is based on lineage. The closer you are to the crown, the higher the level you live on, but you can freely go to any level, except for the top one.

I frowned. By lineage, he meant how blue your blood was, and mine wasn't close to blue no matter that Lukas's blood had been used in my conversion. "Shouldn't I be on one of the lower levels?"

"You don't think we'd let you live so far from us, do you?" Conlan teased. "Goddess knows what kind of havoc you'd wreak if we let you out of our sight for too long."

Kerr snorted. "Because she'd get into no trouble with you?"

"New faeries live with a guardian," Faris explained. "You are old enough for your own quarters, but we thought you'd want to be near us."

"I do. Thanks." The argument they'd had with the faerie upstairs made sense now. He must have put me on a lower level, and they'd forced him to change it.

A bell chimed inside, and Kerr went to admit a dark-haired female. Behind her came a male with his arms full of clothes. Both of them looked surprised to see Kerr and unsure of whether or not they should enter the room.

Kerr motioned for me to join them. "Jesse, this is Sereia. She is here to fit you for your new clothes."

"Hi." I smiled at the newcomers.

Instead of looking at me, their startled eyes went to something behind me. I was confused by their nervous expressions until Conlan and Faris appeared on either side of me. I guessed she hadn't been expecting the crown prince's personal guard to be here.

Sereia said something in Fae, and Faris shook his head. "Speak English only. Jesse does not yet know our language."

She nodded and smiled demurely at me. "Welcome to Unseelie. I hope your stay here will be enjoyable."

Her English was perfect but a little stilted, which I suspected was from lack of use. Still, it was good to know that others here could speak it. Faeries had the ability to pick up any human language after listening to it for a few minutes. I hoped the same would be true for me soon.

"Thank you. It's nice to meet you."

Sereia glanced at the others before her gaze landed back on me. "I have brought you some garments to wear until yours are made."

"I think this is our cue to leave." Conlan turned to me. "We'll come back when you're done."

"Okay." I brushed off an absurd stab of panic. I was a big girl more than capable of taking care of myself. I couldn't expect them to stay with me every minute I was here.

The moment the door closed behind them, Sereia's timid expression vanished, and she assessed me with all the warmth of the Hudson in January. I fought back a laugh because she was about as threatening as the two Texas bounty hunters I'd had a run-in with a few months ago. If her plan was to intimidate the new girl, she had a lot to learn about New Yorkers.

"Where do we start?" I asked cheerfully.

Her delicate brow creased as she appeared to decide what to say next. "I will take your measurements and show you a selection of garments to see what fits you. We will leave some with you to wear until yours are made."

"Sounds good." Except for my prom dress, I'd never been fitted for clothes in my life. Violet would love this, and I wished she was here to share it with me.

Sereia turned to the blond male with her who still held the stack of clothing. "You may put those on the chair and leave us."

He did as she instructed and left without a word. She looked at me as if she was waiting for something, and when I merely stared back, she sighed impatiently. "Undress."

I cocked my eyebrows at her. I had no idea why she was copping an attitude, but I wasn't going to take it.

"Please," she added, looking like she'd tasted something sour.

"Of course." I stripped down to my underwear, and she made short work of taking my measurements. I would have appreciated her efficiency if she hadn't tsked over my frame, which wasn't as tall and willowy as all other female faeries, or made a sound of disapproval when she saw the freckles on my shoulders.

When she was done, she went to the pile of clothes and chose a pair of pants and a top, which she held out to me with a satisfied little smile. I knew the reason for her smile when I saw the linen-colored pants and pastel lilac top. The pants were fine, but most pastels clashed horribly with my red hair and made my skin look washed out.

I accepted the pants and refused the top. "I'd like a different color."

Sereia's mouth turned down as she selected another top. This time it was a tangerine one that would have looked amazing on her. Me, not so much.

"Do you have something blue or green?" I peered around her at the pile of clothes, seeing nothing but more pastels.

"No," she replied a little too gleefully.

I walked over to the clothes and picked through them, ignoring her indignant huff. She hadn't brought much of a color selection, and I was certain that had been on purpose. I found one white top that looked like it might fit me and slipped it over my head. It had clearly been made for a taller female, but it didn't look bad.

The pants were a different matter. When I donned the pair she'd given me, I discovered they were a size too small, and they bunched up at my ankles. Every pair I tried was the same. I gave up after the sixth pair and pulled on the pants I'd worn here. They were the perfect length and size, which meant Lukas had ordered them specifically for me.

"I'll have to wear these until more can be made," I said, earning an appalled look from her.

"You cannot wear the same clothes two days in a row."

I shrugged. "Better than my pants bursting open in public, don't you think?"

Her lips thinned even more. "This is not your human world. It is unseemly to wear the same clothes for more than a day. It's also custom for us to change our outfits for the evening hours."

The bell chimed. Sereia moved before I could and went to answer the door. A male elf entered carrying a tray covered with a white cloth, which he set on a small table. When Sereia motioned for him to leave, he looked at me.

"Prince Vaerik requested a midday meal for you," the elf said timidly in English that was more stilted than Sereia's.

"Thank you." Warmth filled my chest. Lukas might be too busy to be here in person, but he was thinking of me.

The male left, and I walked over to see what he'd brought. There was a thick soup with colorful vegetables, some bread and cheese, a bowl of mixed berries, and a small carafe of juice. The soup's aroma hit me, and I was suddenly ravenous. After my portal debacle, lunch had been forgotten in the rush to prepare for the trip to Faerie.

A sound reminded me Sereia was still in the room. I looked over to where she was gathering up the clothes she'd brought. I went to help her, but she waved me off.

"I will return in two days with several outfits, and you can decide on the rest of your wardrobe then," she said stiffly. "You will have to stay in your quarters until your new clothes arrive."

I had no intention of staying cooped up here until she got around to making my clothes. Based on our short acquaintance, I wouldn't put it past her to take her sweet time. I didn't tell her that though because I wanted her to leave and let me enjoy my lunch.

As soon as she left, I exhaled loudly in relief and carried the tray out to the small table on the balcony. The food was delicious, especially the berries. I'd had some of them before, but there was one kind I'd never tried. They resembled red currants and tasted like a hybrid of mint and cherries. If I hadn't filled up on soup and bread, I would have devoured them all.

After my meal, I wandered around my room – or rooms. There was the main living area, a large bedroom with another view of the valley, and a bathroom with a sunken tub. I loved baths, but they were a rare luxury when you shared a single bathroom with your parents. I had a feeling I was going to get a lot of use from this one.

An hour later, I was bored, and it hit me that I didn't know how to find or contact Lukas or the others. There were no phones in Faerie. I was sure they must use some form of communication, but I hadn't thought to ask.

I was on the balcony passing time by watching drakkans on the distant cliffs when I felt some discomfort in my stomach. I ignored it at first until a small cramp hit me, followed by a bout of nausea. I put a hand to my stomach. This is what I got for eating too much of the rich Fae food at once.

I sat at the table, hoping it would pass soon. It would be just my luck to get a tummy ache on my first day here and when Lukas had promised to have dinner with me.

A stronger cramp knotted my stomach, and I thought I was prepared for the nausea that would follow. I wasn't. I doubled over, clutching the edge of the table for support. By the time it passed, my face was damp with a sheen of sweat, and I was shivering despite the heat of the day.

Needing to lie down, I went inside and got to the couch before the next cramp struck. I moaned and curled into a fetal position as knives stabbed my gut. The pain had barely subsided when my stomach roiled violently, and I threw up all over myself and the couch.

I struggled to sit up and get away from the foul smell of puke that made me want to retch again. I made it to a sitting position in time to throw up down the front of my once-white top. Hot tears poured down my cheeks as I slid off the couch to my hands and knees and crawled toward the bathroom.

My whole body seized with the next cramp, and I curled up on the floor, gasping. I barely had time to recover before another one came. "Oh, God," I moaned. I had survived being shot and a conversion, and now I was going to die here in a pool of my own vomit.

9

———————

Iwasn't sure how long I lay curled up on the floor as wave after wave of sickness hit me. I'd given up trying to reach the bathroom. All I could do now was ride it out. There was nothing left in my stomach to throw up, but I retched until my throat burned.

"Jesse!" Cool hands brushed away the hair that had fallen onto my face, and I was dimly aware of Lukas's raised voice. Was he speaking to me or to someone else? Did it even matter? Nothing mattered except this never-ending agony.

Someone picked me up and laid me on a soft surface. There were more voices, male and female, but I couldn't distinguish any of them. My lips were pried open, and I fought when a bitter liquid dribbled into my mouth. But the hands that held me were too strong, and all I could do was cry as I was forced to swallow the awful stuff.

Two more times I was made to choke down the liquid until the spasms in my stomach began to lessen. The nausea stayed, but I was no longer heaving.

A kind female voice spoke in Fae as gentle hands cleaned my face with a wet cloth. She said something else, but I couldn't understand it.

I didn't have the energy to open my eyes as a second pair of hands lifted me to a sitting position. The two unfamiliar people stripped off my pants and top and ran a warm cloth over my damp skin before they dressed me in a soft, loose shirt. Someone put a glass to my mouth, and I drank deeply, letting the cold water soothe my parched throat.

The next thing I knew, I was lying in a bed with a blanket pulled up to my

96

chest. My whole body hurt, especially my chest and stomach, but I was no longer racked with agonizing pain.

Lukas spoke in Fae from what sounded like the other room, and I shivered at the anger in his voice. No, not anger. He sounded enraged.

Someone answered him. It was the same female voice that had spoken to me. Whatever she said must not have been good because the next person to speak was Faolin, and it sounded like he was trying to calm Lukas down.

What is going on? I wondered, but my head was too muddled to think about it. Sleep pulled at me. Lukas said something else, but it came from a long way off as I let the warm darkness take me.

I dreamed of storms that ripped the sky apart and left towns burning. I watched it all from above, safe from the destruction but unable to help those on the ground. The scene changed, and I was watching my parents in our apartment, holding Finch and Aisla between them as a storm bore down on the building. "Mom! Dad!" I screamed, but my words were lost in the roar of the storm.

"Shhh, Jesse. You're safe. Your parents are safe," said Lukas's soothing voice.

I flailed against the arms wrapped around me, but they were too strong. Didn't he see that my family needed me? I had to go to them.

Conlan spoke in Fae. Then Faris. They sounded worried. Were the storms coming for them too? Suddenly, I was back on the ferry on the Hudson, watching people fall into the river. Only this time it was Lukas, Conlan, Faris, and the others. I tried to reach for Lukas and screamed his name as he disappeared beneath the roiling water.

I was vaguely aware of being lifted and held against a warm chest. "I'm here, Jesse. I'm not leaving you."

A new dream enveloped me.

I stood on my balcony, watching storms rage through the valley. Rain and wind battered me, but I was frozen, paralyzed with fear and helplessness.

"Come, Jesse," said a female voice.

I turned my head to see a tall, beautiful woman with long silver hair. Her face was young, but she radiated the power and wisdom of countless lifetimes. Her kind eyes met mine as she placed a hand on my shoulder. The moment she touched me, the storm muted, and I was able to breathe again.

"Do I know you?" I asked as she took my hand and led me from the balcony to the bedroom I recognized as the one in my new quarters at court.

"Yes." She helped me into the bed and smiled down at me. "We will talk very soon. For now, you must rest."

"But the storms... I need to stop them."

"You will." She laid a cool hand on my forehead, and warm lethargy stole over me. "Now sleep, my child."

I opened my eyes and stared in confusion at the high stone ceiling. It took a minute to clear the cobwebs from my brain and to realize I was in my bed at the Unseelie court. I frowned. Why didn't I remember going to bed?

I moved my legs – or tried to – but couldn't because of a heavy weight across them. Lifting my head, I looked at Kaia sprawled across my lower legs. The lamal opened her eyes and gave me a disgruntled look before she went back to sleep.

The murmur of voices drifted to me from the other room, too low for me to make out what they were saying. In this world, faeries had normal hearing and couldn't hear through doors like in the human world. Thank God for that. I couldn't imagine living in a place where there was no privacy for anyone.

Sitting up, I freed my legs from beneath the annoyed lamal and got out of bed. I was a little shaky, like I'd been one time after a particularly bad bout of flu, and I suddenly remembered the attack of cramps and nausea and lying on the floor. My hand went to my stomach, but aside from feeling empty, it was fine.

I spotted a stack of folded clothes on a chair and went to check them out. They weren't the ones I'd brought with me, and I was relieved when the pants fit. I didn't see my old clothes, and I could only imagine the state they'd been in covered in vomit.

After checking my appearance in the bathroom mirror and grimacing at my pasty complexion, I walked out of the bedroom. Lukas and the others all stopped talking when I entered the living area, and Lukas came to meet me halfway. His eyes were full of concern, and I had a memory of him telling me he wouldn't leave me. Was that real or one of the strange dreams I kept having flashes of?

"I'm okay," I said before he could ask.

His eyes searched my face. "You're pale."

"Thanks for reminding me." I gave him a wry look. "It's nothing a hot shower won't fix. You do have showers here, right?"

Conlan laughed. "I think she's feeling better."

"Yes, there is a shower." Lukas smiled and led me over to where he'd been sitting. He went to the other side of the room and returned with a tray of food.

My stomach growled, but the memory of what had happened the last time I'd eaten made me push the tray away. "I can't."

"It's safe," Faolin said from his seat directly across from me. "You won't get sick from the food again."

"How do you know? Maybe I'm not ready to eat all Fae foods." I eyed the plate warily. It looked delicious, but so had yesterday's lunch.

Lukas's jaw hardened. "You got sick because you ate some acca berries. They are toxic to us and cause stomach upset."

"I only ate what was on my lunch tray, and none of it tasted bad." I tried to recall the assortment of berries that had come with my meal.

"Acca berries are sweet and taste like any other berry," Faolin said. "Young children sometimes ingest them by mistake, but adults know not to eat them."

My mouth turned down. "I wish I'd known that."

"Whoever put them on your tray had to be counting on the fact that you wouldn't know what they were." Lukas's knuckles whitened where they gripped the tray. "They meant to give you an unpleasant stomachache, but the berries had a stronger effect on you because you're a new faerie."

I took the tray from him before he accidentally cracked it in two. "So, they didn't intend to kill me. That's good, I guess."

"When we find the one who did this, their punishment will be the same regardless of their intentions," he said in a hard voice. "And we will find them."

I looked at Faolin, who had a fierce gleam in his eyes, the same one he'd had on our first few encounters. I felt a moment of pity for whomever had played the prank on me – until I remembered writhing in pain in a pool of my own vomit.

Lukas let out a harsh breath. "This should not have happened to you. I promised you'd be safe here, and I didn't keep my word."

"That goes for all of us," Conlan said without his usual grin.

"Stop. None of you is to blame for this." I picked up a pastry and sniffed it before taking a tiny bite. Mmmm. I ate the whole thing before I realized they were all silent and watching me. "What? Don't tell me there is some weird etiquette about how to eat here."

Everyone but Faolin laughed, and Faris said, "It's good you have your appetite back. The color is returning to your cheeks."

"I feel better already."

Faolin stood and looked at Lukas. "The king and his counsel are expecting you to join them shortly."

"Duty calls?" I said as disappointment pricked me.

Lukas nodded. "We are meeting to discuss the damage to the barrier and to see if we can come up with a solution. I'm sorry to leave you so soon."

"Fixing the barrier is a lot more important than keeping me company." I smiled. "I think I can occupy myself with exploring this place."

He frowned. "Perhaps you should stay here and rest today."

"I can't stay cooped up in here all day unless you *want* me to lose my mind. I need to start finding my way around, and I really want to go outside."

"I will escort her and give her a tour." Faris shot me a sly smile. "And do my best to keep her out of trouble."

I opened my mouth to tell them they were overdoing it on the protection thing, but Lukas looked so relieved I let it drop. Besides, I enjoyed spending time with Faris, and I didn't want to go it alone on my first day here. Yesterday had taught me two things: there was a lot I needed to learn about Faerie, and not everyone was happy to have me here.

"Good." Lukas gave me one of those smiles that did funny things to my insides. "I will see you for evening meal, and you can tell me all about your day."

I almost said "It's a date" but stopped myself in time to avoid an embarrassing moment. Instead, I went with, "See you then."

He left, followed by everyone except Faris. Before the door closed, Kaia raced across the room and slipped out behind them.

I looked at Faris. "Do you guys go everywhere with him at court? I thought that was only something you did outside of Unseelie."

"It depends. At court, Vaerik can travel around without us, but everyone wants to talk to the crown prince. We can be a great deterrent. Outside of court, he always travels with at least two of us."

I'd never really considered what life must be like for Lukas in Faerie. In my world, he somehow managed to fly under the radar, but that was impossible here where he was the second most powerful person in all of Unseelie.

"I don't envy him," I said.

Faris shook his head. "Nor do I."

I finished my breakfast and went to shower. It didn't take long for me to decide that the rainfall shower was my new favorite thing. There was an assortment of soaps and shampoos to choose from that carried the mild, pleasant scents of flowers and rain.

After I dressed, I towel dried my hair and watched in amazement as it continued to dry on its own into soft, shining curls. No-frizz, manageable hair was definitely one of my favorite perks of being Fae.

I hurried back to the living area. "I'm ready."

We left my quarters and walked at a leisurely pace down the wide hallway. I still couldn't believe we were inside a mountain, and I felt a bit claustrophobic without windows. One more thing to get used to.

"What would you like to see first?" Faris asked.

"Outside," I answered automatically. "I've always wondered if the real thing looks like the paintings and drawings I've seen."

He smiled. "None of them do it justice."

We took the magical lift to the ground level, and Faris chuckled when I gingerly stepped onto the floating stone. I'd grown up surrounded by magic, but technology powered most things in my world. It was going to take a while to get used to relying solely on magic for certain things.

I caught glimpses of each level we passed, and most of them looked the same to me. A few times, there were faeries walking by, and they gave us curious looks. None of them seemed unfriendly like Sereia or the female we'd passed in the courtyard yesterday, which was encouraging.

The first things I noticed when we stopped on the ground level was that the hallways were narrower, and the walls were rough stone without the polished surface of the upper levels. They had the same lighting, but it felt more confining down here.

"Is there only one way into the mountain?" I asked as we walked toward an open area with wide doors flanked by two male faeries. They wore dark blue pants, matching tunics with silver trim, and long slender swords. Their expressions were impassive, but they inclined their heads to Faris when we approached them.

"This is the exit to the grounds. The main hall is larger and more formal. There are other exits used mainly by the guards and servants."

Faris opened the door, and we walked outside into a courtyard with thick columns and a few unoccupied benches. Beyond it, I saw trees, bright colors, and blue sky.

We crossed the courtyard and stepped onto a path of crushed white rock. I knew exactly how Alice must have felt upon her arrival in Wonderland. Faerie was exquisitely beautiful but so unlike anything in my world. Faris was right. The paintings did not do it justice.

The trees drew my gaze first, in particular the ones that resembled weeping willows but with silver leaves that glimmered in the sun. There were other trees with green or red leaves, but they paled in comparison. Brightly-colored birds flitted among the trees, calling to each other, and what looked like two tiny lavender monkeys fought over some kind of fruit on a branch.

Flowers of every color filled the air with their perfume, but the most stunning were the hydrangea-like blooms that had to be two feet wide. Something moved inside one of them, and a little blue face peeked out at me. It was a sprite that looked so much like Finch I almost said his name.

We left the path to walk on the grass, and I crouched to touch it. It was a deep mossy green, and it was so soft it didn't seem real. I ran my hand over it and marveled at the texture that was like a thick chenille rug.

"Are you going to roll on it?" Faris teased.

I smiled. "Maybe tomorrow."

A cute little creature the size of a chihuahua ran up to sniff my hands. It resembled a black fox with long silver-tipped black hair, silver claws, and beautiful silver eyes. I reached out to pet it, but it ran off toward a couple walking ahead of us.

"What is it?" I asked as I stood.

"A rika. They are popular pets here."

We started walking again, and I jumped when a pixie flew past me, its wings brushing my face. Then I nearly stepped on a white ball of fluff that was almost invisible against the path.

"Cina," cried a child's voice. A little blonde girl ran out in front of us and picked up the hama, hugging it protectively to her chest. She ran back to an adult I assumed was her mother, and I realized she was the first faerie child I'd ever seen. Her skin was like porcelain, and her features looked like they had been carved by a sculptor. If I had to choose one word to describe her, it would be angelic.

The child's mother hugged her and watched me as we walked by. She wasn't the only one. There were other parents with their children who stared until we left them behind us.

"I feel like an exhibit at the circus," I grumbled.

Faris laughed. "They've never seen a red-haired faerie. Don't worry; it'll pass."

The path curved around some gigantic flowering shrubs, and I forgot all about the gawking faeries. Before us, the path branched off in three directions, The right and left paths led to more extensive gardens. Directly ahead of us was a wide stretch of grassy ground dotted with trees and flowers that sloped down to a small sparkling lake. In the middle of the lake was a white pavilion accessible by a wooden walkway.

There were faeries everywhere, strolling along leisurely, sitting on the many benches, or standing in small groups. I had never seen so many Court faeries together. Every adult was at least six feet tall, the females slender and the males with a natural athletic build. Unlike Lukas and his men, everyone had long, straight hair, although some of the females wore theirs in various styles.

Everyone was beautiful and elegantly dressed like we were at a summer yacht party. And though they had different features, they had a sameness about them that I found a little unsettling coming from a world with so much diversity.

"Shall we walk to the lake?" Faris asked.

"Yes." I looked away from the curious eyes. "Can I ask you something?"

"You must have many questions. You can ask me anything."

I thought about the best way to phrase my question. "Everyone looks like they are out for a Sunday stroll. Do Court faeries have jobs? I know some are guards and some work with the king, but what about the rest of the court?"

"Some do, but in general, no."

I shook my head. "That sounds like a boring life for an immortal. How do they stay sane?"

Faris's warm laugh surrounded us, drawing even more curious stares. "They throw many gatherings and parties and spend their time trying to maneuver themselves into better standing at court."

I turned my head, expecting to see a grin, but he wasn't joking.

He nudged my shoulder with his arm. "It's not all that bad."

"For you. You're an elite royal guard." I was starting to see why so many faeries found my world appealing. It was far from perfect, but it was vibrant and at lot more exciting.

A thought occurred to me. "Are there female royal guards?"

"Yes. The consort's personal guard is entirely female and so is Princess Roswen's."

Princess Roswen, I'd learned, was Lukas's younger sister. He also had a younger brother named Kellen. When Lukas said we were coming to Faerie, I'd wondered if I would meet his family. So far, he hadn't brought it up.

"What do you think of the grounds?" Faris asked.

"They're beautiful." I stopped walking and tilted my face up to the sun. "It smells so fresh and clean, and I don't think I've ever been anywhere this quiet and peaceful. It's strange not to see buildings or hear the city."

"My first visit to the human world was jarring," he said. "It's not only the iron. I had never seen a city or automobiles. It's always noisy, and there is this chemical smell in the air that never goes away. It takes a while to adjust to a new world."

I gave him a sideways look. "Point taken."

We continued on our walk. Now that I'd gotten my first look at the place, I was able to notice other things. For one, the parents doted on their children, playing and interacting with them instead of watching them run around like people did in the parks at home. Another thing I saw was how people acted around Faris. If we encountered someone on the path, they stepped aside for us, and they all looked at him with deference. I wondered if this was because he was royalty or a royal guard.

As we neared the lake, the surface rippled, and I caught the flash of a silver tail that was too big to belong to a fish. "What was that?"

"A siren. There are a few in the lake."

"Really?" I craned my neck eagerly, hoping for another look at the creature. I'd read about sirens, but actual sightings of them were rare in my world. They resembled the mythical mermaid, but their singing was so beautiful it was said to mesmerize any human who heard it.

Faris chuckled. "You're not planning to take up your old occupation here, are you? I think King Oseron is particularly fond of the lake dwellers."

I smiled. "My interest is purely academic. I can't wait to tell Mom and Dad about it."

A male faerie in the court livery approached us and spoke to Faris in Fae. Faris nodded and looked at me. "I need to step away for a few minutes. Do you mind?"

"Go ahead. I want to look for those sirens."

I walked to a bench a few feet away, and I'd barely sat down when I heard a soft splash nearby. I thought I caught a glimpse of dark hair, but I couldn't be sure if it was my eyes playing tricks on me.

"Such an unfortunate color. And those curls," a female voice drawled, intruding on my thoughts.

"And her skin," said another. "Humans call those spots freckles."

"I don't know," said a third. "I think it gives her an exotic look."

It took a few seconds for my brain to register the voices had spoken in perfect English – and that I recognized one of them. I schooled my expression to be as serene as the lake as three faeries came to stand in front of me.

Dariyah was flanked by two females I didn't know, her fake smile not reaching her green eyes, which glittered with malice. One of her companions had black hair and bore enough of a resemblance to her to make them sisters or cousins. The third was blonde, and the tiny smile she gave me was hesitant as if she wasn't sure how she was supposed to greet me.

"Josie, how lovely to see you again," Dariyah said with a self-satisfied smirk. "Welcome to Unseelie."

I turned up my smile a notch. "Thank you, Delilah. It's great to be here."

Her blonde friend made a sound and pressed her lips together.

Dariyah's smile slipped a fraction. "It's Dariyah, Vaerik's...friend."

She said *friend* like she was a lot more than that to him. My chest squeezed because I had no idea what she was to Lukas. I'd be damned if I let her know her words had hit their mark.

"My bad." I made an oops face. "I guess I forgot because he doesn't talk about you to me."

This time it was her dark-haired friend who could barely keep a straight face.

Dariyah's smug look vanished, and I half-expected her to lunge at me. She regained her composure so quickly I was impressed.

"We heard you were very ill last night. Pity your first night in Faerie was ruined." She lowered her voice to a stage whisper. "Vomiting all over yourself is nothing to be ashamed of."

I gave her my sweetest smile. "That's what Lukas – Vaerik – said when I woke up this morning. He stayed all night to take care of me."

I had no idea if that was true, but neither did Dariyah. Her lips flattened, and her eyes narrowed to slits. She was seconds away from exploding, but I didn't care. I was not going to be bullied or demeaned, and she might as well learn that now.

Her two friends' eyes widened, and they took a step back. The blonde paled, and the brunette inhaled sharply. I'd been the brunt of one of Dariyah's rages, and her bark was definitely worse than her bite.

It wasn't until I heard other gasps and a few urgently spoken Fae words that I realized Dariyah's friends were staring at something happening behind me. They backed up a few more steps, and Dariyah went with them, her mouth now curved into a malicious smile.

My stomach knotted. Anything that would make her happy did not bode well for me.

10

M Y HEART LEAPT into my throat as I stood and spun to look up the way I'd come with Faris. I expected to see a dozen bunneks coming to tear me apart, but I was greeted by the sight of Kaia making a beeline right for me. Her lips were pulled back into what I used to mistake for a snarl until I got to know her. She looked scary, but at heart, she was a big old softy.

When she reached me, she pounced, knocking me back down to the bench. Her huge paws rested on my shoulders, and she growled playfully before she rubbed her head against mine. I laughed and then sputtered when I got a mouthful of lamal hair.

"Kaia, down." I pushed her away, and she fell back to all fours. Then she jumped up beside me on the bench where she seemed to notice the three females for the first time. She clearly didn't like what she saw because she showed her fangs to them and hissed.

I scratched behind her ear. "Be nice."

Faris returned and smiled at Dariyah and her friends before he looked at me. "Shall we continue our walk?"

I nearly jumped to my feet. "Absolutely!"

Kaia leaped off the bench, and the three females stepped back so fast I thought they would end up in the lake. I won't lie and say I wasn't a tiny bit disappointed when they stayed on dry land.

We resumed our stroll along the lake with Kaia walking beside me, and I didn't miss the strange looks we were getting from people around us. I waited until we were out of earshot of anyone else to mention it to Faris.

106

"Why does everyone look like they've never seen a lamal before? Lukas said some are bred in captivity and domesticated, so Kaia can't be the only one here."

Faris looked over at the big cat. "She's not. But what you probably don't know about lamals is that they imprint on the person who raises them. They will tolerate family members and close friends, but they don't often show affection for anyone except their owner. Everyone at court knows who Kaia belongs to. Her familiarity with you tells them you've spent a lot of time with her and Lukas."

I made a face. "I'm guessing that won't earn me many friends around here."

"On the contrary. I'd say your status at court just shot up considerably."

I could think of at least one person who wouldn't be happy about that, but I didn't mention her. The less I heard her name the better.

As if he knew what I was thinking, Faris said, "I heard part of your conversation with Dariyah. I was ready to come to your rescue, but I'm not surprised you didn't need it."

"Dariyah might be the resident mean girl here, but I'm a Brooklyn girl." I tipped one corner of my mouth up. "And *she* hasn't trained with Faolin."

Faris laughed. "Or hit him with a wooden bat. And that was before you started your training."

"Imagine what I'll be able to do with even more training." I paused. "Will you be able to train me here? It's not against the rules or anything, is it?"

"Few rules apply to the royal guard," he said without a hint of arrogance. "We assumed you'd want time to adjust before resuming your training."

"God, no. When can we start?" The other faeries might enjoy this life of leisure, but I needed something more.

His eyes sparkled with amusement. "I'll talk to Faolin. I'm sure he will appreciate your eagerness."

Ahead, three children raced up a small hill under the watchful eyes of their parents. It reminded me of the conversation Faolin and I had on my first day of training.

I looked at the tall cliffs in the distance and shivered. "Faolin's not going to make me run up a mountain, is he?"

"Not at first." Faris grinned. "He'll save that for a special occasion."

I grimaced. "Forget I asked."

The bell rang, announcing I had a visitor, and I smoothed down my hair as I ran to get the door. Lukas had said he'd be here for dinner, and it was nearing that time. I'd hardly seen him since we got to Faerie, and I was looking forward to spending the evening with him.

I swung open the door to a smiling Conlan, and the second I saw him, I knew Lukas wasn't coming. My smile faltered, and I tried to mask my disappointment. The empathy in Conlan's eyes said I hadn't been successful.

"Is he still meeting with the king?" I asked in an attempt to sound nonchalant.

"The king is having a dinner party, and Vaerik's presence is mandatory. Vaerik asked me to tell you that he won't be able to eat with you tonight."

I let out a long breath. "I guess not even the crown prince can say no to the king."

Conlan sat on the couch. "The king can be demanding of Vaerik's time when he is at home. It's one of the reasons he likes to get away from court."

I bit my lip. I was upset about not seeing Lukas, but he was the one who didn't have any choice in the matter. I'd known when we came here that he had many responsibilities and obligations, and I couldn't expect him always to be available for me.

What I needed was something to occupy my time and to not be dependent on Lukas and the others for everything. At home, I had my family, a job, and my independence. Here, I didn't have to do anything, and I was already missing my life back in New York.

Conlan held up his hands. "Lucky you, you get to have dinner with us tonight."

"Us?"

"Iian and Kerr will be here soon. They are bringing the food."

I joined him on the couch. "You guys don't have to keep me company. What about your own families?" Aside from Faris and Faolin being brothers, I knew nothing about their home lives or their families. Why was that?

"My mother and sister are at our home near the ocean," he said. "My father is one of the king's advisors, and that role keeps him very busy."

His answer surprised me. "I thought all royals lived at court."

He smiled and stretched out his legs. "Many do, but we all have family estates away from here. Some, like my family, prefer the quieter life away from court. Iian and Kerr's family estates are near mine. Faris and Faolin's home is in the Daerig Mountains, but they spent most of their lives here. Their mother is one of the king's advisors, and their father is the head of court security."

"Why am I not surprised that Faolin's father is the head of security?" I said wryly. "Is he a ray of sunshine like his son?"

Conlan let out a laugh. "If you think training under Faolin is bad, you should have seen what Korrigan put us through. I don't think a day went by in the first year of training that at least one of us didn't throw up or pass out."

"How old were you when you started training?"

"Ten."

I gaped at him. "Ten?"

The door opened, and I turned to see Iian and Kerr enter carrying trays of food and drink, which they set on the table in the dining area.

Conlan stood. "Just in time. I was about to tell Jesse what it was like to train under Korrigan."

"Excellent." Iian flashed a smile and gave me a small bow. "Dinner is served."

Hours later, I was on the balcony staring at the stars when my door opened. My heart gave a little leap when Lukas entered with Kaia. I had given up hoping to see him tonight.

Our eyes met, and he smiled, setting off butterflies in my stomach. Neither of us spoke until he crossed the room and joined me on the balcony.

"I wasn't sure if you'd still be up," he said as he leaned against the rail. "I wanted to see how your day went."

"It was good. Faris and I spent half the day outside, and I had dinner with Conlan, Iian, and Kerr."

"I'm sorry I haven't been around much since we got here. This business with the barrier is taking more of my time than I expected. And then there is my father..." He paused, and I waited for him to continue, but he seemed to be lost in his thoughts.

"You don't have to apologize. I know you have a lot of responsibilities here."

His gaze came back to me, and for a second, he looked like he carried the weight of the world on his shoulders. He smiled, and it was gone, but I knew I hadn't imagined it. He was burdened by something, and I wished I knew how to help him.

I faced the valley that was shrouded in darkness. Far off in the distance, lightning flashed over the ocean. The storm was too far away to affect us, but the sight of it sent a shiver through me.

"Are you cold? The nights can be cool this time of year." Lukas turned and put an arm around me, drawing me against his side as if he did it all the time.

I leaned into his warmth and suppressed a happy sigh. It was balmy here compared to New York, but he wouldn't hear that from me.

"I know my parents are safe from Davian on your island, but what if there is a storm, and I'm not there to help them?"

Lukas's hand rubbed the arm not pressed against him. "The storms have only been happening in the cities with the most portal use, so your family is safe in that remote location. And I have four trusted guards posted there for added protection and daily updates."

"You do?" I tilted my head to look up at him, but his face was hidden in shadows.

"Your family's safety is a priority for me. Never doubt that." He stared into the darkness for a long moment. "I'll take you to see them soon."

His words made me giddy with happiness. "Really?"

"I promise."

I rested my head against the crook of his shoulder again. "Am I allowed to ask if you've made any progress with fixing the barrier?"

He raked his free hand through his hair. "We have all come to the agreement that neither Unseelie nor Seelie can do this alone. Arrangements are being made to meet with Seelie so we can work on a solution together."

"How will that work? Queen Anwyn caused all of this when she had the ke'tain stolen."

"That is not common knowledge, and we have no proof of her involvement," he said, sounding as unhappy about it as I was. "But we have to put aside our differences for the good of Faerie."

I scowled at the darkness. I understood the importance and role of diplomacy, but I was glad I didn't have to see or speak to the Seelie queen. I didn't think I could be civil with the person who had nearly destroyed my family.

"I have business to tend to in the morning, but I've freed up my afternoon. How would you like to visit town with me tomorrow?"

I pulled away to look up at him. "Do you even have to ask? I want to see everything!"

He laughed and surprised me when he leaned down to press a featherlight kiss to my forehead. There was nothing sensual about the gesture, but every nerve ending in my body felt it.

Lukas stayed for another hour, and we kept the conversation light. Mostly, we stood quietly, listening to the far-off sounds of the valley. Long after he bid me goodnight, I lay in bed unable to sleep as I thought about our outing the next day.

When I finally slept, I dreamed of Gus, but he was no longer the tiny drakkan I'd known. He was as big as the one I'd seen yesterday, and his red-gold scales moved like flames under the sun. I called to him, but he didn't remember me. Sadness filled me as he flew away until he was no more than a spec in the sky.

"Ready to go?" Lukas asked when I opened my door to him and Kaia the next day.

I stepped outside and closed the door behind me. "Are you kidding? If you'd been a minute later, I would have left without you."

He chuckled as we walked down the hallway. "Have you always been this impatient?"

I made a face. "No, but I've also never had to spend a whole morning getting fitted for a wardrobe. Who knew that could be so exhausting?"

I'd awakened in a great mood, and that had lasted until Sereia had shown up at my door to help me choose a wardrobe. After we'd butted heads once more over what colors went best with my hair and coloring, we had spent another hour arguing over what articles of clothing I needed. If it had been left to her, I would be wearing dresses every day. That might be the style for most females at court, but I preferred pants for everyday use and dresses for more formal occasions.

Lukas laughed again when I recounted my ordeal for him. The sound must have carried ahead of us because when we reached the courtyard on this level, the dozen or so people there seemed to be waiting for him to arrive. It was the first time I'd been outside of my quarters with him, and it was surreal to see everyone bowing or curtsying to him.

I wasn't surprised when I received more than a few furtive glances. Yesterday, I'd been the object of curiosity because I was the "new" faerie. Today, I was in the company of the crown prince.

"Vaerik," said a sultry female voice. It was followed by something in Fae that I couldn't understand.

I turned my head to watch a blonde female approach us from the other direction. It was the same one who'd shot me the death glare the day I arrived, but now I might as well be invisible. She only had eyes for Lukas.

He replied to her in Fae and looked at me. "Jesse, this is Rashari."

"Nice to meet you." I pasted on a smile that was as fake as the one she gave me.

"Ah, yes. Vaerik's little ward," she said as if she were speaking to a child. "How lovely to meet you."

She didn't wait for my reply before she turned her hungry gaze on Lukas.

"I'm so happy I ran into you. I wanted to tell you what a wonderful time I had last night."

My body stiffened, and I felt a tiny stab of pain in my chest. Lukas had told me he'd had dinner with his father.

"The king deserves all your praise," Lukas said courteously. "He enjoys hosting his dinner parties."

Rashari smiled coquettishly. "And I am honored to be invited. I look forward to doing it again soon."

"I am glad you enjoyed it. I apologize for rushing off, but Jesse and I are going to town today." Lukas didn't wait for her to respond before he took my arm and started to walk away. I dared a glance at Rashari, whose pinched smile did not mask her chagrin.

"Enjoy your visit to town," she said halfheartedly.

Lukas and I were quiet when we stepped onto the lift. I stared at the first two levels passing by before I heard him sigh.

"My father often arranges dinners to discuss court business with his senior advisors. Some of his advisors have daughters, whom he considers suitable matches for me, and he likes to invite one of them to dine with us."

I swallowed around the tightness in my throat. "He wants you to choose one of them as your future consort."

Lukas's brows knitted. "How do you know about that?"

I hesitated before answering. I had never intended to tell him about my run-in with Dariyah, but there was no way around it now. I had a sinking feeling that nothing she'd told me had been a lie, no matter how much I disliked the source.

"Jesse?"

"Dariyah told me a few months ago," I finally said.

"Dariyah?" he echoed sharply. "When did you see her other than the day she came to my place?"

Biting the bullet, I said, "She was waiting for me outside my building one day after Tennin shared those photos of you and me online. She told me you have to choose a blue blood mate to produce strong heirs."

Lukas's expression darkened. "She had no right to go to your home or to tell you that. I will make sure she never harasses you again."

Kaia, picking up on his anger, growled in agreement.

I laid a hand on his arm. "It's sweet that you want to protect me, but I can take care of myself. I've handled a lot worse than Dariyah."

The muscles under my hand relaxed, and he smiled. "Yes, you have."

The lift slowed, and I was surprised to see Faris, Conlan, Iian, and Kerr waiting for us on the ground level wearing swords. Lukas explained that an armed detail always accompanied him when he left the court.

We stepped off the lift, and a male in court livery hurried up to us. It was the same attendant who had come for Lukas the moment we arrived in Unseelie, and my heart sank before he spoke. I didn't need to understand Fae to know he was here on behalf of the king.

"Tell my father I have plans for the remainder of the day, and I will see him tomorrow," Lukas replied in English, his words sending warmth through me.

The attendant looked like the last thing he wanted to do was carry that message back to the king. Bowing to Lukas, he turned and hurried away.

We walked to a different exit than the one Faris and I had used the day before. This was the main hall, and it boasted two massive doors I didn't think I had the strength to open on my own. Four guards stood at attention, and they bowed to Lukas when we entered the room.

Instead of leaving through the huge doors, we walked to a normal size door I hadn't noticed. Iian opened it, and we emerged into a circular area paved with flat stones. Standing inside the circle was a white open carriage. It was drawn by four huge black equine creatures called tarrans that had bony faces and two small horns on their foreheads. A liveried male sat on the driver seat holding the reins. Four more tarrans stood nearby wearing light-weight saddles similar to those used by human jockeys but with long stirrups.

Kerr gave me an exaggerated bow. "Your chariot awaits, my lady."

"Why thank you, sir." I walked over to the carriage and let him help me up.

Lukas climbed in beside me. The carriage was big enough to fit six people, but Faris, Conlan, Iian, and Kerr mounted the tarrans and took up positions on either side of us. Lukas called something to the driver, and with a small lurch, we were off.

"Where's Kaia?" I looked around for her, and I was halfway out of the seat when Lukas stopped me.

"She likes to run. It's exercise for her." He pointed to something on his side. "There."

I leaned into him to peer over the side at the lamal loping ahead of the lead tarran. She suddenly crouched and wiggled her rear, and then she took off after something in the bushes.

I settled back into the seat and took a minute to savor the experience. It was a beautiful day, and I was alone in a carriage with Lukas on my first outing to a Fae town. I'd had a rough start to my visit to Unseelie, but this made that awful day seem like a distant memory.

The carriage slowed as we reached a fork in the road. The left one looked more traveled, and the right wound into the trees.

"Where does that go?" I pointed to the right as we started down the left road.

"To the Cadian forest," Lukas said. "There is a small elf village at the edge of the forest, but most of the elves have gone to live in town. The road is mainly used by hunters now."

"How far is the town?" I asked as we cleared the trees, and softly rolling hills came into view.

"Three miles."

I swung my gaze to meet his. "That's not far at all. We could have walked."

Conlan, who rode closest to me, snickered. "The crown prince does not walk to town. He must have more regal transportation."

"Normally, I ride with them," Lukas explained. "But you've never ridden a tarran, and it takes practice."

"You could have doubled up with him, but that would cause quite the scandal in town," Conlan joked loudly enough for the others to hear.

"No, thanks," I said over their laughter.

The gravel road curved, and the hills became farmland. On one side, there were fields of leafy crops and grazing animals, and on the other was an orchard. I recognized some of the fruits I'd been eating back home. The landscape was green and picturesque like the Italian countryside. You could imagine you were in Tuscany until you looked close enough to see that the people working the fields were trolls and dwarves, and the cows were actually small wooly mammoth-like creatures.

It wasn't long before the roofs of buildings came into view. We passed over a stone bridge, and I let out a sound of delight when we entered the town. It was like stepping back in time to a medieval town, but without the knights and peasants.

The gravel road gave way to a flat cobblestone street wide enough for two carriages to pass. The well-kept two- and three-story buildings along the road were white, tan, or brown with lots of windows and balconies that made them look bright and airy. Some of the buildings had shops on the bottom floor, and I wished we could stop and visit them all.

People waved to us from balconies and sidewalks, and wide-eyed children watched us pass. Unlike at court, the townspeople were a mix of court faeries, elves, dwarves, and even some trolls. It was strange to see trolls going peacefully about their business, and it made me wonder if only the troublemakers came to my world.

As we neared the center of town, the streets became more congested, and there were colorful banners up ahead.

"Are they having a fair or something?" I asked Lukas.

"It's market day. I thought you might enjoy it."

I could barely stay in my seat as the crowds parted for us, and we stopped beside a fountain in the middle of the town square. From my elevated position, I had a three-hundred-and-sixty-degree view of the market, and I nearly gave myself whiplash trying to take it all in.

Booths and stalls lined the edge of the square, selling everything from produce, cured meats, cheeses, and baked goods to clothing, jewelry, art, books, and so much more. Music filled the air along with the hum of many voices, shouts, laughter, and the squeals of children. The smells of exotic spices, savory meats, and baked goods made my mouth water.

I saw a few people from court, who stood out in their fine clothing. For the most part, the townspeople dressed more casually in simple pants, skirts, and shirts. Everyone gave the carriage a wide berth, bowing to Lukas when he stepped down. He tipped his head in acknowledgement and helped me down. I could have done it on my own, but it felt like proper decorum for him to assist me. Conlan and the others dismounted and came to stand with us, and Kaia wound through their legs to take her position at Lukas's other side.

"What do you want to see?" Lukas asked me.

"Everything."

Laughing, he placed a hand on my back and guided me toward the nearest stalls. People moved out of our way, making a clear path for us. I got the impression the crown prince wasn't often seen at the market, and this was a treat for them.

The first stall we stopped at sold jewelry, and I was dazzled by the large assortment of sparkling baubles and crystals. There were rings, bracelets, necklaces, hair accessories, and head pieces. I picked up a bracelet made of glowing eyranth and admired the intricate detail in the metal band. When Lukas spoke in Fae, I realized he was translating my praise to the elf vendor, who looked both flustered and honored to have the prince at her booth.

I asked her a few questions about some of the stones and her work until she was more at ease. By the time we moved on to the next stall, she was flushed with pride over some of Lukas's compliments.

The next vendor sold pastries, and it didn't take much coaxing for me to try one. The flaky, sugary pastry melted on my tongue, and I told him, with Lukas's help, that it was the best I had ever tasted. The beaming vendor offered me more, but I told him I had to save room for all the other tasty treats.

Lukas and I wandered from stall to stall. I tried the foods he suggested and talked to the sellers with his help. It was the happiest I'd been since coming to Faerie, and I felt more at home here where it was less formal and had so many different people. Court was beautiful and luxurious, but it lacked the vibrancy and warmth of this place.

Lukas's men stayed close enough to react to any threat to their prince while not crowding us. It wasn't like in my world where they walked beside him as equals. They might be his best friends, but here they looked more the part of a royal guard.

Occasionally, faeries from court approached us, and Lukas stopped to speak a few words to them. Some of the females tried to linger, but he never stayed long with them, to their dismay. I also didn't miss the fact that he always used English when I was beside him.

During one of his conversations, I wandered a few feet away to watch a musician setting up an oblong stringed instrument. He plucked a few strings, and delight filled me. It sounded like a classical guitar. My fingers itched to give it a try. Maybe I could find one like it since I'd had to leave my guitars at home.

The musician saw me watching and waved me over. He said something in Fae, and I shook my head, motioning that I couldn't understand him. A frown marred his brow, and then he smiled and held out the instrument to me.

I took it with eager hands and sat on the stone bench behind him. The instrument was awkward to hold at first, and the strings were made of a fiber I'd never seen. The first few chords I produced made me wince, and it took a minute for my hands to get used to the feel of the strings. As if my fingers had a mind of their own, they started to play "Annie's Song." It didn't sound quite the same as when I played it on my guitar, but I lost myself in the familiar melody. The market disappeared, and I was back in my bedroom at home playing for Finch and Aisla.

The song ended, and clapping brought me back to the present. I looked up to find a small crowd applauding me. Smiling, I stood and handed the instrument to the musician.

"Thank you," I said, and his answering smile said he understood the meaning if not the words.

I turned back to where I'd left Lukas and found him watching me with a thoughtful expression. I raised my eyebrows in question, and he merely smiled. He was hard to read sometimes, but today he looked relaxed and content.

A little elf girl with a rika ran up to me. I crouched to pet the creature, and I was surprised to feel a tug at my hair. I peeked at the girl who was running her little fingers through my hair, a look of wonder on her face.

"*Misse*," she said in Fae.

An adult female elf hurried over and gently removed the girl's hand from my hair. The female's face was anxious like a mother worried her child had done something wrong.

"It's okay," I said, but my words only seemed to cause her more distress. I looked around for help and was relieved when Faris appeared by my side.

He said something to the child's mother, who replied timidly, barely meeting his eyes. When her gaze met mine again, she wore a small smile and appeared less upset. I smiled back, and she bowed before she led her daughter away through the crowd.

"I didn't mean to upset her," I said to Faris in a whisper.

He shook his head. "You didn't. She thought her child would be punished for touching the prince's companion."

I stared at him aghast. "But that wouldn't happen, right?"

"No one would dare hurt a child, but there are some people at court who see townspeople as beneath them. They would have given the mother a harsh word."

I pressed my lips together, my good mood dampened by the reminder that no matter what world you lived in, there would always be *those* people.

"The little girl said something when she touched my hair. What does *misse* mean?" I asked him.

Faris smiled. "It means pretty."

He escorted me back to Lukas, who leaned in to say, "You have never played for me."

The teasing note in his voice sent my stomach into a tumble. "Ask nicely, and I might."

Lukas laughed softly, and my breath caught. Was I flirting with him? And was he flirting back?

We continued our walk, and I spotted a bookseller's stall. "Oh, Lukas, we have to stop there."

A gasp nearby alerted me to my faux pas, and my face grew warm. I lowered my voice. "I keep forgetting you're the crown prince."

"You might be the only person in Unseelie who does," he whispered.

I couldn't tell if he was disappointed in me or not. "I'm sorry."

"I like it." His mouth curved. "That's between us."

I smiled back. "My lips are sealed."

We walked over to the stall that had shelves of books and more in wooden crates. Every book had a fabric-bound cover with a simple embossed title, and most of them were works of fiction, according to Lukas. They were all in Fae, so I couldn't read them...yet. I flipped through some of them, intrigued by the flowing script that was the Fae language. It was hard to believe I would soon be able to speak and write in Fae. And eventually, I'd be able to pick up any human language.

I lifted a green book and discovered that every other page was a detailed drawing of a Faerie plant. When I showed it to Lukas, he said the text on the opposite page described the plant and its medicinal or culinary uses. My parents would love the book, even if they couldn't read it. Knowing Mom, she'd have someone translate it as soon as I gave it to her.

I looked at the bookseller, and then it occurred to me that I had no money to buy the book. I'd seen people exchanging the wafer-thin pieces of metal that was used for currency here, but I didn't have any of my own.

I moved to place the book back where I'd found it when a hand stopped me. Lukas took the book from me and handed it to the seller, who nodded and bowed.

"You don't need money here," Lukas told me. "All the merchants know the court will pay for your purchases. He will bring your book to the carriage."

"That kind of takes the fun out of it," I quipped. "But thank you."

A few minutes later, I discovered a stall selling dried berries that had a crunchy texture and a flavor similar to blackberries. When Lukas told me they were a popular children's treat, I bought a bag for Finch and Aisla.

At another stall I found a tiny purple crystal pendant inside a delicate eyranth cage that Violet would lose her mind over. Eryanth was expensive, so I smiled regretfully at the vendor and moved on.

"Do you want it?" Lukas asked.

I looked behind me to see him standing beside the pendant display. "I thought Violet would like it, but I'll get her something less extravagant."

Lukas turned to the vendor and said something in Fae. She beamed and removed the pendant from the display.

"You don't have to do that," I said when he rejoined me.

"I want to." We continued our walk, and he said, "You've bought things for everyone but yourself. Is there anything you want?"

I sniffed the air as more delicious aromas reached me. "I want to taste whatever it is that smells so heavenly."

He laughed, and we continued doing our circuit of the market. I ate and drank until I was too full to try another morsel.

When I spotted the carriage up ahead, I sighed quietly. It had been a wonderful afternoon, but now it was time to go back to court.

Lukas assisted me into the carriage, where I found my book waiting for me along with a long object wrapped in cloth. I gave Lukas a questioning look.

He smiled. "You can't play for me without an instrument."

I wanted to hug him, but I remembered where we were. "You bought me a...?"

"It's called a bugu."

I laid my hand over his resting on his thigh. "Thank you."

He turned his hand over and entwined his fingers with mine, sending a warm tingle up my arm.

Conlan and the others mounted their tarrans, and the crowd parted as the carriage started forward.

"Did you enjoy your first trip to town?" Lukas asked as we drove back the way we'd come.

"It was perfect."

"My schedule is hectic right now, but I promise it won't always be like that," he said. "We'll have many more days like this."

"I'm going to hold you to that," I said lightly.

He gave me a slow smile. "I hope so."

I didn't know if he was talking about friendship or something else, but the way he looked at me and held my hand promised more. Heat pooled in my belly, and I wanted nothing else in this moment but to feel his lips on mine. I didn't think he could kiss me when we were on full display like this, but maybe when we were behind closed doors...

The heat in my belly rose to my cheeks, and I looked away before he could see me blush and guess where my thoughts had gone. My gaze swung to my left and right into the amused eyes of Conlan who rode beside the carriage. His eyebrows rose knowingly, and he smirked at my poor attempt at nonchalance.

"What did you like most about the market?" Lukas asked as we passed over the stone bridge outside town.

I turned back to him. "It's easier to ask what I didn't like."

"And what was that?"

"Leaving it." I sighed quietly. "I wish this day didn't have to end."

His fingers squeezed mine. "It's not over yet. How would you like to have dinner with my brother and sister?"

My stomach did a little flip. "You want me to meet your family?"

"Only Roswen and Kellan." His eyes lit with amusement. "Unless you feel up to facing my whole family at once."

I swallowed nervously at the thought of meeting the Unseelie king. "Maybe only your brother and sister tonight."

Lukas smiled. "Roswen has been asking when she can meet you, and I can't put her off much longer."

"What?" I made a face of mock surprise. "Someone who can't be ordered around by you?"

He pretended to scowl. "Maybe I shouldn't introduce you two."

I opened my mouth to retort, but I was interrupted by a commotion in a field off to our right. A flock of what looked like pink geese was making an awful racket as the birds ran and flew across the field pursued by a dark shape. A dwarf chased after them shouting and waving his arms, trying to save his flock from the predator that looked *very* familiar.

Lukas called to the driver, and the carriage slowed. Standing, he called, "Kaia."

If the lamal heard him, she was having too much fun to heed his call. She pounced at one of the birds, and I put my hand over my mouth, expecting the worst. The bird took flight at the last second, escaping with all but a few feathers. Kaia leaped up and took off after another one.

"You're going to have to go get her," Conlan said, his voice full of laughter.

"I know." Lukas hopped down from the carriage and set off across the field, followed by the guffaws of his men. Iian and Kerr gave him a small head start before they slid off their mounts and trailed him.

I stood for a better view – and what a view it was. Lukas's muscled body moved with the same powerful grace of his lamal as he strode toward the chaos. He looked every bit the predator himself, one I would not mind stalking me.

A shadow passed over the carriage, and I tore my gaze from Lukas to look up at the sky. My jaw dropped at the sight of the winged shape soaring over us. From a distance, drakkans were big. This close, they were massive. The one above us had to be bigger than a single engine plane.

"He won't hurt you," Faris called, mistaking my awe for fear. "Drakkans never attack people in the valley."

The drakkan flew a quarter of a mile away and turned to come back for another pass. It was lower this time, and its scales flashed like flames in the sun. Reddish-gold flames.

It can't be. My heart jumped. There had to be lots of drakkans with scales that color, and there was no way he could have grown this big in the two months since I'd last seen him.

My eyes were glued to the drakkan as he dipped lower, giving me a good look at the all-too familiar red and gold pattern on his back.

"Gus," I breathed.

His horned head whipped toward me as if he'd heard me, and his red eyes fixed on me like laser beams.

I stared into his eyes, mesmerized. Someone shouted, but I could barely hear it over the flap of leathery wings. I snapped out of it in time to realize he was coming straight at me. This time, I did feel fear as I ducked for cover.

My head snapped back when the huge clawed foot wrapped around me from behind and snatched me from the carriage. I think I screamed as the ground fell away from us. It happened so fast it was a blur. The only thing I remembered clearly was Lukas racing across the field and shouting my name.

11

THE DRAKKAN'S POWERFUL wings beat the air, carrying us away at incredible speed. Within seconds, Lukas and the others were out of sight, and I closed my eyes against the dizzying blur of the ground flying past a hundred feet below. I clung to the foot wrapped around me, terrified that any second it would open and send me falling to my death.

After a few minutes, I couldn't take not knowing what was happening, and I opened my eyes. Beneath me, farms and green fields passed by, and a few people pointed up at us. It probably wasn't a common sight for a drakkan to be carrying a person.

I didn't want to think about what he intended to do with me when we got wherever we were going. He looked like Gus, but that didn't mean he was Gus. And even if he was the drakkan I'd rescued, he had changed so much there was no telling what he'd do.

We passed over a field of grain that looked like wheat, and I stared at the huge shadow cast by the drakkan. I was struck by the overpowering feeling that I'd seen this before. Tiny flashes of a memory taunted me. No, not a memory. It felt more like a dream, but how could I have dreamed of a place I'd never seen.

Up ahead, the wide river cut through the valley, and somehow, I knew before we reached it that he was going to turn left. When we flew over a few boats, I wondered dismally if I'd ever get to take a boat along the river or if this was the last time I'd see it.

I lifted my head and saw we were headed straight for the black cliffs I'd seen from my balcony. We veered away from the river, and the drakkan picked up speed as we neared what had to be his home.

As we approached the base of the cliffs, he started to climb at a dizzying speed that made my stomach roil. I had to close my eyes before everything I'd eaten at the market came back up.

The air suddenly shifted, and it felt like we were floating. I forced my eyes open to see we had crested the top of the cliff and entered a world beyond my imagination.

The craggy cliffs stretched for miles, and as far as I could see, there were drakkans, hundreds of them in every color and size. Some played together or ate, some nested in aeries, and others looked like they were standing on guard watching for threats. Two fought over what looked like a catfish the size of a tuna, and two appeared to be busy making more drakkans.

We flew along the cliffs out of reach of the other drakkans but close enough to see their snarling faces and hear their growls as they watched us. One snapped and jumped at us, making my heart threaten to break through my ribcage. If my captor let me go here, I wouldn't have to worry about the fall killing me. The teeth and claws below would rip me to shreds.

He didn't drop me, and he didn't land on the cliffs like I expected him to. We reached the end that jutted out over the ocean, and he kept going, straight out to sea where there was nothing but the vast horizon ahead of us.

A mile from shore, he lifted his legs so I was tucked against his warm underbelly and sheltered from the wind. I didn't know if he did that for me or because it allowed him to go faster, but I felt less like I was about to fall into the ocean. He was flying at a speed I hadn't known was possible for a living creature.

After several hours, I spotted a dark shape miles ahead. The closer we got to it, the more I could make out the details of an island. It was small, no more than a quarter of a mile wide, with a rocky shoreline, some trees, and a hill at the center. On top of the hill was a stone building that looked like it had grown out of the rock. Except for a few sea birds, the island appeared to be uninhabited.

The drakkan circled the island once before going in for a landing on top of the hill. He touched down lightly on three legs with me still tucked against his belly. I held my breath as he lowered me to the ground and released me.

I stumbled when he set me on my legs, which felt a bit rubbery from the flight. Righting myself, I turned to face him. He towered over me with his wings folded against his body, and his slit eyes watched me with the same wariness I had for him. He resembled Gus, but I'd seen other drakkans with similar coloring on the cliffs. How would I know if this was the one I'd rescued?

I licked my parched lips, wishing I had some water. Clearing my throat, I said, "Gus?"

He cocked his head to one side. Gus had done that too, but all drakkans probably did the same.

I gave him a sad smile. "I wish Finch was here. He'd know if you were our Gus."

The drakkan suddenly dropped down to his belly, his enormous spiked tail swishing back and forth and little puffs of smoke issuing from his nostrils. He rested his head on the ground and stared at me with an expectant expression. I knew that look. It was the same one he'd worn when Finch used to play with him.

"Gus, it *is* you!" Tears pricked my eyes. "I can't wait to tell Finch how big you are."

His tail moved faster at the mention of Finch. Gus might recognize me as the person who'd fed him, but he'd spent more time with Finch than anyone else. What would the drakkan do when he realized Finch wasn't here?

Better questions are where the heck am I, and how am I getting home? I turned toward the stone building, which appeared to be the only structure on the island. It wasn't much bigger than a hut with an uneven roof and a hole for a doorway that was barely tall enough for a Court faerie.

I walked in the direction of the building and began to feel a strange pull toward it. The closer I got, the stronger it was. The logical part of my brain said anything that compelled you to do something could not be good. My gut told me it wasn't a coincidence that Gus had flown all the way to this island in the middle of the ocean. I needed to be here, and I had to find out why.

I stood in the doorway to let my eyes adjust to the dim interior. There were stairs leading down and the glow of light below. I released my breath. This place couldn't be abandoned if there was light.

Encouraged but still cautious, I descended the roughly-hewn steps to a round room less than fifteen feet across. At the center of the room was a narrow stone pedestal on which sat a glass bowl of laevik crystals that cast enough light to allow me to see where I was going. To my right was a narrow tunnel lit by sconces. Across from me was an archway to another room that looked larger and more well-lit.

I crossed the room and peered into the one beyond. My breath caught because I suddenly knew exactly where I was.

The round, sunken room was easily three times the size of the first one, and it had a high ceiling hung with crystal lights. The walls were bare stone, and across from the entrance was a low, white stone altar. At the very center of the altar sat the ke'tain.

I walked down the steps to the room and jumped when I caught movement out of the corner of my eye. On my left were two male faeries in the blue and silver livery of the Unseelie court. I looked to my right and found two more faeries in white and gold tunics that must be the colors of Seelie. All four guards watched me with suspicion, but none of them spoke or approached me.

I turned back to the altar and stared at the stone that had changed my life in ways I was still coming to terms with. Seeing it stirred up a lot of conflicting emotions, and I was torn between wanting to leave this place and needing to move closer to the altar.

The pull of the ke'tain won, and I walked toward it. Four feet from it, I came up against an invisible wall that kept me from getting closer. It had to be the new ward they'd added to the temple to protect the ke'tain.

The ward might keep me from getting near the ke'tain, but it didn't stop me from feeling the power emanating from the stone. As a human, I hadn't been able to sense the ke'tain's magic. As a faerie, the ke'tain's energy was almost overpowering. How had Conlan been able to get within a foot of the thing that day in the bookstore office?

"Can you feel it?"

I started at the female voice and turned my head to see a tall woman with silvery blonde hair standing beside me. She wore a long, white dress adorned with a belt of eyranth, and warmth radiated from her. I didn't know how or where, but every cell in my body told me I'd met her before.

She smiled fondly. "Can you feel the power, Jesse?"

"Yes," I replied softly, unable to look away from her ageless gray eyes.

She nodded, pleased. "Good."

"Why is that good?" I asked when she didn't say more. "Can't everyone feel it?"

"Not the way you can." She reached up and touched the stone hidden in my hair, sending a small jolt of energy through me. It didn't hurt, but it left me breathless and filled with the certainty that my companion was no ordinary faerie.

"Who are you speaking to?" demanded a male voice.

I turned to see one of the Seelie guards a few feet away. He regarded me with leery eyes and one hand on his sword hilt. Looking past him, I found three more sets of eyes on me. Why were they looking at me like that?

And then it hit me. I was the only one in the room who could see the woman.

"I asked who you were talking to," the faerie said.

"Myself," I blurted, shaken. "I do that sometimes."

His hard, assessing gaze swept over me and lingered on my hair. Unless he'd been stuck on this island for two months, he had to know who I was. The downward turn of his mouth told me what he thought of the newest Unseelie faerie.

"Excuse me." I moved around him and headed for the stairs without checking to see if the woman was still there. I practically ran up the stairs, passed through the outer room, and kept going until I emerged into the fading daylight.

Gus was where I'd left him and appeared to be sleeping. His eyes opened, and he watched me lazily as I hurried toward him. He didn't appear to be in a rush to go anywhere, leaving me to wonder how the hell I would get home. Even if he did pick me up and carry me away from the island, he could take me anywhere, and I had no way to tell him where I needed to go.

I took a deep breath. Those guards had to have gotten here somehow. I'd go ask them how to get back to Unseelie. The two from Seelie might not help, but I was not above using Lukas's name to get assistance from the Unseelie guards.

I spun and nearly ran into the strange woman from the temple. I backed up several steps, once again filled with the certainty I'd met her before. But that was crazy, especially if my suspicion about her identity was right.

"Are...you Aedhna?" I asked.

"I am. It is wonderful to see you, Jesse." She smiled, and it banished the trepidation I'd felt only seconds ago.

I stared at her. This was the Fae goddess, the one who had created Faerie and everything in it. I was in the presence of a deity, and all I could think to say was, "Have we met?"

She laughed softly and closed the distance between us to cup my chin in her hand. Images and snatches of conversation filled my mind, whirling and fitting together to form forgotten memories. I saw my body on the ground surrounded by fog, and Lukas and the others were using their power to save me. I remembered pain, but it was muted, and the goddess was there beside me, helping me through the worst of it.

Aedhna let go of my chin to gently wipe away the tears coursing down my face. "You have been so brave and strong. Because of you, the ke'tain is back where it belongs."

"But I was too late. The barrier is weak, and the storms aren't going away." Hope blossomed in my chest. "Are you going to fix it? Is that why you're here?"

She smiled again, but there was a touch of sadness in it. "It can be healed but not by my hand."

"Unseelie and Seelie are going to meet to work on a solution," I said, giddy from her assurance that the barrier could be healed.

"I am pleased to see them coming together, but I fear they have been estranged from each other too long to succeed in this."

My heart sank because she was right. I didn't know much about King Oseron, but from what I'd heard, he was dedicated to fixing the barrier. Queen Anwyn was a different story. She had caused all of this, and knowing what I did about her, I couldn't see her doing anything for the good of others.

"You're the goddess. Can't you make them get along and work together?" I asked.

"When I created this realm and all within it, I gave them free will to live as they choose without my interference," Aedhna explained. "The last faeries to see me were the Asrai who guarded my temple thousands of years ago."

A gust of wind blew my hair into my face, and I brushed it away irritably. "You came to me."

"You were human, and though you are now Fae, you belong to both worlds. You wear the stone I gifted you, and you have proven yourself to be brave and worthy of my blessing and the job I chose you for."

Her praise filled me with warmth. "I'd do it again to keep my family and friends safe."

She laid a hand on my shoulder. "That is why I know you will succeed in what I ask of you now."

"What?" I asked slowly.

"To be my hands. I am going to give you the knowledge to heal my world."

"Me?" I took a step back, and her hand fell away. "I've been a faerie for a few months. Wouldn't it be better to ask someone stronger – like one of the royals?"

"This task requires more than physical strength. You will see that when the time comes. I would not choose you for it if I did not believe in you."

I took a few breaths to gather myself. My head spun, and I felt a little queasy, but I managed to speak. "You didn't bring me here to do it now?"

"The time is not yet right. I will come to you when you need to begin. For your protection, you will be unable to speak of this to anyone."

I shook my head. "Who would believe it?"

She smiled again. "I will see you soon, Jesse."

She disappeared. I spun in a full circle, but I was alone, except for Gus.

Gus stood and flapped his wings as if preparing for flight. He fixed his molten gaze on me, and when I didn't move, he let out an impatient growl I knew all too well. The only problem was that it was the same sound he used to make when he wanted his dinner. I thought about his sharp little teeth devouring the raw chicken I'd fed him at home, and I tried not to imagine what his dragon-size fangs could do to me.

Aedhna would not have left me with him if she thought he'd hurt me. Right? At least, that's what I told myself as I gathered my nerve and walked over to him.

When I was a few feet from him, he stretched out his powerful wings and lifted into the air. I should have been prepared, but I gasped when one of his clawed feet shot out to pick me up and tuck me against his belly. And then we were off.

I dozed off less than thirty minutes into our flight over the ocean. I woke to find that night had fallen, and we were nearing land. Ahead of us was a wide valley ringed by a mountain and tall, glassy, black cliffs.

Lights moved below us as we flew over the valley, and I realized they were torches held by faeries riding tarrans. Was it a search party out looking for me?

I called to them, but my shouts were drowned out by the wind and the flap of drakkan wings. Was Lukas out there with Conlan, Faris, and the others? They must be worried sick, not knowing if I was dead or alive.

The mountain grew closer, and I could make out the lake and the extensive grounds that were lit by torches. People strolled and mingled, oblivious to our approach. I studied them in their court finery and wondered how they could live this life of idle luxury day after day, year after year, without going completely insane from boredom. It had only taken me a few days of life at court to know I could never be happy living like them.

Gus circled the grounds, dipping lower with each pass. Shouts sounded from below, and people scattered when he flew around the perimeter of the lake. One group was too slow to get out of his path, and I heard female squeals and splashes when they went into the water.

He landed on a grassy slope near the lake and set me down gently on the ground. I immediately fell back on my ass. I stood, rubbing my backside, and looked up at the drakkan.

"Thanks, Gus."

He snorted, and smoke billowed from his nostrils. His big head lowered, and he nudged me hard enough to make me stumble. The next thing I felt was a massive gust of wind as he leaped into the air, pushing me back onto the grass. I lay there watching him rise higher and higher until the darkness swallowed him up.

I stared up at the stars winking in the night sky until running feet alerted me to someone's approach. I sat up as two males in guard livery reached me, looking at me like I was an alien that had fallen to earth.

"It *is* you!" One of them hurried forward to give me a hand up. "Are you hurt? Do you require a healer?"

I didn't need his help, but I accepted his hand. "I'm okay, thanks."

"We could not believe it when we saw the drakkan set you down," he went on. "Half the court thinks you are dead."

"The reports of my death have been greatly exaggerated," I joked as I brushed grass and dirt off me.

"How could they not be?" he asked. "You were carried off by a drakkan."

The second guard spoke for the first time. "Prince Vaerik and half the guard are out searching for you. We will escort you inside and send word to him that you are back."

"I don't need an escort. I think I can find my way by now."

He blocked me when I made to move past them. "We have orders to accompany you if you returned before his Highness."

One glimpse of their serious faces told me I wasn't going anywhere without them. I gave them a resigned nod, and they fell into step on either side of me. I could feel eyes on me as we walked to the entrance, but I ignored all the onlookers. I was getting used to being stared at.

We entered the mountain and took the lift to the upper floors. When it stopped, I was surprised to see the large indoor terrace area I'd passed on my first day here. The two black-clad guards posted there were not the same ones I'd seen on my arrival, but they looked every bit as threatening as they faced the lift to see who had dared to enter their territory. When they saw me, their expressions barely changed as they stepped back to allow us entry.

"This is not my level," I protested when I was ushered off the lift.

"We will take her from here," said one of the guards in black. The next thing I knew, my escort had returned to the lift, and the guard who had spoken was steering me toward the courtyard where I had first arrived in Unseelie.

We entered the courtyard and crossed it to the set of double doors I'd noticed my first time here. He laid a hand against one of the doors, and there was a click as it unlocked. Then he opened the door and motioned for me to enter. I did, expecting him to follow me, but all I heard was a soft whoosh as the door closed behind me.

"Hey!" I spun and grabbed the door handle, but it wouldn't budge. I was locked in.

"Not cool," I called irritably, turning to see my prison.

My anger evaporated as I let my gaze sweep the living area that was at least twice as big as my generous suite. This one had more couches than mine and a dining area that could seat eight. It was softly lit by crystal lamps, but the darker fabrics and a collection of weapons on one wall gave it a masculine feel.

I walked over to inspect a charcoal gray shirt carelessly thrown over the back of a couch. I felt a jolt of recognition, and I picked it up to sniff it. It was the shirt Lukas had worn to town, and it still carried his scent. That could only mean I was in his private quarters.

Holding the shirt to my chest, I explored the suite. It was laid out much like mine, only a lot bigger. When I entered the bedroom, I discovered his balcony stretched the entire length of his suite from the living area to the bedroom.

It was his bed, though, that really caught my eye. The black, carved headboard reached halfway to the high ceiling, and the blue coverlet was so dark it was almost black. I had thought his bed back home was huge, but this one could probably fit him and his whole personal guard. I grinned at the mental image of the six big faeries lying side by side in the bed. That image was replaced by one of Lukas and me alone in here, and heat suffused my body.

I gave into temptation and lay back on the bed with my arms splayed. The coverlet felt like silk under my fingers, and Lukas's familiar scent enveloped me. I would have curled up and gone to sleep there, but the last thing I wanted was for Lukas to walk in and find me in his bed like a stalker.

I gave the bathroom a cursory look before I walked out onto the balcony. It was too dark to see much, but the view would be the same as the one from my suite two levels below. Leaning on the rail, I scoured the valley for the torch lights I'd seen when we flew over it, but they weren't visible from this height.

Turning, I spied an oversized chair behind me, and I made myself comfortable on the plush cushions. I tucked my legs under me and tried to process what had happened today. I had met the goddess... again. She'd been with me during my conversion, and it was because of her that I was alive.

Now she wanted me to accomplish a feat that apparently no one else in this realm could do. What if she was wrong about me, and I couldn't do whatever it was that needed to be done to save Faerie?

I rested my head against the cushion and stared at the dark sky. I couldn't think that way because there was too much at stake for me to fail. Aedhna wouldn't trust me with the fate of her world if she wasn't sure I could handle the job. I only wished she'd told me why she'd chosen me. It would make the wait a whole lot easier.

Raised voices startled me, and I realized I must have dozed off. I was halfway out of the chair when a male spoke from inside the suite.

"I brought her here myself, Your Highness, and she did not leave."

It was followed by Faolin's voice. "She must be here somewhere, Vaerik."

I grimaced and walked toward the open balcony doors to the main living area. I was met by Kaia, who rubbed against my legs and nearly knocked me over. Petting her head, I moved to the doors where I saw Lukas with Faolin and the guard who had escorted me here. Lukas and Faolin wore pants and jackets made of some kind of dark leather, and swords hung at their sides.

Lukas's back was to me, but Faolin spotted me the second I appeared in the doorway. He tilted his head in my direction, and Lukas spun to face me. The wild look in his eyes when they locked with mine sent my pulse racing. I couldn't remember ever seeing him like this, and I didn't know whether to be afraid or happy to see him.

"Jesse." He was across the room before I could speak, his arms wrapping around me to pull me tightly against him. "I thought... I didn't know if you were..."

The anguish in his voice made my throat tighten painfully. I slipped my arms around his waist and held on tightly as I breathed in his scent. He smelled of fresh air, leather, and the faint musky odor of tarran that made my nose wrinkle. He could reek of skunk, and I wouldn't care as long as he kept holding me like this.

The door clicked, telling me Faolin and the guard had left, and I finally found my voice. "I'm sorry," I whispered against his shirt. What happened hadn't been my doing, but I couldn't think of anything else to say.

"It wasn't your fault." He loosened his embrace and put a hand under my chin to tilt my face up to his. "I should have kept you safe. If you had been hurt..."

I barely registered his head lowering before his mouth closed over mine. The only thought that went through my mind was *Finally!*

His kiss was hard and possessive, and it set my insides ablaze. I didn't surrender to it. I matched it with all my pent-up emotion and need. My hands slid up his chest and grabbed the neckline of his shirt to keep him exactly where I wanted him.

Lukas's chest rumbled with pleasure, and he lifted me until my legs could wrap around his waist, and my face was level with his. He broke the kiss to look at me, and my limbs turned to jelly at the desire in his eyes. Then he reclaimed my lips with the same fierceness, and I knew that if he asked, I would give myself completely to him.

"Vaerik, I see you've found your missing friend," said an amused male voice from across the room.

I gasped and let go of Lukas like he'd burned me. He caught me easily before I fell and lowered me unhurriedly to my feet. His smile did little to reassure me, and my face was on fire when I turned to face the newcomer.

I did a double take at the sight of the male who could be Lukas's twin. His dark hair was long like that of most faeries, but his face was almost a mirror image of Lukas's. Even though his clothes were in the same elegant style favored by the males at Court, he had a presence that told me he was no ordinary faerie.

Of course! He was Lukas's brother Kellen, whom Lukas had planned for me to meet at dinner tonight. I groaned inwardly and resisted the urge to look down at my crumpled, soiled clothes. This was not how I wanted to meet Lukas's family. I was a mess, and Kellen had just walked in on me making out with his brother.

"It's more like she found us." Lukas's hand gave mine a gentle squeeze. "Father, allow me to introduce you to Jesse James."

It took a few seconds for his words to sink in, and then shock slammed into me. *Father?*

I was standing in front of the Unseelie king...who had witnessed me climbing all over his son and heir.

Where was a drakkan to carry me away when I needed one?

12

———

"J ESSE." KING OSERON walked toward us. "I have heard so much about you."

I had never learned to curtsy, so I gave him a small awkward bow. "It's an honor to meet you, Your Majesty. I've heard a lot about you, too."

He smiled warmly. "Yes, I hear I am a subject of much curiosity and speculation in the human world. Do I live up to the expectations?"

I hadn't expected the Unseelie king to address me so informally, so his manner threw me off balance. How was I supposed to answer a question like that?

"Father," Lukas said in a slightly annoyed tone.

The king waved him off. "There is nothing improper in that question."

Lukas quirked his eyebrows. "No, but I speak from experience when I say that Jesse has no qualms about telling you exactly what she thinks of you."

King Oseron threw back his head and laughed. His gaze met mine again, and I saw that his eyes were blue but not the same midnight blue as his son's. And they seemed older somehow. Up close, there were other differences in their faces. The king's jaw was squarer, and his lips were not as full as Lukas's. Although their smiles were similar, the king's did not have the power to turn my insides to mush. Only one person had ever been able to do that to me.

"I expect nothing less from the girl who returned the ke'tain to us." The king reached out and took one of my hands in both of his. "On behalf of Unseelie, I thank you."

"I... you're welcome," I squeaked when I found my voice. Never in my life had I imagined I would someday be face-to-face with the Unseelie king while he held my hand. Could this day get any crazier?

I discovered the answer to that when the door opened, and a dark-haired female came in. She carried herself so regally I knew immediately that she was Lukas's mother, Maurelle.

Maurelle saw me and smiled. She crossed the room and kissed both of my cheeks. "Jesse, I am so glad you have returned unharmed from your ordeal."

"Thank you, Consort," I stammered.

"Call me Maurelle. Vaerik and his friends speak so fondly of you I feel like I know you already." She stepped back. "I wish we could have met under normal circumstances, but if I waited for my son to present you, goddess knows when that would be."

"Jesse has been in Faerie for two days, Mother," Lukas said in an amused voice. "I thought she might want to settle in a bit before I subjected her to a royal inquisition."

"Vaerik." She shot him an admonishing look.

King Oseron chuckled. "Are you enjoying your first time in Faerie, Jesse?"

I bit the inside of my cheek. Talk about a loaded question. I'd only been here a few days, and already I'd been poisoned and carried off by a drakkan. On top of that, I had to sit by while he tried to match Lukas with a "suitable" mate.

"It's more beautiful than I could have imagined," I told him honestly. "I can't wait to see more of it."

He smiled, pleased by my answer. "There is much to be seen. Are you an adventurer, Jesse?"

"I've only ever lived in the city, but I hope to travel someday. I don't know if that makes me an adventurer, though."

"Then we shall have to find out. As a faerie, you now have the means to explore both worlds. Do you prefer mountains, desert, or ocean?"

"Father." Lukas's tone was sharp this time and held more than a hint of annoyance.

The king frowned at him, and they shared a look I couldn't decipher. I didn't know enough about their relationship to read their body language around each other, but I felt like an intruder on a private conversation.

Maurelle laid a hand on her mate's arm. "Jesse has had an exciting day, and she must be exhausted. Why don't we let her and Vaerik have some time together?"

The king frowned. "There is a matter of importance I wish to discuss with Vaerik first."

My stomach tightened with disappointment. "I'll go so you can talk."

Lukas's hand shot out and took mine before I could move away from him. "It's late, and I'm sure the discussion can wait until the morning."

For the first time since he'd arrived, I caught a glint of displeasure in King Oseron's eyes. "Seelie has agreed to meet in two weeks, and there is much to be done to prepare for it."

"Then it would be best to go over it with the council," Lukas replied firmly. "If you wish, you and I can talk about it at breakfast."

I was sure the king would insist they speak now, and he surprised me when he conceded. He did not strike me as someone whose authority was challenged often. But then, neither did Lukas, so they were evenly matched in that respect.

"I will see you at breakfast," he said to Lukas. His smile back in place, he looked at me. "I am glad you are safely home, Jesse."

My awe of him had subsided enough to hear the sincerity in his voice. I relaxed a little more.

Maurelle gave me a motherly smile. "I ordered a hot meal for you. It will be here soon."

"Thank you."

Lukas walked his mother and father to the door, and they stopped for a moment to speak in lowered voices. It felt rude to watch them, so I retreated to the balcony to wait for him. Kaia followed me, and I rubbed her head as I stared at the distant ocean and hoped there were no more surprises in store for me today. I'd reached my limit, mentally and physically.

I was so lost in thought that I didn't register Lukas's presence until he came to lean on the balustrade beside me. He was close enough for our arms to touch, and I leaned toward him to rest my head against his shoulder.

He slipped his arm around me. "I'm sorry about that, Jesse. The last thing you needed tonight was to meet my parents."

He said it so casually as if he wasn't referring to the Unseelie king and his consort. I tried to sound nonchalant when I said, "It's okay. They were nice."

"They were, but they had no idea what condition you'd be in after what happened to you, and they should have waited for a more appropriate time to introduce themselves." Lukas dropped his arm and turned toward me. "You would tell me if you were injured."

I faced him and laid a hand against his chest. "I promise Gus didn't hurt me. Aside from nearly giving me a heart attack, that is."

"Gus?"

I grinned, feeling suddenly lighter. "You remember the drakkan I rescued back home? Well, he's not so little anymore."

Lukas stared at me. "That was your drakkan? And he remembers you?"

"Yes." I laughed at his stunned expression. "Trust me; I couldn't believe it either, and I was there."

"You need to tell me exactly what happened today." Lukas took my hand and led me inside to one of the couches. Kicking off my shoes, I sat with my back to the arm and my legs pulled up, but he moved them so my feet rested on his lap. When we were both settled, he said, "Talk."

I told him about our flight to the cliffs and then to the island, omitting my encounter with the goddess. That wasn't hard to do because she had done something to me so I couldn't speak of my time with her. I didn't like being controlled, but her hold over me lessened the guilt I felt over keeping something so important from Lukas.

Lukas's brows furrowed. "He flew you straight to the location of the ke'tain?"

"Maybe he's drawn to it since he had it inside of him for a few months," I suggested, hoping it would sound feasible enough to satisfy him.

He mulled it over. "That is possible. The island is in the middle of the Ellyon Sea. Drakkans don't go there because hunting is better close to the mainland."

"Speaking of the island, how do the guards get there?" I asked. "Do they live in the temple until someone goes to relieve them?"

"There are dedicated portals in Unseelie and Seelie that allow travel to and from the island. The guards use those to change shifts once a day."

I mulled over that bit of information. "Can anyone use the portals?"

He nodded. "Yes and no. Anyone from Unseelie can use our portals, but the portals won't work for someone from Seelie. The same applies to their portals."

"That makes sense."

We were interrupted by a bell chime. Lukas lifted my legs off him and went to answer the door. A liveried elf entered carrying a large covered tray, which Lukas directed him to set on the small table near the couch. The elf left, and Lukas lifted the cover of the tray to reveal a bowl of seasoned grains topped with meat in a thick cream sauce. The meat was raha, the Fae version of chicken, and it was one of the foods I liked most so far. There was also a salad of leafy greens, a piece of crusty bread, and a glass of juice.

Lukas lifted the tray and settled it on my lap. My mouth watered, and my stomach growled at the sight of the first food I'd seen since the market, which felt like days ago.

I picked up the fork, touched by Maurelle's kindness. "What about you? You're not hungry?"

He sat. "Faolin and the others made sure I ate while we were searching for you. Can't have the crown prince fainting from hunger and falling off his mount."

A laugh burst from me at the image. "Definitely not." I ate a few pieces of meat to silence my noisy stomach. "I saw a group of people with torches on tarrans when Gus brought me back. Were you with them?"

"It's possible. We had people searching the whole valley for you."

My meal lost all of its flavor, and I set down my fork.

"Do not apologize." He fixed me with a stern look. "Did you call that drakkan and order him to take you away?"

"No, but you have more important things to do than worrying about me. First, I get sick and then carried off by a drakkan. Maybe it would have been better if I had gone to your island with my family."

His jaw hardened. "Jesse, you didn't get sick; you were poisoned, and Faolin *will* find the person who did it. And do you honestly think I wouldn't worry about you if you had gone with your parents? Having you here where Davian can't possibly get to you is the only reason I can focus on the other things."

My heart squeezed at his admission, and I gave him a small smile. "Remember you said that the next time something happens."

"Next time?" He let out a pained laugh. "Were you this much trouble in New York?"

I grinned at him. "Wow, you have a short memory."

Lukas shook his head, laughing. "Eat your food before it gets cold."

I obeyed happily. This wasn't exactly what he'd meant when he had asked me to have dinner with him tonight. It was better. I wanted to meet his brother and sister, but I'd take time alone with him whenever I could get it.

"You like it?"

"It's delicious," I said around a mouthful of bread. I looked up and caught him watching me with a thoughtful expression. "What?"

"I asked that question in Fae. When did the language come to you?"

Swallowing the food, I said, "You spoke in Fae? Say something else."

"You have cream sauce on your chin," he said and grinned when I swiped at it with my finger.

I gaped at him, and then I squealed. "I can understand Fae!"

"You speak it, too. It occurred to me that we spoke Fae the whole time my parents were here. I was too preoccupied to realize it then."

"Is that how it works? I just start speaking the language without even realizing it?" I frowned, trying to remember exactly when it had started.

Lukas seemed to be trying to work that out, too. "From what I've heard, it happens gradually over a week or two. You couldn't understand a word of Fae at the market. Did anything happen on the island that you forgot to tell me about?"

I pretended to think about it because what else could I do? "I entered the temple, saw the ke'tain, and talked to a guard. I guess he was suspicious when I showed up."

"He spoke to you in Fae?" Lukas asked.

"I don't know…" I replayed the encounter in my head, and my eyes widened. "He must have. Everyone here speaks Fae to me unless they are told to speak English."

Lukas nodded. "It has to be the ke'tain then. Or it could be your goddess stone."

"Maybe it's both." I had a strong suspicion Aedhna was responsible, but I couldn't say that.

A knot formed in my gut. I'd been keeping one secret or another from Lukas since I met him, and I'd thought I was done with that. Now I was forced to keep the biggest one of all from him, and I hated it. I suddenly felt the weight of responsibility Aedhna had laid on me, and I wished I could confide in Lukas. He would do everything in his power to help me, and I wouldn't have to lie to him.

"Are you okay?"

Lukas's voice pulled me from my unhappy thoughts, and I gave him a confused look. "Huh?"

"You got quiet for a few minutes." He smiled tenderly. "You've had an exciting day, and you must be tired. Do you want to go to your quarters and rest?"

"No," I blurted. "I mean I'd like to stay here a little longer, unless you have things to do. I know how busy you are. Your father –"

"Can wait until tomorrow." He laid a warm hand on my foot. "You can stay as long as you want."

There was nothing sexual in his tone or the look he gave me, but the thought of spending the night here with him made my stomach flutter. Would he kiss me again? Maybe do more than that?

"Finish your meal," Lukas ordered, thankfully unaware of my thoughts. "You haven't eaten enough."

I resumed eating, and between bites, I talked about my flight with Gus and asked Lukas if they ever used drakkans for patrols. He told me drakkans were too wild and unpredictable to be tamed or domesticated. They were protective of their territory, which made them excellent guardians of the valley, but they'd never attacked or carried off a member of Unseelie. Until today.

I thought about Gus and how he'd behaved with me. There'd been a wildness about him that had scared me at first, but the more time I was around him, the more he was like his old self. He couldn't have been more than a few months old when I'd rescued him, at an age when he would have been in his nest, shielded from the world by his parents. His early childhood could not have been more different than the other drakkans.

"Gus was hatched in my world away from his parents. All he knew until he came home was the people who stole him and my family. He was a grumpy little guy, but I think he felt safe with us. That's why he acted the way he did and didn't hurt me."

Lukas nodded. "You may be right. A lamal can only be domesticated when they are raised by their owner from birth."

I looked at Kaia, who was curled up on a rug like a big house cat. It was hard to believe I was ever afraid of her. "So, no one here has tried to raise a drakkan?"

"It's too dangerous. If you did manage to steal an egg, the parents would pick up the scent and attack until they got their egg back. Your drakkan was taken through a portal, so his parents could not follow."

I laid my fork on the tray. "Poor Gus. Faris told me his parents wouldn't accept him back into their nest. I was worried about him until I saw him today. I wonder if I'll see him again."

"I'm sure you will." Lukas picked up my tray and set it on the table. He sat and gave me a long perusal that made me want to look away. Instead, I poked his thigh with my foot.

"It's not polite to stare."

He smiled. "There's something different about you tonight, and I just realized what it is. You're like the Jesse I knew in New York."

I cocked an eyebrow at him. "Was I supposed to be someone else?"

"No, but you haven't been yourself since you came to Faerie, and I didn't see it until now." His eyes grew troubled. "I know this is nothing like New York, and you haven't exactly had an easy start. Are you unhappy here?"

I inhaled deeply and let it out. "I won't lie and tell you it's been all roses. It's definitely an adjustment, and I miss my family and Violet. But I think the hardest thing has been that I have no purpose here."

He started to respond, and I held up a hand to stop him. "My whole life, I've been working toward something. In school, I worked hard to get into a good college. My parents disappeared, and I had to find them and take care of Finch. Then I had to find the ke'tain and provide for my family. I come here, and all I'm expected to do is wear nice clothes and let others serve me."

Understanding dawned in his eyes. "I was so focused on keeping you safe that I didn't think about what I was taking from you. How can I help?"

"I want to start training again," I said without hesitation. God only knew what Aedhna had in store for me, and I wanted to be ready for it. "That's a start, and then find a job I can do here."

"Training we can do. We'll worry about a job later. Do you want to start tomorrow?"

I nodded eagerly. "Yes. And I don't even care if it's with Faolin."

Lukas chuckled and lifted my feet back to his lap again. "What is that human saying? Be careful what you ask for."

"At least I already know what I'm getting with him." Warm and content, I adjusted the pillow behind me and settled into a more relaxed position. I let out a huge yawn. Maybe eating a full meal this late hadn't been a great idea.

Lukas rubbed my foot. "Tired?"

"Not at all," I lied. "I'm just trying out your couch. It's more comfortable than mine."

Amusement filled his tone. "You're welcome to use it whenever you want."

"Thanks."

"Jesse."

"Mmmm?" I opened my eyes. "I'm awake."

"Good to know." He shifted, and then I felt a soft throw cover me. "Sleep well, *mi'calaech*."

I sighed happily. "You, too."

I woke suddenly and sat up in bed. The dream I'd been having clung to me, and I rubbed my tired eyes as I shook it off. In my dream, I had been flying over the ocean with Gus, but he kept dropping me into the icy water. The last time, he pulled me out right before some monstrous fish had me for dinner.

I flopped back onto my bed, only to shoot up again. This was not my bed.

One glance around the room, which was lit only by a single lamp, told me exactly where I was, and I racked my brain to remember how I'd ended up here. I had been talking to Lukas on the couch. After that, nothing.

I must have fallen asleep, and he'd carried me to his bed – the same bed I'd fantasized about being in only hours ago. However, in my fantasy I hadn't been alone.

Throwing off the covers, I got out of bed. I was still wearing my clothes from earlier, so I ventured out to the main room in search of Lukas. I found him near the door speaking quietly with Conlan, and they turned to looked at me when I entered the room. Their expressions told me they were in the middle of a serious discussion, so I backed up.

"I didn't mean to interrupt you."

Lukas's face softened. "You didn't. I'm sorry we woke you."

"I'm sorry, too." One corner of Conlan's mouth lifted. "There's nothing worse than having a good sleep interrupted."

"Conlan." Lukas shot his friend a stern look. Conlan chuckled and winked at me.

I glanced at the dark sky outside and thought I saw the faint light of morning. Through a yawn I asked, "What time is it?"

"Early. Go back to sleep," Lukas said, and I noticed he was wearing different clothes from the night before. "My father wants to see me before we meet with his council today."

I went to sit on the couch. "I thought only humans were workaholics."

"You don't have to leave," Lukas said when I picked up the shoes I'd discarded last night.

I pulled on the shoes and stood. "You have a busy day ahead, and I doubt I'll be able to get back to sleep now."

What I didn't say was that it would be best if I went back to my quarters while everyone else was asleep. No doubt, I was already the talk of the whole court after yesterday, and I had no desire to give them more to gossip about. Me leaving Lukas's suite in the same clothes I'd worn yesterday would definitely cause a stir.

"I'll see you later today to hear how your training went," he said.

Conlan didn't hide his smirk as he extended a hand to me. "Let me see you back to your quarters."

"I think I can find my way without getting lost," I replied irritably, which only heightened his amusement.

He shrugged. "You never know when a drakkan might come and whisk you away. Or you might run afoul of one of Vaerik's jealous admirers. There are dangers everywhere."

"Funny guy." I curled my lip as I walked past him. "To think you used to be my favorite."

"I am?" he said brightly. "Wait. *Used* to be?"

Opening the door, I looked back at Lukas. "See you later. Have a good meeting."

I was halfway across the courtyard when the door opened behind me, and Conlan said, "I took a bullet for you. I am definitely your favorite."

I kept walking as a grin crept across my face.

"Where is the gym?" I asked Faris as we stepped onto the lift on my level.

The lift started to descend before he answered. "The training room is on the first level."

I turned my head to look at him. "And it's available to everyone at court?"

Faris laughed and shook his head. "I doubt most people here even know where to find it. We don't need to exercise to keep fit like humans do. Some of us train to serve the crown and others because they have roles that could put them in danger."

"Like Lukas?"

"Yes. He has trained alongside us since we were children. After Faolin, he is the most skilled fighter in Unseelie," Faris said, his voice full of pride.

The lift stopped, and we got off. Faris led me down a hallway I hadn't used yet, and we came to a set of rough-hewn wooden doors that reminded me of something from a medieval castle. The whole ground level had that feel, now that I thought about it, and I kind of liked it. It was as if we had gone back in time.

He opened one of the doors and waved me into a windowless room that had to be as big as the gymnasium at my old high school. The walls and ceiling were rough stone, and the floor was covered in gray padding.

On every wall were racks of weapons used for hand-to-hand combat, and a thrill of excitement and fear went through me at the sight of them. None of my previous training had involved weapons, and I was eager to start.

The room was occupied by at least thirty people, who mostly ignored us as they trained alone or in pairs. Two females sparred with swords, their movements so fluid and powerful they would make a samurai jealous. I wondered if I would be that good someday.

We kicked off our shoes at the door and crossed the room to where Faolin was moving through the steps of an intricate staff routine. I'd seen him use a staff at Lukas's place in New York, but it was clear that he'd been holding back. I'd never seen anyone move so fast or with such precision, and trying to follow his movements made me a little dizzy.

Faolin ended the routine abruptly, facing us. "Today, you start weapons training. We will begin with the staff."

"Good morning to you too," I said dryly.

His sharp eyes skimmed me, taking in my blue T-shirt, black leggings, and my hair pulled back into a tight ponytail. It was the same basic outfit I'd worn for our training back home.

"Good morning. I trust you are well rested despite your early rise," he replied with a trace of mockery.

Faris snickered softly beside me, and I huffed out a breath. I should have known Conlan would blab to the others.

Faolin picked up a wooden staff leaning against the wall and handed it to me. I stood it on end, noticing it was shorter than the one he used and had no metal on the tips.

"This is a training staff," he informed me. "You will use it until you are proficient enough to handle a combat staff."

I hefted the weapon. "Okay. Where do we start?"

"First, you will learn how to stand and hold it properly. There are different holds, but this is the one you will begin with." He repositioned my hands on the center third of the staff. Then he demonstrated the various stances and showed me which one to use now.

"We will begin with basic strikes and blocks so you can get used to the feel of the weapon. Once you can execute all the strikes, you will learn how to use them together. After that, you can practice sparring with a partner."

"How long will it take to get to sparring?" I asked.

He walked over to pick up his own staff. "That depends on you."

And so began my first training session with the staff. Faolin demonstrated a strike, and I had to ask him to slow it down and repeat it several times. Then I tried it, and he corrected my position and follow-through. It was tedious work, and he was critical of every move I made, but I was rewarded with a thrill of satisfaction whenever he gave a curt nod of approval and switched to the next strike.

As I got more comfortable with the staff, I noticed how much better my balance and agility were. Some of it was because I was Fae, but I suspected part of it was due to my months of training with Faolin and the others. It was good to know all that running up and down stairs hadn't been for nothing.

After two hours of barking orders at me, Faolin had to leave. He told me to continue practicing for at least another hour today, and we would pick up where we left off tomorrow. My arms and shoulders were tired, but I kept at it, determined to master the strikes he'd taught me so far.

"You are a natural with the staff," said one of a group of female guards who had been training across the room from me. "It took me days to execute one strike to my trainer's satisfaction."

I stopped practicing to face her. She had black hair and a friendly smile, something I wasn't used to seeing on the females at court. There was something vaguely familiar about her, but I couldn't recall seeing her among the guards on duty.

I grimaced. "I don't suppose your trainer was Faolin?"

The guard laughed. "Goddess, no. You are braver than most of us."

"Or I'm not as smart as the rest of you."

The other females joined in laughing, and I took a moment to check out their outfits. They wore fitted black pants and black tops with a laced bodice and thin sleeves. Their feet were bare, and there was a pile of black boots nearby.

"It is good that you don't fear him," said a blonde guard. "If you survive training under him, you will be a fierce warrior someday."

Me, a warrior? I liked the sound of that.

"I like your hair," the brunette said. "I have never seen a color like that."

"I guess you've never been to my realm. It's common there, especially in certain parts of the world."

She shook her head dejectedly. "I hope to go someday."

I waved a hand at their outfits. "I like those clothes. They look a lot more comfortable than the normal court clothes."

"You don't like your clothes?" she asked.

"They're nice," I rushed to say, not wanting to insult the court fashions. "It's just that I'm used to more casual clothes. I always feel overdressed here."

The guards chuckled, and the first one said, "I will send my personal tailor to you. She makes all of our clothes."

"That would be great. Thanks." I stepped forward. "I'm sorry. I haven't even introduced myself."

She met me halfway, her eyes sparkling with laughter. "Oh, I know who you are, Jesse James. I've heard so much about you from my brother."

"Your brother?"

"Vaerik." She gave me a wide smile. "I am Roswen. I had hoped to meet you last night, but it seems a drakkan had other plans for you."

"Princess Roswen," I stammered. I stared at her like an idiot because I had no clue how you were supposed to greet a member of the royal family outside of social settings.

"Please, call me Roswen," she said. "After hearing Vaerik's stories about you, I already feel like we are friends."

"Okay," I replied slowly, wondering what exactly Lukas had told her. "I'd like that."

She beamed as if I'd handed her a gift. I hadn't been sure what to expect when I met Lukas's sister, but it wasn't this friendly, down-to-earth girl who trained like one of the guards.

"These are my personal guards and best friends." Roswen pointed to her four companions, starting with the blonde. "Parisa, Tiannan, Cyrene, and Ellette. Parisa is head of my security, but she's nice and not nearly as scary as Faolin."

"Not unless I need to be." The blonde gave me a pretend snarl that made them all smile.

I smiled back, hoping I would remember their names. "Hi."

"Now that we are friends, we want to hear all about your adventure." Roswen took my hand and tugged me down to sit on the floor with her. The others followed suit, and they all listened raptly as I explained how I'd rescued Gus in New York and had to send him back to Faerie. Then I told them about my reunion with him yesterday.

"The whole court thought you were gone for good," Roswen said, and the others nodded. "Nothing like that has ever happened before."

I made a face. "For a while, I thought I was a goner, too."

Ellette leaned in. "You made quite the entrance upon your return. Rashari and Delphine will not soon forget it."

"Why?" I asked over their laughter. I'd never heard of Delphine, and I assumed Rashari was the same one I'd met.

"Because your drakkan knocked them into the lake," Tiannan said gleefully. "Goddess, I wish I had been there to witness it. I heard they came out covered in slimy mud."

Parisa scowled. "It's past time someone dunked the pair of them. Goddess help us if either of them is chosen as Vaerik's consort."

"Or Dariyah," Cyrene piped in. "She is the worst of them all."

It felt like someone had punched me in the gut. Was it common knowledge and expected that Lukas would take one of his father's acceptable matches as his mate and consort?

"Vaerik is too smart to not see them for what they are, and he will not choose someone to please our father," Roswen declared. She looked at me. "Only a strong, selfless female with a kind heart could win my brother's devotion."

I smiled at her obvious attempt to reassure me, but I couldn't dispel the tiny knot of insecurity that had settled in my stomach. Lukas cared about me, and the way he kissed me left no doubt he was attracted to me. But we'd never talked about our feelings for each other. Was that because he knew there could be nothing more between us, and he didn't want to hurt me?

A liveried male approached us, and Parisa immediately stood to face him. "Yes?" she asked him.

"Consort Maurelle wishes for Princess Roswen to ride with her this morning," the male answered.

Roswen's face lit up. "Tell her I will be there within the hour."

"Yes, Princess." The male bowed to her and left.

The rest of us stood, and Roswen turned to me. "Riding is one of my favorite pastimes. Do you ride?"

"No." I thought about the huge majestic tarrans Conlan and the others had ridden when we went to town. "Not yet."

"Then you must ask Vaerik to take you riding. It is so much fun, and he is a good teacher. He taught me to ride." She retrieved her boots and pulled them on. "I am so happy I finally got to meet you, Jesse. Maybe we will see each other here tomorrow."

"I'll be here bright and early." I picked up my practice staff. "As long as I don't slip and clobber myself with this."

Roswen laughed. "You won't. I can already tell you're a natural."

She gave me a little wave and walked to the door with her guards. A wave of loneliness washed over me as I watched them leave, and I missed Violet so much it hurt. We'd never been apart this long, and I couldn't even pick up a phone and call her.

Shaking off my melancholy, I went back to practicing with a vengeance. The sooner I learned to fight and defend myself, the sooner I could go home without fear of Davian and his goons. I gritted my teeth and repeated the strikes I'd learned over and over until not even Faolin would find fault with them.

A cool breeze tossed the hair that wasn't clinging to my sweaty face as I walked past the siren's lake toward the manicured grounds. I ignored the curious stares of the people around me because I was used to them by now. I would have thought they'd be used to seeing me too, but I'd underestimated the interest span of people with nothing to do.

The water splashed, and I stopped hoping to catch sight of the elusive sirens, but all I got was a glimpse of the tip of a silver tail. Damn, they were fast. I'd walked past the lake twice a day for a week, and I had yet to see one of them.

On my second day of staff training with Faolin, he'd told me about a low rise nearby that would be good for conditioning and building endurance. It was where he, Lukas, and the others had started before they began their real training. I'd asked him to show me where it was, and I'd burst out laughing at the steep rocky hill he called a rise.

My first attempt had me dragging my ass to the top where I'd needed time to recover before I went back down. The second day, I learned to pace myself better. I was now on day five, and I could finish the climb without feeling like I needed an oxygen mask.

The hill wasn't the only challenge I'd thrown myself into. I trained on the staff for two hours every morning with Faolin or Faris. After that, I practiced alone for an hour, and my hard work had paid off. Within a few days, I'd advanced to sparring, which I enjoyed a lot more than going through the moves alone.

Most days, Roswen and her guards were in the training room, and we made time to chat. I liked all of them, and it felt good to be making friends here outside of Lukas and his men. They even took turns sparring with me, although they had to go easy on me. As the personal guard to the princess, Parisa and the others were among the top fighters in Unseelie, and Roswen was almost as good as them.

Feminine laughter drew my attention from the lake to the group of four people walking beside the lake toward me. My good mood dulled when I saw Rashari and another blonde I now recognized as her friend Delphine. They were accompanied by a dark-haired male I'd seen them with before and Sereia, the rude tailor who had made my first wardrobe here. Why was I not surprised to see her in the company of Rashari and her friends?

I thought about cutting across the grass to avoid them, but Rashari had already seen me. There was no way I was letting her think for a second that she had scared me off. I turned back to the lake and waited for the group to reach me.

"She looks positively wild," Rashari said, and I heard the sneer in her voice. "Does she even bathe?"

"Careful. She might be feral," Delphine quipped, and it was followed by titters.

Sereia spoke. "She won't wear the clothes I made for her." She lowered her voice but not enough that I couldn't hear her. "And I heard she trains with the guards every day."

Rashari scoffed. "What do you expect from someone so low-born? I still cannot believe she was given those quarters on our level. It is an affront to us all."

I smiled at the water as I listened to them talk about me. It was no secret they disliked me and my friendship with Lukas, so none of what they said bothered me. They were speaking in Fae, which meant they probably didn't mean for me to overhear their conversation. Only the people I spoke to often knew I was now fluent in the language.

Rashari switched to English as they drew near. "Hello, Jesse. Out for your daily trek in the wild?"

I faced them with my smile fixed in place and replied in English. "It's very refreshing. You should try it."

She looked down her perfect nose at me. "I have better ways to occupy my time."

I knew how they spent their time. Except for those in service to the crown, most of the blue bloods living at court focused their time and energy on gaining or keeping favor with the royal family. It involved a lot of socializing, parties, and scheming, and it sounded like a miserable way to live.

I nodded. "It must take a lot of work to be as beautiful as you are."

She smiled vainly until the double meaning of my words sank in. Then her eyes took on a satisfied gleam, and I knew what was coming next.

"I confess I do like to take a little extra time to prepare when I'm invited to dine with Prince Vaerik at the king's table." She cocked her head slightly to one side. "Twice since he's returned to court."

The barb hurt, but not as much as she intended. Roswen had complained yesterday about having to attend her father's boring "matchmaking" dinners for Vaerik. I hadn't been able to hide my reaction fast enough, and she'd hurried to say that Vaerik hated them even more than she did. According to her, the only people who truly enjoyed the parties were the females invited by the king to sit beside Vaerik.

Delphine slanted a dark look at her friend that told me she was a lot more upset by Rashari's comments than I was. It made me wonder if they were real friends or two competitors keeping their enemies close.

"I can see why Prince Vaerik keeps her around," said the male in Fae as he leered at me. "She's different, and I bet she's a fun plaything when she is clean."

"More like a half-breed pet," Rashari retorted in their language, and they all tittered. "She can't even dress herself properly."

"You don't like my clothes?" I asked in Fae, taking delight in their shocked expressions. "Roswen sent me her personal tailor to make me the same outfits she and her guards wear. I think I look nice."

None of them spoke. Sereia looked a little horrified. The male shifted uncomfortably. Rashari and Delphine seemed to be trying to figure out how to respond without inadvertently insulting the princess.

"But then," I went on cheerfully, "maybe these clothes are not to your taste. I think I heard somewhere that lake slime is the newest fashion."

Delphine sucked in a breath. Rashari's eyes narrowed into slits, and she balled her hands into fists. I tensed in anticipation of an attack that never came.

"Jesse."

The five of us turned to look at Lukas striding toward us. One glance at his serious expression made me forget all about the others. He was supposed to be in meetings with his father all morning, and his presence here could only mean one thing.

I brushed past Rashari and ran to him. "Something happened to my family. Are they okay?"

He placed his hands on my shoulders. "They're okay. Your father sent word that your mother had a small setback, and he asked me to bring you to them."

A setback? Fear churned my stomach. It had to be bad for Dad to send for me, and I knew the thing we'd worried about had happened.

Mom's memory had returned.

13

Dad was waiting for me when Lukas and I stepped out of the portal into the large living room of Lukas's island house. The exhaustion stamped on my father's face had me running into his arms. He enfolded me in a tight embrace for a long moment like he would never let me go.

"God, I missed you," he said hoarsely against my hair.

I hugged him tighter. "I missed you, too. How's Mom?"

He let out a breath and released me. "She's sleeping. I have her sedated with the pills her doctor sent home with her, and she'll be out for a while."

My heart sank. "That bad?"

"She'll be better when she wakes up and sees you."

Lukas set my bag on the floor. "Is there anything I can do to help? I can have a doctor flown here if she needs one."

Dad gave him a grateful smile. "Thank you, Lukas, but I think all she needs is Jesse. Our doctors told us it's normal to have emotional setbacks in the first six months outside the hospital, and it's been harder on Caroline with us away from home."

Lukas nodded and looked at me. "I'll stay in case you need me."

I glanced at my father. His lips were pressed together, and I knew there was more he wanted to tell me, but he couldn't say it in front of Lukas.

"You should go back. The meeting with Seelie is only a week away, and they need you there to prepare for it." I went to him and took his hand. "We have your guards here, and one of them will let you know if we need anything."

150

He tucked a strand of my hair behind my ear. "Are you sure?"

"Yes."

He lowered his head and pressed a featherlight kiss to my forehead. "I'll see you soon."

I could still feel his lips against my skin as he created a portal and stepped through it into his courtyard. I waited for it to close before I turned to my father, who was watching me with a thoughtful expression.

"He cares for you," Dad said.

"I know."

"And you love him."

"Yes." My father knew me too well for me to try to deny it. "He doesn't know."

"If he doesn't see it, then he's a fool, and the Unseelie prince is anything but a fool." He studied me a moment longer. "The most important question is: Are you happy?"

I wasn't sure how to answer him. If I was too honest, it would make him worry more about me. If I lied, he'd see right through it. "I miss you guys and home, but I'm making friends and finding my place there. Faerie is amazing."

The worry lines in his forehead smoothed out, and he pointed to the wide veranda. "Let's sit and talk a while."

I followed him through the open glass doors to the spacious sitting area that overlooked the golden sandy beach. Before us, steps led down into a glass-walled infinity pool that ran the length of the veranda, and beyond that, waves rolled gently against the shore. The house was nestled among tall palm trees in a crescent cove with a dock at the other end.

The warm breeze tossed my hair into my face, and I brushed it aside as I sat. "Wow. This place is beautiful."

"And isolated," Dad replied. "The mainland is an hour away, and we don't see many boats passing on this side of the island."

My gaze swept the beach again. "Where are the faeries Lukas left with you?"

"There's a second house on the other side of the island. They stay there to give us privacy, and they drop by a few times a day." He hitched a thumb over his shoulder. "Behind this house is a trail through the woods. It's less than a quarter of a mile."

"Do you like it here?" I asked. My parents were accustomed to the noise and bustle of New York, and they were used to being active and on the go all the time. This had to be a huge adjustment for them.

"What's not to like?" His voice was light, but he couldn't mask the strain on his face.

I averted my gaze, hating that my family had to go into hiding because of me. They should be recovering at home, surrounded by the things and people they knew instead of being trapped here. A paradise was only a paradise when you were free to leave. Anything else was a prison.

"Don't, Jesse," he said softly. "If you want to blame someone for this, blame the Seelie queen and the people who abducted us, or Davian Woods for what he did to you. You didn't cause any of the trouble that led us here, and your mom and I won't allow you to feel guilty for something you didn't do. We couldn't be prouder of you."

My nose stung as I lifted my eyes to meet his. "Can you tell me what happened?"

He inhaled deeply and let it out. "It was my fault. I've been so good at keeping her away from the internet and the entertainment shows. I made sure there were no magazines or anything else around that might have mention of Prince Rhys. We had a food delivery this morning, and sometimes they will stick newspapers or magazines in the bags. I didn't think to check before she started to put the food away, and she found a copy of Modern Fae. He was on the cover."

My fingers gripped the wooden arms of my chair. "And she remembered?"

"Not at first. She joked about how much the prince looked like me at that age and asked if there was something I needed to tell her. We had a laugh, and I thought we were good." He scrubbed at his jaw. "An hour later, she started crying and asking where you were. Then she asked why Caleb wasn't here. The more I tried to calm her, the more agitated she got until she became hysterical and screaming that the queen took her babies."

I covered my mouth with my hands as the tears I'd held back spilled over. "Oh, God."

"I managed to get her sedated before the faeries came bursting in. They heard her screams all the way on their side of the island and thought we were being attacked. They know about our goren addictions, so I told them it was a relapse and asked them to send for you."

This was exactly what I'd been afraid would happen when Mom's memories came back. Dad and I had agreed we couldn't tell anyone the truth about Caleb, but what if we couldn't get her through this on our own.

"She's strong, Jesse," he said when I voiced my fear. "When she sees you and knows you're safe, she'll be calmer. It's going to be hard for her to relive the past, but it's the only way. It was going to happen eventually, and it's better that it happens here where we can keep it secret."

"Can I see her?"

"Of course. Finch and Aisla have been with her since I put her to bed, but it'll help if you're there when she wakes up."

We entered the house, and he showed me to the master bedroom. He opened the door, and my eyes immediately went to the figure lying in the middle of the bed. My mother looked small and pale, and a fresh wave of grief and anger went through me for all she'd suffered.

A whistle split the air, and a tiny blue shape streaked across the white bedspread. I ran and caught Finch when he leaped at me. For a little guy, he had quite the grip when he wrapped his thin arms around my neck. I rubbed his back and looked for Aisla. I spotted her peeking around one of the bedside lamps. The nixie smiled and gave me a timid wave before she slipped out of sight.

"Glad to see you, too," I whispered to Finch, who leaned back to look up at me. "I can't wait to tell you all about Faerie, but first I need to see Mom."

He let go of my neck to sign, *Mom screamed a lot. It was scary.*

"I bet it was. We're going to help her get better, aren't we?"

He nodded and curled into the crook of my neck. I held him there as I went to the bed and lay down facing my mother. I reached for her hand and held it while she slept off the drugs in her system.

"Jesse?" Mom croaked.

My eyes shot open, and I looked into her red, bleary eyes. "Hey, Mom."

A tear leaked from the corner of her eye and disappeared into her hair. "Are you really here?"

I squeezed her hand. "Yes."

She blinked a few times, trying to shake off the effect of the sedation. Then she rolled to her side and pulled me into a weak hug. "I dreamed about you and Caleb. Only he wasn't a baby. He was a young man, and he..."

Her head jerked back, and she stared at me with eyes full of grief and horror. "Caleb's not dead. My baby boy is alive."

"Yes." It was hard to speak around the rock in my throat. Helplessness washed over me when my mother began to shake and wail like a wounded animal.

Then my father was there. He slid onto the bed from the other side and gathered her into his arms. Loud sobs racked her body, and he murmured to her in a soothing voice until she finally calmed and her cries became hiccups. I'd been through a lot this year, but nothing had been as hard as watching my strong mother come apart like this.

"Should I go?" I whispered to him.

"No," croaked my mother. She reached for me, and I took her trembling hand.

The three of us lay there like that for over an hour. Mom stopped hiccupping, and her breathing returned to normal. Just when I thought she'd fallen asleep, she spoke.

"How long have you known, Patrick?"

"My memory came back two weeks before you left the hospital," Dad told her softly.

She pulled away to look at him. "How could you not tell me?"

"Caroline, you heard what the doctors said. No stress or anything that can cause a relapse. It hit me hard when it all came back, and I couldn't put you through that until you were ready. I decided it was best to wait until your memory returned on its own."

Mom was silent for a long moment. "And Jesse? How long has she known?"

Dad's eyes met mine over her head, and I said, "I was with him when he remembered."

She rolled onto her back and pushed up to recline against the pillows. Her face was drawn and tear-streaked, and her eyes were red. She used the edge of a sheet to blot the moisture from her face and hugged a pillow to her chest. Dad and I were silent as we waited to see how she would respond.

Mom stared straight ahead as if she was seeing something we couldn't. "I knew he was alive. All these years, a part of me could never believe he was gone. Then I saw him. My baby. My Caleb." She looked at me. "When he was born, he had my hair, but I said he would look like his father when he grew up. I was right."

"I know. Dad showed me the photos of him when he was younger. They could have been twins."

She held the pillow in a stranglehold. "They stole my baby boy and tried to make me believe he was dead. Then they changed him into one of them. Why? Why did they take my Caleb?"

"I don't know." My father's voice was gentle, masking the agony in his eyes.

I brushed away the tears streaming down my cheeks. My chest felt like it was being squeezed by a hot metal band, and all I could do was watch my parents suffer.

"The Seelie queen did this. She stole him and raised him as her child," Mom went on as if Dad hadn't spoken. "Did she think we wouldn't know our own son when we saw him?"

"Maybe that's why she didn't want him to come here," I said, remembering a conversation I'd had with Prince Rhys. "When he refused to stay in Seelie, she probably hoped she had changed him enough that you wouldn't see any resemblance. I mean I know him, and I didn't see it until Dad pointed it out to me."

As soon as the words left my mouth, I knew I'd messed up. Dad and I hadn't talked about Prince Rhys around Mom, and that included my friendship with him.

Mom stared at me. "You know him?"

"I've talked to him a few times, but I wouldn't say I know him well."

She reached over to grip my hand. "What's he like? What did you talk about?"

"He's nice, and it was mostly small talk. He found out I was a bounty hunter, and he wanted to hear about it. He didn't talk much about his life in Seelie." I paused. "From what he did say, he had a happy childhood."

Anger flashed in her eyes. "Because he had no idea he was stolen from his real family. How will he feel when he learns the truth?"

"Caroline," Dad began quietly. "We can't tell Prince Rhys the truth." Mom started to object, but he cut her off. "The queen's guard tried to have us killed because we recognized him. They warned Jesse to stay away from him. They've worked too hard to cover up what they did to let us expose them. We have no proof, and all we would do is put our whole family in danger."

She shook her head. "No proof? What about the child we buried? We can have DNA tests done to prove it's not Caleb."

I bit my lip as I waited for Dad to tell her the storm at the cemetery had destroyed the grave. But he knew as well as I she wasn't ready to hear that truth.

"DNA tests would prove that baby wasn't ours, but it won't implicate Seelie in any way. The prince has no human DNA left to test, and not a soul will believe he is Caleb even if there is a close resemblance to me." He placed his hand over hers. "The only people who know the truth are the three of us and Maurice. I wanted him to know in case anything happened to us. We can't let on to anyone that we have our memory back. It's the only way to keep our children safe."

She looked incredulously from Dad to me, and I knew the exact moment she comprehended what he was saying. All I could do was watch as my beautiful, fearless mother crumpled before my eyes.

Dad took her in his arms, and she buried her face against his shirt as she fell apart again. This time, I couldn't bear to witness it. I eased off the bed and slipped out of the room.

Emotionally wrung out, I found a bathroom and splashed water on my face before I went in search of Finch and Aisla. When I couldn't find them in the house, I walked out to the veranda. There I got the surprise of my life when I caught sight of the two tiny figures playing in the sand. Finch, who had never gone outside except for Lukas's warded garden, was outdoors.

I stood quietly by the railing and watched him lie on the dry sand above the water's reach and make a sand angel. Aisla took his hand, pulled him up, and made her own angel. Their joy was almost palpable, and I smiled in spite of my heavy heart.

Aisla saw me and gave me one of her shy waves. I walked down to them and sat on the warm sand, and Finch immediately asked how Mom was.

"She's sad, but she'll be okay. How about you two? Do you like it here?"

They nodded eagerly, and Finch signed, *Are you going to live here with us now?*

"I'm going to visit for a while, but I have to go back." My smile widened when I remembered the surprise I had for him. "Guess who I saw in Faerie."

His eyes widened. *Gus?*

"Yep. He came to visit me. And guess what else. He's big like the dragons in that cartoon you like to watch." I stretched my arms out for emphasis. "He picked me up and flew me around. It was amazing."

Finch demanded I tell them all about Gus. When I said Gus remembered him, he jumped up and down in the sand. *Can Gus come visit us?*

"I don't think so, but I can take you to visit him sometime when Mom and Dad say it's okay."

Finch considered this. Six months ago, the closest he wanted to get to the outside world was through the windows of our apartment. Today, he was playing in the sand on a tropical island and pondering over the idea of visiting another realm. Life had changed so much for everyone in my family.

Can Mom and Dad come, too? he asked hopefully.

"Humans can't go to Faerie, remember? But we can bring back lots of gifts for them and tell them all about the fun we had." That reminded me of my trip to the market, and I grinned. "In fact, I might have something in my bag for you guys."

The two of them were at the veranda steps before I got to my feet. Laughing, I brushed sand off my pants and followed them into the house.

It was two days before my mother was strong enough to leave her room. She didn't need to be sedated, but Dad and I had to fight to get her to eat and drink. When she wasn't sleeping, we took turns sitting with her so she wasn't overwhelmed, and during my time with her, she wanted to know all about Prince Rhys.

When I wasn't with Mom or Dad, I played outside with Finch and Aisla. I showed them how to build sand forts, and I created shallow wading pools that they delighted in for hours. I loved to watch them play together. They took joy in the simplest things and never asked for more than my company. Humans could learn a lot from sprites and nixies about making the most of life. As could Court faeries for that matter.

It wasn't until my second evening there that Dad and I were able to sit and talk again. He asked about Faerie, and once I began, it all came pouring out of me like a dam that had burst open. I described the court, the town, and the people there. His face creased with concern when I told him about getting sick, and he asked a ton of questions when I described the market.

Then I got to my reunion with Gus. I described the nerve-racking flight across the valley and cliffs and over the ocean to the island. I got to the part where I saw the ke'tain in the temple, and I don't know who was more shocked when I said, "The next thing I know, Aedhna is standing beside me, asking if I can feel the ke'tain's power."

My father stared at me as if he wasn't sure whether I was joking or delusional. "Aedhna, the Fae goddess, appeared to you?"

"Yes," I replied hesitantly. When nothing bad happened, I laughed breathlessly. "Her magic gag doesn't work here."

"Jesse, what are you talking about? You're not making sense."

I sank back in my chair. "Wait until you hear the rest."

He listened raptly while I recounted my whole conversation with Aedhna, including her stunning revelation that I would help her repair the barrier between our worlds. I concluded with her disappearing and Gus returning me to court. I left out the part where the king walked in on Lukas and me kissing.

"She said I wouldn't be able to tell anyone about it until after the job was done." I looked around, half expecting a bolt of magic to come at me out of nowhere. When nothing happened, I let out a breath. "Either her magic doesn't work on me here, or it only applies to me telling other faeries."

Dad's brow furrowed. "She didn't give you any clue about what you have to do? Or when?"

"All she said was that I would know when the time is right." I drew my legs up under me. "What can I possibly do for her that Lukas or the king can't?"

"Maybe it has something to do with you being a new faerie. Or it could be your goddess stone. Maybe it allows you to do things other faeries can't."

I'd considered that already. "Then why wouldn't she tell me that?"

He rubbed his chin. "You're asking me to explain the reasoning of the Fae deity?"

"Well, when you put it like that." I heaved a sigh. "I'm in way over my head, Dad. What if she's wrong about me, and I can't do it?"

"You can do anything you put your mind to, and I'm not saying that because I'm your father. You've been like that since you were a little girl. Look at what you've done in the last six months. Aedhna gave you that goddess stone because she saw what I see in you. If she believes you can do this, then you should believe it, too. I do."

I scooted across the couch to hug him. I hadn't realized how much I needed to hear that from him until this moment.

From inside the house a phone rang, and I moved away so he could go answer it. It was the first time I'd heard that sound in weeks, and it amazed me how easily I'd adapted to life without phones and computers. It was going to feel strange when I returned to city life.

Dad came back a few minutes later, smiling. "That was Maurice checking in. He said to say hi. And your mom's up and wants to know what we're having for dinner."

It was the first time Mom had expressed interest in food since I got here. A huge grin split my face. "Whatever she wants."

The moon created a path across the ocean and lit up the beach as I walked barefoot through the sand. A light tropical breeze rustled the palm fronds, and somewhere in the underbrush, a small creature stirred. The only other sound was the gentle lap of water against the shore.

Behind me, the house where my family slept was dark and silent. I didn't know why I wasn't asleep too, only that something had drawn me out here to the beach. It was strange when I thought about it. I'd been on the island for five days, and this was the first time I'd felt the urge for a midnight stroll.

Something made a light splash on the water. A few seconds later, the surface of the water rippled closer to shore. Something white slowly emerged from the ocean, taking the shape of a horse's head.

The kelpie moved toward me, its white coat gleaming like silver in the moonlight. I felt no fear as it left the water and walked up to me. Two feet from me, it lowered its head and dropped something into the sand. Then it looked me in the eye, bent one leg, and bowed to me.

I could only stare at the kelpie as it stood and turned back to the ocean. It wasn't until the majestic head disappeared beneath the surface that I remembered the object it had brought me. I knelt in the sand and picked up a small white stone that immediately turned the color of my hair.

"Jesse," said a distorted female voice. "It is time to come home."

I looked around, but I was alone. "Hello?"

"Jesse," the voice called again.

I stood. "Where are you?"

Something touched my shoulder and gently shook me. "You're dreaming, Jesse. Wake up."

I opened my eyes and stared up at my mother, who was leaning over me. She smiled and straightened. "That must have been some dream."

"It was definitely a weird one." I yawned and rubbed my eyes. "What time is it?"

"Seven-thirty. I was going to let you sleep in, but you kept calling out. How about I make us some breakfast?"

"Pancakes?" I asked hopefully, earning a chuckle from her.

"Of course." She walked to the bedroom door. "They'll be ready in ten minutes."

I stretched my arms over my head and smiled up at the ceiling. The first few days had been rough, but my mother was more like her old self every day. When the time came for me to go back to Faerie, I could do so knowing she was going to be okay.

Tossing the covers off me, I rolled out of bed and froze when I looked down at my feet, which still had dried sand caked on them. Turning back to the bed, I threw back the sheet and stared at the sand where I had lain.

I sat heavily on the edge of the mattress. *It wasn't a dream.* My stomach twisted as understanding dawned.

Aedhna had summoned me back to Faerie.

14

I CRESTED THE top of the hill and let out a whoop as I pumped my fist. *I did it!*

Breathing hard, I bent and rested my hands on my legs. I was hot and sweaty, and my chest ached from exertion, but that did nothing to lessen my jubilation. I'd made my first trek up the steep hill without stopping once to rest, and it felt good.

I walked a few feet and lay on my back on a small patch of coarse grass to smile up at the blue sky. Soft footsteps came toward me, but I didn't turn my head to look at my companion as she flopped down on her belly beside me. I reached out and scratched Kaia's head, and she emitted an aggravated growl.

"Hey, you didn't have to come with me," I told the sulking lamal, who had been accompanying me on my daily outings since my return to Faerie three days ago. She preferred running through the grass because there wasn't much on the hill for her to chase, but she didn't like to let me out of her sight when we were away from the court.

She shifted so her heavy head rested on my stomach. I laughed and rubbed the back of her neck, making her purr. She wasn't the dog I'd always wanted, but she was great company, especially now.

I'd seen Lukas twice since I came back. His days were spent behind closed doors with the king and his advisors, preparing for the big meeting with Seelie. Faolin and the rest of his guard were busy as well, so I trained by myself and spent most of my time alone. Even Roswen and her guard had been absent the last three days.

160

The whole court was buzzing with anticipation of the Seelie queen's arrival today, even though most people wouldn't lay eyes on her. For my part, I was too anxious about when Aedhna would finally send me on my mission to be caught up in the excitement. My gut told me it would happen soon, and the wait was killing me.

When my breathing slowed to normal, I pushed Kaia's head off me and sat up. She grumbled and stood, fixing me with an aggrieved look that made me chuckle. I'd never seen an animal that could portray human-like emotions the way she did.

I started down the hill. Kaia ran ahead of me, and every now and then she stopped to look back and make sure I was still behind her. As I neared the bottom, I was surprised to find Conlan waiting for me. I hadn't expected to see him or any of Lukas's men for the next two days.

"Faolin said you'd be out here," Conlan called. "Looks like you've conquered the hill."

I grinned at him. "You bet I did."

He lifted one corner of his mouth. "Shall I tell Faolin you are ready for a bigger one?"

"Not unless you want me to murder you in your sleep," I retorted.

He snickered, and we began the walk back to court with Kaia leading the way. One second, she was in front of us, and in the next, she was off running through the tall grass. There was a squeak followed by rustling, and I hoped that whatever she was chasing escaped.

"Not that I don't enjoy your company, but aren't you supposed to be with Lukas now for the queen's arrival?" I asked.

"You are never going to call him Vaerik, are you?" he teased.

I huffed softly. "I keep forgetting. He's Vaerik to everyone here, but I got to know him as Lukas."

"Well, *Lukas* sent me to ask if you would like to attend the meeting this morning."

I stopped abruptly to stare at Conlan. "The closed meeting with the king and the Seelie queen that no one is allowed to go to?"

Conlan nodded. "That would be the one. Vaerik told the king that you have earned the right to be there after your sacrifice for Faerie. King Oseron agreed. Vaerik couldn't get away, so he asked me to bring you to the meeting. You'll be an observer only, but you will hear firsthand what is discussed. Do you wish to attend?"

"Do you even have to ask?"

He laughed and motioned for us to keep walking. "Then you're going to need to clean up and change. If we hurry, we will get there before it starts."

I picked up my pace, and in less than twenty minutes, we were at my quarters. He waited on the balcony while I showered and changed. I cast a longing look at my new outfits as I dressed in the court clothes Sereia had made for me. I left my hair down except for two side sections that I pulled back into a braid at my crown.

"How do I look?" I asked when I joined him. I had no idea what the dress code was for something like this.

He smiled approvingly. "You'll do."

We left my quarters and went to the lift. I expected us to go up, but he surprised me by taking us down to the ground level. We walked through a maze of tunnels that took us deeper into the mountain. I was completely lost by the time we came to an open area with two more tunnels branching off from it.

Instead of taking one of the tunnels, we crossed the space to stand before a wall of rock. Conlan raised his hand and muttered something. A few seconds later, the rock shimmered, and a portal appeared. We stepped through it into a room that was entirely white from the walls to the floor to a set of gleaming white doors. The only color in the room was from the stone-faced guards stationed on either side of the doors and along two walls.

"Are we still in Unseelie?" I whispered to Conlan as we walked to the doors.

"Yes. We're in a part of the mountain that can only be accessed via a portal and only to those who have clearance."

He opened one of the doors and ushered me into the room beyond. We moved along the wall to a spot a few dozen feet from the door, and then I turned to check out my surroundings.

We were in an oval room with a set of doors on each end. Two rows of seats were positioned in a semicircle in front of each set of doors, and at the center of the room was a low pedestal with a shallow brazier on top. Instead of fire, the brazier held laevik crystals that glowed softly.

The walls were completely covered in tapestries depicting Aedhna in various scenes. I studied one and was amazed that the artist had captured her exact likeness. Or maybe that was the image she presented to those of us she appeared to.

Conlan and I were the first to arrive. A few minutes later, the door near us opened, and six royal guards came in. After they had positioned themselves along the wall behind the seats, the far door opened, and eight faeries entered to do the same on that end of the room.

More guards entered through the door on our end, preceding King Oseron, who wore a simple crown and a long blue robe. He was accompanied by Consort Maurelle, who wore an ivory robe and a plain circlet adorned with a single blue stone that matched the king's robe. They moved down to take their places in the middle of the first row.

Faolin and Faris came next, followed by Lukas wearing a plain coronet and a belted midnight blue tunic with silver trim. His pants were a lighter blue with the same braid down the sides. It was the first time I'd seen him in his royal uniform, and he literally took my breath away. He looked like the real-life version of a fairy tale prince.

Lukas didn't look our way before he took the seat on his father's other side. Then came a procession of people I'd never seen whom I assumed were the king's advisors. They filled out the remaining seats. Faolin, Faris, and the others took up positions near the ends of the rows.

Finally, the far door opened again, and I sucked in a breath at the sight of the first two to enter. They were the queen's guards who had threatened me in New York and warned me to stay away from Prince Rhys. My eyes moved past them to a blonde in an emerald green dress and matching robe trimmed with gold. I didn't need to see her jeweled crown to know this cool, aristocratic visitor was the Seelie queen.

My gut twisted as Queen Anwyn took her seat directly across from King Oseron. I couldn't look away from the face of the person who had devastated my parents and tried to take away everything I cared about. The knowledge that there was nothing I could do to get justice for my family made my hands clench into fists.

A gentle elbow nudge from Conlan made me aware of how rigid I was and what my expression must be. I forced my body to relax and looked away from the queen to take in the rest of the Seelie contingent. On her right was a blond male wearing a plain coronet, whom I guessed to be her consort. He wore the bored, bland expression of someone who had better things to do than attend a meeting to discuss the fate of the world. I wondered if he had always been that apathetic or if being mated to Queen Anwyn had made him that way.

The queen leaned slightly to her left to speak to the person there, and I gave a small start when I saw it was Prince Rhys. I shouldn't be surprised he was there or that she was more interested in talking to him than her consort. The only thing she seemed to care about was the prince.

Ever since my father told me who Rhys was, I'd been trying to think of why the Seelie queen would take a human child to convert and raise as her heir. So far, I hadn't come up with a reason that made sense. I didn't think Rhys knew the truth, but I was sure the rest of Seelie didn't. If the blue bloods at Seelie were anything like the ones here, status and lineage meant everything to them. They would never stand for a half-breed becoming their king someday.

I was so lost in thought it took a few seconds to realize Prince Rhys's eyes were focused on me. He looked as surprised to see me as I was to be there. He smiled, and I returned it before I averted my gaze. I could feel his eyes on me until King Oseron stood, and everyone's attention shifted to him.

The king bowed to the Seelie queen. "Queen Anwyn, welcome to Unseelie. We are honored to host you and your council for these important talks. I am confident the cooperation of our two regions will result in a solution to heal the barrier between Faerie and the human realm."

Queen Anwyn tilted her head forward in acknowledgement and a hint of a smile touched her lips. "Thank you, King Oseron. We are pleased to be here and look forward to working with you to eliminate this threat to our world."

He smiled, and they began the tedious process of introducing everyone seated on both sides. I barely heard them because I was fuming about the ridiculousness of everyone in the room exchanging pleasantries and pretending that Queen Anwyn hadn't caused the threat that brought them all here in the first place. It was probably a very good thing that I was a spectator only at this meeting because I could not pretend ignorance, even for the sake of diplomacy.

After all the formalities were done, one of the king's advisors stood to present the first of their proposals. "Every time a portal is created, it causes magic to leak into the human world. If we prohibit all travel between the two worlds for a period of time, it could help to slow the drain of energy from ours."

The two sides began to discuss the proposal, weighing the pros and cons and talking about how long a ban on travel to the human world was needed to make a difference. The thought of not being able to go home and see my family for any length of time filled me with anxiety. I could go to them before the ban went into effect, but I had to be in Faerie to do whatever it was Aedhna needed me to do.

Another of the Unseelie advisors stood. "In addition to prohibiting travel to the other world, we think all Court Fae should be summoned home to Faerie. Many of our people have permanent residences in the human realm, only returning home to replenish their magic. Having them all here could help restore the balance of magic."

His suggestion set off another flurry of discussions and caused my anxiety to grow. If they agreed on this course of action, who knew how long it would be before I was allowed to visit my family? Time meant nothing to faeries, but my parents were mortal. They'd already lost their son. I would not let them lose their daughter, too.

Queen Anwyn's imperious voice cut through the din. "These proposals have merit, but they are not enough."

The room fell silent, and all eyes went to her.

"There is only one way to repair the barrier and protect Faerie," she said to King Oseron. "We must seal the barrier between the worlds permanently."

Her words hit me like a punch to the gut forcing all the air from my body. For a few seconds, her face blurred before my eyes, and the sound of the room erupting became a buzzing in my head. I wasn't aware I'd leaned back against the wall until Conlan's hand squeezed mine. It was enough to ground me and help me focus on what was happening around me.

"There are two sides to the barrier," Lukas said to the queen. "Sealing us off from the human realm might not repair the damage done to their side."

No one spoke as we waited for her response. She did not make us wait long.

"That is a possibility but a chance we must take." She placed a hand over her heart as if it pained her to say the words. "Our first duty is to protect Faerie and all who live here."

Anger boiled inside me. All of this was her fault. It was she who had stolen the ke'tain and taken it from Faerie. She caused the damage to the barrier, and now she planned to wipe her hands free of it by destroying my world and everyone I loved. And every damn person in this room knew it.

Queen Anwyn's gaze suddenly shifted away from Lukas and locked with mine. I stared back, not trying to hide my animosity. Recognition flared in her eyes, and they narrowed on me, but I held her stare, refusing to look away first.

I was aware of several people turning in their seats to see what had captured the queen's attention. I could also feel Conlan's hand gripping the back of my shirt to keep me from going anywhere.

The queen broke our stare down and returned her cool gaze to Lukas as if nothing had happened. They resumed their discussion, but I was too consumed by anger to pay attention.

Conlan leaned down and whispered, "I think it's time to go."

I didn't resist when he took my arm and quietly guided me out of the room. We crossed the outer room, and he created the portal to take us to the tunnels. It wasn't until we were back in an area I recognized that he spoke.

"Queen Anwyn has been pushing for years to seal the barrier, and she sees this as an opportunity to press her agenda. But King Oseron won't agree to that unless it is the last resort."

I stared straight ahead. "But it's a possibility if they can't repair the damage."

"Yes," he said honestly. "Don't worry, Jesse. We will find a solution before that happens."

I nodded but didn't say much as we took the lift to my level, and he walked me to my door. When he started to follow me inside, I held up a hand to stop him. "I'd like to be alone for a while."

He frowned. "Are you sure? I don't want to leave you when you're upset."

"It was a lot to take in, seeing her for the first time and then her saying that." I dug down deep and summoned a smile for him. "I think I might go to the training room and get in some more practice on the staff. Exercise always helps clear my head."

He visibly relaxed. "That's a good idea. I will let Vaerik know you are well."

"I doubt he even knows we left," I said as I kicked off one of my shoes.

"He does. He could not come after us, so he signaled me to make sure you were okay."

I stumbled in the process of removing my other shoe. "He did? I didn't see that."

Conlan smiled. "You were not supposed to see it."

He walked away, leaving me staring after him. I shut the door and bent to pick up my discarded shoes. Even in the midst of such an important meeting, Lukas had been concerned about me. I wished I could see him tonight, but he would be tied up until Queen Anwyn left.

I let out a sigh and turned toward the living area, coming up short at the sight of the woman standing by the balcony door. The shoes slipped from my fingers and clattered to the floor.

"Aedhna," I said in a hushed voice. "Is it time?"

"Yes." She held out a hand to me. "Come here, my child."

My heart thudded against my ribs as I walked to her. When I reached her, she took my hand in hers, and calm descended over me.

She smiled. "Is that better?"

"Yes, thanks." I looked away, embarrassed that she had sensed my fear.

"Today, I will explain what must be done to heal Faerie and the human realm. Tomorrow, your work will begin."

I swallowed hard, unable to think of a thing to say.

Aedhna released my hand and walked to the balcony rail. "Do you remember what I told you about the ke'tains during our first conversation?"

Ke'tains? Plural? I dug through my memory of talking to her during my conversion. It was still a bit hazy, but it all came back to me.

"You said there are four of them, and their energy keeps Faerie alive. And that the three hidden stones were weakened because they had to work harder when the fourth one was taken from Faerie."

She nodded. "Now we must correct the imbalance created during that time."

I followed her to the rail. "But you said the world would heal on its own once the ke'tain was back."

"It can, but it will take a long time and only if it is closed off completely from the human world. That will save Faerie, but not the world you still call home."

"That's what Queen Anwyn wants to do." I braced my hands on the stone rail. "I can't let that happen."

"King Oseron will argue against it, but eventually, he will accept it is the only way," Aedhna said, and every word was like an arrow in my heart. "Unless we can restore the balance."

Understanding dawned. "You waited to come to me because you knew what Queen Anwyn was going to say in the meeting, and you wanted me to hear it."

"Yes."

I spun to her. "Tell me what to do, and I'll do it."

Aedhna clasped my hands in hers. "The ke'tain in the temple must be restored to its full power. To do that, it has to replenish its energy from the three other stones."

"How?"

"You will take the temple ke'tain to each of the hidden stones," she said as if it was no big deal. "After each pairing there will be storms, but do not be alarmed by them. As the temple ke'tain grows stronger, Faerie will begin to heal itself."

I couldn't tell if my heart was racing from excitement or fear. "The ke'tain is under constant guard in the temple, and it's protected by wards. How am I supposed to take it without getting caught?"

"The stone I gifted you will allow you to increase your own magic to enter the temple unseen and pass through the wards around the ke'tain."

My excitement dimmed, and I grimaced. "I've only used my magic once to create a portal, and it didn't go as planned."

She laughed softly. "I will teach you how to use it."

"Am I going to create portals to get to the other ke'tains?"

"No portal can take you where you need to go," she said. "Your drakkan will fly you there."

"Gus is not exactly my drakkan," I reminded her. "How do I find him and tell him where to go?"

Aedhna squeezed my hands. "I will teach you that as well."

Apparently, she had thought of everything. I puffed out a breath. "Okay then. Where do we start?"

I got off the lift and walked to the main hall. The guards attentively watched me approach, but none of them spoke when I crossed the hall and opened the smaller door. I stepped outside and gave a little wave to the two other guards posted there before I set off toward the road to town.

It wasn't until I rounded a curve and the entrance to the mountain was no longer visible that I was able to breathe normally. People left court all the time to go to town, so it was the perfect cover for my absence today. With Lukas and the others fully occupied by the Seelie visit, there wasn't anyone who would miss me. I'd left a note in my quarters in case one of them did go there looking for me.

The fork in the road came into view, and I glanced around to make sure I was alone before I took the road to the right. The trees were so tall they formed a canopy over the road and blocked out the sun, giving the impression I was in a long eerie tunnel. A shiver went through me. I was a city girl, and I could handle alleys and dark buildings. The woods, not so much.

Half a mile in, I came to a spot where the trees thinned out to show a wide patch of blue sky. I stopped and listened, but all I could hear was birds.

I reached up and touched the goddess stone in my hair. Closing my eyes, I pictured Gus, and an image formed of him perched on the edge of a cliff eating some kind of fish with tentacles. *Gus*, I called in my mind, and he responded by cocking his head to the side. I called again. *Come to me, Gus.*

He dropped the fish and stood. Stretching out his wings, he leaped off the cliff and flew in my direction.

It worked! I let go of the stone and jumped up and down exuberantly.

Having nothing else to do but wait, I sat on a fallen tree at the side of the road and whiled away the time going over my plans for what to do when I got to the island. Aedhna had spent hours with me last night, patiently teaching me how to create illusions, but I wasn't as confident about my ability as she'd been. Everything hinged on this, so I could not fail.

A branch cracked, and I jerked my head in the direction of the sound. I sucked in a breath as the biggest boar I had ever seen shuffled onto the road a dozen yards from me. The creature was at least six feet tall at the shoulder with spiky, black hair and bottom tusks that reached his ears.

I scrambled to remember what I'd read about Fae boars. In my world, wild boars could be vicious, so I expected no less from those in Faerie. Drakkans kept most dangerous creatures out of the valley. Predators preferred to stick to the forest where game was abundant, and they were sheltered from the drakkans. I'd never come this close to the forest or considered the dangers lurking inside.

The boar ambled to the other side of the road and sniffed at the ground. I sat very still, barely breathing and hoping the animal was too busy foraging for food to notice me. I thought about hiding behind the tree I sat on and dismissed that idea because moving might draw the boar's attention. I had the staff and one of the knives I'd gotten for my birthday with me, but they'd be useless against a creature the size of a bull moose with a hide thicker than that of a rhinoceros.

A bird took flight from the underbrush, and the boar lifted its snout from the ground. It sniffed the air and swung its head slowly in my direction until its beady black eyes found me.

Neither of us moved. The boar grunted and sniffed. One of its front hooves scuffed the ground, drawing my eyes to the short, pointed horn protruding from each hoof.

I tensed as my fight-or-flight mode kicked in. Outrunning a wild boar wasn't an option and neither was fighting it off. That left one avenue of escape. The lowest branches on most of the large trees were too high to reach, but I spotted one I might be able to climb. The only problem was I didn't know if I could get to it before the boar got to me.

The boar growled. I sprang to my feet as it charged.

I fell backward as a drakkan dived through the opening in the tree canopy and snatched up the boar in his massive claws. I barely caught a glimpse of red and gold scales before the drakkan and boar disappeared into the trees. I covered my ears to block out the terrified squeals and the sound of ripping flesh as Gus made up for the meal he had abandoned to answer my call.

I'd stopped shaking by the time he walked out of the woods, licking his snout. He paused to chew on something stuck in his claws, and a full body shudder went through me when I saw it was a curved tusk. He tossed it to the side of the road and trotted toward me, looking calm and sated.

I cleared my throat. "Hey, Gus."

Gus stopped close enough for me to smell the scent of fresh blood on his breath. He lowered his head, and I tried not to gag as I reached up to pat the end of his snout.

"Good boy," I said and stepped back so I could breathe. "You want to take a little trip with me?"

He shifted restlessly and angled his head to look at me with one big red eye as if he was awaiting instructions.

I shivered at the intensity of his stare. "I need to go to the temple on the island."

I should have been prepared, but I wasn't. One second, I was standing on the road, and in the next I was rising into the air in Gus's claw. I barely had time to do the glamour to make me invisible before we were flying over the main road. The people below looked up but didn't point or anything, so I assumed my glamour was working.

I couldn't take any chance of someone seeing me, so I held the illusion until we were out to sea. I relaxed and dozed on and off until the island came into view. Then I created a new glamour to hide me. Drakkans didn't normally go to the island, but no one would make a big deal of it unless they saw he wasn't alone.

Gus landed in the same spot as before and let me go. I plucked the stone from my hair and clutched it in my fist as I walked to the building that housed the temple. I stood in the doorway, my heart thudding at the realization of what I was about to do. I had to take a few calming breaths before I could continue.

The circular room at the bottom of the steps was as I remembered it. I crossed it and peered into the main chamber below. From here I could not see the guards who were stationed on either side of the stairs to give them a full view of the altar.

My stomach quivered. What if my glamour wasn't strong enough? What if I tripped and broke the illusion? What if...?

I shook off my nerves. I was here, and there was no going back now. Aedhna believed I could do this, so I would.

I descended the stairs and looked back at the two Seelie and two Unseelie guards who were so still they could have been statues. Lukas had told me it was a great honor to be chosen to guard the temple, and every court guard asked to be in the rotation. The job was mostly ceremonial since it was the ward that protected the ke'tain, but that didn't matter to the guards. I felt guilty for deceiving them when they took their duty so seriously, but if all went as planned, no one would ever know the ke'tain had left the temple.

I felt the ke'tain's energy as I approached it, but it wasn't overpowering like it had been my first time here. Now, there was no invisible wall that kept me from getting close to the altar.

I looked down at the ke'tain that glowed from within. For months, I'd lived in close proximity to it, and I'd held it in my hands for a short time, but I'd never had the time to study it because I'd been too busy being kidnapped and getting shot. If one small stone could hold enough power to affect the balance of magic in the realm, I understood why Aedhna had kept the existence of the others hidden. I didn't want to imagine the damage someone like Queen Anwyn would do with all four ke'tains.

Glancing at the guards again, I stuck my free hand into my pocket and pulled out a small cloth sack. Inside it was the plain blue stone Aedhna had given me last night. It was the same size and shape as the ke'tain, and if I created the illusion correctly, it would look like the real thing to anyone who entered the room. The illusion only worked as long as no one got close to the stone, but the wards would keep people away from it.

Holding my goddess stone in my right hand and the blue stone in my left, I focused my gaze on the ke'tain. Then I closed my eyes and visualized the blue stone taking on the physical properties of the real thing. The fingers on my right hand tingled, and it intensified as a current flowed up my arm, across my chest, and down my left arm. The sensation faded, and I opened my hand to reveal the exact replica of the ke'tain lying in my palm.

Almost there. More confident now, I moved to the last step. I pushed out the illusion that hid me until it enveloped the altar. The tricky part of this was to portray an image of the ke'tain sitting on the altar so the guards could not see me switching it out for the fake. It was the one step that Aedhna had needed to work on the longest with me last night, and I was about to find out if her tutelage would pay off.

Using one hand, I made the switch. My hand prickled uncomfortably when it touched the ke'tain, but as Aedhna had promised, it didn't harm me. I carefully placed it in the sack that had held the fake and put it in my pocket. Then I held my breath and pulled the illusion back to me.

One of the Seelie guards took a step forward, his eyes narrowed on the altar. "What was that?"

I froze.

"What do you see?" his partner asked.

"The ke'tain... It moved."

The other guards jumped to attention. One grabbed the hilt of his sword as the four of them crossed the room toward me.

15

M Y MOUTH WENT dry, and my heart pounded so hard I was afraid they would hear it. Thoughts of what would happen to me if I were caught stealing the ke'tain made my stomach roil.

The guards reached the ward and spread out, but their eyes remained focused on the ke'tain. One of the Unseelie guards lifted his eyes and stared right at the spot where I stood. Could he see me?

He turned his head toward the Seelie guard who'd spoken first. "I see nothing out of place, and the wards are working."

The Seelie guard scowled but kept his eyes on the altar. "I know what I saw."

"It looks normal to me as well," said the second Unseelie guard. "But if you are certain, it is protocol to send for our heads of security."

I bit my inner cheek so hard I tasted copper. I was as good as dead if they sent for reinforcements. My only option was to try to slip past them and pray to the goddess that the fake ke'tain held up under scrutiny until I could return the real thing.

The first Unseelie guard shifted his stance. "Korrigan is attending the conference with the king today. I do not think it would be wise to interrupt them unless we are sure there is a problem."

The two Seelie guards exchanged a fearful look. The one who hadn't sounded the alarm said, "Bauchan is with the queen as well. Do you want to send for him?"

"No." The first guard glanced from his partner to the Unseelie guards and back again. "The wards are up, and no one but the goddess could walk through them. It must have been a trick of the light."

I let out a breath. It was evident by the guards' expressions that no one in the room wanted the heads of security coming to the island. Now, if these guys would return to their stations, I could get out of here. The illusion made me invisible, but it wouldn't hide me if I brushed up against someone.

As if by mutual silent agreement, the four guards turned and walked back to their spots at the wall. They looked more alert than earlier, but as long as they stayed there, I should be okay.

I stepped back and moved slowly around the altar. On shaky legs, I crossed the room and ascended the stairs. I didn't breathe until I stepped out of the building into the bright sunlight. Bending over, I braced my hands on my knees and took a few deep breaths. I was too shaken by my close call to revel in what I'd done. And this job was far from over.

I straightened and hurried over to Gus who lay waiting for me. His head came up as I approached, reminding me he could see through my glamour. I stopped in front of him and pulled out the sack containing the ke'tain. His nostrils flared, and he lowered his head to sniff at the sack.

"You remember the ke'tain, don't you?" I whispered. "There's another one like this far away in the Duergar Mountains. I need you to take me there."

Gus stood, and I tucked the ke'tain away. He picked me up, and we were off.

He flew back the way we'd come, but when land came into view, he veered north and flew along the coast. Small towns were scattered here and there, but we were too high for me to make out any of the details. Maybe someday, when I wasn't busy trying to save the world, I'd come back for a closer look.

Hours passed, and the terrain changed, slowly rising to form a mountain range that stretched as far as I could see. Gus turned inland, and the temperature dropped. I was warm tucked against his belly, but I could feel the bite of cold air on my face when I lifted my head to look around.

We dropped lower as we flew over the foothills that were covered in dense forests. It was a little warmer down here, and I enjoyed the myriad of colors from the green valleys dotted with wildflowers and lakes so blue they didn't look real. A few times, we passed other drakkans, but they kept their distance from us. One thing I didn't see was signs of civilization, and it started to feel like I was the only person left in the world.

The hills became steeper and the vegetation sparse. The air stung my face as Gus crested mountains that got higher and higher the farther we went. We passed several crags with families of drakkans, and I noticed that the mountain drakkans were smaller than the ones that lived on the cliffs in Unseelie. A pair of them flew out to snap and growl at us for being in their territory, but they kept their distance from Gus who was twice their size.

We climbed above the snowline where the air was thinner and so cold it burned when I took a deep breath. I had to cover my face to protect it, and the next time I peeked out, I was shocked to see nothing below me but clouds.

Gus suddenly changed course and headed for one of the snow-covered peaks. I thought he was going to land on the summit until he dipped at the last minute, and I saw the dark spot in the face of the rock. The cave.

He landed lightly on the wide ledge at the mouth of the cave and carefully set me on my feet. My legs wobbled, and my feet felt numb after so many hours in the air. I leaned against his foreleg to steady myself until I could stand on my own.

"Oh, my God," I said through chattering teeth when I stepped away from Gus's warmth. The cold didn't seem to bother him, but I was shivering so hard my bones ached.

Gus nudged me with his snout, a not so gentle reminder that I was here for a reason. The sooner I did what I came to do, we could leave this frozen place.

I pulled out the laevik crystal I'd brought with me, and it illuminated the cave that was roughly twenty feet deep. Walking to the back of the cave, I found a tunnel opening hidden from view by a protruding slab of rock. I held the crystal in front of me and entered the narrow tunnel.

A few feet in, the tunnel branched into two directions. I paused and frowned at them. I'd dreamed of this place. Just like that, I knew exactly where I was going.

I took the left tunnel, not surprised when it began to slope downward. It was as quiet as a tomb inside the mountain, and even my footsteps sounded muffled. At times, the tunnel was so narrow I had to turn sideways and suck in my stomach to squeeze through. I had never been spelunking, and until now, I hadn't known how much I disliked enclosed spaces.

Aedhna had hidden this ke'tain well. If by a remote chance someone ever managed to find the cave, they'd have a lot of trouble fitting through some of the tight spots in the tunnel unless they were my size. No adult faerie I'd seen could make it.

I was questioning my sanity for being here when I noticed a change in the air. It was charged with electricity, and I felt a strong compulsion to keep moving. I didn't know if it was Aedhna telling me I was close, or if it was the two ke'tains sensing each other.

I came to a spot where the ceiling was so low I had to crawl. On the other side, the ceiling leveled out, and I found myself at a dead end.

I laid my palm against the cold wall. Immediately, the ke'tain in my pocket thrummed with energy, and the hairs on my body stood on end. From deep within the rock, I felt an answering pulse, and the wall grew warmer. I withdrew the sack from my pocket and tipped the ke'tain onto my hand. I pressed the stone against the wall and waited.

Ripples spread across the wall like tiny waves on the surface of a lake. When the disturbance subsided, the rock was crystalline, and deep in its depths was a small glowing object. The object rose slowly to the surface, until finally I could make out a luminescent green stone the same size as the one in my hand.

The two ke'tains made contact, and my body jolted like I'd been struck by lightning. Every cell ignited, my vision turned white, and pain lanced through my chest. I would have fallen, but my hand was fused to the wall.

In seconds, the pain vanished, and my sight returned. Beneath my hand, the ke'tains pulsed and I could feel the one from the cave feeding the one from the temple. The energy was pure and immeasurable, and its divine beauty made tears spill down my cheeks. It should have reduced me to ashes, but my goddess stone protected me as Aedhna had promised it would.

I didn't know how long I stood there like that before the ke'tains separated. I stayed where I was, watching the green stone recede until it disappeared, and the wall was plain gray rock again. It was done.

I secured the ke'tain in my pocket and wiped my wet cheeks with my sleeve. Then I made my way back to the main cave, knowing I would never be the same after this experience.

Gus's head swung toward me when I climbed out of the tunnel and came into view. I smiled and walked over to stand beside him in the mouth of the cave.

"Have you ever seen anything like that?" I gazed at the snow-capped peaks that resembled islands in a sea of clouds. It was breathtaking and frightening at the same time, and I'd never felt so alone, even with Gus at my side.

An icy wind stole my breath, and I shivered. "Let's go home, Gus."

I fell asleep before we reached the foothills and didn't wake until Gus growled to let me know we were approaching the island. The same four guards were on duty when I entered the temple, but they were more relaxed than when I'd left them. I was ready for this day to be over, but I took my time exchanging the fake ke'tain for the real one. Another misstep like the last one and the guards would call in backup for sure.

It was dusk when Gus set me down on the road near the forest. If I'd thought the place was creepy during the day, it was ten times worse in the near dark. I was too tired to create another invisibility illusion, but I had enough energy to run to the main road.

I was rounding the curve near the mountain when Iian and Kerr came into view riding tarrans. The moment they saw me, they dismounted and waited for me to reach them.

"We were coming to look for you," Iian said. "Vaerik found the note you left in your room, but he thought you would be back from town by now."

"You know me. There's so much to see and do, and I have to look at everything," I answered. Hearing that Lukas had taken time out of the meetings with Seelie to visit me made my weary body feel lighter. Combined with the exhilaration over what I'd done today, it was a heady sensation.

"You look tired," Iian said.

I rolled my eyes. "Just what every girl wants to hear."

They chuckled as we started toward home. Kerr looked at my empty hands. "You did not buy anything?"

"Maybe next time."

"Did you see anything interesting in your exploring?" Iian asked.

Images of my day flashed through my mind. "Oh, you know. The usual stuff."

"Looks like it's you and me tonight," I said the following evening to Kaia, who was curled up on the other end of the couch with her head on my feet.

She cracked an eye to look at me and closed it. Her loud purrs filled the room.

I sighed. As much as I loved her company, I wished I had a companion who could talk to me.

Tonight, the king was hosting a lavish dinner in honor of the queen's visit, after which she and her people would return to Seelie. Tomorrow, the court would go back to normal, and I'd see Lukas, Roswen, and the others again. For now, I was on my own.

The bell rang, signaling someone was at the door. Kaia leaped off the couch and padded ahead of me when I went to see who was visiting. I was surprised to find Gelsey, Roswen's personal tailor who had made all my wonderful new clothes. Gelsey's arms were laden with dresses, shoes, and other items, and I rushed to relieve her of some of her burden.

"Did we have a fitting I forgot about?" I asked as I draped the clothes over a chair. I eyed the long dresses in confusion. We hadn't discussed her making formal clothes for me.

She set the rest of it on the couch. "I have been instructed to help you dress for the queen's dinner. I've brought some gowns I have been working on for Princess Roswen. A few adjustments and one of them will be perfect for you."

I held up a hand. "I think there's been a misunderstanding. I'm not going to the dinner."

Gelsey's brow furrowed. "Oh, but you must. Prince Vaerik himself asked me to tend to you."

Lukas wanted me to go to the dinner with him? Warmth rushed through me, and I gave her a wide smile, brushing aside the fact that I had never been to a formal Fae affair and I had no clue what to do at one. I'd be with Lukas, and he would guide me through it.

I touched one of the dresses, a deep green one that felt like silk in my fingers. "Roswen won't mind you trimming her dress for me?"

"It was her idea to use one of these." Gelsey arranged the three floor-length dresses so we could see them better. In addition to the green one, there was a pale blue one, and one in midnight blue, all in different styles. They were beautiful, and any of them would work with my coloring and hair.

She picked up the green dress. "Why don't you try on each of them, and we'll see which one suits you best."

Two hours later, I stood in front of the mirror in my bedroom, hardly able to believe I was looking at my own reflection. After some deliberation, Gelsey had decided on the dark blue gown, and I could see why Roswen would have no one else make her clothes.

The off-the-shoulder sheath dress fit like it had been made for me. The form-fitting bodice adorned with lace and tiny blue crystals tapered down to a skirt that hugged my hips and fell gracefully to my feet. The skirt was over-laid with a gossamer veil that trailed a foot behind me. It was open at the front and flared out gently from the sides when I walked.

On my feet were low-heeled shoes the same color as the dress and trimmed with blue crystals that winked in the light. Gelsey had arranged my hair into an elaborate loose braid adorned with tiny white and blue flowers that draped over one shoulder, leaving the other shoulder bare.

"You are breathtaking," Gelsey said from behind me, her eyes glistening with the sheen of tears.

I smiled at her. "Thanks to you."

She shook her head. "I merely framed your natural beauty. With your unique hair and coloring, you are incomparable, and I am honored to be the one to dress you."

I dabbed at my eyes. "It's a good thing faeries don't wear mascara, or I'd be a mess now."

Gelsey laughed. "I have heard about the colored powders and creams humans put on their faces. Is it true they also wear false lashes and change their hair color?"

"Mostly women wear makeup and false eyelashes, but some men do, too." I grinned at her shocked expression. "And both men and women dye their hair."

"It is a very different world you come from," she said as she adjusted the back of my dress. "I think I would like to see it someday."

I turned to face her. "I'll be happy to show you around when you decide to go."

The bell rang, and her eyes lit up as she ran to answer the door. I took one last glance at the mirror and pressed a hand to my stomach to calm the butterflies there. Then I followed Gelsey to the living room to greet Lukas.

I came up short when I saw the unfamiliar dark-haired male standing in the entranceway with Gelsey. He was dressed formally in cream pants and a matching tunic with dark blue trim, and his eyes widened in appreciation when he saw me.

"Can I help you?" I asked him.

He gave a small bow. "I am Joreth. King Oseron sent me to escort you to dinner."

"But..."

Joreth came over and took my limp hand in his. "I heard about our lovely new faerie, but the stories do not do you justice. You are a vision, and I will be the envy of every male there tonight."

"Thank you." I shot a helpless look at Gelsey, who seemed to be as surprised as I was by his arrival.

A growl came from behind me, and Joreth dropped my hand. He took a few steps back as Kaia came to stand between us.

I stroked her head. "Kaia, be nice."

She stopped growling but continued to stare at him. I remembered that look from my first encounter with her.

Joreth cleared his throat. "We should go. We cannot be late for the dinner."

I stepped around Kaia and walked with him to the door. Gelsey smiled weakly as we approached her. "I will collect the other dresses before I go. Have a wonderful time tonight."

"We will," Joreth answered for me.

"Can you let Kaia out when you leave?" I asked Gelsey, who nodded.

Outside, Joreth tucked my hand into the crook of his elbow, and I let him escort me to the lift. It wasn't his fault I'd been expecting someone else as my date, and there had to be a good reason why Lukas didn't come for me.

The few people we passed eyed us enviously. When we stepped onto the lift, Joreth happily confided that tonight's dinner was a big deal, and invitations were highly coveted. Dressed as we were, it was no secret to anyone where we were going.

The lift stopped on the top level, and we were met by six guards. A male in court livery directed us where to go, and we walked down a long hallway until we came to an open archway guarded by two more guards. Passing through it, we entered a large terrace. Half the terrace was enclosed by walls and a ceiling, and the other half was open to the night sky. The entire space was laid out like a formal dining room.

At the back of the terrace, tables were arranged in a semicircle on a low dais. Smaller four-person tables were placed around the room to allow every occupant a view of the main table. The overhead lights had been dimmed, and on every elegantly set table was a small dish of laevik crystals that gave off a soft warm light.

A female in livery took us to our table on the other side of the terrace near the rail. We were as far from the dais as you could get; however, the location offered us an unobstructed view of everyone entering the room. Joreth looked a little put out by our seating arrangement, but I was content to sip the juice brought to me and watch the other guests arrive.

It was like watching the red-carpet event at the Oscars as elegantly-dressed couples entered and were shown to their seats. Rashari and Delphine were among them, and I felt a surge of relief that neither of them was Lukas's date. It was going to be hard enough to see him with someone else without it being one of those two.

Before long, the smaller tables were full, and another couple named Fayette and Cleon had joined us at our table. Joreth made introductions, but our table companions were more interested in watching the room than talking to us.

A murmur went through the room, and I looked up as King Oseron entered with Queen Anwyn, and they walked to the dais together. Before I could wonder where their consorts were, Lukas's mother entered on the arm of Queen Anwyn's consort. All eyes were on the Unseelie king and the Seelie queen as they sat in the two large chairs at the center of the dais with their consorts on either side of them.

Queen Anwyn was resplendent in an ice blue dress and a crown that was bigger than the one she'd worn to the meeting. When she smiled at something the king said, it was almost hard to believe that a cold, vile heart beat inside such a delicate, beautiful person.

"I am not surprised Dariyah is on his arm tonight," said Fayette, who was seated across from me. "Her father is one of the king's advisors after all."

I followed Fayette's gaze to the entrance, and my gut hardened when I saw Lukas with Dariyah at his side. She was radiant in a white form-fitting dress, and her haughty smile told every female in the room that Lukas was hers. We'd see about that.

My gaze moved to Lukas, who paid no attention to his date as he scanned the terrace. When his eyes locked with mine, he smiled. For a few seconds, no one else in the room existed. With one look, he said it was me he wanted by his side, and he didn't care if the whole room saw it.

He shifted his stare to Joreth, and his eyes narrowed slightly. Warmth burst in my chest, and I had to bite back a stupid grin. Lukas was jealous of my date.

Dariyah tugged on his arm, and he turned his head to look at her as they continued to their table. I wondered if she had seen our silent exchange, and I got my answer when they took their seats at the head table beside his mother. Dariyah's smile was a lot less smug, but the glare she shot me promised I hadn't won, not by a long shot.

I smiled at her. *Bring it.*

Someone took the seat on Dariyah's other side. I slid my gaze to them and saw Roswen with a dark-haired male, who, based on the resemblance, had to be her brother Kellen. A few seats down from them, I was surprised to see Faolin and Faris. I knew they were princes in their own right, but I'd had no idea their blood was blue enough to place them at the head table.

I looked around for Conlan, Iian, and Kerr and found them at tables near the dais. They were dressed formally and had dates, but they were also close enough to Lukas to protect him should the need arise.

"So, it is true that you and Prince Vaerik are close friends," Joreth said in my ear, startling me by his nearness. "He rarely befriends anyone outside his close circle."

At first, I thought he was insinuating something sordid between Lukas and me, but there was nothing sly or suggestive in his expression.

"We are." I noticed Fayette and Cleon listening to us and didn't elaborate.

Joreth took my reply as an invitation to delve further. "Before your conversion you were one of those hunters I've heard about? You hunted down faeries who broke the law in your world?"

"Yes." *Unless they were above the law.* I looked to where Queen Anwyn was speaking to King Oseron. She and her personal guard would never pay for the terrible crimes they had committed.

"Fascinating." Joreth slid his chair a little closer. "Is that how you met the prince?"

"You could say that. I was looking for someone, and he offered to help me find them."

"Did you find them?" he asked.

I nodded. "Yes, I did."

"Then you returned the ke'tain to us," Joreth said in wonder. "And to reward you, the crown prince made you Fae."

I stared at him at a temporary loss for words. Good God, was that what people here thought? If so, I needed to set the record straight.

"It wasn't a reward. I nearly died, and he did the conversion to save my life."

"And here you are now, a guest at the king's party," Joreth replied cheerfully, oblivious to the edge of annoyance in my voice. "I am fortunate enough to be your escort. I hope that by the time this night is done, you and I will be friends, too." He gave me a secretive smile and lowered his voice. "Or maybe more."

I had no response to that, so I took a sip from my glass instead. Thankfully, servers chose that moment to arrive with our first course, and I was saved from having to reply.

Talk was sparse and light through the five-course meal. Even Fayette and Cleon joined in at times, mostly to talk about who was seated with whom and what they were wearing. The conversation was so shallow I was bored nearly to tears by the time dessert arrived.

I tried not to stare at Lukas and Dariyah, but I couldn't help myself. I wished I hadn't whenever I saw her smile and lean in close to say something to him. It killed me to admit it, but she looked like she belonged there with the royal family. And she knew it.

At one point, she had looked straight at me as if she'd known I would be watching. Her lips curved into a satisfied smile, and she'd laid a hand on Lukas's shoulder in a way that suggested they were more intimate than dinner dates. Lukas had been talking to his mother and hadn't reacted to her touch, but it bothered me all the same.

I wasn't the only one unhappy with Dariyah's display. The few times I glanced at Rashari and Delphine, the pair looked like they were plotting her demise. Dariyah seemed to revel in her competition's jealousy, which only riled them up more. If I were her, I wouldn't be taking strolls down any dark hallways after this.

Servers came to clear away the last of the meal, and people at the small tables began to leave their seats to mingle around the room. As soon as Fayette and Cleon left us, Joreth placed a hand over mine on the table. "I hear there is going to be a special light display after dinner. Why don't we take to the gardens and watch it together?"

I had to stop myself from jerking my hand away when his thumb stroked it. Smiling, I eased it from under his and rested it in my lap. "I think the view would be so much better up here. Don't you agree?"

He leaned in so close our heads touched, and his voice dropped to a husky whisper. "It will be crowded here, and we can spend some time getting to know each other better. I would love to hear more about your life before you came to Faerie."

I laughed. "You'd be better off taking a trip to my world and seeing it for yourself."

"Is this not your world now?"

"I haven't been here long enough for it to feel like home," I replied honestly.

"Then we shall have to make you feel at home here," he persisted, clearly not getting the message.

I picked up my glass and took a sip, scanning the room for an escape. I caught Faris's eye, and the look he gave me said he wanted to help but couldn't. My gaze slid down the table to the spot I'd been avoiding for the last half hour, and my pulse jumped when I found Lukas staring in my direction. His eyes and jaw were hard, and my breath caught before I realized his glower was not directed at me.

Joreth pulled away from me as if I'd burned him. I didn't need to look at his face to guess he had also seen Lukas.

"If you don't mind, I'd like to say hello to some friends of mine," he said, already half out of his chair.

"I don't mind at all." I waited until he left to return my gaze to Lukas, who looked slightly appeased. I smiled and gave him a tiny shrug, and his answering smile sent a delicious shiver through me. Even with a room and a hundred people between us, I could feel his presence as if he was beside me.

His mother said something to him, and he looked at her, breaking the spell between us. I stood and walked to the rail, wondering what the proper etiquette was for these dinners. How long was I expected to stay here? Was it rude to leave before the king did?

I became aware of the whispers nearby just as a voice said, "Jesse James, I hoped I would have an opportunity to talk to you during our visit."

I turned to face Prince Rhys, who stood a few feet away with Bayard and another of his personal guards. The prince was smiling, but his two guards looked none too happy to be there.

"Prince Rhys... how nice to see you," I stammered.

"I thought you agreed to call me Rhys," he said in a teasing voice.

I smiled. "Rhys, how are you enjoying your visit to Unseelie?"

"It's been rather dull until now," he confessed.

I gave him a disbelieving look. "I spent an hour in the first meeting, and it was anything but dull."

His mouth turned down. "It is when you sit in them for three days and are not permitted to participate. My mother believes I am too young and inexperienced to contribute."

His frankness was unexpected. "Why did she bring you if you can't take part in the discussions?"

He leaned in conspiratorially. "Appearances. It's a show of strength. Where one crown prince goes, so does the other."

Bayard made a disapproving sound, but as usual, Rhys ignored him. I sensed something was off between Rhys and the queen. When he'd talked about her the day we went to lunch, his tone was affectionate. Tonight, there was a note of aggravation in his voice.

They were blocking my view of Queen Anwyn, but I knew she would not be happy to see the prince talking to me of all people. I was safe from her in Unseelie, but that fact did not stop a chill from slithering down my spine.

"What do you think of Faerie so far?" he asked me. "I see you have mastered the language already."

"I'm a quick study. What I've seen of Faerie so far is beautiful, although it's definitely an adjustment after living in New York my whole life."

"Yes, it's nothing like the human cities. I have not been home long, and I miss that world already." He stared thoughtfully at the darkened valley. "I have realized during this visit that there is so much of Faerie I have not seen. The Unseelie court is very different from ours. This mountain is quite large, but I cannot imagine living in close quarters with so many others."

"You call this close quarters? You've never been inside my apartment in Brooklyn."

Rhys laughed. "In Seelie, only the royal family and their guards live in the palace. We have servants as well, but everyone else lives in nearby estates or in the town."

I tried to imagine what it must have been like for him living in a palace with only his parents and guards for company. It sounded like a very sad and lonely way to grow up.

Bayard stepped closer to the prince. "Rhys, the queen is signaling for you to rejoin her."

"I am surprised she waited this long." Rhys released an inaudible sigh. "It was good to see you again, Jesse."

"It was great to see you, too," I said and realized I meant it. Despite being raised by Queen Anwyn, he was a genuinely nice person. As he walked away, I wondered what it would have been like if we'd grown up together as brother and sister. I felt a pang of sorrow for what we'd lost.

I glanced around the room, ignoring the people still staring at me after my encounter with the Seelie prince. The diners, except for most of those on the dais, were walking around the room and engaged in conversations. It was as good a time as any to slip out without anyone noticing my departure.

The thought had barely crossed my mind when I caught sight of Rashari and Delphine headed in my direction. Their intentions were written all over their faces. They couldn't rip into Dariyah while she was with Lukas, so they thought they could take out their spite on me.

I groaned inwardly. *Aedhna, you're testing me, aren't you? You couldn't let me make my getaway?*

A flash lit up the sky. I looked out, expecting to see the king's light display, but I was greeted by the sight of purple lightning streaking through the sky toward the mountain. A deafening boom sounded directly overhead, and my ears hurt from the sudden change in air pressure.

Then the mountain shook.

I stumbled back from the rail as a basketball-sized rock struck the floor a foot away. I looked up in time to see more rocks break off from the side of the mountain and tumble toward us.

People screamed and pushed at each other to get away from the open section of the terrace. I whirled to run to the nearest wall and spotted Delphine frozen like a deer in headlights. Rashari was nowhere to be seen.

Changing direction, I raced to Delphine, dodging the smaller rocks coming down around me. I plowed into her and shoved her forward with all my strength. Seconds later, something big crashed into the floor behind me.

I pushed at Delphine's back, yelling for her to keep moving. But when I tried to follow, I couldn't. I looked back at the boulder pinning my train to the floor and gulped at how close it had come to flattening me. Gripping the material, I yanked hard, and it tore free.

Pain lanced through my skull. I staggered as something warm ran down my temple, and the room dimmed. My knees gave out, and I heard someone shout my name before the noise faded to a dull buzz. Then everything went black.

"Jesse, Jesse, talk to me," Lukas begged in a voice edged with fear. "Please, *mi'calaech*, open your eyes."

Faolin's steely voice rang out, making me flinch. "I said stand back. Do not make me say it again."

Warm hands cupped my face. "That's it, Jesse."

I coughed and immediately winced at the sharp pain in my head. "Ow," I groaned. "Who hit me?"

"The mountain," Faris said in a teasing voice. "She's okay, Vaerik."

Opening my eyes, I stared up into Lukas's dark ones. "You guys really know how to throw a party."

Male laughter came from nearby, and Lukas's mouth softened into a smile that made me forget about my throbbing headache.

"A healer will be here shortly, Jesse," Faris said. "Do you hurt anywhere besides your head?"

"No." I moved my arms and legs, and everything worked. "All good. Can I sit up now?"

Lukas gently picked me up. I suddenly became aware of my surroundings. Faolin, Conlan, Iian, and Kerr formed a barrier between us and a curious audience, but I heard people talking excitedly and a few crying.

"Let's get you out of here." Lukas stood and spoke to Faris. "Send my healer to me."

"I can walk," I insisted, but he ignored me. "I thought you were done carrying me around like this."

His chest rumbled with laughter as he turned to Conlan. "Tell my father I will talk to him after I see to Jesse."

Conlan moved away, giving me a clear view of the onlookers. At the front was Dariyah, who looked close to having steam come out of her ears. The thought made me giggle, and I covered my mouth with my hand. That movement brought the pain back, forcing me to close my eyes as Lukas carried me out of the room.

I didn't say anything when he took me to his quarters instead of mine. He laid me on his bed and went to admit the healer, who cleaned the cut on my head and gave me something sweet to drink.

I didn't protest when she helped me out of my torn dress and into one of Lukas's shirts before tucking me into bed. By the time she began to pack up her bag, the pain in my head had receded to a dull ache.

"Your head wound will heal by tomorrow, and you have no other injuries." She smiled at me. "I hear you were hurt saving someone's life. That was very brave."

"Thank you." I smothered a yawn. "Did you give me a sleeping potion?"

She shook her head. "Menak is strong, and it can have a sedative effect on the young. You are a new faerie, so it will affect you the same way."

"Oh." I closed my eyes and listened to the soft murmurs of her talking to Lukas in the other room.

"Jesse." Lukas's hand touched my cheek, and I forced my eyes open.

He smiled, but his eyes were troubled. "My father has called an emergency meeting, so I have to leave you for a few hours."

I lifted my head. "I'll go back to my room then."

"I'll feel better knowing you are here." He tucked the blanket around me. "Elva will stay until I get back in case you need anything."

I assumed Elva was the healer, so I nodded.

Lukas leaned down and lightly brushed his lips against mine. "Rest. I'll return soon."

"Okay," I said groggily.

I heard him leave the room. A minute later, the bed dipped slightly, and a warm weight laid across my stomach. I reached down to pet the furry head. "Hey, Kaia," I said before I drifted off to the sound of her purrs.

The next time I woke, I was curled against Lukas's warm body with my head in the crook of his shoulder. He was still wearing his formal clothes, minus the coat.

"I didn't mean to wake you," he said softly. "Go back to sleep."

"What time is it?"

"Early." His fingers played with my hair that had come partially free of the pretty braid Gelsey had done for me. "How do you feel?"

I did a self-inventory. "Better. Was anyone else hurt?"

"Minor injuries. It could have been much worse." He drew in a breath. "I have always admired your bravery, but when I saw you push Delphine to safety and almost get hit by that boulder, my heart nearly stopped beating."

I laid my hand on his chest. "You have to know by now that it'll take more than a storm to get rid of me."

His other hand came up to capture mine, holding it over his heart. "If you had been with me at the dinner, you would not have been in danger. That was my father's doing, and I've let him know it will not happen again."

"There was no way he could have known there'd be a storm," I said as my heart soared at his words.

Lukas's voice hardened. "I don't blame him for your injury. But he went too far when he arranged for someone else to escort you to dinner and tricked me into taking Dariyah. I've tolerated his interference for too long, and I made it clear I am done with it."

I wanted to believe the king would stop trying to match his son with a suitable mate, but it was a futile effort. I wondered if Lukas knew that, too.

I tilted my head back to look up at him. "You were in the meeting for a long time. How did it go?"

He pressed his lips together as if he was formulating what to say next. "My father and Queen Anwyn agreed to a temporary travel ban between the realms. Faeries in the human realm will be notified that they have three days to come home before the ban."

The air squeezed from my lungs. The one thing I was trying to prevent was happening, and there was nothing I could do to stop it.

"It's a temporary ban, Jesse." The hand in my hair moved down to rub my back. "You'll see your family again soon."

"But they'll be alone if your men come home. Who will keep them safe from Davian?"

Lukas gave me a reassuring smile. "Faolin has been working with a security firm he hired to track down Davian Woods. These are ex Special Forces, and they're trustworthy. He's going to arrange for the firm to take over protection detail until we return. It's not a matter of if but *when* the team will find Davian. If that happens before the travel ban ends, they will take your family home to New York, unless your parents wish to remain on the island longer."

His confidence in the security team eased my fear, and I relaxed against him. I rested my head on his chest, and the steady rhythm of his heart coupled with his fingers in my hair soon began to lull me back to sleep.

"I should probably go back to my room," I murmured.

Lukas stopped toying with my hair. "Do you want to go?"

"No. I don't want people to talk when they see me walking back to my quarters in my dress."

Chuckling, he tugged the blanket up to my shoulder. "You're already the talk of the court after that dinner. What's one more rumor."

"Ugh." I groaned into his shirt. "You're not helping."

He wrapped his arm around me. "Will you stay if I tell you it will help me sleep having you near?"

Warmth spread all the way to my toes, and I snuggled against him. "Yes, I'll stay for that."

When I woke, I was alone in the bed, but the spot beside me was still warm. I slid out of bed to go find him, and I made it to the open bedroom door before I realized I was wearing nothing but Lukas's shirt. I was looking around for my dress when King Oseron's voice stopped me in my tracks.

"I like the girl, Vaerik. She has many traits I admire, and the service she did Faerie can never be repaid," the king said. "But that does not change the circumstances of her birth. She is neither Fae-born nor royalty."

I recoiled as if he'd slapped me. I wanted to retreat to the bed where I couldn't hear any more of the conversation, but my feet refused to move.

"Father, we have discussed this," Lukas replied in a low, angry voice.

"You are drawn to her. I understand that. She is lovely and spirited and brave. Were I your age, I would find her appealing as well. But in the end, I would fulfill my duty to Unseelie." There was a quiet pause before the king said, "Think about it, Vaerik. Remember Onagh."

Onagh? Lukas had never mentioned that name before. Who was he, and what did he have to do with Lukas and me?

The sound of the door closing sent me tiptoeing back to bed. I lay down and pulled the blanket up a few seconds before Lukas came into the room. I debated whether or not I should pretend to be asleep and decided I wasn't a good enough actress.

He sat on the edge of the bed and looked at me with apologetic eyes. "How much did you hear?"

"Enough to know your father doesn't hate me, so that's something," I said lightly.

His mouth tightened. "My father's intentions are good, but he is too set in his ways to see past his vision of the future for his children. He does not consider what we might want."

"What do you want?" I asked, realizing we'd never talked about that.

Lukas's head dipped. "This," he whispered against my lips, and then his mouth took mine in a slow, drugging kiss. I floated on a cloud as his lips blazed a trail to the hollow of my throat. "This," he said before his tongue darted out to taste my skin. I let out a tiny moan as every nerve ending in my body lit up.

"Lukas," I breathed. I wanted his mouth back on mine as much as I wanted him to not stop what he was doing to me.

He pulled away, and then he was on top of me. He raised up on his forearms, but the rest of his hard body pressed me down into the bed. The possessive gleam in his eyes sent a shiver through me as he recaptured my mouth, telling me without words that I was his.

I was breathless when he moved to lie beside me, propped up on one arm. His lips continued their assault as his free hand tugged the covers down to my waist.

My breath caught when his fingers touched the shirt button between my breasts, and he lifted his head to look at me. I nodded my permission, and he smiled as he flicked the button open with ease. His warm hand slipped beneath the soft material, and I arched into his touch when he cupped my breast.

"I've wanted to touch you like this for so long," he said thickly.

I reached up to pull his head down to me again. "Then don't stop."

Our lips had barely made contact when the bell sounded. Lukas groaned and fell onto his back beside me. "If that is my father, I am going to disavow him."

A pained laugh slipped from me because I shared his frustration. He went to answer the door while I lay there reliving the most sensual experience of my life. I imagined what would have happened if the bell hadn't rung, and I silently cursed our visitor, who had the worst timing ever.

Lukas came back to the bedroom, carrying a small bundle of clothes. "Roswen sent Gelsey with a change of clothes for you." He tossed the clothes on a chair. "You won't need those for a few hours."

My heart thudded when he rejoined me on the bed. He rose up on his elbow and leaned down to brush a featherlight kiss against my lips. "Now where were we, *mi'calaech*?"

Mi'calaech...my fire flower. The translation of the endearment formed in my mind, and I wrapped my arms around his neck to kiss him back wantonly.

The sound of the bell again had Lukas pulling away from me, swearing. I pitied whoever was at the door this time because he looked a little scary when he strode from the bedroom. He returned with a resigned expression and carrying a food tray, which he set down on the foot of the bed.

"My mother sent breakfast and hopes you are feeling better this morning." He arranged the pillows behind me, and I reclined against them. Picking up the tray, he settled it over my lap and sat facing me. "We'd better eat before it gets cold, or she will want to know why you didn't touch the food."

I grinned and picked up a pastry. "That sounds like something my mom would say."

Lukas moved up to sit beside me. "What would you like to do today?"

"With you?" I asked around a bite of pastry. Last night was the most I'd seen of him in days, and I assumed the king would keep him even busier after what had happened.

He laughed. "Yes, with me. I have more free time for the next week, and I intend to spend it with you. We can do whatever you want...as long as we stay in Unseelie."

My chest expanded so much I thought it would burst. If not for the tray on my lap, I would have straddled him and kissed the hell out of him.

"I'd love to see more of the valley. It's so beautiful from up here." I would have been happy walking to the lake as long as I did it with him, but it would be nice to get away from court for a few hours.

"A day outside sounds perfect," he said.

After breakfast, Lukas went to let his men know of our plans while I showered and changed into the clothes Gelsey had brought. In the living room, I found my favorite combat-style boots I used for outdoor training and made a mental note to thank Gelsey. I was lacing them up when Lukas returned looking a little put out. My shoulders slumped as I waited for him to tell me he couldn't go out after all.

"I hope you don't mind some extra company," he said, walking to his bedroom. "Roswen stopped me to ask after you, and I foolishly told her our plans for today. She's meeting us outside."

"Oh, good! I haven't talked to her since I got back from visiting my family."

Lukas said something I couldn't make out.

"What was that?" I called.

He appeared in the bedroom doorway. "I'm glad you two like each other, but this was supposed to be our time together." With that, he yanked off his shirt, giving me a tantalizing view of his hard chest and defined abs before he disappeared into the room. I stared dreamily after him until Kaia jumped onto the couch and jolted me to my senses.

When he emerged ten minutes later, his hair was still damp from the shower, and he was dressed in riding clothes like the ones he'd worn the night he had gone out searching for me. We left his suite, and I was surprised none of his men were waiting for us. I couldn't believe they would let him leave the court with only Kaia for protection.

It wasn't until we exited the mountain that I saw Conlan and Faris waiting for us with Roswen and a group of others. I recognized Roswen's personal guards, but who were all of these other people?

"Jesse!" Roswen grabbed someone's arm and pulled him over to us. I didn't recognize him until they were standing in front of us.

"Jesse, this is our brother, Kellen. Kellen, meet Jesse," she said.

I smiled at the sixteen-year-old prince. "It's nice to meet you, Prince Kellen."

"Hello," he said stiffly as if we were at a formal event. I couldn't tell if he was a snob or socially awkward.

Roswen waved a hand dismissively. "Call him Kellen."

Kellen shot her an annoyed look, which she ignored. He huffed softly and walked away to pick up the reins of a beautiful white tarran. The animal lowered its head to him, and he rubbed its forehead affectionately. I forgave his rudeness when he took a treat from his pocket and fed it to the tarran.

Two elf servants approached carrying large baskets, which they secured to the back of one of the tarrans with straps. I gave Roswen a questioning look, and she smiled.

"It's such a lovely day. I thought we could ride to the river and have our lunch there."

"That sounds great," I said before the rest of her sentence sank in. "There's one tiny problem."

Roswen took the reins of the tarran Parisa led to her. "What's that?"

"I've never ridden a tarran."

"Then you will have to ride with me," Lukas said from behind me.

I turned to find him astride a glossy black tarran. He smiled devilishly and leaned down to extend a hand to me. My heart gave a little flutter as I walked over and took his hand. He lifted me with ease, settling me in front of him.

"Comfortable?" he asked as his arms encircled me to take the reins.

"Uh-huh." I glanced around at the other riders, most of whom were watching us curiously. Even Roswen was openly staring, but she looked pleased, too.

I licked my dry lips. "Are you sure it's a good idea for me to ride with you like this? Won't people talk?"

"Yes." He flicked the reins, and his tarran started walking. Conlan and Faris flanked us, with the rest of our party falling in behind. Kaia ran ahead, already on the hunt for something.

We set off across the grounds, skirting the main gardens and lake. When we reached a narrow hard-packed trail, Conlan took the lead with Faris behind us. They put enough distance between us so Lukas and I could talk privately, and it felt like we were in our own little world.

The valley was a riot of colors that were even more vibrant up close. Wildflowers of every hue grew among the tall grasses on the gently rolling hills, and they attracted bright yellow and blue birds no bigger than butterflies. There were trees that looked like pines with silver needles and others with giant red leaves that resembled clusters of open umbrellas.

Lukas pointed out things we passed such as a livestock farm, an orchard, and a small village inhabited mostly by artisans. When I asked why they didn't live in town, he said they preferred the quieter village.

Further on, a low group of buildings came into view. They were too far away to make out much detail, except for a few people walking around and what looked like tarrans in a fenced area.

"That is a training camp for new recruits," Lukas explained. "We have another camp on the mountain for advanced trainees."

"The same mountain your trainer made you run up and down?"

He laughed. "That's the one."

For the next hour, he entertained me with tales from his childhood and training years. Most of his stories had some or all of his friends in them, and it was easy to see why they were such a tight-knit circle.

We reached a low rise, and hoofbeats interrupted our conversation. Roswen raced past us laughing with Kellen hot on her heels and half a dozen of their guards chasing after them. Roswen looked back over her shoulder and taunted her brother before she leaned over her tarran's neck, and they shot forward. She crested the rise and raised her arms in the air with a victorious whoop.

"Roswen and Kellen have always been competitive riders," Lukas said. "He's never been able to catch her, but he keeps falling for her challenges."

I smiled at the comradery between his siblings. "Is she better than you?"

"She's better than everyone," he answered proudly.

We followed them up the incline. As we neared the top, Lukas said, "Close your eyes."

I did. A minute later, we stopped moving, and I was bursting with anticipation when he said, "You can look now."

I opened my eyes and stared at the view laid out before me. Less than half a mile away, a wide, sparkling river moved slowly as if it had all the time in the world. The far bank of the river was lined with tall trees, and beyond them, the black cliffs rose in the distance.

Between us and the river was a field of undulating flames. No, not flames. They were flowers with reddish-orange blossoms that resembled fire under the sun. The illusion was so realistic, it looked like flames were licking at the legs of the tarrans ahead of us.

"Wow."

Lukas urged our tarran forward. "Calaech flowers. They grow all over the valley, but they are most plentiful along the river."

"Beautiful," I murmured, mesmerized.

We caught up to the others as they were dismounting at a grassy spot beside the river. Two grooms led the tarrans to the water to drink, while we began to set out our picnic.

Roswen was helping me spread a blanket when she scowled at something over my shoulder. "They never give up."

"Who?" I turned and found another riding party coming around a bend in the river. Rashari was at the front beside the same male who had been with her at the lake. Behind them rode Delphine, Sereia, and two males I didn't recognize.

Cyrene made a face. "Someone should tell Rashari that desperation is not a good look for her."

I looked to where Lukas stood by the water talking to Kellen, Conlan, and Faris. Conlan saw the newcomers first, and he said something to Lukas, whose smile disappeared.

"Hello, there," Rashari called, feigning surprise at seeing us. "I see we are not the only ones drawn to the river today."

"I'd like to throw her in the river," Parisa muttered.

Roswen snickered, and I smothered a grin. I would not let anyone spoil this day for me. It didn't matter how many people crashed our outing as long as I was with Lukas.

Movement behind Rashari's group caught my eye, and I looked at the blond straggler riding into view. He saw us and waved a hand, and I thought my grin would split my face.

"Tennin!"

"You know Tennin?" Roswen asked.

"He's a good friend of mine," I said as he approached. "I'm surprised to see him with Rashari and her friends, though."

Parisa stepped up beside us. "He's most likely here because of Delphine. They are cousins."

I made a face. "I won't hold that against him."

The group reached us and dismounted. Tennin handed his reins to one of our grooms and came over to us. He gave Roswen a small bow. "Princess Roswen, you grow more beautiful every day."

She laughed affectionately. "I see the human world hasn't changed you at all."

"And I see you have the same impeccable taste in friends." Tennin looked at me. "How are you, Jesse? I hope you're not finding Faerie dull after living in New York."

Roswen burst out laughing. "Only if you consider being carried away by a drakkan dull."

"Or surviving a rock slide at the royal dinner," Parisa added. She lowered her voice. "Although, I believe you were less in danger of the rocks than some of the death glares you received when Prince Vaerik carried you out of there."

Tennin's eyes widened. "Do tell."

Roswen, Parisa, and Cyrene took great delight in recounting the events of last night. In their version, Lukas had vaulted over the head table and run for me as soon as the first rock fell. I thought they were embellishing the story until I met Roswen's eyes, and she nodded.

"Jesse," said a quiet female voice.

I turned to see Delphine approaching me. Her hands were clasped, and she wore a demure expression, which put me on my guard. She stopped beside Tennin, and for the first time, there was no scorn in her eyes when she looked at me.

"I wanted to thank you for what you did last night." She swallowed nervously. "You saved my life. I am sorry you were injured helping me."

I was *not* expecting those words from her. It took me a few seconds to reply. "You don't have to thank me for that. I'm glad you're okay."

She smiled timidly. "I am happy you are well, too. If you ever need anything, please ask."

"Thanks... that's very nice of you."

I was saved from figuring out what else to say when Rashari called for her friend. Delphine smiled at me, curtsied to Roswen, and went back to the group she'd arrived with.

I stared after her, not sure what to make of this transformation. Rashari's frown told me she was as confused as I was and not happy about her friend's little defection.

Roswen raised her eyebrows at me. "That was unusual."

"Not if you know her mother, Maraja," said Ellette, who had joined us. She looked at Tennin, and he shrugged good-naturedly.

"There is very little about my aunt that will surprise me." To me he said, "Delphine's father and mine are brothers. My family prefers to live at our estate in the north. Delphine's parents prefer court life."

I had been at court long enough to know the meaning in his words. Delphine's parents were courtiers, who cared only about status and gaining the favor of the royal family.

"What does Maraja have to do with it?" Roswen asked her friend.

Ellette leaned in. "I saw Delphine's brother Aslan this morning, and you know how much he hates his mother's scheming. Aslan told me Maraja was livid when they came home from the dinner last night. She's been grooming Delphine for years to be the prince's consort, and she knows that will never happen now. Everyone at the dinner saw how Vaerik looked at Jesse and the way he ran to her when she was hurt. There is no way he will take Delphine as a mate."

Happiness bubbled up inside me. I thought about kissing Lukas and what we had almost done in his bed this morning. Parisa gave me a knowing smirk, and heat crept up my neck.

"Maraja told Delphine they'll have to make the most of it," Ellette continued. "If Delphine can't be the prince's consort, she will be the consort's friend."

"Are you serious?" I shook my head as my happy buzz turned to anger. "Lukas is a person, not some object they can use to get what they want."

Roswen smiled, looking pleased by my outburst, and Parisa asked, "Why do you call him Lukas?"

"That's the name he gave me when I met him, and *no one*" – I glared at Tennin – "cared to tell me he was Prince Vaerik. I got to know him as Lukas and I keep forgetting to use his real name."

Tennin laughed. "You already know why I couldn't tell you. And look at it this way. No one can accuse you of getting close to him because of who he is."

His comment made me think of how angry Lukas had been when he'd thought I had done exactly that. Now that I'd seen what he had to deal with here, I could understand why he had reacted so strongly when he'd believed I had betrayed him.

"Speaking of getting close to Vaerik." Cyrene cocked her head sideways in Lukas's direction.

We all turned our heads to follow her gaze. I felt a flicker of irritation when I saw Rashari standing beside Lukas. It faded when he shifted, putting some space between them.

"I think Lukas can handle it," I said lightly. "Let's get this picnic set up."

It didn't take long with all of us helping to unpack the baskets and put out the food and drinks. Roswen called everyone to join us, and I smiled when Lukas detached himself from Rashari to sit by me. Conlan and Faris sat on his other side, and Kaia suddenly appeared to lie beside me.

Lunch was fun and the conversation light. No one talked about last night except when Tennin said he had come back to Faerie before the travel ban. He was staying at court for a few days before he traveled to his family home.

After the meal, Lukas stood and extended his hand to me. "Will you walk by the river with me?"

I put my hand in his and said playfully, "I would love to, Your Highness."

He pulled me to my feet so we stood mere inches from each other. "I am Lukas to you, or Vaerik if you so choose. But never Your Highness."

My stomach fluttered at the tenderness in his eyes. "A walk would be great, Lukas."

I could feel all eyes on us as we walked away from the picnic. That was something I'd have to get used to if I wanted to be with Lukas, but it was a small price to pay.

Footsteps behind us signaled that Conlan and Faris had accompanied us. They stayed back out of earshot but close enough to react to any threat. Kaia sped past us, darting in and out of the tall grass and making me smile at her antics.

"It's so peaceful by the river," I said when we were out of sight of the group and all we could hear were birds and the water lapping at the bank. "Thank you for bringing me here."

He took my hand, lacing our fingers together. "Then we'll come back soon but without bringing half the court with us."

I laughed at the trace of vexation in his voice. "Oh, come on. Roswen and her friends are fun. And we're alone now."

"Not quite." Lukas changed course and pulled me down into a large patch of calaech flowers growing along the river. Before I could utter a word, we were lying on the mossy grass and hidden from sight. Above us, the reddish blooms looked like a ring of fire against the blue sky.

Lukas rose up over me and brushed away the hair that had fallen into my face. "Now, we are alone."

My lips parted eagerly, and he did not make me wait. He brushed his mouth against mine once, twice, with agonizing slowness before he swept his tongue inside. I kissed him back fervidly as if it had been weeks, not hours, since we made out on his bed. My fingers raked through his hair, and the answering rumble in his chest made me want to roll him over and climb on top of him.

Lukas suddenly let out an "oof" and fell forward, crushing me with his weight. I wheezed as he pushed up on his hands and something landed on the ground behind him. Instead of the alarm I expected to see on his face, he was grinning.

Then he rolled off me to lie laughing in the grass with Kaia standing over him. He scratched the side of her neck, and that was all the invitation she needed to squeeze into the sliver of space between us.

I laughed and turned my face toward Lukas. "This is the third time someone has interrupted us today. Do you think the universe is sending us a message?"

"Yes. It's telling us we need to get better at hiding." He propped himself up on his elbow again and gave me a sensuous smile that promised no one would disturb us next time.

A thrill of anticipation went through me. It was probably for the best that Kaia had stopped us before things got more heated. Lukas and I couldn't have gone any further out here in the open with Conlan and Faris standing guard. The thought of them knowing what we were doing in the grass sent heat straight to my cheeks.

Lukas reached toward me and plucked something from my hair. It was a calaech flower that had broken off its stem. Holding the base of the bloom, he glided the soft petals down the side of my face and across my lips. I breathed in the flower's mild spicy fragrance, and lost myself in his warm blue eyes.

"Do you remember the morning we found you on North Brother Island?" he asked, surprising me with the shift in conversation.

I arched my eyebrows. "How could I forget?"

Lukas's eyes took on a faraway look. "When Faolin told me you were one of two hunters presumed drowned after a kelpie hunt, it felt like he had punched me in the stomach. I convinced myself it was guilt for not repaying you after you had warned us of the assassination plot. After we found you, I told myself my debt to you was repaid.

"Then the men attacked you in your apartment the following night, and I wanted to kill them for hurting you. I could no longer deny that I cared about you. Somehow, you had slipped beneath my defenses, and I never saw it coming."

I started to speak, but he pressed a finger to my lips.

"You didn't want to become Fae. It killed me to know you were hurting and that I couldn't go to you after the conversion. But at the same time, I was selfishly happy because I wouldn't have to give you up. I brought you to Unseelie, but I allowed my father and Faerie's problems to keep us apart. I won't do that again."

My throat tightened, and the only response I could come up with was, "Good."

He smiled. "In two weeks, my father and I will go to Seelie to continue the discussions about the barrier. I'll have work to do here until then, but I intend to spend part of every day with you. We can do whatever you want, but I am going to court you as you deserve."

"Is Fae courting the same as dating?" I asked a little breathlessly.

He tucked the flower he was holding into my hair. "Yes."

I bit my lip as my stomach fluttered nervously. When I opened my mouth, I couldn't stop the words that tumbled from me. "Does this make you my boyfriend? I've dated, but I've never had a boyfriend. Are boyfriends and girlfriends even a thing in Faerie?" My face flamed, and I clamped my mouth shut to stop my rambling.

Chuckling, he dipped his head to kiss me long and slow until I forgot to be embarrassed. When we finally came up for air, he said, "I am whatever you want me to be."

"Vaerik," Faris called, and there was no mistaking the laughter in his voice. It wasn't hard to guess what we were doing down here.

"Yes?" Lukas answered.

"There is a storm coming. We should head back before it hits."

I shot up to a sitting position. "A storm?"

"Not the kind you think. It's a rain storm." Lukas got to his feet unhurriedly and held out his hand to me.

"Oh." I took his hand, feeling foolish. Of course, they got rain here.

Lukas pulled me up and smirked as he brushed grass and dirt off me. He took my hand, and we walked to Faris and Conlan, who smiled knowingly at us.

"Did you enjoy your *walk*?" Conlan asked me when we drew near.

I smiled back. "Immensely."

We headed toward the group, and Lukas pointed out the dark clouds in the distance. "It's coming in from the ocean, and those storms bring the most rain. They usually hang around for a day or two and give the valley a good soaking."

Roswen and the others had also seen the approaching storm. They were packed up and ready to leave by the time we returned. Lukas's sister took in our joined hands and practically beamed at us. His father would not be so happy about us dating, but at least, one member of his family approved.

Tennin looked pleased as well, and he winked at me as he took his reins from one of the grooms. A few feet from him, Rashari stared at us with a sour expression. Whatever she'd hoped to accomplish today had not gone as she had planned. I was not at all sorry to be the cause of her disappointment.

Lukas mounted and lifted me to sit in front of him again. I leaned back against his chest, and it felt more intimate after our time alone. I sighed happily as we started home, neither of us feeling the need to fill the silence between us.

We were still a few miles from the mountain when the first raindrop hit my face. Lukas spurred his tarran into a gallop, but there was no outrunning the storm. We were both soaked to the skin and laughing by the time we made it home.

He dismounted and helped me down. "I'm sorry the rain ruined our outing," he said as he brushed dripping hair off my face.

"It didn't." I smiled up at him. "It was a perfect day."

"*Was?* It's not over yet." He took my arm, and we headed inside. "Dinner tonight?"

I shook my head. "Sorry. I think I'm having dinner with my boyfriend."

He kissed the top of my head. "Yes, you are."

17

I LOOKED DOWN at Gus's huge shadow on the water and sighed. I never thought I'd get sick of seeing the ocean, but this flight had proven me wrong. We'd left the island hours ago, and there was still no land in sight.

Closing my eyes, I focused on much more pleasant thoughts, most of them involving Lukas. The last two weeks with him had been some of the happiest of my life. We'd spent time together every day doing whatever I wanted, whether it was training, visiting town, teaching me to ride, or talking. He had refused to attend more of his father's special dinners, opting to dine alone with me in my quarters. And we ended each night making out on my couch until I thought I would combust.

While Lukas's kisses and touches left no doubt how much he wanted me, he had taken it no further than that since the morning after the royal dinner. He kept our alone time out of the bedroom, and to my eternal frustration, he went back to his quarters at the end of the night.

I wondered if this was how Fae courting worked, but I didn't have anyone to ask. Though Roswen and I were friends, there was no way I was talking to her about me wanting to have sex with her brother. I missed Violet so much, and I wished I could talk to her about this. She would know what to do.

Lukas, the king, and the Unseelie contingent had left yesterday for the meetings in Seelie. That gave me two days to figure out how to talk to him about us when he got back. If he was waiting until I was ready for sex, I had to let him know I was. Or I could jump him and show him what I wanted. I smiled to myself. The latter option sounded a lot more fun.

Gus growled, and I opened my eyes to stare at the horizon. I squinted. Was that land? Please, let it be land.

Last night as I was having my first solo dinner in weeks, Aedhna had come to tell me that today, I would take the ke'tain to the Mab desert, which happened to be on the other side of the Ellyon Sea.

Fortunately, I had a drakkan who could make the trip in six hours instead of the three days it would take by ship. Unfortunately, flying in the claws of a drakkan wasn't the most comfortable way to travel, and my whole body felt cramped from being in the same position for so long.

Half an hour later, I could make out a white land mass in the distance. At first, it looked like we were flying toward a glacier, but as the details became clearer, I realized it was huge sand dunes.

It was another twenty minutes before we reached the coastline where the water was a pale aquamarine and waves rolled against a blindingly white beach. Vegetation here was sparse except for a few clumps of grass, and the wind felt hot against my face.

The flat beach soon gave way to the desert dunes that stretched as far as the eye could see. The air turned arid and gritty, and I had to close my watery eyes against the glare of the sun off the white sand. Gus had known where to take us in the mountains, so I'd have to trust him to find the hidden ke'tain in this vast desert.

We flew for another hour before we came to a small canyon. On the canyon floor, dozens of columns of white rock rose from the ground. There was no pattern or uniformity of size to the columns, so I assumed they were natural formations. Aside from some spiny bushes, there were no signs of life in the canyon.

Gus circled the columns and found a space big enough for him to set down. We had been in the air so long I felt the landing in every one of my stiff joints. He put me down, and I fell back on the sand. I was going to need a few minutes to recover before I got to work.

"Ouch!" I scrambled to my feet and touched the back of my neck, which felt like I'd pressed a hot flat iron against it. The ground was so hot it had burned me. I crouched and held my hand a few inches above the sand. It was like hovering over a hot stove.

Standing, I surveyed my inhospitable surroundings. Aedhna sure knew how to pick places to hide her ke'tains. Now I needed to find the one I was looking for.

I walked to the nearest column. It was roughly four feet in diameter, and up close, it appeared to be made of some kind of porous rock with tiny holes in the surface. Circling it, I discovered a hole on the other side big enough for me to fit into. A faint clicking came from inside, and I took a step closer to listen.

Something moved inside the column, and I heard the unmistakable sound of claws on stone. I jumped back, my heart racing. No way was I going in there. I'd seen *Pitch Black*, and it had not ended well for those people.

I walked among the columns, making sure not to get too close to any of them. Once again, Aedhna had not been specific about the exact location of the ke'tain. All she'd said was that I would know when I was close to it. So far, my *spidey–sense* was not tingling.

I approached the two biggest columns, which I had been avoiding because they also had big holes in them. I had no desire to see what lived inside those creepy dark holes.

Keeping a wide berth, I studied the columns. There was nothing to mark them as special, but then Aedhna wouldn't have made it easy to find the ke'tain. I'd hoped the ke'tain I carried would be drawn to the other one like it had in the cave, but so far, it wasn't picking up anything. I was going to have to get closer.

I stepped up to the columns, trying to block out the scratching sounds echoing from the holes. The moment I stood directly between the columns, the ke'tain in my pocket began to vibrate softly. I didn't move as the ground rumbled and the sand in front of me sank, slowly revealing a set of stone steps disappearing into darkness.

I pulled out a laevik crystal and went down the first three steps with it held before me. It illuminated the bottom of the stairs and the floor of what looked like a tunnel.

She wouldn't have sent me here if it was too dangerous, I reminded myself. She needed me to do this for her to save Faerie, and I still had one more after today. With that encouraging thought, I descended the rest of the stairs.

The first thing I noticed when I reached the bottom was the drop in temperature. It was over one hundred degrees outside, but down here, it felt about thirty degrees cooler. The second thing I noticed was that, unlike the tunnel in the mountain cave, this one was not a natural structure. It was also much shorter. After ten feet, it opened into a low round room with a smooth stone floor.

The room was about fifteen feet in diameter with a small, plain circle etched into the center of the stone floor that was covered in a fine layer of sand. I stepped inside the room, and my hair lifted, crackling from the static electricity in the air. I was definitely in the right place.

I took the ke'tain from my pocket and walked to the center of the room. After the first step, the bottoms of my feet started to tingle, and by the time I reached the circle, the tingling had become a serious case of pins and needles that had spread to my calves.

I studied the area inside the circle and blew away the sand. It was roughly a foot wide and bore no special markings. There hadn't been any markings in the cave either, though. I held the ke'tain over it, and the stone began to pulse with energy like it had last time. Leaning down, I laid it in the center of the circle. The moment it touched the floor, I felt the energy signature of the other ke'tain, and my excitement built as I straightened and waited for the hidden ke'tain to appear.

The floor inside the circle rippled once and went still. I stared at it. Had I done something wrong?

Crouching, I reached for the ke'tain. The instant my fingers made contact, the floor began to move again and lose its color. When it was fully translucent, it was like looking into a deep well with a faint purple light at the bottom. The stone under my hand quivered, and then it sank into the floor.

"What the...?" I watched in confusion as it slowly moved toward the purple glow. Was it supposed to do that? In the cave, the other ke'tain had come to me.

The ke'tain reached the bottom and began to glow. Seconds later, a blast of energy came from the floor, knocking me back on my ass. My body went rigid as the power surged through me, and for one terrifying moment, I thought my heart would stop under the onslaught.

When I thought I couldn't take it a second longer, the power receded, leaving me limp and gasping on the floor. I wasn't sure how long I lay there before I was able to move. My limbs felt rubbery when I rolled over and pushed up onto my hands and knees. I crawled to the circle and looked down at the pulsing lights of the two ke'tains. There was nothing left for me to do but wait.

It took half an hour for me to regain the full use of my legs. I paced the room, frequently stopping to look in on the ke'tains. A few times, when I got close to the walls, I heard faint scratching inside them. I shuddered and tried not to think of what was living in there.

Looking for a distraction, I walked to a section of the floor where my boots hadn't scuffed the layer of sand. Grinning, I bent and wrote *Jesse was here* in English in the sand. If someone ever found this place many eons from now, my message would give them a mystery to puzzle over.

After what felt like hours, the blue ke'tain separated from the purple one and rose to the surface. I reached for it hesitantly and cried out when it shocked me. The pain didn't last long, but it was enough to bring tears to my eyes. I tucked the stone away in its pouch, wondering if I would be able to touch it at all when it reached full strength.

I picked up the laevik crystal I had dropped when I'd fallen and walked through the tunnel. At the base of the stairs, I spotted a narrow crevice in the wall at eye level, and I held the crystal up to it. Call it morbid curiosity or the academic in me, but I would never come back to this place and have a chance to see what kind of creature could live in this hostile ecosystem.

I let out a small scream when a black claw shot out of the crevice. It looked like a crab claw, and it made clicking sounds as it grabbed at me. My curiosity fled, and so did I. I sped up the stairs and back into the world of blinding sun and suffocating heat.

"Let's get the hell out of here," I yelled as I ran to Gus.

We were in the air, seconds later, and rising from the canyon. My heart was still pounding when he set off across the desert toward the ocean.

Less than ten minutes into the flight, I detected a faint rumbling sound over the flap of wings. I craned my neck to look around us, but all I saw was sand. Tucked against Gus's belly, I couldn't see much of the sky.

Gus dived suddenly, and my stomach lurched. The ground came up to meet us, and I squeezed my eyes shut for the impact. The crash never came, but he touched down a little less smoothly than normal.

He set me on the hot sand, and I backed up as he began digging. His strange behavior alarmed me, and I turned in a circle to see what could have caused it.

I inhaled sharply when purple and green lightning streaked across the sky. But that wasn't nearly as frightening as the monstrous sandstorm speeding toward us. The wall of sand had to be one hundred feet tall, and I could already hear the howl of the wind that drove it. It was travelling so fast it would be on us in minutes.

I spun back to Gus, who stood over a large hollow he had dug in the sand. He looked at me expectantly, and I realized he wanted me to get into the hole. I jumped in, and he settled down over me. He wrapped his leathery wings around us with his head tucked beneath one, and we waited.

The storm hit with such force it nearly pushed Gus over. He held fast as the howling wind and sand slammed into him. Some dust blew in under his wings and made me cough, but I was safe in my shelter.

The light grew dim as the storm raged on until I was nearly in darkness. I took out the laevik crystal, thankful I wasn't claustrophobic. I was more afraid of suffocating as the air got hot and stuffy. To take my mind off it, I thought about Lukas. He would be home tomorrow evening, and as soon as we were alone, I planned to let him know I wanted to be with him in every way. I loved him, and I knew he felt the same for me even if we'd never spoken the words. What were we waiting for?

I didn't realize the wind had stopped until Gus shifted above me. He grunted as he stood, and I saw the reason when he dumped two feet of sand off his wings.

I sucked in cool air as it hit me that night had fallen. I stared at the dark desert landscape in dismay. It would take us six hours to reach the island and another two to get back to Unseelie after I returned the ke'tain to the temple. If I stayed out all night, someone would notice and there'd be questions I couldn't answer.

We took off, and this time we made it to the ocean without any problems. It wasn't until we were an hour out to sea that I wondered if the storm had been caused by the joining of the two ke'tains. It had happened faster than the last one, but that could be because the ke'tain was getting stronger.

I had never been so happy to see the island. It took ten minutes for me to sneak in and return the ke'tain, and then we were on our way again. I was exhausted, but it was impossible to sleep when I still had no clue how to get past the guards at the mountain entrance. I could make myself invisible, but the guards would be suspicious when the door opened and no one was there.

The sun had cleared the horizon by the time we reached the valley. I'd already created a glamour to make us invisible, but that didn't help with the bigger problem. My stomach was in knots as I tried to figure out how to get inside the mountain without being seen.

"Next time, maybe I should hang a really long rope from my balcony."

That's it! Why hadn't I thought of that all along?

"Gus. I need you to take me to my balcony," I called, hoping he understood me as well as I thought he did.

He did. As we neared the mountain, he stayed on a straight course instead of turning toward the road where he'd picked me up. It was too early for most court occupants to be up and about, but there were people working on the grounds.

Most of the balconies looked the same from the outside, so I had to figure out which one was mine. Gus surprised me when he headed straight for one of them. Drakkans had a sharp sense of smell, but I had no idea he could detect my living space that easily.

I realized the flaw in my plan when we reached the balcony. There was no easy way for Gus to get close to the rail, and he was far too big to land there. I was trying to think of a solution when he turned and flew away in a downward arc. Several levels down, he changed direction and flew straight up the wall of rock. Before I understood what he was doing, he came abreast of my balcony and tossed me inside.

I landed facedown with my arms protecting my head. The impact knocked the wind out of me for a few seconds, and I lay there gasping for a minute. When I finally managed to stand, Gus was speeding toward the black cliffs.

I stumbled to my bedroom, kicked off my boots, and stripped. I showered away the day's grime along with some of my aches and pains, and I was half asleep by the time I left the bathroom. My hair was still damp when I crawled into bed and fell into a deep, well-earned sleep.

"Jesse," someone called.

I hurried through the short tunnel to the stairs. I placed my foot on the first step as a black claw shot out of the crevice in the wall and grabbed my shoulder. A scream tore from me, and I spun, punching the faceless creature emerging from the hole.

"*Disir!*" swore a male voice. "Jesse, it's me, Conlan."

I came awake with a start and looked up at a frowning Conlan beside my bed, sporting a red welt below his eye. "Conlan, what are you doing here?"

"You didn't answer your door, and I was concerned, so I let myself in." He touched his cheek. "I thought you might be ill, but that punch says otherwise."

I sat up, rubbing my bleary eyes. I couldn't have gotten more than a few hours of sleep, and I was bone tired. "That's what you get for coming into my room and waking me up."

"I wouldn't have if you'd answered your door." He gave me an assessing look. "It's close to midday. Why are you still in bed?"

I scowled at him. "Why are you here and not in Seelie with Lukas?"

"He asked me to come home and make sure you were okay after that storm hit this morning."

Another storm had hit here? I must have slept through it. Was it connected to the one in the desert or a separate one entirely?

"You haven't answered my question," Conlan said. "Why are you still in bed?"

I flopped back on the pillows. "What are you, the sleep police? If you must know, I couldn't sleep last night, and I didn't doze off until this morning."

Conlan's shrewd gaze swept the room and landed on the boots and clothes I'd worn yesterday and left in a pile on my floor. My mouth went dry, and I cursed myself for being so careless. If he checked them, there would be no explaining away the fact that my pockets and boots had sand in them from a desert across the ocean.

"If I'd known someone would barge into my bedroom, I would have tidied up," I quipped in a tone snarky enough to draw his attention back to me.

He arched his eyebrows. "Have you always been this grouchy in the morning?"

"Only when I don't get enough sleep."

"Then by all means, go back to sleep." He smirked. "We wouldn't want you grumpy when Vaerik returns today."

My heart leapt at the reminder I'd see Lukas in a few hours. My face must have betrayed me because Conlan chuckled softly.

"I apologize for waking you, and I'm glad you are well...if not in the best mood. I'll leave you to your rest."

"Conlan," I said as he left my room. "I'm glad I have friends like you who care about my welfare."

He stopped in the doorway and looked back at me. "Does this mean I'm still your favorite?"

I snorted a laugh. "Yes, but don't tell the others."

"Oh, they already know." He grinned and disappeared from sight.

I tossed aside the book I was trying to read, startling Kaia, who lay on the other end of my couch. Getting up from the couch, I walked to my balcony with the lamal on my heels. It had become our ritual of the last few hours as we waited for Lukas to return from Seelie. He'd told me they would be back before the evening meal, but that hour was fast approaching.

It was possible they had already arrived and his father had him tied up with something. I hadn't seen the king since Lukas had made it known to the whole court that we were dating, but I couldn't forget his words to Lukas about me the morning after the royal dinner. King Oseron would never think I was a suitable mate for his heir, and he didn't strike me as someone who gave up easily.

"Enough of this." I slapped the stone railing and turned to look at Kaia. "Let's go for a walk."

She ran inside and went straight for the door where she waited for me to pull on my shoes. I let us out, and we walked to the lift, returning the greetings from people we passed. Ever since it had become common knowledge that Lukas and I were together, I'd become a lot more popular at court.

There were some who didn't hide their resentment of my relationship with Lukas, and chief among them were Dariyah and Rashari. They were all smiles whenever he was around, but they didn't spare me their looks of loathing when I was without him. I ignored them. They would get over it eventually…or they wouldn't.

It was a beautiful day for a long walk, but I decided to keep to the grounds this time. Not in the mood to stop and chat with everyone, I choose the relative privacy of the gardens over a walk to the lake. I followed one of the many white stone paths through the extensive gardens where the trees, thick flowering shrubs, burbling fountains, and animal noises blocked out the sounds of the other people around me.

Kaia and I had been walking for a few minutes when one of the liveried elf servants making their rounds in the garden offered me a drink from the tray he carried. I sipped the cold fruit nectar as I continued to stroll and wonder how things had gone at the meetings with Seelie.

No doubt Queen Anwyn had continued her push to seal the barrier. I needed King Oseron to hold out against her long enough for me to finish the task of restoring the ke'tain's power. If they closed the barrier before that happened, no one would ever believe their solution wasn't the reason the storms had ended. And with the barrier sealed on one side, the damage to my world would be irreversible.

Weighed down by my thoughts, I suddenly felt tired despite sleeping until noon. I entered one of the many secluded alcoves, which had been designed for a romantic interlude judging by the oversized chaise. I set my drink on the small table and reclined on the chaise to rest a bit while Kaia wandered off to do her own thing.

It wasn't long before the comfortable chaise and the soothing sounds and scents of the garden lulled me into a light sleep. I could still hear the birds and people's voices, but it was as if someone had turned down the volume around me. I floated in a warm, blissful haze and dreamed of kissing Lukas among the calaech flowers by the river.

I came half-awake as a hard body lay beside me on the chaise and an arm wrapped around my waist to tug me closer. "Lukas," I murmured drowsily as warm lips pressed to mine.

I frowned. Something didn't feel right. I turned my face away from his kiss as my fuzzy brain tried to understand what was wrong.

"What is this?" demanded a harsh male voice.

My eyes flew open to find Lukas standing six feet away, staring at me with a mix of anger and confusion that pierced the fog in my head. "Lukas?" I turned my head to look at the dark-haired male lying beside me, one who I didn't remember ever seeing before.

"Get off me!" I shoved him away from me and came unsteadily to my feet. My stomach lurched at the memory of the stranger's mouth on mine, and I felt violated. I *had* been violated.

I rounded on the male who hadn't moved from the chaise. "How dare you?"

He smiled lazily. "Are we playing another one of your little games, *mi'dhu*?"

Mi'dhu, my sweet.

"Jesse." The dangerous edge in Lukas's tone had me turning back to him. That was when I saw he wasn't alone. Conlan and Kerr stood on Lukas's right, and standing on his left was Dariyah wearing an expression of smug satisfaction she didn't bother to hide from me.

"What is going on here, Jesse?" Lukas bit out. "Who is this male?"

I met his furious gaze. "I have no idea. I woke up and thought it was you beside me."

The male in question sat up. "Come now, *mi'dhu*," he wheedled.

"Don't call me that," I snapped, taking a step back. I turned to Lukas and saw a small crowd of onlookers gathering outside the alcove.

Dariyah scoffed. "You want us to believe you mistook *him* for Vaerik?"

"I don't care what *you* believe." I looked at Lukas, and pain pricked my chest at the uncertainty in his eyes.

The crowd moved in. Conlan and Kerr immediately stepped between them and Lukas, while Dariyah used the opportunity to get closer to Lukas. I narrowed my eyes on her in time to catch the conspiratorial look she shot at the male behind me. Just like that the pieces fell into place. The drink, the sudden need to lie down, the brain fog. I had been drugged. I glanced at the table only to find my glass conveniently missing.

"You!" I took a step toward Dariyah as anger boiled inside me. I was over these court games and manipulations. "You did this."

She pressed herself to Lukas's side. "I had nothing to do with your infidelity. Do not try to blame me to cover your lies."

The male on the chaise, whose name I still didn't know, stood and reached for me. Lukas moved toward him, but I was faster. My fist plowed into the male's smiling face. His eyes widened in shock before they rolled back into his head, and he dropped like a rock. I shook my head in disgust. Court faeries might be stronger in the human realm, but here, most of them were lazy and weak.

I caught the glint of pride in Lukas's eyes as I spun and stalked toward Dariyah, who was no longer smirking. Real fear filled her eyes as she cowered behind Lukas. I pointed a finger at her. "I told you once not to come at me again. This is your final warning."

"Jesse." Lukas laid a hand on my arm, and I shook it off.

I turned accusing eyes on him. "I never would have doubted you. Not for one second."

Moving past him, I found my exit blocked by our captive audience. When I looked for another way out, I found Dariyah clinging to Lukas's arm like a damsel in distress. The fact that he did not look happy about it didn't matter. For the first time in my life, I knew what it meant to see red.

I closed the distance between us, and before either of them could react, I slugged her right in her lying, spiteful mouth. The satisfaction that filled me as she went down did nothing to ease my anger, but damn, it felt good.

Turning to the gaping crowd, I growled, "Move."

This time, they scattered. I didn't look back as I stormed off. I had been so excited for Lukas to come home, and now I wanted to be as far away from him as possible.

"Jesse." Lukas's voice rang out loud and commanding. Around me, people froze as if he'd spoken to them, but I picked up my pace.

"Go away, Lukas," I called without looking back. Gasps came from nearby, and I didn't need to look to know people were scandalized over the way I'd spoken to their crown prince. I couldn't care less what they thought of me.

"Jesse, stop." There was no mistaking the warning in his tone this time. What was he going to do? Lock me up for not heeling like the pet these people thought I was to him?

I exited the gardens and turned toward the lake. I needed to work off my turbulent emotions, and I knew just the place to do it. I wasn't dressed for a hike up the hill, but going to my quarters to change wasn't an option.

I started down the grassy slope. One second, my feet were on the ground, and in the next, they were in the air as I was lifted and slung over a wide shoulder. Momentarily stunned, I didn't react at first as my captor wrapped his arm tightly around my legs and turned to walk back up the hill.

"Let me go," I yelled when my senses came back to me. I squirmed and pummeled his back with my fists to no avail.

"No," Lukas said in an unyielding voice that gave me pause. Maybe he *was* going to lock me up.

I hung stiffly over his shoulder as he entered the mountain. I expected him to put me down when we reached the lift, but he carried me all the way to the top floor. It wasn't until we were outside his door that I realized we weren't alone.

"We are not to be disturbed by anyone," Lukas ordered as he opened the door.

"And if it's the king?" Conlan asked with a note of amusement in his voice.

Lukas entered his quarters. "Especially my father," he said, shutting the door with a solid click.

"Are you done being a Neanderthal?" I demanded as he crossed the room.

"That depends. Are you ready to talk rationally?"

"Oh, that's rich coming from someone who thinks I would cheat on him, and then tosses me over his shoulder and carries me off against my will."

Lukas set me on my feet and placed his hands on my shoulders to steady me when I swayed. "I would *never* believe that of you, Jesse, and I'm sorry if my reaction made you think I doubted you. I was angry but not at you."

I pressed my lips together as I replayed the incident. "It was all a setup. They timed it so you'd come upon us and think the worst." I lifted my eyes to his. "How did you find me?"

His jaw flexed. "When I couldn't find you or Kaia, I assumed you'd gone outside. I ran into Dariyah, who told me she'd seen you enter the gardens."

Anger surged in me again. "They played us perfectly. There had to be something in the drink the servant gave me that made me sleepy."

Lukas's eyes darkened, and his fingers tightened on my shoulders. "Someone drugged you?"

"I can't prove it, but I was fine when I went outside. I drank the juice, and not long after, I had to lie down. You know what happened next."

He released a harsh breath. "The male's name is Fafnir. I got that from him before I followed you. Kerr detained him, and Faolin will get to the bottom of this. Fafnir will wish he had never touched you."

My anger abated, leaving me drained. "Will it always be like this? People scheming and trying to come between us?"

He wrapped me in his strong embrace. "No. If Dariyah was involved in this, I will have her sent away from court. For her, that would be worse than banishment. I'll make it known to all of Unseelie that the same punishment awaits anyone who dares to try something like this."

"If they do, I want five minutes alone with them first." I snaked my arms around Lukas's waist, trying to erase the memory of Fafnir's touch.

"After watching you knock out Fafnir and Dariyah, I'm not sure anyone would survive five minutes with you," he teased.

I leaned away to look up at him. "You would."

Heat flared in his eyes, and an answering fire ignited low in my belly. He smiled, and it was as if the last twenty minutes had never happened.

"I missed you," he said gruffly.

I frowned. "Were you gone? I hadn't noticed."

He brought his hands up to frame my face, and he captured my mouth in a scorching kiss that left me dizzy and boneless.

"Okay… I might have missed that," I panted.

Lukas chuckled and silenced me with his mouth as his hands slid down my body to cup my backside. He lifted me, and I eagerly wrapped my legs around him without breaking our kiss. I barely noticed he was walking until my back was pressed against the wall.

His mouth left mine, and I rested my head against the wall, intoxicated by the sensations flooding me. Every time he touched me, it was better than the last, but this felt different. There was an urgency to our kisses that said we were headed toward something and I would never be the same after.

"Look at me," he ordered roughly.

I lifted my heavy-lidded eyes to his, which were dark with desire.

"If you are not ready for this, tell me now. We will wait as long as you need to. Otherwise, I am going to take you to my bed, and we are not leaving it until I know every inch of you."

My body quivered at the promise of what was to come. This was what I wanted, but I was also a little scared. I trusted him completely, and I knew he would be a skilled lover. What if I was so bad at it that he didn't want me afterward?

"Jesse," he said in a gentler voice. "It's okay if you need more time."

I licked my kiss-swollen lips. "No. I mean I don't need more time. I want you now."

Lukas searched my face, and whatever he saw there made his lips curve into a carnal smile. His eyes took on a predatory gleam that sent my heart into an erratic rhythm. A tiny primeval part of my brain urged me to flee, but I pressed closer to him instead.

He let go of my bottom, and my legs, strong from weeks of training, held tightly around his waist. He slid his hands with tantalizing slowness up my body, his touch setting my blood on fire as his hands skimmed my ribs and along the outside curve of my breasts through my clothes. I wanted more, but his hands continued their path to my shoulders and along my arms, which were clasped around his neck. Before I knew what he intended, he had my hands imprisoned in one of his above my head.

His free hand cupped my chin and tilted it up to him. I managed a small sound before he claimed my mouth with a hungry possessiveness I'd never sensed from him before. He pressed me into the wall, and the feel of his arousal made me squirm as a hot bolt of lust went through me.

"Lukas," I whimpered against his lips, unable to verbalize what I needed.

He released my hands, and I clung to him as he carried me to his bedroom. My legs loosened around his waist when he reached the bed, and he lowered me to the floor.

I pushed up the bottom of his shirt and ran my hands over the taut lines of his stomach. Satisfaction rippled through me when he inhaled sharply and ripped the shirt off over his head. Emboldened, I kissed one of his pecs while my hands played over the hard planes of his back, and I was rewarded when a tremor went through him.

Lukas took a step back. I opened my mouth to protest, and it died on my tongue when he stripped off the rest of his clothes and stood before me in all his naked perfection. My gaze moved down his body, and I averted my eyes when I caught myself lingering on a certain part of him.

He reached out and gently turned my face toward his. "I love it when you look at me."

I swallowed hard. "Lukas... I've never been with anyone else."

"Do you want to stop?" he asked softly.

"No," I blurted. "I thought you should know in case –"

I didn't get to finish because he pulled me flush against him and bent his head to speak gruffly into my ear. "Feel how much I need you, Jesse. By the time this night is over, you will never again doubt that you are the only one I want."

He kissed me, slowly at first and then deeper until I could no longer remember why I'd been afraid. I felt drunk when he broke the kiss long enough to slip my top off over my head. His expert hands freed me from my pants, and I shivered when his warm fingers brushed against the bare skin of my stomach.

Picking me up, he placed me on the bed, and I knelt facing him. Smiling, he ran his fingers through my hair and let it fall across my shoulders.

"I don't know what I did to please the goddess, but she blessed me when she brought you into my life, Jesse James."

My throat tightened, and I choked out the words I had been holding close to my heart for so long. "I love you."

"I love you, *mi'calaech*," he said huskily. Then he lowered me to the soft coverlet and spent the whole night showing me how much.

18

———————

From my seat on the right side of the throne room, I watched Lukas speak quietly with the king, Korrigan, a male I recognized as one of the king's advisors, and a female I didn't know but who looked familiar. Their voices didn't carry to me, but their solemn faces told me the conversation was not a pleasant one.

The advisor said something, and Lukas responded with a firm shake of his head. This prompted the female to turn her head and shoot me a look of angry resentment that was so much like another's I knew immediately who she was. Dariyah's mother, Marceline. That meant the male advisor beside her was Dariyah's father, Tyrion.

I had heard Dariyah's parents' names mentioned numerous times in the week since the incident in the gardens. Word had spread quickly, and soon the entire court had been buzzing with the deliciously scandalous story. The people who didn't like Dariyah – and there were many of them – were delighted to talk about her fall from grace and speculate on how it would affect her parents' elevated positions at court.

By now, *everyone* had heard about how Lukas had run after me, thrown me over his shoulder, and carried me to his quarters. We had emerged a day and a half later and had spent every available hour together when he wasn't dealing with court business.

I was too happy to care about the rampant gossip. I spent my nights with Lukas and woke up every morning in his arms. Soon, I'd complete the job

Aedhna had given me, and the damage to both worlds would be repaired. I couldn't wait to tell Lukas everything and bring him home to visit my family.

I met Lukas's serious gaze as he crossed the room toward me. He sat beside me and leaned in to say in a low voice, "They are bringing her in now. It'll be over soon."

As he spoke, the king took his throne, and Korrigan stood behind him on his left. Dariyah's parents moved to sit opposite from us on the other side of the room. Normally, every seat would be occupied for something like this, but King Oseron had limited it to only the people involved out of consideration for his friend Tyrion. As long as the end result was that I no longer had to deal with Dariyah, I didn't care how it was done.

The door opened at the back of the room, and Dariyah entered escorted by Faolin. It was the first time I'd seen her in a week because she had been confined to her quarters. Her arrogant demeanor was gone, but she walked with her head high, her gaze straight ahead.

They stopped ten feet from the king, and she dropped into a graceful curtsy. When she rose, she lowered her eyes to the foot of the throne, and silence fell over the room as we waited for the king to speak.

"Dariyah." King Oseron said her name as if he was speaking to a misbehaving child. "I have known you your whole life, and it saddens me greatly to have you before me like this today."

I tensed at the familiarity with which he spoke to her. He didn't sound like someone about to mete out a punishment.

Lukas's hand covered mine, and I relaxed a little. He had assured me Dariyah would not get away with her actions this time, and I trusted him. I didn't have the same faith in his father, who, until now, had favored Dariyah as a potential mate for Lukas.

"Fafnir confessed his part in your scheme and provided Faolin with the name of the elf servant who gave Jesse the drink laced with menak." The king's expression changed to one of censure. "Under interrogation, the servant admitted he was also the one to slip Jesse acca berries on her first night here, making her very ill. He said you had threatened his family with banishment when you became consort if he did not carry out your bidding."

I gasped audibly. I wasn't surprised to learn Dariyah was behind the acca berry incident, but to threaten banishment to a servant if he didn't go along with her schemes was beyond cruel.

"As king, I have many responsibilities, but none are more important than protecting the welfare of every Unseelie citizen, no matter their station. Causing harm to another or using a position of power to threaten someone weaker than you are two things I cannot condone."

Dariyah appeared to shrink under his reproachful stare. Watching her, I realized that until this moment, she thought she would get off with a slap on the wrist. Her father was a close friend and advisor to the king. She had been raised to believe she was better than most and groomed to become the consort one day. I would bet she had never been punished for a single wrongdoing in her life.

King Oseron pressed his lips together as if it pained him to say what came next. "You will leave here tomorrow morning and travel to your family's estate in Galia. Henceforth, you are forbidden to return to this court."

Dariyah made a small choked sound and looked at her parents. Her father wore a grim expression, and her mother couldn't have looked more devastated if the king had sentenced Dariyah to death. Lukas was right. This was the worst possible punishment Dariyah could have been given. It didn't matter that she would live in luxury at her family estate and be able to come and go as she pleased. The one thing she wanted would be forever denied her.

"This will not sever your ties with your parents. They are free to visit you whenever they want," King Oseron told her kindly, clearly misinterpreting the reason for her distress. "Your father is needed here now, but I will understand if he and your mother wish to live with you away from court after the barrier crisis is over."

I watched Dariyah's parents for their reaction. Tyrion's expression hadn't changed, but Marceline looked decidedly uncomfortable. Based on what I'd heard about her this week, she loved her prominent status at court, and she was quick to remind people that her mate was one of the king's most trusted advisors. She was not giving that up for anyone, including her own daughter.

A wave of longing hit me. I wished I could hug my mom and tell her how lucky I was to have her as my mother. She was strong and loving, and she would do anything for her children. I couldn't have asked for a better role model.

"Have you anything to say before you leave?" the king asked Dariyah.

"No, Your Majesty," she answered in a subdued voice. Dariyah wasn't stupid. She knew nothing she said now would change his ruling.

He nodded once. "You have the remainder of today to pack and make your farewells. You may go."

It was over. Faolin escorted Dariyah out of the room, and the king rose from his throne to speak to her parents. Lukas stood and held out a hand to me. I took it, and we quietly left the room.

"I'm glad that's done," I said as we walked to Lukas's quarters. "How far away is Galia?"

He chuckled. "Far enough. I suspect Dariyah will be spending more time in the human realm once travel is permitted again."

My heart leapt. "When do you think that will happen?"

"I can't say for certain, but our tests have shown a slight strengthening in the barrier since all portals were closed."

I stopped abruptly to stare at him. "You are only telling me this now?"

"I learned of it this morning. We are waiting on Seelie's tests results." He smiled ruefully. "I should not have mentioned it until after they confirmed it."

"I'm glad you did." Elated, I resumed walking. The ke'tains were starting to repair the barrier. I wished more than anything I could tell Lukas the truth, but there was no way around the gag Aedhna had put on me. It felt wrong to start our life together on a lie, and I prayed that when all this was done, she would finally allow me to confide in him.

Queen Anwyn was due in four days for more discussions. Lukas had told me that they'd made little progress during the meetings in Seelie because the queen was still set on the idea of sealing the barrier for good. She couldn't do it alone so they were at an impasse.

"What would you like to do today?" he asked when we neared the lift.

"You're free?" The king had been pulling Lukas back into meetings the last few days to prepare for Seelie's visit, so I had expected to not see him until dinner.

"I'm all yours for the rest of the day."

"In that case..." I lowered my voice so the guards couldn't hear me. "Can we stay in?"

His answering smile made my breath quicken. "I think we can arrange that."

I winced at the pain in my wrist and shoulder as I dressed after my shower. It served me right for agreeing to spar with Parisa. That girl was a savage when you put a weapon in her hands, and she handled the staff like it was a part of her. Thank God I wasn't practicing with blades, or she would have sliced me to ribbons.

I never thought the day would come when I'd wish I was training with Faolin. He and the others were busy preparing for Seelie's visit tomorrow, which had left me training alone until Parisa had offered to show me some of her techniques. It was no wonder she was Roswen's head of security.

Kaia growled softly and jumped off my bed to run out of the bedroom.

Seconds later, the bell rang. I smiled at my reflection in the mirror and hurried after her. Lukas had said he'd be here for dinner, but his work must have finished up early. No matter how many times I told him he didn't have to ring the bell, he did it anyway. It was all a part of the courting thing.

I swung the door open, and my smile froze at the sight of the male standing there. "Your Majesty."

"Hello, Jesse," King Oseron said pleasantly. "May I come in?"

I came to my senses and moved aside for him. "Of course."

He entered my quarters, and I noticed two of his personal guards standing behind him. They took up positions in the hallway, leaving me alone with the king of Unseelie.

"Would you like to sit?" I discreetly rubbed my damp palms on my pants. I could think of only one reason why he would visit me, and it wasn't good.

In the weeks since Lukas and I had become an official couple and he'd informed his father he was done with the matchmaking, the king had been very quiet on the matter. I hadn't believed he would give up that easily, but whenever I mentioned it to Lukas, he told me not to worry and that he would handle his father.

I trusted Lukas, but the fact that I hadn't spoken to his parents since we got together told me the king was not happy about our relationship. Now, he was here to take matters into his own hands.

"Yes. Let us sit," he said warmly. He took one of the large chairs and looked around him. "I have not visited private quarters on this level since before I was king. That was so very long ago."

I perched on the edge of the couch, too anxious to relax. My throat had gone dry, and my stomach was twisted in knots.

If he noticed my emotional state, he did not show it. "Are you comfortable here?"

"Yes."

"Faerie is very different from your old home in the human realm," he noted. "You must miss it."

I nodded. "I mostly miss my family."

"The separation must be difficult for you. I am sorry about that."

I heard the sincerity in his voice, and I managed a small smile. "I'm hoping I'll be able to see them soon."

"I hope that as well." He settled back in his chair. "I have often wished I could visit that world. When I was young, I loved to travel. I would have been happy to do it my whole life if I had not become king. Did you know I was not the original heir to the throne?"

My mouth fell open at that revelation. "No."

He smiled at my reaction. "I am not surprised. It was so long ago that most have either forgotten it or were born after that time in our history." He touched the round eyranth medallion, which was only worn by the Unseelie king or queen. "Queen Belisande, the last monarch, is my mother, and she ruled Unseelie for eight hundred years. When she stepped down, my older brother Onagh became king."

I didn't say anything as my mind raced. Had Onagh died? What other reason was there for the current king to take his brother's place on the throne?

"My brother had been groomed and trained his whole life to be king, and he did everything our mother asked of him but one," the king went on. "Before she abdicated, she selected a high-born female to be his consort, but Onagh refused her. He was in love with a non-royal named Asherah, and he took her as his mate and consort."

My stomach bunched into a knot because I knew where this story was headed. I said nothing, and he continued.

"Seven years after they mated, Asherah gave birth to a daughter, and Unseelie celebrated our new heir." King Oseron sighed. "Fae infants are most vulnerable in their first three months, so she was under constant watch. Sadly, she did not thrive and died before she was a month old."

"Oh, no." I covered my mouth.

"It took fourteen years for Asherah to conceive again. She bore another girl, and this baby lived. We soon discovered, however, that the child's magic was weak. A son came seven years later, and like his sister, his magic was not strong enough for him to be the next monarch.

"People soon began to worry because the strength of Unseelie depends on the strength of its leader. Onagh was strong, but he and Asherah were unable to provide a successor, which made our future uncertain. Fear spread, and there were calls for other high-born royals to challenge for the throne. There were some who were only too willing to wear the crown, but those challenges would have fractured Unseelie. We could not allow that to happen."

"So Onagh abdicated to you?" I asked.

He nodded solemnly. "I ascended to the throne, and Onagh and his family went to live with our parents in one of the royal retreats. They prefer life away from court and have been happy there to this day.

"I vowed I would not make the same mistake my brother had. Though I loved another, I took the female my mother had chosen for Onagh, as my consort. Maurelle and I worked hard for years to bring back stability to Unseelie. Here at court, there were still rumblings from those who had wanted to challenge for the throne. It was not until Aedhna blessed us with a strong, healthy son that the people's faith in their monarchy was fully restored."

King Oseron stood. "Come with me."

I followed him out to the balcony where he looked out at the valley for a long moment before he said, "It is beautiful, is it not?"

"Yes. It still takes my breath every time I see it."

He turned to give me a warm smile that reached his eyes. "I love Unseelie almost as much as I love my children, and I would do anything in my power to protect them both. From Vaerik's accounts of you, you would do no less for your family."

"Yes." I straightened my shoulders and tried to prepare myself for what was to come. He was going to order me to stay away from Lukas. Or maybe he planned to send me away to some distant town like he had with Dariyah.

He took one of my hands in his. "You have so many qualities I admire, Jesse, not the least of which are your courage and fortitude. I doubt there are many who could handle all you have been through with the same poise. I can see why my son loves you, and I can see that you love him."

My chest squeezed painfully, and I whispered, "Yes."

"As a father, I want more than anything for my children to be happy. As the king, I must also do what is best for Unseelie." His eyes grew sad. "I have seen firsthand what happens when someone of weaker blood is chosen as consort. The future of Unseelie depends on a powerful line of succession. Vaerik's magic is strong, but you are not Fae-born. There are those who will never accept you as consort and might challenge Vaerik because of it. If that does not happen, there is the high risk of you bearing weak heirs as Onagh and Asherah did."

The pain in my chest spread through me and formed a hard, cold lump in my stomach. I had no argument to make because he was right. I could not change the circumstances of my birth, and I'd experienced enough disdain and condescension to know he spoke the truth about some people not accepting me. They were nice enough to me now that I was with Lukas, but what would they be like when I officially became his mate and the future consort?

"What are you going to do?" My voice nearly broke on the last word, but I held the emotion in.

"Nothing," he answered softly. "Vaerik loves you, and he will choose you as his mate. I cannot prevent that any more than my mother could stop Onagh from choosing Asherah."

"I don't understand. Why did you come to see me if not to break us up?"

King Oseron looked at the valley and back to me. I saw the answer in his eyes before he said the words. "The only person who can stop Vaerik from making a choice that could destroy his future is you. I came here to tell you about Onagh in the hope that history will not repeat itself."

I leaned against the rail, feeling as weak as the day Lukas had exposed me to iron. However, this time the chain was around my neck and pressing against my chest. The king wasn't going to force me away from Lukas. He was asking me to walk away from the man I loved.

I felt a light squeeze on my hand, reminding me the king still held it. I looked up into his troubled eyes.

"You deserve to be happy after all you have endured, and I wish there was another way. The last thing I want is to hurt Vaerik or you."

He released my hand and walked away. When the door closed, I sank to the floor, wrapped my arms around my knees, and let the tears come. I couldn't do it. I couldn't give up Lukas and watch him take someone else as his mate.

When Aedhna's arms encircled me, I curled against her like a little girl. She stroked my hair and hummed a soft melody as I cried until I had no tears left.

"I can take the pain away," she offered gently.

My throat was so raw it hurt to speak. "Can you make it so Lukas and I can stay together?"

She shook her head. "That is a decision you and he must make."

"But the king said there's no other choice."

"Oseron made sacrifices for his people, and his fear of unrest drives him to expect the same from his son. He forgets there is more to being a ruler than the ability to produce strong progeny. Onagh did not have the right strength to lead, but Oseron did. Vaerik possesses it, too."

Hope kindled in my chest, and I lifted my head to look at her. "Does that mean no one would challenge him for the throne if I was his consort?"

She wiped away the wetness on my cheeks. "It means he could rise to the challenge as you rose to the one I gave you. You did not believe you were up to the tasks, yet here we are on the eve of the final one."

My stomach fluttered with a mix of excitement and fear. "It's tomorrow?"

"Yes." She stood. "Come. I must prepare you."

I followed her inside where she gave me instructions as she had the first two times. Then she removed all evidence of my emotional meltdown and left a second before the door opened and Lukas came in.

"All ready for tomorrow?" I asked, surprised by how composed I sounded when I was anything but.

"Yes." He came over to join me on the couch. "I'm sorry I've left you on your own the last few days. I won't see much of you while Seelie is here."

I moved over to snuggle against his side. "I understand. Hopefully, soon you won't need to have any more of these meetings with Seelie."

"I hope so, too." He wrapped an arm around me. "How do you feel about a change of scenery after Seelie leaves? I have a private retreat in the Daerig Mountains where we could get away from all of this for a week."

"That sounds amazing." The thought of going away with him made me instantly feel lighter.

Lukas leaned in to press a light kiss to my mouth. "I'll tell Faolin to prepare for a trip in three days."

I smiled at him and rested my head in the crook of his shoulder. Aedhna had given me a sliver of hope about my future with him, and time away from court was exactly what I needed to figure things out. I understood the king's concerns, but I wasn't giving up my prince. Not without a fight.

I hurried along the tunnel that wound in a wide circle down into the rock beneath the temple. It led to a room where portals were created by people coming to the island, and I hoped there were no visitors until I got out of the tunnel. There wasn't room here for someone to pass without bumping into me.

I reached the portal room, which was nothing more than a cave with sconces high on the walls. It looked like a dead end until I walked to the left side and found the slab of rock that Aedhna had told me about. It blended with the wall unless you were standing beside it, and behind it was a space so narrow I wasn't sure I would fit inside.

Squeezing behind the slab, I had to contort my body to get through the cramped space. Six feet in, it opened up into a tiny cave with water dribbling down the sides. I sniffed the air and picked up the smell of seaweed and brine. I was under the ocean.

I went to the dry section of wall and touched the ke'tain to it. The wall rippled, and the outline of a doorway appeared in it with steps leading down into the darkness. I shook my head in wonder. No matter how many times I witnessed magic like this, I would never get used to it.

Here I go. I took out my laevik crystal and descended the long flight of stairs. At the bottom, wind whistled, and there was enough light to see without my crystal. I was in what appeared to be a tall rock crevice inside a mountain. The air was warm, so I ruled out the Duergar Mountains, but I was definitely no longer on the island.

I walked toward a sliver of daylight up ahead. A few minutes later, I emerged in a place so beautiful I wasn't sure I could find the words to do it justice.

I was in a small green valley beneath a sky so blue, it hurt my eyes to look at it after the gloom of the tunnel. The valley was ringed with snow-capped mountains, but here it was warm and smelled of flowers, fruit, and sunshine.

Shielding my eyes, I looked toward a lake sparkling in the sun, and I did a double take at the sight of a small herd of kelpies grazing beside it. Closer to me, a pair of fluffy, white hamas romped in the grass, and a nixie began to sing from her perch in a tree.

I turned in a half circle to take in my surroundings and stopped when my gaze landed on a pristine, white stone building with thick columns that reminded me of an ancient Greek temple. I walked toward the building, and as I drew closer, I could make out some of the interior through the wide arched entrance. The building appeared to have only one room with tall windows and a raised dais at the far end on which stood a throne.

A ninny drew my gaze back to the lake where a white kelpie stood slightly apart from the rest, looking at me. As I walked toward it, I remembered the night in the East River when I'd nearly been drowned by a kelpie before I'd grabbed the goddess stone from her mane. That night felt like a decade ago.

The kelpie walked out to meet me when I neared the lake. It was smaller than the rest of the herd, which told me it was still a foal. For a second, I wondered if it might be the same foal that had lain beside me and kept me warm through the night on North Brother Island. There was no way to know, but wouldn't that be something?

I stripped down to my underthings and walked to the water with the ke'tain in my hand and the foal beside me. At the water's edge, I grabbed a handful of the kelpie's mane, and we entered the water. I held on while the kelpie swam to the center of the lake.

The lake wasn't wide, but it was deep, and the water was so clear I could see all the way to the bottom. We stopped at the deepest part of the lake, and far below was a dim yellow glow.

I looked at the kelpie. "I'm ready if you are."

He sank below the surface, and I sucked in a deep breath before he took me down with him. It was a reflex action because Aedhna had said the goddess stone would help me breathe in this lake. Even so, I held the air in my lungs as long as I could before I had to let it out.

Down, down we went into the eerie underwater world where schools of colorful fishes darted away from us. Once, I thought I saw the flash of a large silver tail, but whatever it was disappeared before I got a better look.

The ke'tain began to pulse, and it grew stronger the deeper we went. By the time we reached the bottom, it was emitting a soft blue glow, and it thrummed with so much energy my fingers started to feel numb.

The yellow glow came from below the surface of the soft mud. I let go of the kelpie, and it swam away as if it knew what was about to happen. I wished I could go with it because I had a feeling this last pairing was going to hurt a lot.

Bracing myself, I lowered my hand until it hovered a few inches above the glow. Then I laid the ke'tain on top of the one in the mud.

A bright green flash lit up the lake bed a second before a shockwave slammed into me. Excruciating pain enveloped me, and it felt like every bone in my body had been crushed. I welcomed the blessed oblivion that followed.

When I came to, I was floating on my back on the surface of the lake with the kelpie beside me. My body no longer hurt, and I moved my arms and legs to make sure everything worked. I stared at the sky, still dazed. That blast should have killed me.

It took me a minute to notice the strange glow surrounding me. I looked down and sucked in a mouthful of water. The entire lake glowed bright green, and I could no longer see the bottom or the ke'tain. I hoped that meant it was doing what it was supposed to, and I hadn't accidently turned the lake radioactive.

The shockwave hadn't killed me, but I felt weaker, and I soon grew tired treading water. The kelpie must have sensed it because he nudged me until I wrapped an arm around his neck. Eventually, I nodded off.

His ninny woke me, and the first thing I noticed was that the green glow was gone except for one spot far below. I watched it until it faded away to a soft blue.

The kelpie turned his head toward me in a silent question. I let go of his neck and took hold of his mane. "Let's go."

This time, I didn't take in a gulp of air first. We dived down, and my eyes were too focused on the blue glow to enjoy the view. My feet hit the bottom, and I wasted no time reaching for the ke'tain without stopping to wonder if it might be too powerful for me to touch now.

A painful tingle rushed from my fingertips to my shoulder, and I almost dropped the ke'tain. I held the stone tightly in my fist until the pain lessened to a dull ache. It was then that I felt a faint vibration at the back of my head. I reached up with my other hand to touch the quivering goddess stone. It had to be somehow absorbing the power from the ke'tain to protect me.

I turned to where I'd left the kelpie, and let out a small scream. Floating a dozen feet away from me were two sirens. Their long hair swirled around them to below their waist where their tails began, and their large eyes resembled those of a Disney princess. Their features were beautiful but so sharp they looked cruel. One had silver hair, and the other's hair was a darker shade of red than mine.

The red-haired siren motioned at my braid with her webbed hand. Realizing what she wanted, I unraveled my braid so my hair flowed free like theirs. I didn't move when she swam over and ran her fingers through my hair. She spoke to her friend, and it sounded like dolphin speech. Her friend responded, and I shivered when I saw pointed teeth like those of a shark.

The kelpie was suddenly beside me even though neither of the sirens had shown aggression. I didn't know if he was being protective or possessive, but his bared teeth were enough to send the sirens racing away through the water.

We rose to the surface, and on the way back to the shore, I couldn't stop thinking about the sirens' behavior. It wasn't until my feet touched the rocky bottom that it occurred to me the sirens had never seen a red-haired faerie. They must have wondered what the heck this creature was with red hair and the legs of a land walker. I smiled to myself. I couldn't wait to tell Mom and Dad about this.

The other kelpies watched us curiously when we walked out of the lake. For the first time since coming to Faerie, I wished I had a camera. No one back home would ever believe me when I told them I'd seen a whole herd of the creatures.

I picked up my coat to tuck the ke'tain away in the pocket, and I was overcome with euphoria. *I did it.* The ke'tain had been restored, and now Faerie could heal itself.

Throwing up my arms, I let out a whoop and laughed when some of the kelpies snorted and neighed in response. They were probably snickering at the crazy female dancing in her underwear, but I didn't care.

I waited a few minutes for the sun to dry my skin before I got dressed. My hair was still damp when I braided it again. It would dry by the time I got back to the temple.

The kelpie foal walked up to me when I was fully dressed. I stroked his nose, and he sniffed my face.

"I guess this is goodbye. Thank you for helping me." I gave him one last pat and turned to walk back to the crevice in the rock. I stopped when I saw the white building, torn between my desire to see inside and my pressing need to return the ke'tain to the temple. Need won, and I entered the crevice, leaving the valley behind.

Ten minutes later, I silently descended the stairs into the main room of the temple. My eyes and ears were alert for any movement from the guards as I crossed the room and passed through the wards around the altar. Standing behind it, I took a few slow breaths to calm my nerves. This didn't get any less nerve-racking no matter how often I did it. Thank God this was the last time.

Casting another glance at the guards, I pushed out the illusion surrounding me to blanket the altar. This was my least favorite part, and I never forgot how close I'd come to getting caught the first time I'd done it.

I took the ke'tain from my pocket. It shocked me again, but I was ready for it. I reached out and deftly switched it with the fake one on the altar.

Noises came from the antechamber above. I froze as two blond males appeared in the entrance and started down the stairs. One I'd never seen before. The other male I didn't know by name, but I'd recognize him anywhere. He was one of Queen Anwyn's personal guards.

My heart began to pound. What was he doing here? He should be with the queen in Unseelie.

I withdrew my shaking hand and pressed it to my chest as the two males approached the altar and stopped outside the wards. My eyes were fixed on the queen's guard, so I didn't miss the way his gaze moved over the altar and the space around it. To the guards behind him, his stance was relaxed, but they didn't see the calculating gleam in his eyes when he studied the ke'tain. He was up to something.

Surely, Queen Anwyn wouldn't attempt to steal the ke'tain again. If the barrier failed, Seelie would be destroyed along with the rest of Faerie.

I glanced toward the two Seelie guards on duty. One look at their faces told me they were as surprised as I was to see the queen's guard here.

My gaze slid to the other newcomer, who was looking reverently at the ke'tain without a hint of suspicious behavior. Maybe he and the queen's guard weren't together, and they had merely arrived at the same time.

Maybe I was so on edge I was making something out of nothing. Tennin had told me once that it would take four or five strong court faeries to get past the ward that protected the ke'tain. And that was before more powerful wards had been added after the ke'tain was returned. I was able to pass through them only because of my goddess stone.

The queen's guard lifted his eyes from the altar and looked straight at the spot where I stood. His mouth barely moved when he said, "Well?"

I tensed. Was he talking to me?

"It will work," the other male murmured quietly. "It has to be an older one and the hide must be fresh. The scales will fall off after a day, and it will lose its magic."

Hide? Scales? Bile rose in my throat. Drakkans were impervious to wards. Gus was able to come and go through the powerful ward Lukas had put on my apartment, and he'd only been a young drakkan.

What if someone managed to kill an older drakkan, wrapped themselves in the hide, and were able to walk right past the wards? They'd have to knock out the guards first, but then the ke'tain would be theirs for the taking.

One of the Unseelie guards on duty shifted restlessly, his watchful eyes trained on the two visitors, who had been standing in front of the altar a little too long. The queen's guard smiled, and the sight made my stomach lurch. He turned away from the altar and ascended the stairs as if he hadn't a care. Ten seconds later, his co-conspirator followed him.

I looked down at the ke'tain and pressed my lips together. I was not going to give Queen Anwyn another chance to destroy everything I loved.

I needed to warn the king about what she was up to, and I had to do it without revealing how I'd come by this information. I'd worry about that part later. First, I had to take the ke'tain and hide it somewhere safe – like that hidden cave in the mountains. It was a long trip, but no one would ever find it there.

I extended the hand that held the replica, and I had to pull it back because it was shaking. I took a few deep, calming breaths. *Get it together, Jesse.*

My hand was steady when I tried again, but I was distracted by what had happened, and I forgot to brace myself for the jolt when I touched the ke'tain. Hot needles of pain shot from my fingertips to my shoulder, and I barely managed to bite back a cry.

For a second, I lost all feeling in my hand, long enough for the ke'tain to slip from my grip. It landed in its spot on the altar with a soft thump that might as well have been a gunshot in the tomblike room.

The four guards came to life and rushed toward the altar. I barely breathed as the Unseelie guards scanned one side of the altar, and the Seelie guards checked the other side.

"Do you see anything?" one of the Unseelie guards asked.

"No," replied a Seelie guard. "You all heard the noise?"

The second Unseelie guard craned his neck, trying to peer around the altar. "Yes, but I can see nothing out of place."

"I do not like this." The first Unseelie guard looked at the two from Seelie. He was the same guard I'd seen watching the visitors like a hawk, and he did not try to hide his suspicion. "I am going to send for Korrigan."

My body went cold, and sweat broke out on my upper lip. If Korrigan came, so would Bauchan, the queen's head of security. More guards would accompany them, and I'd be trapped here. The glamour made me invisible, but they could still touch me. If they took down the wards to investigate, I was done for.

"Then I will send for Bauchan," said one of the Seelie guards, who looked anything but happy about it. He followed the Unseelie guard who had already started up the stairs.

I looked at the ke'tain as indecision flooded me. If I left it here, I risked Queen Anwyn getting her hands on it. If I tried to take it, I risked getting caught.

I bit the inside of my cheek. The chances of the queen's men managing to hunt and kill an adult drakkan by tomorrow were slim. But the odds of me being imprisoned if I was caught were much higher. If that happened, I wouldn't be able to protect the ke'tain from the queen.

Resigned, I quietly returned the fake ke'tain to my pocket. I kept a close eye on the two remaining guards, who stood facing the altar, as I crept around it. I had to hug the wall to sneak past the Unseelie guard, and I was afraid to breathe until I was halfway up the stairs. In the antechamber, I paused to listen for the presence of others. I released a shaky breath. That had been too close.

I jumped at a sound to my left, and I whirled to see a stone-faced Korrigan stepping out of the tunnel. Behind him were the guard who had been on temple duty and several others I couldn't see. Damn it. They'd gotten here fast, which meant the Seelie people would arrive any second. It was about to get crowded in here, and I needed to get out before that happened.

More people spilled from the tunnel, and at the front was a blond male with a glacial expression. I saw why the Seelie guards had been so afraid to summon Queen Anwyn's head of security. Up close, he was terrifying. I suddenly felt like a mouse dropped into a cage with a cobra.

I darted to the steps that led outside. In my haste, I brushed against the bowl of crystals atop the pedestal in the center of the room. The glass bowl rocked, and the crystals clinked against the sides.

I took two more steps before someone slammed into me, taking me down hard to the cold stone floor. Black dots swam before my eyes as I was rolled roughly onto my back and found myself looking up at Faolin's shocked face.

19

FAOLIN STARED AT ME like he thought his eyes were playing tricks on him. "Jesse?"

"What treachery is this?" Bauchan towered over us. He held a sword in one hand and looked seconds away from plunging it into me. My heart banged painfully against my ribs, and I could barely hear over the roaring in my ears.

"Stay your hand, Bauchan," ordered a commanding voice. Korrigan strode forward. He didn't hold a weapon, but his glare could have sliced me to ribbons. "Jesse James, what are you doing in the temple?"

Bauchan didn't wait for me to answer. "She was cloaked by a glamour. No one is strong enough to do that here, least of all someone like her."

Korrigan nodded gravely, and his eyes pinned me. "You will tell us how you came to the island and how you were able to hide yourself from us."

I swallowed dryly and croaked, "A drakkan brought me."

"Impossible," Bauchan spat. "Drakkans cannot be tamed."

I looked at Faolin, who still held me down. "Gus. He's outside."

Comprehension flashed in his eyes, and he lifted his head to look at his father. "It was the young drakkan she rescued in the human realm. The same one that carried her off the day we went to town."

One of Korrigan's men ran outside and returned wearing a stunned expression. "She speaks the truth."

Korrigan's lips formed a thin line, and I could tell he didn't believe me. "Did this drakkan somehow make you invisible?"

I glanced at Faolin and back to his father. "No."

"What then?" Bauchan demanded.

"I can't tell you."

"Insolence!" Bauchan loomed over me. "I have ways to make you speak."

Faolin shot to his feet and blocked Bauchan as he reached for me. "You will not touch her," he growled.

Bauchan stood chest-to-chest with him. "You have no authority here. On this island, she is subject to a different rule of law that is neither Seelie nor Unseelie. I have the right to interrogate her about her crime."

"There is no evidence yet of a crime," Faolin replied, undaunted.

"No crime?" Bauchan laughed harshly. "She entered the goddess's temple cloaked in magic. I can think of only one reason someone would do that."

Faolin jabbed a finger at me where I lay on the floor. "Do you forget who she is? Jesse nearly died returning the ke'tain to Faerie. She is the last one who would attempt to steal it. And there is no law against cloaking yourself with magic in the temple."

"There is no law because it should be impossible," Bauchan shouted.

"Enough." Korrigan's voice echoed off the stone walls. "Bauchan is correct. No one, not even the king or queen, is strong enough to create an illusion like that in this temple. I do not know of any object that can do it, but that does not mean one does not exist."

Bauchan gave a triumphant nod and waved one of his men over. "Search her."

I shrank away from them as horrific images of being strip-searched flashed through my mind.

Faolin blocked the guard with his arm. "*I* will search her." He leaned down and took my hands, helping me to my feet. His eyes flicked to mine before he began to methodically pat me down and check my pockets. I held my breath when he reached into my coat pocket that held the cloth sack containing the fake ke'tain. He drew the sack out slowly and frowned at me as he loosened the string and tipped the plain blue stone onto his palm.

"What is it?" Korrigan asked.

"Nothing but a stone." Faolin passed it to his father and resumed searching me.

Korrigan studied the stone. "I feel no magic in it." He gave the stone to one of his men who carried it to Bauchan.

Bauchan rubbed the stone and examined it like it would suddenly reveal its secrets. When it didn't do as he wished, he turned his accusing eyes on me again. "Why do you have this? What does it do?"

"It doesn't do anything," I answered, relieved when my voice didn't shake. "It's a pretty stone I found. I've been saving it for my brother."

Faolin straightened and held up my laevik crystal. "This is all she has on her."

His father took the crystal. "There is nothing special about laevik."

"You missed something," Bauchan accused Faolin. "Remove her clothes."

"No!" I pulled the edges of my coat together as Faolin stepped protectively in front of me.

Korrigan scowled at Bauchan. "She will be taken to Unseelie where a female guard can perform a search in private."

"Do you expect me to trust you with this investigation?" Bauchan said with a sneer.

"Do *not* question my integrity." Korrigan seemed to grow in size, and his eyes took on a dangerous light. "You are welcome to have one of your females assist in the search, and you may participate in the interrogation. But Jesse is Unseelie, which puts her under my authority."

Bauchan's jaw hardened. "When her guilt is proven, Seelie will demand justice."

"If she is guilty of a crime, the king will demand it as well." Korrigan looked at Faolin. "Take her to a holding cell. Bauchan and I will join you after we inspect the temple wards."

Faolin nodded and took my arm in a firm grip. Wordlessly, he led me down the tunnel I'd used earlier. In the room below, he placed his free hand against the wall, and a portal opened.

We stepped through and emerged in a small room I'd never seen before. It was devoid of furnishings, and it had a narrow archway that opened to a hallway. We navigated a series of similar hallways until we came to a winding flight of stairs.

I shivered when we descended the stairs. The level with the holding cells was deep below the ground, and with every step, I conjured images of dungeons and torture chambers. It didn't help that Faolin was silent the entire time, leaving me to wonder what horrors waited for me.

We reached the bottom level, and my pulse kicked up a notch when he steered me down another hallway that was more of a tunnel. He stopped us at a solid wood door and opened it to reveal a long room with a crude table, two chairs, and three doors along the inner wall. Each door had a small window at eye level with a purple crystal above it.

Faolin pressed his hand to the middle of the first door, and it swung inward. The cell was nothing more than a room carved out of stone with a sleeping niche containing a pallet. The thought of being alone in the cold barren cell made me yank against Faolin's hold when he started inside. I was no match for his strength, and he pulled me into the room.

"Faolin, I –"

He spun and gripped my shoulders, his hard eyes searching mine. "We don't have much time. If I am going to help you, you have to be honest with me. What were you doing at the temple?"

I opened my mouth, but nothing came out. Desperation clawed at me. "I...can't."

"Do you understand the trouble you are in?" His fingers dug into my shoulders. "You used magic no one should possess to sneak into the goddess's temple. You have to explain it and prove you were not there to steal the ke'tain as Bauchan claims. I will do what I can for you, but you have to trust me."

Tears of frustration stung my eyes. "I do trust you. I want to tell you, but I can't."

"What is stopping you?"

I tried to say her name, but my mouth refused to form the word. I wanted to scream. I'd done everything Aedhna had asked of me. Why couldn't I speak of it now?

Faolin's head tipped back, and he frowned at me. "You are physically unable to say it?"

I gave a jerky nod as relief flooded me.

"You can't say who or what did this to you?"

I shook my head.

He released me and stepped back. "Did this person or thing force you to go to the temple?"

"No," I answered hoarsely.

His eyes widened at that admission. "You freely went to the island and entered the temple, but something prevents you from speaking of it."

"Yes."

He raked his fingers through his short hair. "I don't have to tell you how bad this is. Tensions are high, and everyone is on edge about the storms and the fate of our world. You could not have chosen a worse time to do this."

"I didn't choose the time." I wished I could tell him I'd done it for Faerie and my world, but the truth was locked inside me.

Faolin's head came up. "So, it is someone and not something who is doing this to you?"

I pressed my lips together and nodded again.

Muffled voices came from the hallway, and my heart began to race. I looked at Faolin, unable to hide my fear. What would Korrigan and Bauchan do when their interrogation got nothing from me? I didn't know if Korrigan would resort to torture, but Bauchan wouldn't hesitate to do it. I'd seen it in his eyes when he'd threatened me at the temple. He'd enjoy it.

"I will not let them harm you," Faolin vowed fiercely. "Vaerik will kill anyone who dares."

My chest tightened. What would Lukas say when he found out what I'd done? He'd protect me, but would he feel the same about me knowing I had deceived him? The thought of losing his trust scared me more than anything Korrigan or Bauchan could do to me.

The outer door opened. Through the open cell door, I watched Korrigan enter, followed by Bauchan and two females. One of the females was an Unseelie guard named Rossa I'd seen in the training room on multiple occasions. The other, I assumed, was Seelie.

Korrigan cast a somber glance at me and turned to Rossa. "You and Alva will do a thorough search of Jesse's clothing. Remove every item and check for jewelry or other objects on her body. If you find anything, call to us."

"Yes, Korrigan." Rossa's wide eyes met mine as she and Alva entered the cell. I could only imagine what was going through her mind at seeing me down here.

Faolin walked out, closing the door behind him. The back of his head was visible through the small window when he took up a position outside the door to make sure no one looked inside.

"Please, remove your coat and hand it to me," Rossa said with an apologetic look.

I complied without speaking. The sooner I got through this, the better.

She went over every inch of the coat before she passed it to Alva, who did the same. Next went my boots, pants, and top, until I was left standing in my underwear. I'd undressed around other girls in the school locker room plenty of times, so I wasn't embarrassed by that. It was the thought of being naked and groped like a new prison inmate that brought heat to my cheeks.

I bit down on my lip and stared ahead with all the dignity I could muster as I removed my underwear, and the two females ran their hands over my body. They made quick work of it, and Alva looked as sorry as Rossa to put me through the humiliating experience.

When Rossa unraveled my braid to check my hair, I felt a moment of panic. But as it had before, the goddess stone hid itself from detection.

"You may dress," she said at last. She and Alva faced the door while I hastily pulled on my clothes. Then she walked to the door and said, "We are done."

The door swung open on Korrigan and Bauchan's expectant faces. Faolin's expression was unreadable as he waited for Rossa to speak.

"We found nothing," she informed them.

Bauchan looked at Alva, who murmured in agreement. I couldn't tell if it was anger or disappointment in his eyes, but he was not happy.

"Thank you. You may leave," Korrigan told them.

Rossa tossed me a sympathetic look before she and Alva walked out, leaving me alone with Faolin, Korrigan, and Bauchan. I stood in the center of my cell, dreading what was to come.

Korrigan folded his arms across his chest. "Are you ready to tell us how you cloaked yourself in the temple?"

"I can't."

Bauchan's lip curled. "Can't or won't?"

"Why were you at the temple?" Korrigan asked.

"I can't tell you that either." I clasped my hands together and sent a silent plea to Faolin to not share what I'd told him. It would only raise more questions I couldn't answer.

Korrigan caught the look I gave his son and addressed Faolin. "Did she confess to you while you were alone?"

"No, Father."

"Do you know what I think?" Bauchan held up the blue stone Faolin had taken from me in the temple. "This is the same size and shape as the ke'tain. You intended to steal the ke'tain and put this in its place."

Korrigan looked at him like he'd lost his mind. "Even if she could somehow make it look like the ke'tain, it would not give off the same power signature. No one would mistake it for the real thing."

"She entered the temple undetected. Who knows what she can do?" Bauchan retorted.

"I would *never* steal the ke'tain," I said vehemently.

Bauchan barked a laugh. "We should take your word on that? Your occupation in the human realm was hunting faeries, was it not? Perhaps you brought your hatred of us with you into your new life, and you seek to destroy our world."

"Do you actually hear yourself?" Anger replaced my fear. How dare he, of all people, preach to me about hate and dishonesty? "The last time the ke'tain was stolen, it hurt both worlds, and I almost lost my family. If anyone wants to keep the ke'tain safe, it's me." I held his cold gaze defiantly. "I was human when it was stolen. Maybe you need to look a little closer to home for the real thief."

For a moment, no one said a word. I had pretty much accused Seelie of stealing the ke'tain, and I braced myself for the fallout.

Bauchan's eyes took on a predatory gleam right before he turned away from me to look at Korrigan. "This is getting us nowhere. There is only one way to learn what she is hiding from us."

Faolin stepped forward. "No."

"It is an acceptable interrogation technique," Bauchan said casually.

"For enemies," Faolin argued. He looked at his father. "You cannot permit this."

My stomach roiled, and I swallowed back the nausea trying to rise. They were talking about torturing me. I took several breaths to ward off the dizziness that threatened.

Korrigan rubbed his jaw. "I do not like it, but it may be our only option. Jesse says she did not intend to steal the ke'tain, but she refuses to tell us why or how she entered the temple. That makes her a potential threat to the ke'tain and to Unseelie."

Faolin spoke through gritted teeth. "Vaerik will never allow it."

"I answer to the king," his father reminded him. "It is my duty to investigate all possible security risks, no matter who is involved."

Bauchan wore a thin smile. "It is settled then. Let us do this and be done with it."

A cold sweat broke out all over my body when Korrigan crossed the room to a spot out of my sight. Before I could imagine what kinds of torture devices he was getting, Faolin entered the cell and took my arm to lead me to one of the chairs in the outer room. His grim expression did nothing to ease the fear clawing at my insides.

Korrigan joined us, carrying what looked like medieval manacles made of dark metal. Pea-sized white stones were embedded into the cuffs that were connected by a thick chain. He set them on the table with an ominous clunk. "Do you know what this is?" he asked, taking the chair across from me.

I shook my head, afraid my voice would come out as a squeak.

"This is a dannakin. The metal was forged in drakkan fire and these" – he pointed at the white stones – "are pieces of drakkan bone. It locks around the wrists like shackles, and it forces the wearer to truthfully answer any question they are asked."

I cleared my throat. "How does it do that?"

Bauchan walked over, one corner of his mouth turned up. "If you lie or refuse to answer the question, the dannakin sends drakkan fire into your body. The longer you hold out, the worse it gets. It doesn't leave physical damage, but the pain is excruciating. I have seen aged warriors scream and cry while wearing it. Some soiled themselves."

I felt the blood drain from my face. "That's barbaric."

Korrigan nodded. "It is. We have not used the dannakin here in many years."

"But you're going to use it on me?" I asked weakly.

"That is up to you." He laid the device on the table. "I will offer you the same choice I have given others who came before you. Speak the truth willingly, or wear the dannakin."

He didn't want to use the device on me, I saw that in his eyes. But he would. I couldn't stop my body from shaking because there was no getting out of this one.

"I wish I could tell you what you want to know, but I can't."

I didn't realize Faolin's hand was on my shoulder until his fingers flexed. "Father, don't do this."

"It is the only way. You may leave if you do not wish to witness it."

"I will stay," Faolin bit out. He released my shoulder and moved around the table to where he could see my face. "Answer as honestly as you can, Jesse."

I refused to look at Bauchan as Korrigan fitted each cuff of the dannakin around my wrists and locked them in place. My breaths were coming in fast, and I was in danger of hyperventilating by the time he finished.

He sat back in his chair with his hands clasped on the table. "Jesse James, how did you get to the island today?"

I unclenched my teeth. "A drakkan flew me there."

Nothing happened, and he nodded. Since they already knew about Gus, he must have asked that question to test it.

"How did you cloak yourself when you entered the temple?" Bauchan asked.

"I created a glamour," I answered honestly as Faolin had instructed.

Korrigan stepped in. "How did you create the glamour?"

"I –" My fear mounted, and every muscle in my body tensed. "I can't tell you that."

I squeezed my eyes shut and waited for the fire to consume me, but none came. Cracking open my eyes, I saw Korrigan's frown, Bauchan's scowl, and Faolin's relief.

"Why is it not working?" Bauchan demanded.

"It is working," Faolin told him. "She said she can't tell us how she did it, not that she won't."

Korrigan eyed me closely. "Why can't you tell us?"

I shook my head helplessly.

Bauchan cut in. "Did you go to the temple to steal the ke'tain?"

"No," I said easily because it was the truth.

His look of surprise when the dannakin didn't react was followed by a glower. "Then why did you go to the temple?"

"I can't tell you that either."

He slapped a hand on the table, making me jump. "This interrogation is a farce. That dannakin does not work."

"We can test it on you if you'd like," Faolin said dryly.

Ignoring him, Bauchan fixed me with a calculating look that sent a cold shiver down my spine. "How did you survive the conversion?"

"What does that have to do with this line of questions?" Faolin asked.

"It has everything to do with it," Bauchan said, not taking his eyes from mine. "No human her age has ever survived the process, and I am not the only one who has wondered what makes her unique. I believe whatever she used in the conversion is helping her now."

Faolin looked at me, and I could see his mind working as he started to fit the pieces together.

I opened my mouth and knew immediately that Aedhna had not blocked me from talking about my conversion or my goddess stone. There was no way I could tell Queen Anwyn's head of security about it. If Queen Anwyn learned of my goddess stone, she'd try to take it or use me to get what she wanted.

I closed my mouth and tried to steel myself for the pain, but nothing could have prepared me for what came next.

My fingers twitched as a painful prickling sensation began. It intensified and grew hotter until I had to grit my teeth against the searing pain.

"Answer the question, and it will stop," Korrigan said.

I shook my head and tried to stand, but I was paralyzed. I could do nothing as the heat raced up my arms and spread through my body, setting my bones on fire. I screamed.

"Answer me," Bauchan shouted.

There was no end to the agony as the fire filled my chest and threatened to burn my heart to a blackened lump. It consumed my lungs until I couldn't breathe, and darkness crowded my vision.

Please, make it stop, I begged to the only one who could help me now.

Something light pressed against my chest, and blessed cold poured into me. It wasn't enough to douse the flames, but it lessened their intensity and let me breathe again. I remembered Aedhna's touch doing the same during my conversion, and I opened my eyes, expecting to see her there. The only sign of her presence was the weight of her cool hand on me.

I let my head fall forward. *Thank you.*

"That is enough." Faolin's angry voice echoed off the walls.

"It is not enough until she tells us what we want to know," Bauchan shot back.

Dimly, I was aware of someone touching the manacles. There was a click, and then the fire receded from my body, leaving me a hollow burned-out husk.

"If she has not spoken by now, she won't," Korrigan said. Was that a note of admiration in his voice?

I lifted my head to look at him, but he wore the same serious expression as before. My gaze moved to Faolin, who looked as furious as I'd ever seen him.

"Are you okay?" Faolin asked me.

I tried to shrug, but my body from the neck down did not want to move for me. "Ask me in an hour," I slurred.

The room started to tilt, and Faolin caught me as I fell sideways off the chair. He picked me up and carried me into the cell where he laid me on the sleeping pallet. I heard Bauchan and Korrigan arguing, but it sounded like a long way off.

"You never cease to amaze me," Faolin said in a low voice.

I gave him a crooked smile. "I knew you liked me."

He huffed a laugh. "Rest. I will be outside."

The door clicked shut. I tried to concentrate on the conversation in the other room, but my head felt like it was full of cotton. I guess that happened when you were cooked from the inside out by drakkan fire.

I hadn't lain there long when the din of voices on the other side of the door rose suddenly, and a very pissed-off Lukas demanded, "Where is she?"

The door to the cell flew open. There was no time to worry about how angry he was before he was standing over me, his furious eyes taking me in.

"Lukas," I rasped.

He sat beside me and brushed away the damp hair plastered to my face. "I'm so sorry, Jesse. What they did to you was unforgiveable."

"She was caught committing a crime against Faerie and refuses to confess. She deserves much worse than what she received," Bauchan said from somewhere behind him.

"Get him out of here," Lukas barked over his shoulder.

"I will leave, but I will be back," Bauchan said coldly. "Seelie will demand justice even if you do not."

Lukas turned back to me. "Do you trust me, Jesse?"

"With my life," I whispered.

His thumb stroked my jaw. "Then you have to tell me what you were doing out there so I can defend you against these false charges."

"They're not all false," I said hoarsely. "I did use a glamour to hide myself, but I swear on my life that I did nothing wrong. I would never do anything to hurt you or Faerie."

"I believe you, but my father and Queen Anwyn won't be satisfied with your word," he warned. "She is already demanding that you be banished."

I tried to get up, but he pressed me back gently. "I will never let that happen."

Faolin appeared behind Lukas. "Father and Bauchan have gone to speak with the king and queen. There are guards posted in the hallway, but we are alone in here for now."

"By alone, he means all of us," Conlan called from the outer room.

"They will return soon," Faolin told us. His meaning was clear. We didn't have long to talk.

"Can I sit up?" I asked Lukas, whose hand was still on my chest.

He stood and helped me to a sitting position. I was still weak from the dannakin, but it felt better to be upright. The first thing I saw was Conlan, Faris, Kerr, and Iian standing outside the cell, looking as serious as I'd ever seen them. I didn't need any of them to tell me how much trouble I was in.

"It's the goddess stone," Faolin said, drawing all eyes to him. "You used it to cloak yourself in the temple. It's why you refused to answer Bauchan's last question."

I folded my hands in my lap. "Yes."

"Is the stone preventing you from telling us why you were there?" he asked.

I started to say no and stopped. Until that moment, I'd assumed Aedhna had put some kind of glamour on me, but she didn't need one. I had a vague recollection of her touching the stone in my hair the first time we met in the temple.

"Jesse?" Lukas pressed.

"Yes, it is." I met his confused eyes. "I never wanted to keep this a secret from you, but I couldn't say anything. Please, believe me."

He took my hand in his. "I do."

I let out a breath as a weight lifted from my chest. As long as I had his trust, I could get through this.

"Faolin said Gus flew you to the island. How did that happen?" Lukas asked. "Does it have anything to do with the first time he did it?"

"Yes."

Faolin moved closer. "How many times have you flown with the drakkan?"

I avoided his sharp gaze. "A few."

Conlan whistled. "From bounty hunter to drakkan rider."

"Let's discuss the drakkan later." Lukas tugged on my hand to make me look at him. "My father and Queen Anwyn will demand answers from you. Can you tell us anything we can use in your defense?"

"Nothing that will satisfy them," I replied.

He sighed. "Then there is only one thing for us to do. We have to tell my father about the goddess stone. He'll understand your reluctance to share such a secret with Seelie, and he will believe you meant no harm to Faerie. Aedhna would not bestow her blessing on someone unworthy of it.

"I agree," Faolin said. "You are the first goddess-blessed faerie. The king will never banish you."

I looked between him and Lukas. "What about Queen Anwyn? She won't let this go."

Lukas squeezed my hand. "Let us worry about her."

A loud rap sounded on the outer door, and Kerr went to answer it. He came back frowning. "Vaerik, your father has requested you join them. Bauchan and the queen are demanding that "the prisoner" not get special treatment." He looked at me. "Sorry, Jesse."

"She is in a cell, and they used the dannakin on her," Faris growled, sounding angrier than I'd ever heard him. "How is that special treatment?"

Kerr shook his head. "The king has ordered us all to leave the cells. The guards will remain outside."

Dread coiled in my stomach at the thought of being alone in a cell below ground. The king might not banish me, but he could keep me locked up down here for days or weeks.

Lukas wrapped me in his arms. "I'll be back after I speak to my father. It may take a few hours to get him alone if he's with the queen."

I nodded against his chest, not trusting myself to speak.

He tilted my face up to his and kissed me so sweetly it made my chest ache. Without words he told me he loved me and promised that everything would be okay. I didn't want to let him go, but I dropped my arms to my sides when he stood. The sooner he left, the sooner he could return.

Faolin shut the cell door behind them, and the click of the lock replayed in my head for several minutes after they'd gone. It wasn't until it stopped that I remembered the vital piece of information I'd forgotten to tell them. I had to let the king know what I'd seen and overheard at the temple. Seelie was going to try to steal the ke'tain again, and I was the only one who knew about it.

I ran to the cell door and shouted through the window. If the guards posted in the hallway heard me, they ignored my calls. I finally gave up and lay on the pallet to wait for Lukas's return. When the oppressive silence of the room pressed down on me, I sang the lyrics of some of my favorite songs to keep it at bay.

At least two hours had passed before the outside door opened. I rolled off the pallet and ran to the window, but my gut tightened at the sight of a smiling Rashari on the other side.

"What do you want?" I looked from her to the guard who stood near the outer door, averting his eyes from us. It didn't surprise me that she could bribe or coerce her way in here.

Her smile widened. "I came to personally thank you for getting rid of all the pesky obstacles in my way. You have outdone yourself."

I crossed my arms. "What are you talking about?"

"Let's see." She started counting on her fingers. "First, you took Delphine out of the running for consort, although she was never much competition. Then you had Dariyah banished from court. That was quite the feat." Her eyes gleamed with satisfaction. "And now, you have removed the last person between me and my future as consort. You."

I let out a peal of laughter. "Happy to burst your bubble. I'm not going anywhere."

"Aren't you? No one is saying what crime you committed, but it must be grievous indeed for them to stop the meetings and lock Vaerik's little play-thing in a cell. I heard Queen Anwyn is demanding you be banished and that King Oseron is going to agree to it. What do you say to that?"

"I say you shouldn't believe everything you hear." I smiled secretively, knowing it would aggravate her more than anything I could say.

She sneered. "If you think Vaerik will protect you, think again. He might be fond of you, but he will want nothing to do with you after this."

I could have told her Lukas had already come to see me, and he might be, at this very moment, giving the king proof of my innocence. I chose to let her crow over her false victory. She'd learn the truth soon enough.

Rashari's expression soured at my lack of reaction. "I have always been the king's favorite to be Vaerik's consort, and now it will happen just as I planned." She flicked her long hair over her shoulder. "If somehow you manage to avoid banishment, you'll never go near Vaerik again. I will see you married off to a male in a distant city, and you will be forbidden to show your face at court."

"You might want to put those plans on hold." I gave her a bored look. "Now, if you don't mind, I'd like to go back to my nap."

She gnashed her teeth. "You should know I always get what I want in the end. I have ways of making things work out in my favor."

Whirling away from me, she stalked to the outer door and flung it open. The guard followed her, and I called to him.

"I need to speak to Prince Vaerik. It's urgent."

He didn't stop. "The prince is with the king and not to be disturbed."

I flattened my hands against the cell door. "Then get Korrigan, please."

The guard looked back at me with contempt. "Prisoners do not make requests. Korrigan will come here in his own time."

"Tell him I want to confess," I yelled desperately, but the guard stepped out and let the door close without another word.

I jerked awake and stared at the stone ceiling above me. It took a moment to remember where I was and why. I must have dozed off but how long ago? There was no way to tell down here.

A soft scraping sound came from the other room. I slid off the pallet and went to peer through the window, expecting to see the guard. The room was empty.

"Hello?" I called.

The answering silence sent a small shiver through me. Something didn't feel right. I rubbed my arms through my coat. Where was Lukas? He should have come back by now.

The door to the hallway opened, and I instinctively took a step back. Two blond males entered the room, and my blood turned to ice when I saw their faces. They were Seelie royal guards, and they should not be here.

One of them was named Aibel. I knew this because he had been at Teg's one night, and Orend Teg had pointed him out to me. I didn't know the name of the second one, but I'd never forget him. I'd watched him create a portal to Seelie from inside Davian's penthouse. And he had waylaid me outside a grocery store to warn me to stay away from Prince Rhys.

I backed up until I was against the wall. How did Seelie guards get in here? Where were Korrigan's guards?

Aibel glanced dispassionately at me before he went to work on the cell door. I looked frantically around the room, but there was nothing I could use to defend myself. Not that I had any hope of fighting off two royal guards.

I groped for my goddess stone. If I could make myself invisible, maybe I could slip past them. I needed to calm down and focus before they –

The cell door opened. There was no time to react as Aibel crossed the cell in several quick strides and pinned me against the wall with one hand over my mouth. Terror-fueled adrenaline coursed through me, but it was no match for his strength.

He spun me around until I was facing the door with him behind me. I saw the other guard filling the doorway as Aibel's arm came around my throat, cutting off my air.

I clawed at his arm, but it was no use. The edges of the room started to darken, and tiny pinpricks of light floated before my eyes. He was going to kill me.

A sob welled in my chest as the darkness closed in. Lukas's face flashed through my mind, and it was the last thing I saw before the room disappeared for good.

20

———————

I ROLLED ONTO my side with a groan. My body felt stiff, and I had a killer headache. The last time I'd ached this much was after I'd been stupid enough to spar with Parisa.

Wincing, I cracked open my eyes. It took a moment for the room to come into focus and another few seconds for me to register I wasn't in the cell anymore.

I jolted upright and groaned again at the sharp pain in my skull as it all came back to me. Two of Queen Anwyn's guards had knocked me out and brought me here to this unfamiliar room. That could mean only one thing. I was in Seelie.

The room spun a little when I stood, and I had to steady myself before I could take in my surroundings. I was in a circular room with a wooden floor, white walls, and no furnishings except for the thin pallet I'd been lying on. The room was lit by the natural light from four narrow windows.

I went to one of the windows, which had no glass, and looked down at a wide river far below. On the other side of the river was a forest that went on for miles. Through the opposite window I saw spires, turrets, and the white stone walls of what had to be the Seelie palace. The position of the sun told me it was late morning, which meant I'd been here at least half a day.

The door opened behind me, and I spun to see Aibel enter with the other guard who had helped abduct me. Behind them came Queen Anwyn in a pale green dress and a jeweled diadem. She stopped a foot inside the door and smiled at me, but it wasn't enough to melt the ice in her eyes.

245

"You are awake at last," she said with a note of irritation, as if my lack of consciousness had been my fault. "Welcome to Seelie."

I crossed my arms. "Why am I here?"

She smoothed an invisible wrinkle in her sleeve. "I have heard so much about you, Jesse James, and I thought it was time you and I talked face-to-face."

Her guards had broken into a secured part of the Unseelie court and kidnapped me. What could be so urgent that she would have them take such a risk?

My stomach plummeted. She'd found out that my parents had their memories back.

No, that wasn't possible. They'd been in hiding since before I came to Faerie, and Lukas had assured me no one knew about his island. Even if she suspected the truth, she couldn't get to them.

I lifted my chin defiantly. "Prince Vaerik will know you took me, and he'll come for me."

Queen Anwyn laughed. "No one is coming for you. By now, the entire Unseelie court thinks you escaped and fled to the human realm."

"Vaerik won't believe that." Lukas knew I'd never leave him that way, especially not when he'd gone to speak to his father on my behalf.

"Aibel and Conard are very good at what they do." She cast a fond look at her two guards. "And they had a little inside help from someone. She was more than happy to have you out of the way."

"Rashari." I curled my hands into fists. I knew she was desperate to become consort, but to help Seelie kidnap me? She'd be lucky if Lukas didn't kill her himself when he found out what she'd done.

Aibel nodded. "She was quite helpful. She even provided a witness who saw you create the portal."

"I do hope you like your accommodations." Queen Anwyn waved a hand at the room. "The view from up here is lovely, and you have the whole tower to yourself for the duration of your stay."

I refrained from asking how long that stay would be. My gut churned at the thought of how this was going to end for me, and I hoped my face didn't give away how scared I was.

"What will Rhys think of you kidnapping me and keeping me prisoner?" If the time I'd spent with him had told me anything, it was that he was a good person despite having been raised by her. He considered me a friend, and he'd be angry about what she'd done to me.

Her mouth tightened for a second. "*Prince* Rhys has gone to one of my retreats for an extended stay. I see no need to include him in this unpleasant business, and you will be long gone before he comes home. He will never know you were here."

I shivered and hugged myself tighter at the words *long gone*. "Why exactly am I here?"

"Right to the point. I like that. Although, from everything I've heard about you, I thought you would have already guessed the reason for your visit." Her disdainful gaze swept over the length of me. "I want to know why you were in the temple yesterday and what magic you used to cloak yourself."

Something flickered in her eyes, an urgency not reflected in her voice. She hadn't accused me of trying to steal the ke'tain. She was more interested in the why and when details of my visit to the temple.

Suddenly, it all made sense, and I understood Bauchan's reaction when they caught me and the rush to kidnap me. He knew one of his men had been at the temple, which meant he also knew I had to have seen and over-heard the plot to use drakkan hide to get past the temple wards. They couldn't risk me sharing that information with Unseelie, so they'd taken me before I could talk.

Aibel stepped forward, and I noticed for the first time that he had some-thing in his hands. I thought it was another dannakin until he held it up and revealed a circlet made of the same metal and embedded with bits of drakkan bone.

A fresh wave of fear shot through me, and I backed away. Conard caught me and dragged me backward. Cold metal clamped around my wrists, and he yanked my arms high above my head to fasten the shackles to a hook bolted into the stone wall. He gripped my head and forced me to be still while Aibel fitted the circlet snugly on me.

"A traditional dannakin did not work on you, so we must use a different technique." Queen Anwyn walked over to stand two feet from me. "My people have experimented with creating a more effective version that I am told makes the old dannakin feel almost pleasant. One taste of it and you will beg to tell me what I want to know. Feel free to scream. No one will hear you up here."

The two guards stepped away from me. "It is ready," Aibel said to her.

She tapped her chin with one slender finger. "Bauchan is still in Unseelie, so I will pick up where he left off. Let us begin with the last question he asked you. How did you survive your conversion?"

I pressed my lips together and gripped the chain between my shackles. *It's only pain,* I chanted over and over in my head as the metal band around my head grew warmer. *You're strong, Jesse. You can get through —*

A scream tore from me when flames engulfed my head. I thrashed in agony as my skin blistered and my hair shriveled. The smell of burnt flesh and hair filled my nose and throat until I could no longer breathe.

Aedhna, please, I silently screamed because my charred lips were no longer capable of forming words.

Her cool hand touched my forehead, and the fire lessened like it had the last time. The pain was still there but bearable, and I could draw air into my lungs.

As suddenly as it had started, the fire was gone. I hung from the shackles with my chin resting on my chest and tears pouring down my cheeks. My arms hurt from the strain, but I couldn't summon the strength to stand tall and take the weight off them.

A hand cupped my chin and lifted my head. I opened my eyes and met the queen's icy gaze. She looked equal parts angry and curious as she studied my face before she let my head fall forward.

"Fascinating. That is quite impressive." She tapped a foot on the floor. "I should tell you it only gets worse with each treatment. You may as well answer my questions now and save yourself the pain. Eventually, you will break, and I will get what I want. I always do."

I knew in that moment I was not leaving here alive. Even if I gave her what she wanted, she couldn't let me go after kidnapping and torturing me. Worse, she might figure out a way to use me and my goddess stone against the people I loved. I didn't know what her endgame was, but I'd die before I gave her that kind of power.

It took a superhuman effort to lift my head and several tries before I was able to utter, "You can't break me."

I had the brief satisfaction of watching Queen Anwyn's composure slip before she smiled and said, "Let's try this again."

Then I knew nothing but pain.

My shivering woke me. I opened my dry swollen eyes and stared into the darkness as I carefully unfurled my stiff body from its fetal position on the cold floor. Everything hurt, even my eyelashes, and my throat was so raw and parched I could barely swallow.

I groaned when I finally managed to roll onto my back. Panting, I rested while I took stock of my body. My clothes were soaked with sweat that made them stick to me, and the pungent odor of urine surrounded me. I grimaced at the realization that I had wet myself, and I was still wearing my soiled pants.

My teeth chattered. The room was so cold I was sure I'd see my own breath if there'd been any light to see by. I forced myself to my hands and knees and crawled around searching for the pallet I'd woken up on before. My fingers brushed against rough fabric, and I fell on top of the meager pallet. It didn't protect me from the cold breezes coming through the windows, but at least it was a barrier between me and the icy floor.

I curled into a ball and distracted myself with thoughts of Lukas. I knew he was out there searching for me, but did he know where to look? Would he fall for the lies and believe I had fled on my own, or would he know Seelie was behind my disappearance? And even if he did suspect Seelie, what could he do about it without proof of their involvement? Hadn't they gotten away with the ke'tain theft for that same reason?

My mind shifted to much less pleasant thoughts, and I let out an involuntary whimper at the memories that assailed me. I had no idea how long Queen Anwyn and her men had used the dannakin on me, only that it was Aedhna's cool hand that had kept me from going insane from the pain. What I didn't understand was why Aedhna had allowed this to happen to me when one appearance from her would have stopped it. Was it some kind of test to see if they would break me?

They hadn't. I would never forget the look of rage on the queen's face when she realized no amount of pain would make me give up my secrets. She had screamed at me and spittle had flown from her mouth as she ranted and threatened to destroy everything I cared about. Even her two guards had stared at her like she'd gone insane.

Despite my discomfort, I slept again. The next time I opened my eyes, the faint outline of the sky was visible through the windows. I stayed where I was, miserable and cold, while the day broke and the morning light slowly filled the room.

It wasn't until I heard the scrape of the door that I rolled over to see who had entered my prison. I expected the queen and her guards, but it was a dark-haired female in a plain dress like the ones the female elves wore in Unseelie. She came up short when she saw me watching her, causing the guard that accompanied her to run into her back.

"I have brought fresh clothes for you." She held up the bundle in her hands.

"Thanks," I rasped and followed it with a burning cough. My throat felt like I'd gargled with broken glass.

She set the bundle on the floor and fled without another word. The guard followed her, and the door closed with a loud click.

I let out a breath, grateful they'd left me to change without an audience. Standing, I went to pick up the clothes. My body still hurt, but I was able to undress without much difficulty. I made a face as I tossed my damp pants away from me, and I sighed when I donned the clean, dry clothes. The air in the room was warmer, and it was a small relief to finally stop shivering.

The door opened again, and I couldn't stop my body from recoiling when Bauchan entered carrying a pair of shackles. Queen Anwyn had taken delight in telling me how good her head of security was at making people talk, and what a pity it was that he'd needed to stay in Unseelie to keep up appearances.

"Hold out your arms, and do not try anything," he ordered. What did he think I was going to do? I had no weapon and barely enough strength to keep from swaying on my feet.

I did as he said, and he shackled my hands in front of me. Taking my arm in his bruising grip, he marched me out of the room and down the tower's winding stairs. We left the tower and navigated a maze of hallways that all looked the same to me. Every one of them had a white floor that resembled marble, white walls, and wooden doors. Occasionally, we passed a small table holding a vase of white flowers. The only color came from the glimpses of sky and trees through the windows we passed.

We stopped at a set of double doors with a guard on either side. Bauchan didn't spare the guards a look as he opened one of the doors and shoved me inside. It was a large living area done mainly in white with some splashes of color in the tapestries on the walls and in the rugs on the floors. Large windows gave a panoramic view of the river and beyond.

The room had a feminine feel to it, and I didn't have to wait long to see its owner. A door opened, and Queen Anwyn entered wearing a long blue gown that trailed the floor and a small jeweled diadem that caught the light as she moved. Unlike me, she looked well rested and fresh, and her face practically glowed with health and beauty.

She saw me and smiled as if she'd hadn't spent hours torturing me yesterday. "Jesse, you are a marvel. Anyone else would be a mindless lump after that interrogation, and yet here you are."

I didn't respond. If that bothered her, she didn't show it. She reclined on a chaise and motioned to Bauchan, who pushed me forward and forced me down onto a chair across from her. He stayed behind me, out of my sight but close enough for me to feel his threatening presence.

"Bauchan brought me the news that King Oseron believes you are hiding somewhere in the human realm. Prince Vaerik and his guard are going there today to search for you." Queen Anwyn paused to let that news sink in. "No one is coming to save you. The sooner you accept that, the sooner we can move on to more important things."

I folded my trembling hands in my lap. "Like you stealing the ke'tain again?"

She had said enough during my torture session to make it clear why I was here. If I was going to be subjected to more of that, I was determined to get answers to the questions that had plagued me for months. Everyone in Faerie had to know or suspect by now that she was behind the theft, but no one had evidence to bring against her.

Queen Anwyn didn't bother to deny it. "Yes."

"Why?" I implored. "You saw what happened when the ke'tain was taken from Faerie. Why would you want to do that to your own world?"

Her mouth twisted. "It was never my intention to harm my world. I took the ke'tain to save Faerie."

I shook my head. "That makes no sense. You had to know that removing something so powerful from Faerie would upset the balance of magic between the two worlds."

"Of course, I knew that," she snapped. "The ke'tain was only supposed to be in the human realm long enough to cause minor instability. Then my men would recover it and return it to its rightful place. Our mistake was including humans in our plan. We will not do that again."

"I don't understand," I said more confused than ever.

"My men took the ke'tain to a human known for selling valuable Fae objects. His job was to keep it safe until another human named Davian arranged to buy it from him. In turn, Davian would return it to me." She huffed in irritation. "It would have worked out well had the first human not lost the ke'tain."

"I know all of that. What I don't understand is why you wanted to make the barrier unstable."

She scowled at my interruption, and for a moment, I thought she wasn't going to answer me. Her actions had caused so much harm, and people had died. I'd nearly died, and I deserved to know why.

"I have never understood the fascination faeries have for your world." Her lip curled. "It's dirty and contaminated, and humans are so frail and prone to diseases. After my son was born, I knew the only way to protect him and his future was to cut off all contact with your world. I warned Oseron that this filth might one day spread to our world, but he dismissed my concerns. I cannot seal the barrier alone, and Unseelie has refused to do it.

"When Rhys came to me and said he wanted to explore the human world, I knew I had to take matters into my own hands. I had the ke'tain taken from

Faerie to show how fragile the balance of magic is and to prove Faerie is not safe as long as the barrier is open. I will do anything to protect my son and my world."

You mean my brother. I bit my lip to keep myself from saying those words to her. Anyone else might believe her act as the doting mother and selfless monarch, but I knew what she was. And as the missing pieces began to fall into place, I realized her true motive for taking the ke'tain. She did want to coerce Unseelie into closing the barrier, but not for the good of Faerie.

Twenty years ago, she'd taken a human child, secretly made him Fae, and passed him off as her son and heir. When he announced he was going to the human world, she knew there was a risk, however small, of someone discovering his real identity, and she would do whatever she could to keep her secret safe.

What I still didn't know was *why* she had stolen my brother. She didn't hide her revulsion of humans. Why would she convert one and raise him as her own child? What was I missing?

"That brings us to our current dilemma. After all that has happened, Unseelie is still unconvinced we must close the barrier. And now they insist it is healing faster than expected." Queen Anwyn sat up and fixed me with an accusing stare as if she somehow knew I was behind that. "The only way to change their minds is to take the ke'tain and force their hand."

"You can't do that." I tried to stand, but Bauchan's hand clamped on my shoulder, roughly pushing me down into the chair.

"Don't you see what will happen if you take it out of Faerie again?" I asked her. I thought about everything I'd done to restore the ke'tain's power. It had pulled energy from the other ke'tains, and I didn't know if they had enough power in them to do that again so soon without weakening them too much.

She looked at me like I was a simpleton. "The ke'tain will stay in our world. I don't need to change the balance of magic this time because people already know what could happen. Their fear will drive them to do what needs to be done."

"They won't close the barrier if they think the ke'tain was taken from Faerie," I said.

She nodded, looking pleased with herself. "That is why it will be found along with the thief. We were going to pick a random person from Unseelie and make it look like they were the culprit. That was until your timely capture in the temple. Your mysterious ability to get past the temple wards and your unwillingness to explain it make you the perfect suspect. Add to that your escape from the cells, and no one will believe you are innocent. I could not have planned it better myself."

A sour taste filled my mouth because she was right. It didn't matter if Lukas believed in me or if he told his father about my goddess stone. The evidence against me was damning. Not that it would matter to me because I'd be dead. There was no way Queen Anwyn would let me leave Seelie alive knowing what I did.

I lifted my chin, refusing to show her my fear. "Is that why you had me brought to your quarters? You wanted to tell me about your plans and gloat?"

"I do not gloat." Piqued, she stood so she could look down at me. "I told you all of this so you would know you have nothing to gain by not cooperating with me. Whether it happens today or in a week, I will have the ke'tain in my possession. How you spend your last days *does* depend on your cooperation."

She smiled at her head of security behind me. "Bauchan has creative ways of extracting information. If you wish to die with all of your body parts intact, you will tell me what I want to know."

I swallowed convulsively as cold spread through me. It was one thing to endure the dannakin, which didn't cause any real physical damage. I could not hold out against the kind of torture she was talking about.

A door opened on the right side of the room, and I started as Queen Anwyn turned that way. I followed her gaze and gasped when Prince Rhys strode into the room.

"Mother, I know you asked me to stay at the mountain house, but I –"

The prince stopped walking so fast he nearly tripped. His stunned eyes met mine before they went to Bauchan and then the queen. "Mother, what is going on? Why is Jesse here?"

Before anyone could speak, he took a few more steps into the room and caught sight of my shackled hands. His nostrils flared, and he started toward me. "What is the meaning of this?"

Queen Anwyn moved with surprising speed to intercept him. "Rhys, what are you doing home?"

"I think my question is more important, don't you?" He pointed at me and demanded, "Why do you have Jesse in shackles?"

She let out a pained sigh. "I didn't want you to see this. I know you are fond of Jesse, and I wanted to spare you."

He shifted his gaze back to her. "Spare me from what?"

"Come sit down." She took his hand and led him over to sit beside her on the chaise. "Bauchan and the Unseelie head of security were summoned to the temple two days ago. They caught Jesse in the act of trying to steal the ke'tain."

"That's not true!" I cried and winced at Bauchan's bruising grip on my shoulder.

Queen Anwyn went on as if I hadn't spoken. "She was taken to Unseelie and questioned, but she refused to talk. I learned she was going to be released because she is Prince Vaerik's lover, and I could not let such an injustice stand."

Rhys gave me a confused look, and I shook my head. His expression said he didn't want to believe what she was saying.

"You abducted her?" His tone was incredulous when he faced the queen. "Mother, what are you thinking? You have to send her back."

A tiny spark of hope flared to life in my chest. She had sent him away so he wouldn't know what she was up to. Now that he was here, could he actually intervene and help me?

"I did what is best for Seelie and Faerie," she said as if she was speaking to a child. "When you are king, you will understand the difficult decisions we have to make for the good of our people."

I don't know who was more surprised when he retorted, "I hardly think starting a war with Unseelie is good for our people."

It was clear from her expression that she was not used to him challenging her. It took her several seconds to recover. She let out an indulgent laugh. "War? It's not like we stole the consort. And she will be returned to them after we interrogate her."

Rhys did not look convinced. "You could have done that in Unseelie. You did not have to bring her here."

"I tried to question her, but Korrigan allowed his son to stop the interrogation before she could answer me," Bauchan said. "The safety of the ke'tain is too important to risk her going free before we know what she was planning to do with it."

"It was Jesse who returned the ke'tain to us," Rhys reminded him. "Why would she want to steal it?"

Bauchan's fingers dug into my shoulders. "That is what we want to know."

The look Rhys gave me was pleading. "Jesse?"

"I didn't. I…"

"You see?" Queen Anwyn laid a hand on Rhys's arm. "She will not even tell you the truth, and you are friends." Her lip curled slightly on the last word. "A few days in the tower with no food or water will make her more willing to talk."

"The tower? With no food or water?" Rhys stared at her aghast, and I realized how naïve and sheltered he was if he thought that was so awful. He had no idea what happened in an interrogation or how cruel and ruthless the queen and her guards could be.

She patted his arm. "I'm sorry you have to be here for this, but it must be done."

"But –"

"You know I would do anything for Seelie, don't you?" She stroked his hair as a mother would, and a ball of anger formed in my chest. She had no right to touch him like that. It was one of a million things she had stolen from my mother – our mother.

Rhys nodded, but his eyes were still troubled when he looked at me.

"Then you have to trust me on this." Queen Anwyn stood, and he did the same. Taking his arm, she walked him to the door. "Do not worry about Jesse. I promise when all of this is over, she will go home to Unseelie."

She lowered her voice and said something to him I couldn't hear. Then she ushered him out of the room and shut the door before he could say another word. Her mouth was pressed into a thin line when she turned back to us.

"Bayard was supposed to keep him away until I summoned him home," she said tightly.

Bauchan eased his hold on my shoulder. "Rhys's guards are as loyal to him as yours are to you. They will not go against him when he wishes to do something unless it puts his life in danger."

Something in his voice told me this was a discussion he and the queen had had before, and her answering pout said she was not happy about it. At least, it answered a question I'd had about whether or not Rhys's guards were in on her plot.

She went to a side table and poured herself a glass of juice. "It complicates things, but we will proceed as planned. Take her back to the tower for now."

I said nothing as I stood, and Bauchan took hold of the chain between my wrists. He pulled me to the door like I was a dog on a leash. I should be glad the chain was on my hands and not around my neck. He'd most likely take perverse pleasure in leading me through the palace that way.

"Jesse," Queen Anwyn called as we reached the door.

I looked back and met her brittle eyes.

Her smile was more of a sneer. "You have earned a brief reprieve while I deal with this. You should use that time to rethink whether you want to cooperate or have Bauchan extract what we want from you. The choice should be an easy one."

When I didn't respond, her mouth tightened, and she looked at Bauchan.

"Have Aibel give her another taste of the dannakin. We would not want our *guest* to get too comfortable."

I shivered and curled myself into a tight ball on the pallet that stunk of old sweat and urine. The sun had gone down less than an hour ago, and already it was freezing in the room. It was going to be a long, miserable night.

My teeth chattered so hard they hurt. Desperately, I reached up and plucked the goddess stone from my hair. It had helped me create powerful glamours. I should be able to use it to keep myself from freezing to death.

Holding it in my fist, I imagined a warm bubble around me, as I did for the glamour. The stone grew warm in my hand and then...nothing. I tried again with the same result. Then I attempted a glamour to see if I could do that, at least. Nothing.

I sank down onto the pallet, defeated. Either the stone didn't work here for some reason, or I was too weak from the two hours of the dannakin I'd endured earlier. I should be thankful that my clothes were dry because I had avoided the humiliation of wetting myself this time.

My stomach rumbled painfully, adding to my discomfort. I couldn't remember the last time I'd eaten, and I couldn't tell if my weakness was from hunger or cold. I smacked my cracked lips together and tried to swallow, but my mouth and throat were too dry. I didn't know what was worse: the bitter cold or the extreme thirst.

I was so wrapped up in my misery that I didn't hear the door open or notice I was no longer alone until my visitor spoke.

"Jesse." Rhys's voice was harsher than I'd ever heard from him.

I lifted my head sluggishly to peer at his outline in the doorway. I saw movement, and then a laevik crystal filled the room with light. I put a hand up to shield my eyes after being in almost complete darkness. It took a moment to realize he wasn't alone. Bayard must have entered ahead of him and another of his guards stood behind him.

"Rhys," I croaked and dissolved in a fit of coughing that caused my parched throat to burn.

"Water," he ordered briskly.

A few seconds later, a flask touched my lips, and I drank like someone who had been lost in the desert. The water hit my empty stomach, and I immediately retched it back up onto the floor. It soaked into Rhys's pant legs as he knelt beside me, but he didn't seem to notice it as he lifted my hair out of my face. His hand grazed my cheek, and he swore.

"Kaelen, get some blankets and a clean pallet," he said, laying the back of his warm hand against my icy cheek.

"The queen will not be pleased if we interfere with her prisoner," his guard replied.

Rhys looked over his shoulder. "I will handle my mother." Anger laced his voice when he looked at me again. "They put her up here without heat or a blanket. Even the tarrans are covered with a blanket on cold nights."

Bayard came to stand behind the prince. He wore his normal hard expression, but for the first time, I didn't think it was directed at me. I was probably hallucinating from hunger and cold.

"Oh, Jesse, how did you come to this?" Rhys asked softly.

It felt like forever since I'd heard a kind voice in this horrible place, and a tear leaked out to drip onto his hand. He wiped it away tenderly and whispered, "It will be okay."

Kaelen wasn't gone long before he returned with a new pallet and several soft wooly blankets. Rhys picked me up and sat me on the new pallet, and Kaelen wrapped the blankets around me.

"T-thanks," I said through chattering teeth, already feeling my body getting warmer under the thick blankets.

Rhys held the water flask out to me, and I took it with shaking hands. This time I sipped it, letting the water soothe my throat and quench my thirst.

"Here." Bayard took the flask from me and pressed something else into my shackled hands. It was warm and wrapped in cloth, and when I opened it, I wanted to cry at the sight of the meat pastry.

"Eat it slowly," he ordered when I started to take a large bite. I remembered throwing up when I drank too fast, and I took a tiny bite, chewing it well before I swallowed. My empty stomach growled so loudly at the first food I'd had in days that it sounded like a wild animal was hiding under the blankets with me.

"Is that better?" Rhys asked when my stomach finally stopped making noises.

I nodded and continued to eat, half expecting Bauchan to burst through the door at any second and snatch the food from my hands. I needed all the nourishment I could get to help me stay strong for whatever Queen Anwyn had in store for me.

Rhys sat beside me. The expressions on his guards' faces said they weren't happy about their prince sitting on the floor, but they said nothing.

"Jesse," he began kindly. "How did this happen? No matter what my mother says, I cannot believe you would ever steal the ke'tain."

I wiped my mouth with the back of my hand. "I wouldn't."

"Why are they saying you were caught trying to take it?" he asked. When I didn't answer, he said, "I want to help you, but you need to trust me."

I glanced up at Bayard and Kaelen and whispered, "Just you."

"No." Bayard crossed his arms. "I am not leaving you alone in here, Rhys."

Rhys arched his eyebrows at his guard. "She is shackled, weaponless, and as weak as a newborn hama. If I am not able to defend myself against her then you, my friend, are a very bad trainer."

Bayard's scowl slipped for a second, but it was back in place when he looked at me. "We will be right outside the door."

I waited until after the door closed to speak. I didn't agree to talk to Rhys because I thought he could save me from the queen. He might try, but he was not strong enough to go against her and her guards. I did it because I knew I would probably die here, and there were things I needed to say to him before it was too late.

"I was caught at the temple, but not trying to steal the ke'tain. I can't tell you why I was there, only that I was trying to help Faerie. I understand if that's not enough to convince you I'm telling the truth, but it's all I can say about it." I paused to take a sip of water. "It's true that Bauchan questioned me in Unseelie, and he was angry when I wouldn't answer all his questions. But that's not why he arranged to have me kidnapped and brought here."

Rhys was hanging on every word. "Why then?"

I hesitated for a moment and plunged forward. "He did it because when I was in the temple, I overheard one of the queen's guards talking to someone about how to get past the wards to steal the ke'tain. He had to get me out of Unseelie before I told someone what I knew, so two of the queen's guards snuck into my cell and took me. They made it look like I escaped and used a portal to go to my world."

Rhys inhaled sharply. "Bauchan wants to steal the ke'tain? I have to tell Mother."

He started to rise, but I snagged his sleeve to stop him. "The queen knows. Bauchan is acting on her behalf."

"No. You are mistaken." Rhys shook his head.

"I'm not," I said firmly. "She told me so herself. Just like she admitted she had the ke'tain stolen the first time."

He shot to his feet before I could stop him. "That is impossible. My mother would never do anything to harm Faerie."

At his outburst, the door opened, and Bayard leaned in. "Is everything okay?"

I looked up at Rhys's agitated face and waited for him to say no. He surprised me when he said, "Yes."

He paced to the other side of the room and back. "Tell me this. What possible reason could the Seelie queen have for stealing our most sacred relic and endangering our world?"

I heard the challenge in his voice, but in his eyes, I caught a flicker of uncertainty. It was enough for me to keep going. He either believed me, or he didn't. What did I have to lose?

"I don't think she ever intended to harm Faerie," I said. "But it was *her* actions that led us to where we are now. I've known that since long before I came to Seelie."

He stopped pacing and spun to stare at me. "How?"

I wasn't sure if he was asking how the queen had stolen the ke'tain or how I'd known all this time. I also didn't know if he was ready to hear all of this, but I was running out of time.

I patted the pallet beside me, and he sat. Then I moved so I was facing him. "It all started when I went on a job at a black-market dealer's house the Agency had raided."

I told him about Lewis Tate, the dealer whom the Agency suspected had the ke'tain, and how I'd connected Tate to Davian Woods. That led to the party at Davian's where I'd seen one of the queen's guards create a portal and speak to her about the ke'tain. Rhys tried to interrupt me at that point, but I put up a hand to stop him. He could ask all the questions he wanted when I was done telling my story.

Rhys fell silent as I talked about Faris and what he had suffered after he'd discovered who had taken the ke'tain. Rhys's eyes widened in horror when I described Faris wrapped in iron in that basement and Faris's own account of it.

Rhys hadn't been in the human world long, but like every faerie, he knew how deadly iron was and what long-term contact like that would do to a Fae body. The queen's men could have killed Faris, but they chose instead to torture him for months. Kind-hearted Rhys struggled to process that level of brutality from people he knew.

I continued my story, telling him about Gus and how he'd had the ke'tain inside him all that time. I recounted how Davian's men had kidnapped Conlan and me, and Davian had told me about his deal with Queen Anwyn. How I'd been shot by one of Davian's men during our escape and would have died if Lukas and his men hadn't attempted the conversion.

"What I could never figure out was why the queen would take the ke'tain from Faerie," I said half to myself. "Today, I got my answer. She told me she did it to upset the balance of magic just enough to show everyone how dangerous it is to keep the barrier open. She wanted to use it to convince Unseelie to seal the barrier for good. But then the ke'tain was lost, and things got out of control."

Rhys looked like I'd punched him in the gut. "My whole life, Mother has talked about sealing the barrier. At times, I felt like she wanted to do something about it, but I did not think she would take it this far."

"She's going to try again. This time, she's not taking the ke'tain out of Faerie, but she's going to use it to force Unseelie's hand." I paused. "And she's planning to make it look like I was the one who stole it."

"How could she? She has to know you will tell them the truth about her and..." He stared at me for several seconds, and then he vigorously shook his head. "No. She may be guilty of those other things, but my mother would not resort to killing an innocent. I cannot believe that of her."

My stomach twisted as it did every time he called Queen Anwyn his mother. His real mother – our mother – was a good, strong, loving, fiercely protective woman who had been robbed of her son by that monster.

I looked into his blue eyes, identical to our father's, and I was suddenly overcome with longing and grief. I was never going to hear my dad's laugh again or feel the warm security of his hugs. And my mom would never recover from losing another child. My death was going to destroy our family, and Queen Anwyn's victory over us would be complete. And there was nothing I could do to stop it.

I reached for Rhys's hand and clasped it between mine. I might not be able to change my fate, but I could give something back to my parents before I died.

My father and I had been wrong. We'd thought the only way to protect our family from the queen was to keep the truth about Caleb a secret. What we should have done was tell our story to anyone who would listen. Most would not have believed us, but enough people would have. If we had exposed her and something had happened to us, then people would know who did it. More importantly, Rhys would know.

"There is something else I have to tell you. I believe it's the real reason Queen Anwyn is trying so hard to seal off Faerie from the human world."

He frowned. "I know her reason. She has talked about keeping our world free from the impurities of the other realm."

"That's what she tells you and everyone else, but it's a lie," I bit out the last word as the anger and pain I had been carrying for months threatened to spill from me. "She wants to close the barrier to protect her secret, to keep people from finding out about the horrible thing she did."

"Jesse, I fear the stress of imprisonment is affecting your mind. I think I should summon a healer." He tried to pull his hand from mine, but I refused to let him go.

"I don't need a healer. I need you to listen to what I have to say."

He sighed and assumed a placating expression. "Okay. What is this awful thing my mother did, and how do you know about it?"

I took a deep breath. "I know about it because she did it to my family."

I didn't know what he saw in my eyes, but he paled and spoke in a hushed voice. "What did she do?"

"Twenty years ago, Queen Anwyn stole something precious from my parents, and it nearly destroyed them. They've never gotten over it."

Rhys's hand flexed in mine. "Twenty years ago? That's the year I was born."

"I know," I said softly.

He swallowed convulsively and covered my hand with his other one. "What did she take from them?" he whispered urgently.

"My brother."

21

RHYS PULLED AWAY from me so fast he fell backward. He scrambled to his feet and stared down at me, words of denial already forming on his lips. His eyes, however, conveyed a different emotion. He knew, maybe not consciously, but a part of him knew the truth.

"My brother's name is Caleb," I went on as if nothing had happened. "He was two months old when he died suddenly in his crib. Or so everyone believed, except for our mother. She tried to tell people that the dead baby wasn't hers, but they dismissed her as a grieving mother."

I tugged the blankets tighter around me. "I was born later, so I never knew Caleb. Whenever Mom and Dad talked about him, it made them sad, so I tried not to mention him often."

"You were unhappy?" Rhys asked.

"No." I sniffled quietly. "I had a very happy life, but there were moments when one or both of my parents let their guard down, and I could see their pain. I think Caleb's birthday was the hardest for them. We go to the cemetery to visit his grave on his birthday every year."

Rhys came back to join me on the pallet. "I am sorry for your loss and the pain your family has suffered. But nothing you have said implicates my mother or proves your claim that I am your brother."

"I'm getting to that." I swiped away the wetness on my cheeks. "Do you remember when those photos of you were leaked weeks before your debut?"

"Yes." His brows drew together, and I could almost hear him wondering where I was going with this.

262

"The photog who took those pictures is a friend of my family. You met him the night the paparazzi cornered me at Navi. He showed the photos to my parents, who had never laid eyes on the Seelie prince."

Rhys sucked in a breath. I kept going.

"My mother recognized you first. You have blond hair instead of Caleb's red, but you look too much like my father at that age for it to be a coincidence." I let that sink in for a few seconds before I continued. "They found out you were at the Ralston, so they went there to see you in person."

"I never saw them," Rhys said in a small voice.

"Some of the queen's guards were with you, and they got to my parents before you could see each other."

"I remember that night." Rhys stared past me. "Mother... she insisted on Aibel and Conard coming with us for our first trip. There was a commotion outside the room where we were doing a photo shoot, and they told me they'd taken care of a security breach. They made me return to Faerie immediately after."

I let out a bitter laugh. "Yeah, they took care of it. One of them told my parents they should have killed them twenty years ago when they took you. Then they called a goren dealer to do their dirty work for them and to dispose of my parents. It was sheer luck that someone else took the call and kept my mother and father alive and hidden by drugging them with goren. My parents had to spend months in rehab after I found them, but at least they're alive."

"This cannot be real." Rhys ran his hands through his hair, and I couldn't tell if he was upset or in shock. He moved suddenly to put his hands on my shoulders. "Why did you not tell me? Your parents never tried to see me after that. I met your father, and he said nothing."

My heart constricted at the hurt and confusion in his eyes. "At first, they didn't remember what happened because of the goren. When they did get their memory back, we were too afraid of what Queen Anwyn would do if she found out. You have no idea what it's doing to them to know you're alive and not be able to tell you. Mom nearly had a relapse when she remembered."

"Why are you telling me now? Are you no longer afraid of what my mother would do?"

"I'm terrified," I admitted. "But I wanted you to know in case...something happens to me. You deserve to know that you have a whole family out there who loves you. Lukas...Vaerik has them hidden for now. I hope you can help to keep them safe from the queen."

"Prince Vaerik knows about me?" Rhys asked.

"No." Guilt and sorrow sliced through me, and for a moment, I couldn't breathe. I'd carried the burden of my family's secret all this time, and my fear had kept me from confiding in the one person I should have.

Rhys got up to pace the room again. "My...mother... she wasn't always affectionate like other mothers. She treated me well and gave me everything I wanted, but I always felt like something was missing."

"What about your...father?" I asked. I'd never thought much about the queen's consort. Was he in on this, too?

"My father is a quiet person. He does his duty as consort, but outside of that, my parents are rarely together. He is a loving father, but he did not have much input into my upbringing."

I tried to imagine what it had been like for him growing up here with an absent father and a mother who didn't show him the kind of love I'd known. He was a prince raised in absolute luxury, but I felt like the one with all the riches.

He went to one of the windows and stared out into the night. I watched him for several minutes, wondering what was going through his mind. When Dad had told me Rhys was Caleb, it had shaken my world. What must it be like for Rhys to discover his whole life was a lie, to learn not only that he was stolen from his real family, but he was not even from this world?

More minutes passed, and the silence in the room became too much for me. I cleared my throat. "Rhys, are you okay?"

"No." He turned to look at me with bleak eyes. "I cannot believe my mother is capable of the things you said."

My heart sank. I'd hoped he would believe me, but I couldn't blame him for siding with the only mother he had ever known. It was too much to ask of him.

"From our first encounter, I felt inexplicably drawn to you. Bayard teased that I was infatuated with a pretty human, but that wasn't it. I felt connected to you somehow, and it grew stronger every time I saw you. When I met your father, I felt it with him, too, and I assumed it was because of my interest in his work." Rhys let out a ragged breath. "I didn't know. I didn't know."

I tossed the blankets off me. Shivering, I stood and went to him. I couldn't hug him with my wrists shackled, so I laid my hands against his chest. "You couldn't have known. Even my father didn't know until his memory came back."

He wrapped his arms tightly around me, and it broke the damn of emotions inside me. I cried for him, our family, and everything we'd lost. It wasn't until I felt him shake that I realized he was crying, too.

"I have a sister," he said hoarsely, and my chest expanded with bittersweet joy.

We were still holding each other when the door opened. I lifted my head as Bayard entered and eyed us impatiently.

"This is no time for a tryst, Rhys," he growled. "Donan says Bauchan will come for her within the hour."

I shuddered as the reality of my situation came crashing down on me once more. How could I have forgotten, even for a second, what was waiting for me?

"I will not let them hurt you again," Rhys said fiercely. "We will get you out of here."

"We?" Bayard glared at him. "You want us to help a prisoner of the queen escape? That is treason."

"It is not treason if the crown prince commands you to do it." Rhys released me and scowled at his head of security.

Bayard raised an eyebrow, and I got the impression Rhys rarely issued commands to him. It was confirmed when his mouth twisted into a wry smile. "Of course, Your Highness. How are we to smuggle your little friend out of the palace? She does not exactly blend in, and Bauchan has strengthened the wards. We cannot even create a portal inside the palace."

Rhys thought for a moment. "We could take her to the door in the servants' wing that we used to sneak out as children."

My breath bottled up in my chest as I dared to hope for the first time in days.

Bayard was quick to squash it. "It's on the other end of the palace. We'd never make it without being caught."

"Perhaps we could hide her," Kaelen said, joining the conversation. "She would fit in one of those large baskets used to collect bed linens."

"We would not look at all suspicious carrying a linen basket," Bayard retorted. He turned to Rhys. "Anything we try will be risky. Is she worth incurring the queen's wrath?"

"Yes," Rhys answered without hesitation.

Bayard's surprised gaze flicked to me. "Why?"

Rhys laid an arm over my shoulders. "Shut the door, Kaelen."

Kaelen obeyed. He and Bayard stood together watching us expectantly. Rhys didn't make them wait long.

"Because Jesse is my sister."

"What?" The two guards exclaimed at the same time.

Bayard pointed an accusing finger at me. "That is impossible. What lies did you tell him to make him believe such a ludicrous claim?"

"Do not speak to her that way," Rhys ordered in a hard voice.

"You cannot believe this." Bayard shot him an incredulous look. "She is using you to help her escape."

Rhys looked at me, and I nodded. The truth had to come out eventually, and we might as well start with the people he trusted the most. I needed them if I had any hope of getting out of here alive.

Ten minutes later, Bayard and Kaelen were staring at me like they'd never seen me before. Bayard wasn't one hundred percent convinced by my story, but he admitted that Aibel and Conard had been acting strange that night at the Ralston. And Bauchan had told him multiple times to keep Rhys away from the James family. The reason given had been the queen's disapproval of her son associating with bounty hunters.

"You have the same eyes," Kaelen declared, looking from me to Rhys. "How did I never see it?"

I smiled at Rhys. "We have our father's eyes and our mother's hair. Yours was as red as mine once."

Bayard held up a hand. "We still need to address the why and how of this?"

"The how is pretty obvious," I said. "The queen's guards stole Caleb and put a dead baby in his place. They glamoured the medical examiner to cover it up. Then Queen Anwyn secretly went to my world and did the conversion herself."

"You are forgetting one important detail," Bayard said. "Queen Anwyn delivered a son. I know this because my mother was present at Rhys's birth. After the queen lost her first baby, all of Seelie followed her second pregnancy closely."

"The queen lost a baby?" I asked, surprised.

Rhys nodded seriously. "It was a stillbirth, fifteen years before I was born."

"My mother has told me how all of Seelie celebrated for days when Rhys was born," Bayard said. "How do you explain that?"

I shook my head. "I can't."

He looked at Rhys. "We also need to remember the queen's dislike of humans. She has made no secret of the fact she considers them weak and inferior. Would she take one of them to pass off as her own child? Her heir?"

"He's right," I said deflated. "When you think about it that way, it sounds insane."

Rhys faced me. "Do you believe I am your brother?"

"Without a doubt. If you could talk to my parents and see the pictures of my dad when he was your age, you wouldn't have to ask me that."

He nodded firmly. "Then we will go to your parents. First, we have to get you out of Seelie."

My relief was so strong it made my legs wobble, and he had to reach out to steady me.

Bayard let out a harsh breath and looked at Kaelen. "Tell Donan, Ash, and Mitah to meet us at the bottom of the tower and to bring a weapons bag from the training room."

Kaelen left, and Rhys smiled broadly. "Brilliant. No one will question you carrying a weapons bag."

I almost spoke up and said I could create a glamour to hide me, but I remembered my failed attempt before they arrived. I bit my lip. I felt like I could confide in Rhys, but could I trust Bayard with my secret? What would he do if he found out I had a goddess stone? Would he still help me or turn me over to the queen? If I showed them the stone and I couldn't create a glamour, I would have risked it all for nothing.

"What is it, Jesse?" Rhys asked. He and Bayard gave me questioning looks.

"Nothing. I think the bag is a great idea."

"We should head down now," Bayard said. "We need to get out of here before Bauchan comes for her."

I held up my shackled hands. "Would it be possible to remove these?" I would have done it myself, but there hadn't been a thing in the tower I could use to pick the lock.

Bayard frowned. "Only Bauchan has the keys to his shackles. We will have to wait until we get away to free you from them."

We left the room with Bayard in the lead and Rhys taking up the rear. There was a sense of urgency in our steps as we descended the stairs, and I sent up a silent prayer that we got out of here before Bauchan came for me.

The door at the base of the tower opened as we reached the bottom, and I fell backward into Rhys when Bauchan appeared in the doorway. Queen Anwyn's head of security looked more furious than surprised to see us.

"This explains why the guards I stationed here are nowhere to be seen," he snarled at Bayard. "Where do you think you are going with our prisoner?"

Rhys moved around me. "That tower room is not fit to house an animal, and there are plenty of warmer rooms in this wing where she can be kept. I'm taking her to one of those."

"I will save you the trouble. I am here to bring the prisoner to the queen," Bauchan said, entering the tower. Aibel came behind him along with Conard. The tower suddenly seemed very small and cramped.

Bayard tensed, but there was no room in here to fight, even if he hadn't been outnumbered three to one.

"Then I will accompany you to see my mother," Rhys said imperiously.

"As you wish." Bauchan reached around him and grabbed my arm in his steely grip. "But we will escort the prisoner."

I looked desperately at Rhys before I was led from the tower. He gave my shoulder a quick squeeze and followed us. As we walked down the hallway, Kaelen and another of Rhys's guards approached from the other direction. We'd been so close. If Bauchan had come a few minutes later, we might have made it out.

Kaelen and the other guard were expressionless as they fell into step with Rhys and Bayard behind me. My stomach was a solid lump of dread over what I was walking toward, but the presence of Rhys and his men told me I wasn't alone anymore.

We stopped outside the queen's quarters, and Bauchan exchanged a look with Aibel before he opened the door to push me inside. Rhys entered behind us, but to my relief, the rest of the queen's guards stayed outside.

Bauchan put me in the same chair I'd sat on last time and took up his position behind me. Rhys stood rigidly beside my chair, the image of a protective brother, and it made the ice in my chest thaw a little.

Queen Anwyn swept into the room, and her graceful steps slowed when she saw Rhys. I couldn't see his face, but whatever she saw in his expression caused her smile to falter.

"Rhys, why are you here? You know I don't want you involved in this." She spoke to him like he was a bothersome child as she walked to her chaise.

"I caught the prince taking the prisoner from the tower, Your Majesty," Bauchan informed her. "He said he was taking her to another room, but I believe his real intent was to help her escape. Bayard was with him."

The queen's head jerked back. "Rhys, tell me this is not true."

"It is," he answered evenly.

Her shock morphed into a mask of anger. "You were going to free *my* prisoner? She tried to steal the ke'tain, and only the goddess knows what she planned to do with it. You would release her so she could attempt it again? She is a traitor to Faerie and Seelie. Why would you betray me for her?"

"What brother would do less for his sister?" Rhys asked in a biting tone that sounded like it came from someone else.

Queen Anwyn's open mouth was the only change in her expression. "Sister?" She turned her glittering eyes on me. "What disgusting lies have you contaminated my son's mind with?"

I sat up straighter, bolstered by his presence. "He's not your son."

Bauchan grabbed my hair and yanked my head back so fast I saw stars. "Hold your tongue, or I will rip it out of you."

"Let her go," Rhys demanded, but Bauchan only tightened his hold. Pain lanced through my skull, and I feared he was going to rip my scalp from my head.

Rhys spun to face the queen. "I know what you did, Mother. Silencing Jesse will not change that."

"What do you think you know?" Her voice held a note of amusement as if she was humoring a teen that was acting out.

"I know you stole a baby from Patrick and Caroline James twenty years ago, and then you tried to have them killed when they discovered I was their missing son."

Queen Anwyn scoffed. "Do you hear how ridiculous that sounds? I gave birth to you, Rhys. The whole court was witness to my pregnancy. How can you believe this half-breed traitor over me? She is lying to get you to help her escape."

"I am not that gullible," he retorted. "I could not believe it at first, but the more I heard, the more I knew it was true. Bayard believes it, too, and he trusts no one outside his friends."

"If I did this horrible crime, where is the evidence of it?" she asked in feigned indignation.

Bauchan released me, and tears sprung to my eyes when I raised my head. I resisted the urge to rub my injured scalp as I met the smug challenge in her eyes.

"There is no evidence. Your guards took care of that. Just like they tried to get rid of my parents," I said with all the loathing I'd kept bottled up inside me for months.

"How convenient that you have nothing to prove this outrageous claim." She looked at Rhys. "You believe the word of someone you hardly know over your own mother?"

I shook my head. "I do have something to prove it."

Her gaze snapped back to me. "And what is that?"

"Rhys. You changed his hair and his DNA, but you couldn't erase who he is. He looks so much like a younger version of our father they could be twins."

She waved a dismissive hand. "A physical resemblance? If that is all you have, you have nothing."

"If it's nothing, then why are you suddenly so desperate to seal the barrier?" I asked, satisfied when I saw that my change in direction had taken her off guard. "Rhys's face is everywhere in my world. You know someone is eventually going to see the resemblance between Patrick James and the Seelie prince. People will talk, and the media will pick it up because they love a juicy story about a royal. The only way to stop the story from reaching Faerie is to make sure no one can travel between the worlds."

The room was quiet for a moment, and then she chuckled. "That is quite the imagination you have. I see how you were able to convince my son to believe your story."

"It is not a story," Rhys said tightly.

She sighed heavily. "This is one of the reasons I did not want you to go to that world. You are innocent, and I worried an unscrupulous human would take advantage of you. I allowed you to go, and this is the result." She pointed at me. "If I had known she would try to poison you against me, I never would have brought her into the palace. The only thing I can do now is prevent her from doing more damage."

She exchanged a quick look with Bauchan, and he stepped out from behind me. He went to the door and opened it to admit Aibel, Conard, and three other males. It was her entire personal guard, and their arrival did not bode well for me.

I shot out of my chair, and Rhys moved to stand in front of me. "I am not going to let you hurt her."

"You are still too young to understand the things we must do for the good of Seelie," Queen Anwyn said with an indulgent smile. "Time will change that, but for now, I am afraid I will have to confine you to your quarters."

Rhys stared at her dumbfounded. "You are going to lock me up?"

Her smile never faltered as she walked over to him. "It is for your own good. And you can hardly compare your quarters to a cell."

"What of my guard?" he demanded.

"Bayard and the rest of your guard have been detained until they can prove themselves loyal to the crown," Bauchan said with a vicious gleam in his eyes that chilled me.

Rhys took a step toward Bauchan. "If you have hurt them –"

The queen cut him off. "Do not worry about your friends, Rhys. You will see them as soon as all of this is over." She waved at her guards. "Escort my son to his quarters, and see that he does not leave them."

"Yes, Your Majesty," Aibel said. He inclined his head, and two of the guards came to stand on either side of Rhys.

Rhys looked at me with devastated eyes. "I will find a way to help you. Do not lose hope." He held his hand out to me, and I clasped it in mine for a second before he was led away.

Queen Anwyn rounded on me the second the door clicked behind them. Her slap was so hard my cheek went numb and my ears rang. "I should have had you disposed of the moment I heard of my son's interest in you. You have caused me nothing but aggravation."

I straightened and gave her a look of such hatred she took a step back. Bauchan and Aibel were immediately on either side of her. How brave would she be one-on-one without her guards to protect her?

"He's not your son," I said through gritted teeth. "You can drop the act. Everyone in this room knows what you did."

She sneered at me. "He is my son. I gave him my blood. I gave him immortality and a life few could ever dream of. What could your human mother have given him that I did not?"

"A real mother's love."

"That is another human flaw I despise. You are so sentimental." She turned her back on me and crossed the room to her chaise.

"Why did you do it?" I asked, desperately needing to know why my family had suffered so much. "Why did you take my brother?"

Queen Anwyn sat and took time to arrange her skirt before she answered me. She spoke as casually as someone talking about what they had for breakfast. "I needed a strong infant boy, and Aibel found one for me."

Her apathy nearly left me speechless. "And the dead baby he left in the crib? Did he kill someone else's child to help cover up your crime?"

An emotion crossed her face, but it was gone before I could figure out what it was. "No. That baby was already dead."

I had the answer to Bayard's why. There was only one reason Queen Anwyn could have for stealing a human baby and passing him off as her own after she had given birth to a son. The real Prince Rhys had died, and she'd switched him with another baby so no one would know.

Snatches of my conversation with King Oseron came back to me. He'd told me Onagh and Asherah couldn't provide a strong heir, and they knew someone would challenge Onagh for the throne. So, he'd abdicated to Oseron.

That was it. Queen Anwyn had feared a challenge if people found out her son had died. She had covered it up to keep her throne. She'd taken my brother Caleb and put her dead son in his place. It would have been easy enough for her to glamour a dead Fae baby to look like Caleb. That was why they'd destroyed his grave and the body in it. If my parents ever claimed the prince was their son, an exhumation would prove the child they'd buried was a Fae changeling.

"I should allow Bauchan to carve some parts off you for causing me this strife with Rhys," she said. "But I have other plans for you that require your body to be intact."

A shudder went through me, and I didn't know whether to be relieved or terrified.

She paused, savoring whatever she was about to tell me. "I no longer need to know your secret of how to pass through the temple wards. In two days, I will have the ke'tain, and you will have outlived your usefulness to me." She tapped her chin with a finger. "I think I will have Aibel go to your world tomorrow and pay one last visit to the James family. Should I send them your love?"

Blood roared in my ears. I didn't make it two steps in her direction before Bauchan caught me. He spun me around, and there was no time to prepare before his fist plowed into my stomach. I doubled over, gasping for air and heaving at the same time. A punch to my side sent me to my hands and knees where I threw up every bit of the meat pastry Bayard had given me.

A boot struck my shoulder, and I curled up in a ball with my hands over my head. The last thing I heard before the final blow came was Queen Anwyn's bored voice.

"Try not to kill her, Bauchan. I have one more use for her."

22

"Get up."

I jolted awake to a sharp pain in my lower back. Suppressing a moan, I rolled onto my back and pushed down the blanket I was burrowed under. Above me stood Bauchan looking ready to kick me again if I didn't move fast enough. He liked to kick people when they were down, something I'd learned well during the last two days.

I staggered to my feet, letting the blanket fall to the pallet. Bauchan had visited me once each day in the two days since he'd beaten me unconscious in front of the queen. On his first visit, he'd demanded to know where my parents were after Aibel reported they were nowhere to be found. Laughing at him probably hadn't been my best move. He'd bashed my head against the door a few times until I nearly blacked out. When I collapsed to the floor, he'd kicked me twice for good measure.

On his second visit, he came in while I was asleep. Sharp pain in my side had awakened me, and I thought someone had stabbed me until the boot struck me again. He didn't speak as he kicked me over and over, and I was too weak to do anything but lie there and take it.

I tensed my body for the first blow and faced him. If he expected me to cower, he was in for disappointment. I was past fearing him, and the way his jaw hardened told me he knew it.

He held up a pair of leg shackles. "Your presence has been requested."

I stood still while he locked the shackles around my ankles. It was the first time they'd bound my feet, and it filled me with dread. It was also the first time I'd seen him wear a sword since they'd brought me here.

This was it. Whatever Queen Anwyn had planned for me, it was happening now. I would have been lying if I said I wasn't scared, but I was going to face it with my head high. Before I died, I wanted her to know that all her attempts to break me had failed.

We left the tower room, and Bauchan held my elbow in his hard grip as we descended the stairs. It wouldn't do for me to trip over the leg shackles and break my neck before the queen got what she wanted from me.

At the bottom, two of her other guards waited to accompany us. We took a different route through the palace and stopped outside a set of tall wide doors with two guards posted outside. The guards each grasped a handle and pulled the heavy doors open.

The room was as big as a church with a high glass roof and a row of windows along the upper half of two sides. The floor was polished white stone, but the walls and ceiling were covered in intricate murals depicting the lives of past Seelie monarchs. Along two sides of the room were chairs, half of which were occupied by the queen's advisors and other people I didn't recognize.

At the far end of the room was a dais on which sat a magnificent throne made of eyranth with a back that was at least ten feet tall. On the throne sat the Seelie queen in a royal blue dress and a glittering crown that looked too heavy for her slender neck to support.

On either side of the throne were two smaller ones. The throne on her right where her consort should sit was empty. On her left sat Rhys watching me with an expression of helpless anger as I was led into the room.

The room fell silent except for the clink of my leg shackle chain against the floor. Bauchan took his time escorting me toward the throne, no doubt to build the suspense and excitement of those in attendance. It worked. All eyes were riveted on me as we approached the dais.

We stopped fifteen feet from the throne, close enough for me to see the gleam of anticipation in Queen Anwyn's eyes that belied her serious, regal expression. The knot in my stomach grew, but I kept my face impassive. I would not give her the satisfaction of seeing my fear.

"Kneel before the queen," Bauchan barked. He pushed me down hard, and pain shot through my knees when they hit the floor.

Rhys shifted in his chair like he was struggling to move. It was then that I noticed his arms were bound to the sides of his throne. He was as much a prisoner here as I was. A quick sweep of the room's occupants revealed that none of his personal guards were here.

Queen Anwyn stood and addressed the room. "I have summoned you all here because today, a heinous crime was committed against Faerie."

Murmurs spread through the room. A few people leaned forward to get a better look at me. I could imagine what a spectacle I was in my dirty, stained clothes and shackles. The people at the Unseelie court had gotten used to my red hair, but it was a strange oddity here, making me look even more like an outsider.

"Five days ago, the prisoner, Jesse James, was apprehended at the goddess's temple trying to steal the ke'tain." The queen paused dramatically as murmurs turned to loud gasps. "She was brought to Unseelie and detained, but she escaped from their custody and was believed to have fled to the human world. In truth, she was still in Faerie, hiding until she could make another attempt to steal the ke'tain. Today, she was successful."

Shouts went up from her audience as outrage spread through the room. People stood, making angry gestures as the noise level rose to a loud buzz. Queen Anwyn gave them a minute to get worked up before she raised her hands and called for order.

"It was by the grace of the goddess that Conard and Gans chose that time to visit the temple. They found all four temple guards slaughtered and the ke'tain gone." The queen put a hand to her chest as if imagining it was too much for her. "They ran outside and caught Jesse James trying to escape. If they had not gone there at that exact time, she would have gotten away."

My stomach roiled in horror, and the room erupted again. Her men had murdered four innocent guards, two of them her own people.

It wasn't as easy for her to calm the room this time, and she had to shout to be heard. Her cheeks grew flushed with the effort, and annoyance flashed in her eyes. She wasn't used to people not jumping to attention when she spoke.

"I share your anger and pain, my friends." She spoke in a consoling voice, the picture of empathy. "We will have justice for our fallen, and you will bear witness to it."

The door opened, and every head turned toward it. I couldn't see it from my position, but I heard someone enter and walk toward us. My heart pounded as my mind conjured images of what was behind me. I pictured an executioner with a sword and wondered if I would see the blow coming before it ended my life.

The footsteps drew closer until Aibel appeared carrying a box the size of a shoebox at arm's length. He stopped a few feet from me to bow his head to the queen, and his teeth were gritted in an effort not to grimace in pain. I looked at the box that appeared to be made of some kind of thick leather.

Drakkan hide probably. I didn't need him to open it for me to know what it held because I could feel its power.

"Show us," Queen Anwyn said, indifferent to his discomfort.

He lifted the hinged lid, and I was close enough to hear his hiss of pain. All eyes in the room except mine and Queen Anwyn's locked on the ke'tain. I looked at the queen, who was watching the faces of the people she had brought here to witness this spectacle. She shifted her gaze to me. She was careful to keep her face solemn, but for one second, she let me see the triumph in her eyes.

"I believe in my heart that Aedhna called Conard and Gans to the island so they could capture the thief and save the ke'tain," Queen Anwyn said. Her voice rang with emotion when she added, "We are indeed goddess blessed."

I raised my eyebrows at her performance. If she pulled a goddess stone out of her pocket next, even I was going to applaud her.

The queen looked at me. "For the crimes of theft, murder, and desecrating the temple there can only be one punishment. Death."

Cold suffused me as angry murmurs of agreement spread through the room. Rhys gave the queen a pleading look and whispered, "Mother, please."

She turned her head and shot him a warning look that made him go still. I didn't think she would harm him, so she had to be threatening Bayard and his other guards. If Rhys was as close to them as Lukas was to Faolin and the others, he would do anything for them.

Queen Anwyn swept her gaze around the room. "These crimes were committed with the purpose of stealing our most precious artifact. It is only fitting that the ke'tain carry out the sentence before we return it to the temple."

Aibel set the box on the floor in front of me. I winced and leaned away from the ke'tain. In the days since I'd taken it to the lake, it had grown much stronger, and the energy it gave off was like thousands of tiny needles piercing my skin.

"Touch it," the queen ordered me.

"No." I stared back at her defiantly. Did she honestly think I would submit to her will when her torture hadn't worked?

Her lips curved slightly. "You cannot escape justice. Prolonging it will only make it worse for you."

"This isn't justice. The only one here guilty of murder and theft is you," I shot back.

She waved a hand at the room. "Look around you, Jesse James. There is no one from Unseelie to believe your lies, no Prince Vaerik to shield you this time. Surrender to the ke'tain, and let the power of Aedhna cleanse you of your sins before you leave this life."

Bauchan pressed the tip of his sword against my back and whispered, "Do it or I will kill you myself."

I looked down at the ke'tain. After everything I'd gone through to return it to Faerie and then to restore it to full power, it would not end like this. All I could do was hope the goddess stone was strong enough to protect me.

The room went deathly quiet as if every single person in it was holding their breath. I leaned down and reached out my shackled hands. The ke'tain began to emit pulses of soft blue light, and the tiny needles in my skin became a swarm of angry bee stings. I gritted my teeth against the pain as tears ran down my cheeks.

My fingertips touched the ke'tain, and it was like someone had pressed a live wire to the center of my chest. Stars exploded before my eyes, and every muscle in my body seized. I couldn't breathe or move as my heart began to slow.

An image of Rhys's tormented eyes floated through my mind. Even though he was older than I was, I felt like the older sibling. He had been sheltered his whole life, and he was so naïve about the world. He blamed himself for not saving me, and I wished I could tell him none of this was his fault. I was grateful for the time I got to spend with him, not as a prince but as my brother.

I thought about my parents, Finch, and Aisla and the days I'd spent with them on the island. If I'd known it might be the last time I saw them, I would have made the most of every second of my time with them. But the most important thing was that they were together and safe.

Lastly, I thought of Lukas. We'd had so little time together, and it was unbearably cruel to know I'd never see his smile again or feel his arms around me. It wasn't enough to know he'd never believe the lies Queen Anwyn would spread about me. I wanted the life with him that I would never have.

The pain ended abruptly and all I felt was peace. It was everywhere, in me, around me. I opened my eyes and looked at Aedhna who knelt in front of me.

Her eyes shone with love as she laid a hand against my cheek. "You have been so brave, Jesse. I have one last job for you."

I wasn't sure what I could do for her, being dead, but I asked anyway. "What?"

"Bring my ke'tain home," she said before she disappeared.

I looked down at the stone that was no longer pulsing. It was a familiar solid blue glow that extended to my fingers. I reached both hands into the box and scooped up the ke'tain, expecting a jolt of power that never came. The glow covered my hands and spread rapidly up my arms to envelop me in an unpleasant sensation. It was like being wrapped in a scratchy wool blanket.

I stood and heard clinks and the rattle of chains as my wrist and leg shackles fell to the floor. Around me, there were shouts and cries, but my eyes were on Queen Anwyn, who stood frozen in front of her throne. Her mouth was open, and her eyes were wide with disbelief and fear.

Something hit my back, and I stumbled. Righting myself, I stared down at the tip of a sword protruding from my chest. It was a strange sight because I felt no pain. I watched in awe as the blade crumbled, and the hilt struck the floor behind me.

A male screamed. I turned to see Bauchan engulfed in blue flames. He writhed in agony, his screams echoing in the room as the fire consumed him. Suddenly, the screams were cut off, and there was a blue flash. All that remained of the queen's head of security were the ashes drifting down to the spot where he had stood.

People screamed and ran for the doors while others cowered in their seats. I didn't care about any of them. I turned to look for Queen Anwyn, who was no longer near her throne. I found her running for a closed door behind the dais with Aibel, Conard, and her two other personal guards.

I went after them. Conard tried to open the door, but it would not budge. He rammed his body into it as Aibel and the other guards spun to face me. Aibel grabbed a wooden staff from one of them and struck out at me.

I caught the end of the weapon and yanked him toward me. Ripping the staff from his hands with my free one, I struck him hard in the temple before he registered what had happened. He went down without a sound. I wasn't a killer, so I couldn't bring myself to end him, even after all he had done to my parents and me. He would be brought to justice, but not by me.

The two other guards brandished swords at me. These were some of the most elite warriors in this world, and the sight of them used to strike fear into my heart. Now they were nothing more than obstacles between me and what I wanted.

They had seen Bauchan die, so they knew they didn't stand a chance against the power of the ke'tain. They were willing to sacrifice themselves to give the queen time to escape.

The first one rushed at me. I whipped the staff across his knees with my borrowed strength and speed and heard a bone break. He fell forward, and I stepped back to avoid touching him. I made short work of knocking him out as I had with Aibel.

I faced the last guard. Instead of waiting for him to attack, I moved in. I swung the staff in a one-handed figure eight spin that Faolin had taught me. The staff moved so fast it was invisible, and when the guard tried to block it with his sword, the metal blade snapped in two. He dropped the useless sword and backed up, looking around for another weapon. I took him down with a well-aimed blow to the head.

I turned to Queen Anwyn and Conard who were still trying desperately to open the door. I hadn't done anything to seal the door, so it must have been the ke'tain's doing.

Queen Anwyn saw me coming and cowered behind her guard. Conard drew his sword and assumed a fighting stance, even though he knew he could not win. I heaved a sigh, tired of all the violence. It was all I'd known since I was brought to Seelie, and I just wanted it to end.

"Lay down your weapon," I told him, already knowing he wouldn't comply.

"You will have to go through me to get to my queen."

I nodded. "I can do that, but when you're unconscious like the others, she'll be alone. Is that what you want? To leave her to face justice alone or would you rather stand by her side?"

He lowered the sword. "I will stand with her."

I pointed to the floor, and he laid his sword at his feet. I used the staff to push it out of his reach in case he had a change of heart.

"Walk ahead of me around the dais," I ordered.

"Do you honestly believe my people will let you leave Seelie alive if you kill me?" Queen Anwyn snarled. Her eyes were wild, and her crown was slightly askew, making her look unhinged.

I answered by prodding her with the end of the staff. She swatted at it with her hand, and Conard took her arm to lead her past the still bodies of her guards. She didn't so much as look at them or show any concern for their wellbeing. How could they give their loyalty so faithfully to someone who didn't return it?

We came to the open area in front of the throne and stopped at the sight of the group of people huddled in front of the main entrance. Whatever had locked the queen's getaway door must have locked all the doors. The people Queen Anwyn had summoned to witness my death stared at me in fear. They probably thought they were all going to die like Bauchan.

I looked at Rhys, who was still bound to his throne. "Are you okay?"

"I think I am supposed to ask you that," he answered in a shaky voice.

I turned to our audience and motioned one of the male advisors forward. I recognized him from the first meeting I'd attended at Unseelie. He stayed a good six feet from me, and I remembered I was still sporting the ke'tain aura.

"Would you please free the prince?" I asked him.

He nodded jerkily and did as I asked. Rhys stood, rubbing his wrists, and joined us.

I looked at Conard. "Put the queen on her throne and secure her there with the binds you used on the prince."

Queen Anwyn shouted at the crowd by the door. "I am your queen. Are you going to stand by while this criminal treats me this way?"

No one spoke or moved. Someone pounded on the other side of the main doors. Her reinforcements were here.

"You have been lied to and misled by your queen," I told the scared onlookers. "It was she who stole the ke'tain the first time, and it was her guards who murdered the temple guards and stole the ke'tain today. She wanted to force Unseelie to seal the barrier between Faerie and the human world."

"Lies!" Queen Anwyn shrieked.

I winced as her shrill voice started a dull ache in my head. "Secure her," I ordered Conard. "And gag her while you're at it."

"Jesse, are you okay?" Rhys asked, his voice laden with concern.

"Yes." I turned toward him, and the room tilted. "I don't know."

"You don't look well." He pointed at the dais. "Perhaps, you should sit."

I waved him off. "I'm tired. I haven't slept much." I looked down at my hand that held the ke'tain and saw that the blue aura around me had faded to a bluish white. I lifted my arm, and it trembled from the effort. My limbs felt heavy, and my headache was getting worse.

It wasn't until my goddess stone began to pulse erratically that I realized what was wrong. My body was too weak from days of abuse and lack of nourishment to channel the ke'tain's full power this long. Not even the goddess stone could protect me from that much power indefinitely.

I took a step toward the dais and staggered, falling to my knees in the same spot I'd knelt before. I lost my grip on the staff, and it clattered to the floor. The ke'tain slipped from my other hand and rolled to rest against the side of the box Aibel had carried it in.

Behind me, the doors crashed open, and court guards poured into the room. I lifted my head to look at Queen Anwyn, who stood in front of her throne.

"Seize her," she commanded victoriously.

Two guards grabbed my arms and hauled me to my feet. I stood between them and watched her step down from the dais and stalk toward me. I expected her to strike me, but she leaned in to speak in my ear.

"You should have killed me when you had the chance. Your humanity made you weak, Jesse James. You should know by now that you cannot win against –"

The ceiling exploded. Queen Anwyn screamed, and the guards released me to cover her body as glass rained down on us. I dived for the ke'tain and snatched it up, bracing for the jolt of power that never came. Someone shouted as I got to my feet, but nothing was going to stop me.

The queen saw me coming, and she screamed at the guards to move, but they were too intent on protecting her from the glass to notice the real threat until it was too late.

"You want this?" I shouted at her over the screams and sounds of shattering glass. "Take it."

"Noooo!" Her eyes went wild in terror, and she bucked her guards off her as she tried in vain to get away from me.

I shoved the ke'tain at her, and her hands came up instinctively to protect her face. The ke'tain touched her palm, and for several seconds, we were fused together until a blast of energy sent me sprawling on my back.

In front of me, Queen Anwyn stood with the ke'tain in her hand and her mouth open in a silent scream as she experienced the power of the goddess. Blue fire poured from the ke'tain and engulfed her body as it had with Bauchan. There was a blinding flash, and the Seelie queen was no more. In her place was the ke'tain lying next to a blackened crown in a pile of ash on the floor.

"Mother!" Rhys cried out.

"Get her," Conard shouted.

A roar shook the room. I stared up at where the roof used to be and met the eyes of one very pissed off drakkan. He growled, and flames shot from his nose and mouth.

"Gus!" I scrambled to my feet.

He folded his wings and dropped down to the floor, making the guards scatter. I ran to him and threw my arms around one of his forelegs. "I have never been so happy to see you."

I looked for Rhys and found him and a few others taking cover behind the throne. He stood, staring in shock at what was left of the queen, and the anguish on his face was unbearable. Queen Anwyn had been a horrible, ruthless person, but she had also been the only mother he'd ever known.

"Your Majesty!" Aibel ran around the dais and stopped short at the sight before him.

If he was awake, the others would be soon. It was time to go. I ran to the ke'tain and picked it up. Placing it in the box, I went back to Gus.

"Jesse?" Rhys asked, confused.

"I have to go, but I'll see you soon," I said as Gus wrapped his claws around me and rose straight up into the air. There was barely enough room to accommodate his wingspan, but he managed it.

I looked down at the stunned faces below and waved to Rhys as we cleared the roof. I wished I could stay for him, but it wasn't safe for me here. He gave a tentative wave as Gus flapped his wings, and the room disappeared from sight. I tucked the box in beside me and settled in for the long flight. I was exhausted, but I kept my eyes open long enough to see Gus put Seelie far behind us.

It was dark when we landed on the island. I patted Gus's leg and headed to the temple. I was in a hurry to return the ke'tain so I could go home to Lukas. I wanted to wrap my arms around him and never let him go.

I didn't bother to create a glamour before I entered the building. The first thing I saw when I descended the steps to the outer room was the four Unseelie guards posted at the entrance to the altar room. They all watched me approach with similar hostile expressions.

One of the Unseelie guards opened his mouth to speak. The words never came as his eyes glazed over, and he stood as if he had been petrified. I looked at the other three guards, and they were in the same state.

"Hello, Jesse."

I spun to face Aedhna, who smiled at me like my mom had when I'd gotten acceptance letters to Cornell, Stanford, and Harvard. The pride in her eyes made me feel like there wasn't anything I couldn't do.

She held out her hand to me. I took it, and we entered the main room together. I gasped at the sight of Korrigan and at least a dozen others from Unseelie who were frozen like the guards upstairs. Korrigan was hunched in front of the altar, examining the spot where the ke'tain used to sit.

I turned to look at the back wall where the guards on duty always stood. I put a hand over my mouth at the sight of the four cloth-covered bodies on the floor. I had been so happy to leave Seelie that I'd forgotten about the temple guards who had lost their lives here.

We walked to the altar, and she released my hand. I took the ke'tain from the box and placed it on the altar.

"Faerie and your world are healing now." Aedhna touched my hair like my mother used to, and it made my heart ache. "You have done well, Jesse."

"What if someone tries to steal it again?" I asked. "Wouldn't it be better to hide the ke'tain like you did with the others?"

Aedhna touched the stone. "This is more than a source of energy for Faerie. It is an object of worship that helps the people of this world feel connected to each other and to me. It does not matter if they are from Seelie or Unseelie. The ke'tain tells them they are a part of something greater than all of them."

"We have religious symbols in my world, too," I said. For the first time, I understood the true power of the ke'tain. Unlike the human world, Faerie had one religion and only one sacred symbol of their faith.

I pointed at the altar. "Unseelie and Seelie created the strongest ward they could around the altar, and someone used a drakkan hide to get past it. Can't you create one that no one can get through?"

"I cannot." She smiled at me. "But you can."

"Me?" I gaped at her. "How could I possibly create a ward like that? My goddess stone helps me create glamours, but it's the ke'tain that has the real power. It's only when they're together that... Oh."

I pulled the stone from my hair and cupped it in my hand. It had come to me when I needed it, it saved my life during the conversion, and it had done its part to save Faerie. The thought of parting with it saddened me, but I didn't need it anymore.

I held my hand over the altar and looked at Aedhna for guidance. She nodded in approval, and I placed the stone on the altar beside the ke'tain. Immediately, the stone changed from the color of my hair to iridescent blue to match the ke'tain. Then it slowly sank into the surface of the altar and disappeared.

The air above the altar shimmered, and a dazzling column of light appeared above the ke'tain. The column expanded until it encompassed the altar and rose all the way to the ceiling. When the light faded, the altar was enclosed inside what looked like a clear glass case with tiny blue currents running through it.

I reached out to touch it without stopping to wonder if it was safe. I no longer had my goddess stone to protect me from the ke'tain's power. It felt like warm glass, but there was an almost undiscernible vibration that made my palm itch. I looked at Korrigan. He was in for quite a surprise when he woke up.

"The ke'tain is safe now?" I asked.

"Yes." Aedhna laid a hand on my shoulder. "Not many would give up such a gift. Your courage is exceeded only by your goodness."

I flushed and looked at the ke'tain. "What happens now?"

She looped her arm through mine. "Now you go home and live a good life."

"Will I ever see you again?" I asked as we walked to the stairs.

"Someday."

We emerged from the building, and Gus lifted his head to watch us. I turned to Aedhna and hugged her impulsively. She hugged me back and kissed my forehead. Then she was gone.

I ran to the drakkan. Sensing my excitement, he stood and stretched his wings eagerly.

"We did it, Gus!" I said as he picked me up. "Let's go home."

23

G US LIKED TO make an entrance. It was late when we reached the court, but there were more people than usual wandering the grounds at that hour. Since I could no longer hide us with a glamour, he decided to make the most of it. He blew out puffs of smoke and small flames as he circled the grounds, drawing the attention of everyone there.

"Showoff," I called, and he snorted in reply.

He landed at the top of the grounds and set me down near the door. It wasn't until I stood in front of him that I realized this might be the last time I saw him. Our job was done, and I no longer had my goddess stone to call him.

"Don't be a stranger, okay?" I said hoarsely.

He extended his head and nudged me playfully, knocking me over. Laughing, I patted his snout. "I'll see you around."

I backed up to give him room for takeoff. I was about to call a warning to the people gathering a little too close to us, but Gus took care of it. He swished his long tail, sending the onlookers scrambling to get out of the way. He leaped into the air and bathed the crowd in a cloud of smelly black smoke before he flew away.

Grinning, I turned to the door. I couldn't wait another minute to see Lukas. I nearly ran into the two serious-faced guards standing there.

"Jesse James, you are to come with us," one of them said.

I pulled back when he reached for me. "Where?"

"To the holding cells," the other guard said. "You will be detained until Korrigan can see you."

This was not the homecoming I'd spent the last few hours imagining. I crossed my arms. "Forget it. I've had enough of being a prisoner to last me a lifetime. If Korrigan wants to talk to me, he knows where to find me."

"You do not have a choice," the first one said as they advanced on me.

"I will take her from here," said a voice behind them. I had never been so relieved to see Faolin. If he was here, then Lukas had to be close by.

"How did you know I was back?" I asked him when the two guards left.

Faolin opened the door for me. "You and your drakkan were impossible to miss. Going by your appearance and the manner of your arrival, I am guessing you have a story to tell us about your absence."

"You have no idea." I grimaced at how I must look and smell. I hadn't showered or changed clothes in a week. "Is Lukas here?"

"He's in the human world looking for you. I have already sent for him," Faolin said as we stepped onto the lift.

My stomach fell. "He believes I escaped the cells and went home? Does he think I tried to steal the ke'tain, too?"

"He knows you would never do that. We thought someone threatened you, and you used your goddess stone to escape. We've all been looking for you. I'm only here now because my father summoned me."

I nodded. "Because of what happened at the temple?"

His eyebrows shot up. "You were there?"

"After the fact." The lift stopped on the top floor, and we got off. "Are we going to see your father?"

"Yes."

"Then I'd rather wait to tell the story so I don't have to repeat it a bunch of times. It's not one I'm going to enjoy talking about."

We walked down the hallway that led away from Lukas's quarters and stopped at a door. Faolin opened it and ushered me inside. When I saw the occupants, I came up short, and he ran into me.

We were in a large living area even bigger than Lukas's and richly furnished. But it wasn't the room that had taken me off guard. King Oseron and Maurelle were there, along with Korrigan, and two of the king's advisors. They all wore grim expressions and stopped talking when we entered the room.

"Jesse!" Lukas's mother stood, her hand to her throat. "Should I send for a healer?"

I found my voice. "No, thank you. It's nothing a shower and sleep won't fix." *And Lukas.*

"Please, sit. You look very tired." She pointed at one of the chairs.

I looked at the pretty upholstery and shook my head. "I'd rather stand. I don't want to soil the furniture."

"It is only a chair." She looked at Faolin, who took my arm and made me sit. It did feel good to rest, and I let out a quiet sigh.

I looked up to find everyone watching me expectantly. I was trying to figure out what to say when the king spoke.

"We would very much like to know why you ran away and where you have been. Your disappearance caused quite the upheaval here," he said in an admonishing tone. "First, I must ask if you have knowledge of the terrible incident that happened at the temple today."

"I do."

Korrigan leaned forward in his chair. "Were you involved in the murders of those guards?"

I flinched at his sharp tone and shook my head. "It was two of Queen Anwyn's personal guards."

King Oseron shot to his feet. "That is a serious accusation. What proof do you have to support it?"

"I don't have any physical proof, but I'll tell you what I know." I clasped my hands in my lap. "First, I should tell you that Queen Anwyn is dead."

"Dead?" Korrigan and King Oseron said together, and everyone began talking all at once.

"You killed the Seelie queen?" asked one of the horrified advisors.

I pressed my dry lips together. "Technically, the ke'tain killed her. It's a long story." I looked at Faolin. "Can I have some water?"

He left the room and came back with a glass of water. I was so thirsty I drained the glass, and he went to refill it.

"Does this have anything to do with that goddess stone Vaerik told me about?" the king asked as he sat.

The two advisors stared at the king in shock. Clearly, he hadn't shared that information with them.

I nodded. "It has everything to do with it."

The goddess stone was gone and with it, the magic that prevented me from talking about Aedhna and the ke'tain. So, I told them about meeting Aedhna and the job she had given me. I didn't mention the other ke'tains or their locations, only that she had charged me with taking the one in the temple to various places to restore its power.

I had an enrapt audience as I described how I'd used the goddess stone to create glamours powerful enough to walk through the temple wards. And how Gus had flown me wherever I needed to go.

"Incredible," murmured one of the advisors.

"This is why the storms suddenly stopped," said the other.

I nodded and looked at Korrigan. "The day you caught me in the temple, I'd just returned the ke'tain after the final task. I was still bound by Aedhna's magic, so I couldn't tell you why I was there."

He pressed his lips together thoughtfully. "Is that why you escaped the cells and ran away to the human world? You thought no one would believe you?"

"I didn't run away. Queen Anwyn's guards came into my cell and took me to Seelie."

"Impossible." Korrigan scowled. "That area is warded, and only authorized people can enter. No one from Seelie could have gotten in without permission."

"Not unless they had inside help," I said.

He crossed his arms. "They would have required the help of a guard. None of the guards here would go against my orders."

"At least one of them did. I'd start with the one who let Rashari in to see me."

"Rashari?" Maurelle echoed.

"She visited me in the cells before I was taken, and Queen Anwyn said she was the one who gave me up."

The king shook his head. "I refuse to believe Rashari would betray us to Seelie. Why would she do that?"

I stared at him. Was he serious? Hadn't Dariyah shown him the lengths some people would go to become the next consort?

My head began to ache, and I wrapped my arms around my middle. Where was Lukas?

Maurelle laid her hand over the king's. "Korrigan will get to the truth of this. Let Jesse tell us everything first."

"You are right." King Oseron tipped his head at me. "Please, continue."

I held nothing back. I described my imprisonment, torture, and beatings, my conversations with the queen and her reasons for stealing the ke'tain the first time. Korrigan and the king tried to interrupt with questions, but I refused to stop until I got it all out. I told them about Rhys and who he really was, and I made it clear he had no clue what the queen had done.

"Her guards used a fresh drakkan hide to get past the wards at the temple," I told Korrigan. "It couldn't make them invisible, so they killed all the temple guards, even the two from Seelie. She told people there that I did it. Her plan was to kill me by making me touch the ke'tain in front of them."

"But the goddess stone saved you," Maurelle said.

"Yes." I inhaled deeply and told them what happened after I touched the ke'tain. "I didn't want to kill anyone, but I'm not sorry she and Bauchan are dead. They tried to kill me first."

Korrigan turned to the king. "This explains why Seelie has not responded to our message about what happened at the temple."

King Oseron nodded grimly and looked at one of the advisors. "Summon the council."

The advisor stood and hurried from the room. The other one leaned forward eagerly. "May we see the goddess stone?"

"I don't have it anymore." I told them how I'd used the goddess stone to create a new ward so no one else could ever steal the ke'tain.

Korrigan was dumbstruck. "I could not understand how the ke'tain suddenly appeared on the altar with a new ward. You are telling me Aedhna was there in the temple with us?"

"Yes."

"Jesse must speak to the council," the advisor said to the king.

"Can we continue this tomorrow?" I asked wearily. "It's been a very long day."

"Of course," Maurelle said before anyone else could speak. "You need to rest and recover from your ordeal. Take as long as you need."

"I would like to speak to Jesse alone," King Oseron said when I started to stand. He looked at me. "I will not keep you long."

I nodded and sank back to the chair as the others left the room. Maurelle was the last to go, and she gave the king a look that said *be nice* before she walked out. I shifted uncomfortably. The last time the king had asked to talk to me, I'd ended up a wreck. I didn't have the physical or emotional strength to go through that again.

King Oseron was quiet for a moment. "You will hear this many times when your deeds are known to everyone, but I want to be the first to thank you for what you did for Faerie."

"You don't have to thank me. You would have done the same."

He nodded. "I would have. I would do anything for my people. But you were the one Aedhna asked to shoulder the burden of saving our world. You are young and new to Faerie, yet you took on this enormous responsibility alone."

I smiled weakly. "Aedhna can be very persuasive."

"The goddess is also wise. She saw the strength in you that I did not, and for that, I apologize. I am sorry I said you were weak because you are not Fae-born or royal. You are one of the strongest people I have ever met, Jesse, and I cannot imagine a better match for my son."

I swallowed around the rock lodged in my throat. I'd wanted so much to hear those words from him, but they couldn't be real. It was his gratitude talking, and he'd change his mind when things calmed down.

"The goddess stone made me strong," I said, my voice cracking. "There is nothing special about me anymore."

The king stood and came over to me. He shocked me when he went down to one knee and took my cold hands in his. "It is because you are special that Aedhna blessed you, and in doing so, she blessed us all."

I blinked, and the tears I'd held at bay filled my eyes and ran down my face. I was too tired to care if the sight of them showed him I wasn't strong after all.

The door burst open. I barely registered the sound before the king stood and Lukas was in his place.

"Jesse," he said roughly. His hands framed my face, and his dark eyes were stormy with emotion. Then his strong arms were around me, and I felt a shudder go through him. "I thought I'd lost you."

During this hellish week, I'd thought of all the things I would say to Lukas if I could have one more minute with him. Suddenly, I was drowning in a tsunami of emotions, and all I could do was bury my face against his chest and cling to him as loud, gulping sobs racked my body.

I heard voices, but they sounded far off. The king and Maurelle were there and another female voice I didn't recognize. They were talking about me, but my mind couldn't process the words. It wanted to shut down so I couldn't feel anything at all.

Lukas picked me up and cradled me in his arms. I curled into him as he carried me. I didn't care where we went as long as he didn't let me go. He was the only thing keeping me from splintering into a million pieces.

He laid me on his bed and positioned us so we were on our sides. His arms stayed around me as I tucked my head beneath his chin and cried myself out. At some point, I became aware of Kaia's warm body pressed to my back, and I began to feel safe for the first time in many days.

I didn't know how many hours we laid there like that. Eventually, I stirred, and the first thing that hit me was the stench coming off me. It was so bad I had no idea how Lukas could stand it. I rolled away from him as far as Kaia would let me, and he rose up on his arm to look at me. My eyes were so swollen and scratchy I could hardly make out his features in the dim room.

He stroked my cheek. "How are you feeling?"

"Filthy," I rasped. "I need a shower."

"I think we can arrange that," he said, and I heard the smile in his voice.

He scooped me up and carried me to his bathroom. My emotional breakdown had left me so drained I didn't have the strength to stand on my own for longer than a minute. He took care of that by stripping us both and getting into the shower with me. After he helped me wash and dry myself, he dressed me in some of my sleep clothes I'd left there and took me back to bed. Curled up with him under the covers, I fell into a deep dreamless sleep.

It was daylight when I woke. Food had arrived, and Lukas made me eat and drink a little before exhaustion claimed me. A few hours later, he did it again. It went on like that for the whole day, or maybe two. I lost track of time. He never asked about what had happened to me in Seelie, and the only words we exchanged were his questions about how I was feeling.

Each time I woke, I felt a little stronger and more like myself until finally, I was able to talk. We lay facing each other in the dark, and he listened as my story poured out of me. He had already heard a lot of it from his father and Faolin while I'd slept, but he knew I needed to tell him everything in my own words. I didn't hold anything back, and I cried as I described my darkest moment when I'd believed I would never see him again. These were healing tears, though, and I felt better afterward.

"I should have told you about Rhys," I said later when he held me. "I'm sorry."

"I wish you had, but I understand why you felt you had to keep your family's secret." He rubbed my back gently. "I don't want you to ever feel like you can't tell me something."

"No more secrets. I promise."

He rolled onto his back, and I laid my head on his chest. "Has there been any word from Seelie?"

Lukas sighed. "Seelie is in chaos. Rhys told their council what Anwyn did to your family. There is no proof he isn't the rightful heir, but he has stepped aside. Anwyn's younger sister Coralia has taken the throne for now, but there are already challengers. It will take a while for them to recover from this."

I thought about my brother. His life had been ripped apart, and everything he'd believed about it had been based on a lie. Then he had watched the person he'd believed was his mother die. I was glad he had Bayard and his other friends to help him through this, but I hoped he would reach out to our parents and me when he was ready to take that step.

"I guess the council here is waiting to talk to me, too," I said without any enthusiasm.

"Don't worry about them. They will wait until you are ready to speak to them." He paused. "Korrigan and Faolin questioned Rashari. She admits to going to see you in the cells but denies any involvement in your abduction."

I scoffed. "Did they actually expect her to cop to that?"

"No. They've started questioning the guards, and they will get to the bottom of it. You won't have to see her ever again."

"Well, that's one good thing to come of this," I said dryly.

Lukas chuckled. "I have some good news for you. Davian Woods was apprehended in the south of France four days ago. The Agency is holding him until his trial, which I'm told will happen late next year."

I rose up to rest my chin on his chest. "Does this mean my family can go home?"

His lips curved. "They'll be back in their apartment today. The team Faolin hired is going to stick around until they're sure none of Davian's men are going to cause trouble."

Excitement rippled through me. Now that the storms had stopped, the king would allow travel to the human world to resume.

"I want to go home," I blurted.

His hand stilled. "For good?"

How did I explain this to him? I needed to be back in a familiar setting, somewhere I could feel like the old me again. This life had been thrust on me, and I'd never had time to get used to it before I was running around trying to save the world and getting kidnapped. Anwyn hadn't broken me, but I felt banged up emotionally. I needed to go home to heal.

"No," I answered. "For now."

I adjusted the strap of my backpack on my shoulder and exited Widener Library. Outside, Harvard's mostly deserted campus was blanketed in several inches of snow and more was falling. Inhaling deeply, I pulled up my coat collar and started down the steps.

Bad to the Bone started to play in my pocket, and I grinned as I pulled out my phone. "I'm leaving right this second."

"You're still at school?" Mom huffed out a breath. "I thought your last exam was this morning."

"I had to return a few books."

There was a clamor in the background, and Mom called, "No, not like that."

"What is going on there?" I asked as I avoided a patch of ice on a step.

Mom sighed heavily. "Finch said you were taking too long, so they started decorating the tree without you. If you love me, please hurry home."

I snickered. "Be there soon. Love you."

The call disconnected, and I returned the phone to my pocket. The back of my hand brushed against the metal rail, and a shudder went through me. Six months back in my world, and I was still getting used to being a faerie in a human world. Iron was everywhere, especially in the city. I was adjusting and slowly building up immunity to it. Sometimes, I missed my goddess stone, but I didn't have a single regret about giving it up.

Ducking around the side of the steps, I raised my hands and felt for the traces of magic in the barrier. Creating portals was something else I'd had to learn since coming home. They weren't as easy when you didn't have a goddess stone amplifying your magic. I was getting pretty good at them, but I only used them to travel home because they required a lot of magic, especially when you had to shield whatever you were carrying.

The portal formed, and I stepped through it into a familiar courtyard. I immediately created the second portal, and I emerged on the landing outside our apartment. There was a big wreath on our door and a matching one on Maurice's. Christmas music and laughter came from inside our apartment.

The smell of warm gingerbread and fresh pine greeted me when I opened the door, along with the sight of Bayard leaning against the breakfast bar, eating the head off a gingerbread man. He wore his usual detached expression, but he gave me a chin lift, which was practically a friendly greeting from him.

I dropped my backpack and coat on a chair and turned to the living room where Finch was directing Rhys where to hang ornaments on the tree. Above them, Aisla flitted about dropping pieces of glittering tinsel on the branches.

Finch spotted me first and let out a piercing whistle as he scampered toward me. Mom and Dad jumped up from the couch and hurried over. "Hey, Buddy." I scooped up Finch and gave my parents one-armed hugs.

A year had passed since my parents' ordeal, and no one would ever guess they were recovering goren addicts. They'd been back at work since the summer, and Levi had plenty of jobs for them. I helped them out sometimes with research, but I left the hunting to them. I missed it sometimes, but school kept me pretty busy.

Over Mom's shoulder, my eyes met Rhys's, and he smiled boyishly. He looked less like the Seelie prince every day, and the transformation suited him. It had taken him months to come to terms with Queen Anwyn's death and the things she had done, but he was doing a lot better now.

"How is the new place?" I asked him.

His face lit up. "I like it very much. Caroline is helping me choose furniture."

I glanced at my mother. She was happier than I'd ever seen her, and she had called me no less than five times when Rhys told her he'd bought a house in Crown Heights. A mini mansion was more like it, but it had to fit him and his five personal guards, who had refused to leave him after he had relinquished his title.

"How many rooms did you say it has?" I asked.

"Seven bedrooms and four bathrooms," he said. "It has a total of fifteen rooms I believe."

"Sixteen," Bayard corrected wryly.

I raised my eyebrows. "That is a lot of rooms to furnish."

Rhys nodded. "Everything has been done for me my whole life, so I knew nothing about owning a home. Did you know you must pay the city to have running water in your house?"

A laugh burst from me at his wide-eyed innocence. "Yes, I knew that."

"He's learning fast," Dad said. "He'll be a Brooklynite in no time."

The fond look that passed between him and Rhys made my chest swell. We had lost so many years with Rhys, but he was quickly fitting into our family like the missing piece of a puzzle. He had spent Thanksgiving with us, and now we were having our first Christmas together as a whole family.

Aisla whistled impatiently from her perch on top of the tree where she looked like an annoyed angel, complete with a tinsel halo. I followed the others to the living room to help with the tree.

The doorbell rang, and I hurried to get it. Violet had texted me earlier to let me know she was coming over this afternoon. I opened the door and found her straining under an armload of presents.

"Merry Christmas, Jameses," she sang as she entered the apartment. She saw Bayard and added, "And grumpy faerie who is definitely on Santa's naughty list."

Bayard's lip twitched. I held my breath for the smile that didn't materialize, but I swear I caught a glint of amusement in his eyes.

She frowned at him. "Don't just stand there. Take these before my arms fall off."

He relieved her of her burden and set the presents on the table. Then he swiped another gingerbread cookie and bit the head off it.

Violet pulled off her cap, and I gasped when she revealed her short hair that came to just above her ears.

"You cut your hair!" I reached out to touch the messy pixie style that accentuated her almond-shaped eyes. She had trimmed her hair many times, but she'd never worn it above her chin.

"It's for the show," she said, referring to the series she had just been cast in. "My character has short hair, so it's either this or a wig. Have you seen how bad some of those wigs are?"

"I love it."

"Zoe likes it, too." She smiled dreamily. Zoe was her new girlfriend, a costume designer she'd met while filming the movie. Violet and Lorelle had parted on friendly terms in the spring, and Violet had started dating Zoe over the summer.

"How does it feel to be a celebrity?" I asked her. The movie Violet had filmed in the spring hadn't been released yet, but she had made such an impression that she'd been offered one of the leads in a new sci-fi series. She was already making the rounds of the nighttime talk shows and being touted as the next Hollywood darling.

"Like you need to ask." She tilted her head to study me. "How does it feel to be done with your first semester at Harvard?"

"It feels great." Faeries didn't attend college, so I stuck out there in the beginning. Not to mention my celebrity status because of the conversion. Things had settled down after a month when the other students were too busy to focus on me. Now, I was a student like everyone else.

"Jesse," Mom called. "I made some cookies for Mrs. Russo. Can you bring them down to her? They're in the blue container."

"Sure." I found the container and took it to our elderly neighbor, who invited me in for tea and cookies. I told her I couldn't do it today, but I'd come by tomorrow.

When I returned to the apartment, Finch and Aisla were arguing over who got to help Dad put the star on top of the tree. For the first ten years of my life, that had been my job. I had been so excited when we adopted Finch that I'd let him take it over. Finch did not look happy about having to share this tradition with Aisla.

I turned to close the door and let out a startled cry. "Didn't anyone ever tell you it's rude to creep up on people?"

"I may have heard that somewhere once." Lukas took my hand and tugged me against him. "Sorry I'm late."

I slid my arms around his waist and smiled at him. "I'm in a good mood, so I'll forgive you this time."

He chuckled. "How were your exams?"

"I'm pretty sure I aced them all."

"I hope so after you stayed away from our home for the last two weeks." He lowered his voice to a soft growl. "I plan to make up for lost time tonight."

Heat flooded my belly. "Is that so?"

"Most definitely."

"Then you'd better turn on that princely charm if you have any hope of Mom letting me go home tonight."

He groaned because he knew as well as I that there was little chance of changing her mind about this. She already had my first night home from college planned.

I giggled and stretched up to kiss his chin. "The wait will make it that much better."

"That is what people say to console themselves," he grumbled.

"Come in, and shut the door," Dad ordered in a teasing voice. "We aren't heating the whole building."

Chuckling came from behind Lukas, and I looked over his shoulder at Faris and Conlan standing outside. They came in, and our small apartment seemed to shrink with so many people in it. I looked around, and it suddenly hit me that every person I loved in the world was right here in this room. Everything that had happened in the past year had brought us here together, and I would go through it all again for this.

"Oooh." Violet pointed at Lukas and me. "Guess who is under the mistletoe."

I looked up, and sure enough, there was a sprig of mistletoe above us. I grinned at Lukas, who clearly had no idea what it meant. "It's tradition to kiss under the mistletoe."

"I like this tradition." He pulled me into his arms and kissed me long and slow. I forgot my whole family was watching us until Dad cleared his throat loudly.

Lukas smiled against my mouth. "Remind me to hang mistletoe all over our house."

My phone vibrated in my pocket. "Hold that thought," I said as I reached for the phone. As I pulled it out, it emitted a long distinctive beep. Mom's and Dad's phones went off at the same time, and I looked down at my phone as they went for theirs.

The Agency insignia was displayed on the phone, and underneath it was the words **LEVEL FIVE BULLETIN.**

A level five? I looked up and met Dad's shocked eyes. Then I clicked on the alert.

A large drakkan has been sighted above Manhattan. Last seen flying over Brooklyn Bridge toward Brooklyn. National Guard is enroute. Requesting all available bounty hunters to respond. Approach with caution.

I stared at the message, and Mom said, "A drakkan in New York? How is that possible?"

"There are still weak spots in the barrier," Lukas told her. "A drakkan could fly through one of them, although I can't see drakkans being attracted to this world."

Finch whistled and jumped up and down on the back of the couch. *Maybe it's Gus coming to visit us for Christmas!*

I laughed. "I don't think Gus knows where we –" I spun to look at Lukas. "You don't think...?"

"You did say he always knew where to find you," Lukas said slowly.

"I thought it was because of the goddess stone." I pushed between Conlan and Faris and grabbed for the door. "Oh, no!"

I flew down the stairs with Lukas on my heels. We were at the first floor by the time I heard the others running after us. I burst through the main entrance, barely feeling the cold as I ran down the steps to the snow-covered street.

Standing in the middle of the street, I scanned the gray sky as fat snowflakes hit my face. A horn blew behind me, but I didn't move as I caught sight of the dark shape soaring over the rooftops toward me.

A quarter of a mile away, horns blared, followed by the crunch of metal. I grimaced but couldn't take my eyes off the shape that was now close enough to make out its reddish gold scales and thirty-foot wingspan.

"Oh, my God!" Violet squealed.

"You don't see that every day," Mrs. Russo said.

Somewhere down the street a man yelled, "It's a dragon! Betty, come look at this!"

When Gus was two blocks away, he roared, letting me know he'd spotted me. He dipped lower, flying straight down our street, his wings almost brushing the buildings on either side. How on earth was he going to land without damaging the vehicles parked along the street?

Gus swooped in like a hawk going for a mouse. At the last second, he pulled back his wings and landed twenty yards away with the scrape of large claws on pavement. His red eyes fixed on me, and he shook his head in an agitated way.

"Hey, Gus," I said as I started walking toward him.

He growled and swung his spiked tail, taking out a minivan on one side of the street and an Audi on the other. The Audi's alarm blared, and Gus brought his tail down on the car, flattening it.

I held up my hands, crooning, "It's okay, Gus."

"Jesse," Lukas called from behind me in a warning tone that said he was two seconds from coming after me.

"I'm good," I called back. "Gus is just a little upset. He won't hurt me."

"My car!" wailed a man from the doorway of a building near the destroyed Audi.

Gus jerked his head to the side and growled, emitting a stream of smoke and flames. The man was too far away for the fire to reach him, but he screamed and ran back inside, slamming the door.

"Finch," Mom cried, and the fear in her voice had me whirling to look at her. I nearly fell over when I saw the little blue figure coming around the wheel of a parked car. Finch, who never left home unless he was tucked inside one of our coats, was running down the street toward me, his tiny feet leaving a birdlike trail in the powdery snow.

I moved to intercept him and pick him up, but he evaded me and headed straight for Gus. He stopped a few feet in front of the massive drakkan, stretched out his arms, and whistled.

The air seized in my lungs when Gus went still and tipped his head forward to look down at Finch. Tendrils of smoke still curled from his nostrils as he focused on my tiny brother, and all I could think was one misstep and Finch would be gone.

Finch whistled again, and Gus cocked his head to one side. Then Gus lowered his head until it rested on the pavement, putting them almost eye-to-eye. The drakkan didn't blink as Finch reached out and touched his snout as he had the first time they'd met in our apartment.

Gus made a sound like a dog's whine. Finch shocked me when he climbed up to sit on Gus's snout and began whistling and signing to the rapt drakkan.

"Would you look at that?" Dad said.

I walked over to Gus and rubbed his head. "I guess you got homesick, too."

He let out a contented huff, and Finch looked up at me. *Can Gus stay with us?*

I chuckled. "I don't think he'll fit. Besides, he belongs in Faerie where he can hunt and be with the other drakkans."

My brother's eyes grew sad. *But he misses us.*

"I know. We can visit him, though. Would you like to do that?"

Finch nodded eagerly.

The sound of sirens got louder, reminding me we were about to have a lot of company, including hunters looking for a fifty-thousand-dollar bounty. There wasn't a net or cage that could hold Gus, but that wouldn't stop them from trying anyway. Things were about to get very messy. There wasn't any time to think, so I did the first thing that came to mind.

I picked up Finch, and Gus's head came up. Placing a hand on his snout, I said, "Gus, will you take Finch and me to Unseelie?"

Finch whistled and clapped his hands, and Gus shot to his full height. I held Finch against my chest with both hands and turned to face everyone as Gus's claws wrapped around me.

"Jesse," Lukas shouted, running toward us.

"We're okay," I yelled back as Gus's powerful wings spread out, and he lifted into the air. I looked down at Lukas and my family and friends standing in the middle of the street staring at us. "We're taking Gus home. We'll be back for dinner, Mom."

Finch waved both arms wildly at them and whistled. Mom raised her hand and gave a weak wave in reply. Dad gaped at us. Lukas shook his head, looking both aggravated and amused. I smiled at him to let him know I'd make it up to him later.

We rose into the snowy air and cleared the rooftops as a stream of red and blue lights spilled onto our street. Gus rose higher and tucked me against his warm body. I looked out over the city, and it hit me that for the first time in a year, I was free to do whatever I wanted. No hunting, no school, no trying to save the world. It was just me, my brother, and our drakkan.

And two National Guard helicopters closing in on us.

"Let's get out of here, Gus," I shouted, laughing. Exhilaration filled me. I'd missed this.

He banked sharply toward the Hudson and put on a burst of speed. I let out a whoop, and Finch whistled happily as we set off on our next adventure.

~The End~

ABOUT THE AUTHOR

When she is not writing, Karen Lynch can be found reading or baking. A native of Newfoundland, Canada, she currently lives in Charlotte, North Carolina with her cats and her three adorable rescue dogs: Dax, Des, and Daisy.